FOUR YEARS WITH JHUNTI

Book One of the White Drekesh series

BY JULIET SUMMERS

Published in Australia by
Young Earth Books
Postal: PO Box 570 Daylesford 3461
Email: admin@julietsummersbooks.com.au
Website: www.julietsummersbooks.com.au

First published in Australia 2020
Copyright © Juliet Summers 2020

National Library of Australia Cataloguing in Publication entry

A catalogue record for this book is available from the National Library of Australia

Summers, Juliet
Four Years with Jhunti: Book One in the White Drekesh series

ISBN: 978-0-9954168-0-2 (paperback)
ISBN: 978-0-9954168-3-3 (large print)
ISBN: 978-0-9954168-1-9 (epub)

Cover design by Estella Vukovic
Typesetting by Sophie White

Printed by Ingram Spark

PRAISE FOR *FOUR YEARS WITH JHUNTI*

Four years with Jhunti is a story that is enthralling to the reader and difficult to put down. It is imaginative and certainly will appeal to a wide range of readers both young and old.
- **Barbara Sharp**

I loved the beautiful descriptions of the environment and was enthralled by the portrayal of the Jhunti culture. Four Years with Jhunti got me thinking about a way of life where people have to be self-reliant in order to meet their own material needs. I found myself immersed in the Jhunti's various beliefs and roles such as those related to Healers and the claiming season. It also made me appreciate the pivotal role of storytelling in a culture without the written word.

I was struck by the narrow-mindedness which can arise from people in isolation and the similarities between people from vastly different worlds. From Nemid's desolation and grief for dead loved ones and the compassion he shows the runaway boy Kal, to the pettiness, spitefulness and small-mindedness of people like Aunt Talks Too Much.

A beautiful book that I have now read three times and enjoyed every word.
- **Frances Annal**

Four Years with Jhunti is an engrossing story, well-written, entertaining and moving. It will appeal both to adolescents and their parents.

Juliet Summers is a talented author with the power to make an imagined world startlingly real.
- **Katharine Betts**

Four Years with Jhunti Book 1 of the White Drekesh series is a wonderful story told through the eyes of Chris Daniels, known as Kal. Kal is a young white boy who runs away from an abusive father. He ends up living with a secretive tribe called the Nahill. Through Kal's experiences we are given a sophisticated discussion of the positive and negatives of traditional and Western cultures. All the contradictions and challenges of the meeting of these two cultures are explored. If this sounds tedious it isn't. The story is riveting and I cannot wait for Book 2 and learn what Kal does next.
- **Carolyn Worth**

JHUNTI SEASONS CHART

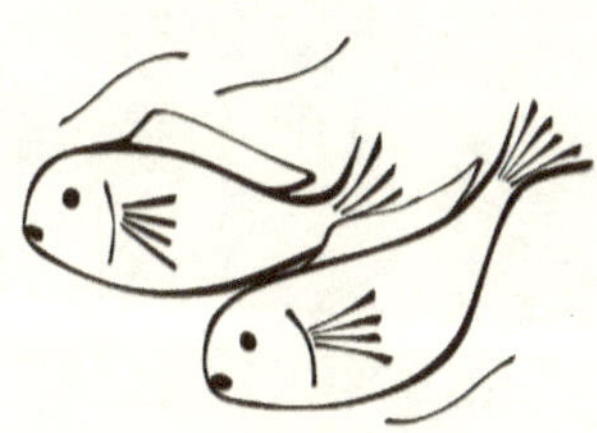

Salmon
Spring
September/October

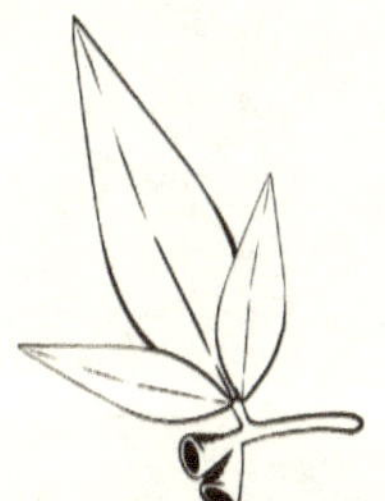

New Leaves
Spring
October/November

New Wings
Spring
November/December

Butterflies
Summer
December/January

Dried Grass
Summer
February/March

Apples
Autumn
March/April

Fungi
Autumn
April/May

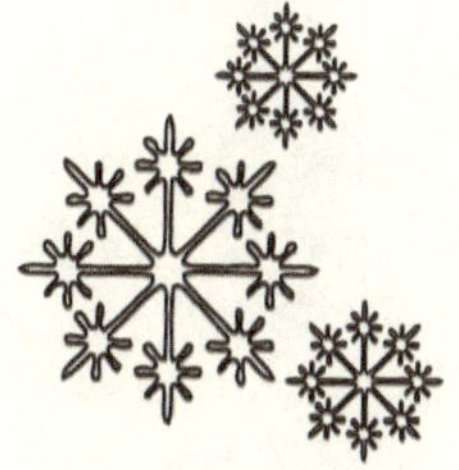

First Snow
Winter
June/July/August

Snow Thaw
Winter
August/September

1

It had happened again, and Nemid still could not believe it. Cross-legged at the base of a large tree, he looked like he was part of the gnarled limbs rooted sturdily in the earth. Nemid was a Jhunti and a member of Water clan from the Nahill tribe. Squat and solid from a lifetime of hard labour in the fields, he appeared to be in his fifties but was actually thirty-nine snows old. His weathered skin resembled bark and was browned by the sun.

He had full lips and dark brown eyes framed by a bush of black eyebrow. His nose had been slim when he was younger, but the combination of its being broken a few times and age meant that there was now a flattened kink in the middle. While he was not handsome, he had a kindly expression that put people at ease. Nemid wore a linen tunic and leggings of light yellow, and his normally long black hair was newly shortened to show he was in mourning. His sleeves were pulled up to his elbows, and there were fresh grieving cuts on each arm, one cut to represent each loved one who had gone on ahead. Seven fresh cuts and twenty old ones lined his arms.

His bare feet were caked with dirt, and the soles and underside of his toes had thick callouses from long days spent in the fields. His usually inquisitive brown eyes were shot with red and dulled from crying. In his hand was a leaf from the family tree of his late wife. This tree was now being nourished by her ashes and the ashes of their children. These same ashes he'd packed into his grieving cuts so he would carry a part of them with him forever.

There by the tree, Nemid sang the grieving song. Chilly winds swirled the leaves of the huge forest trees that made up the majority of the Jhunti reservation in the mountains. The air smelt of eucalyptus and moist earth. He sang of his first wife Trinuxa, how the pair had never attracted any baby souls to her body, but it hadn't mattered. For many snows, they were happy. Then she got sick. Despite sacrifices to appease the Great Spirits and beseeching every Healer to help them remove the curse that was afflicting her, Trinuxa died after seasons of terrible pain. Tears ran down his face. He had thought this loss was the worst of his life, and he had struggled to accept Trinuxa's death according to Nahill doctrines. As there were so few Nahill women, he'd resigned himself to seeing out his days as a bachelor, but then he'd met Leath.

Leath, with the sun in her smile and the wisdom of the ages in her eyes, had captivated Nemid's heart from the moment they'd met. He had been amazed when she claimed him, and living with her had been the happiest time of his life. Her body had attracted many baby souls, of which only eight had stayed. Six had survived past infancy, and Leath and their children had been the reason Nemid got up every day with a smile on his face. It was what gave him strength after a hard day in the fields when his body ached from the never-ending physical toil and his head pounded from the hot sun.

Tragedy struck again. Leath and their children drowned in the lake when their raft capsized. This time the will of the Great Spirits knocked him to the ground, and Nemid no longer had the strength to get up. All were gone, he sang, leaving just him. While he understood that a person lived or died at the pleasure of the Great Spirits, he couldn't help but think what had happened to him wasn't fair. Again, he sang, again he had found his mate and had made a happy home, again she had been taken from him, and he missed her so. And why had the Great Spirits also called his children home? It wasn't fair. He'd give anything to have them back. His wives and lovers, his beautiful children – they were what had given his life meaning, and now he felt empty like the discarded skin of a fruit.

He knew he shouldn't be thinking like this. He was a Nahill, and the Nahill accepted death as a part of life.

'I miss my family!' he yelled out to the trees.

Birds added their calls to his, crying out their sympathy and condolences at the news. A gust of wind shushed through the leaves. Crickets chirped, and there was the thump thump of a kangaroo in the distance. The constant buzzing of flies and other insects filled the air. Listening to the life all around him, Nemid waited for his disillusionment to lift and to again feel one with his surroundings, but this time it didn't come. He felt alone, miserable and angry at his family for leaving him. He also felt guilty.

How often had he comforted the bereaved by reminding them that the Nahill accepted death as part of the pact they had made with the Great Spirits? Now he wanted nothing more than to lie down forever and be with his family. What a terrible example he was setting.

Resentment stirred in him. He resented having to accept this terrible thing and to resume the yoke of normal life. He could not imagine going out into the fields day after day with nothing to come home to. What was the point? Why should he help to feed other people's children and families when he had nothing? No, he thought, he must not think like this, but … what a failure he was. He put his face in his hands and hung his head. What would his strong, beautiful wives think of him? Were his children looking down on him with disbelief? Could they see his thoughts now? Oh, what a failure he was. Fresh tears began to fall.

A large spider crawled slowly down the tree to Nemid's shoulder. After pausing for a moment, it waved tentative feet towards the cloth of his tunic. In one fluid movement, the spider transferred itself from the bark to Nemid and made its way down his arm. The movement caught Nemid's attention. He sniffed and allowed the spider to crawl onto his hand, staring at the creature's slow but deliberate passage along his skin.

'We are in you, and you are in us', he whispered the traditional greeting, which brought him some comfort.

Nemid lifted the spider and stared straight into its beady black eyes.

It was the Great Spirits' way of reminding him that he was not alone.

'Thank you for coming to comfort me', he said. 'Please tell Spider clan that Water clan sends their thanks.'

He gave it a wan smile then placed the spider back onto the bark of the tree. When he looked up, a large male kangaroo stood nearby studying him. Nemid recognised him at once.

'Hello, Dadek', he said. 'Thank you for coming. How are Nelis and the little ones?'

He searched behind the huge kangaroo and, sure enough, not far away were two females, each with joeys at foot. Dadek stood alert for a while longer before recommencing chewing the stalk of grass in his mouth. His wives resumed cropping the ground as the joeys stayed close to their mothers. Nemid gave them a final wave and continued his grieving song, a new peace to his tone.

If Nemid had been paying attention, he'd have noticed Dadek's scrutiny shift to another human in their midst. A stone's throw away, another set of eyes watched Nemid. These belonged to a scrawny eleven-year-old white boy who was peering around a tree from the other side of the clearing. The boy's thin face was sunburnt and smudged with dirt. His name was Chris Daniels. He had straight, unkempt blonde hair, and his eyes were the colour of a stormy green ocean. A trickle of sweat ran down his cheek as he watched, and he absently brushed it away with the back of his grimy hand. His chest rose and fell rapidly with both fear and exertion as he stood unsure what to do. He wore sneakers, jeans, a T-shirt and a lightweight brown jumper. Over one shoulder was a limp canvas bag containing his most prized possession – a hunting knife. The fingers of his right hand tapped lightly against a fishing spear he had laboriously carved himself. He'd been on his way to test it out when he'd heard the crying and came to investigate. His stomach rumbled, but he ignored that, swallowing to try to moisten his dry throat. He noticed his fingers tapping and stopped them. The tapping was a nervous habit he'd picked up over the last two years. It occurred to him that since he'd entered the forest two days ago, he hadn't caught himself tapping once.

He quickly scanned the forest around the man, reassuring himself that they were alone. His wide-eyed gaze fostered an impression of innocence and trust. The set of his jaw was the only outward indicator of his inner steely determination and courage.

Nemid let out another wracking sob and shook his head, muttering to himself before resuming the grieving song. Chris frowned. He'd never seen a grown-up cry before.

As Nemid let out a loud wailing chant, the child automatically ducked, half expecting a smack across the face from some invisible hand. Nemid held his arms out wide, praying to the Great Spirits to help him, to heal him, but there were more tears, and his voice became tight and high-pitched as he beseeched them. The boy knew that this was the sound of desperation. Nemid was grieving for someone who'd left a hole inside. Chris knew that pain too; he felt it every time he thought of his mother. This thought spurred him to action, and he carefully made his way forward.

From nowhere, small fingers gently stroked Nemid's hair.

'Shh', said a child's soft voice. 'There, there. Everything will be alright.'

Nemid's eyes, red from crying, shot open, and stared into the big green eyes of the boy crouched beside him. The boy had a hungry look about him that Nemid was all too familiar with.

'What are you doing here?' Nemid said tersely in Nahill. 'This is Nahill land.'

The boy moved back a few paces, regarding him uncertainly.

'You shouldn't be here', Nemid said.

He hastily wiped his tears, annoyed that even in the middle of his tribe's forest, he could get no privacy from white people. When the boy didn't move, he swapped to English.

'White people aren't allowed on Nahill land. Go home!'

The boy bent down, picked up his spear and walked deeper into the forest. Nemid frowned after him.

'Not that way', Nemid called and pointed in the direction of the nearest road, 'that way!'

The boy changed direction and took off at a run, chastising

himself. He knew adults were trouble, and who needed them anyway – not him! He could fend for himself by hunting, fishing and living off the land. He increased his pace and was soon out of sight. Nemid muttered to himself about the rudeness of white people and started his grieving song again.

'Oh my love', he sang. 'So many seasons of joy and then you were taken from me.' He sang the in-between notes, a long, haunting melody that sounded like wailing. 'My beautiful loved ones', he sang. 'You and our children gone. All gone, leaving just me.'

He was about to start wailing again when he had a sudden thought about the white boy. What if the stupid child was lost? He told himself not to worry. It was only half a morning's walk to the boundary track. Any fool could find it.

'Oh, my first love', he sang again. 'Many seasons of joy and then…'

But what if he didn't find it? Nemid glanced up at the sky. There would be no moon tonight and a frost. That boy had not been dressed very warmly, particularly for this season. He gave himself a shake. A lost white boy was none of his affair. He was in mourning.

'My beautiful wife', he sang. 'You and our children…' What kind of a person would dress like that with the snows only a moon or two away, he thought? Had the boy no sense? He leant forward and peered in the direction the boy had taken. Nemid sat back and resolutely told himself to clear his mind and return to his mourning. He opened his mouth to recommence his chant then groaned and got to his feet.

'Very well', he muttered to himself. 'If I cannot get a moment's peace, I will find this boy and take him to the boundary track myself.'

Still muttering, he followed the distinctive patterns made by the boy's sneakers. They went in the direction of the track, made a large semi-circle and returned to the Jhunti reservation.

'Idiot', he muttered.

Nemid followed the small footprints through several gullies and then down a steep hill to a river. He shaded his eyes and scanned along the river's edge. Suddenly he heard a splash and a yell. *He's fallen in the water*, Nemid thought in horror. *He will drown, just like my family.*

Nemid ran frantically, the memory of his children's death pushing him forward. When he was not far off, he heard a whoop of delight. Stopping and peering through the trees, he saw the boy triumphantly holding his spear aloft, complete with a wriggling fish. The boy grinned from ear to ear as he removed it from his spear. It was only the size of his palm, barely a snack, Nemid noted, but from the way the boy acted, he obviously thought it a valuable prize. The boy pulled out a hunting knife that was far too big for him and cleaned the small fish with gusto.

Chris had known he'd be able to do this, to live off the land and fend for himself. He was just like a modern-day Robinson Caruso. Ignoring the pain that was shooting through his back, he sang the grieving song that the old man had been singing. He even threw in a few Nahill words he'd heard and began to embellish the tune, making it sound happy instead of sombre.

Nemid could stand it no longer. He walked out from between the trees. 'Stop that', he yelled in English. 'White people are not allowed to do that!'

The boy stared at Nemid as if he were seeing a ghost and ran away as fast as he could. Nemid studied the boy's abandoned possessions with guilt: the knife, spear and little fish. He knew he would never be able to catch the boy, and he didn't want to frighten him any further by chasing him.

He picked up the spear and examined it. The boy had used a wood that the Nahill called Tinder wood; it was great for lighting fires but no good for hunting weapons. And he had bound the wooden prongs with flax, which was good, but the knots would soon loosen and fail. Nemid decided they'd gotten off to a bad start. It was time for them to meet each other properly. He put the spear and fish down and walked along the bank till he found a clump of bulrushes. He pulled off a few of the dry heads. As he walked back, he teased the bulrush heads, which erupted into a white fluff like cotton wool. He collected some sticks and branches then pulled off a handful of fibrous bark from one of the nearby trees. All these he brought back to the sandy river bank where he dug a small hole.

This is not a bad spot, he mused. There were berries just up the way, and the logs would be filled with bugs and grubs that made very good eating. The fungi were in full bloom, and as he looked around, he could see many of the most delicious varieties there for the taking. In the distance, he could see a smudge of smoke-coloured grass, which signified a large tract of wild rice. Those seed heads would be fat and ready for picking after the recent hot weather. They would also be attracting many birds and small rodents, all of which were easy to catch. He glanced up at the bird nests in the tree branches. They would be empty now, but the feathers inside would be excellent for providing a warm padding for a jacket.

Dropping to his knees, Nemid placed the white fluff from the bulrush into the hole, pulled out a necklace with a finger-sized locket on it and removed two pieces of flint and steel. Bending down, he struck them together into the cotton wool, and eventually, one of the sparks made the tinder smoke. He blew gently till it began to smoulder and carefully sprinkled bark shreds over it. With that, the tiny flame came to life. He added small sticks and then larger ones until the fire was crackling happily. With the fire going, he removed his hunting knife and finished cleaning the boy's fish. Once it was cooked, he hung it safely on a tree branch and walked along the river bank. He knew the big fish would be lurking by that hole near the bank but that it would be indelicate for him to tell the boy he was fishing in the wrong place. Even a boy had his pride.

As Nemid walked, he snatched up a few herringbone ferns and quickly wove them into a basket. He waded into the water and dug out a clump of water lilies. He gave them a rinse to reveal the walnut-sized root balls underneath. Twisting the root balls off, he tossed the rest away and placed the lily roots into his fern basket. Climbing up out of the river bed, he walked into the forest and stopped at a clump of bracken. Squatting down, he used a stick to dig out the rhizomes, or root balls, and added them to his basket. Next, he went to a clump of grass with fat seed heads. He pulled the tops off and added them to his haul along with some green shoots from the nearby bushes.

By the time he returned to the fire, it had burnt down to coals. The fish, knife and spear had gone. In their place were a fresh set of footprints leading towards a nearby clump of trees. Nemid knew he was the one being watched. He restoked the fire and held up a lily root.

'These are Yama roots', he said loudly. 'Very good to eat.'

He remembered his uncles showing him how to do this very thing when he was a young man. He missed his uncles. Nemid had been the youngest child of the youngest daughter, and over the seasons all but two of his siblings had died. There was a large age gap between himself and his remaining siblings, so he had more in common with their children, his nephews and nieces. He thought of his favourite family member. He was Nemid's twenty-year-old cousin Ashekii. Nemid had taught Ashekii many things just like this over the seasons. He placed the Yama roots into the fire and covered them with embers. He placed a flat rock on top and left it to heat up in the glowing coals.

Taking the grass heads out of his basket and expertly stripping the seeds, he dropped them into a rock with a dish-shaped hole. Using a river rock as a pestle, he pounded the seeds to a fine powder. Next he washed the long roots from the bracken fern. He placed them onto the rock and mashed them. A sticky starch ran out. He channelled this into the grass-seed flour and mixed it into a paste. Taking a handful, he dribbled the paste onto the flat rock. The mixture hissed as it hit the surface. Nemid watched the paste.

'See the bubbles?' he called out while pointing to the batter. 'When you see them, these cakes are ready to flip over.'

Using two sticks, he prised the edge up and expertly flipped it. Chris studied the old man, wondering why he was doing this. Was it to torture Chris? If so, it was working. Chris's stomach gave another painful twist of hunger. A waft of the cooking pancake made his stomach gurgle, and Chris licked his lips.

'You should come closer to see how this one is done', Nemid beckoned without looking up.

Nemid smiled when he heard soft footfalls approaching. Food often won battles that no words or force could, he mused. Using two sticks again, he removed the pancake and held it out to the boy.

'Careful, it is hot.'

The boy hesitated before taking it, and Nemid scooped out another handful of paste. Chris took a bite. It was the most wonderful thing he'd tasted in a long time. Hot and a little gritty, it had a nutty taste that reminded him of sesame seeds with a hint of smoke adding to the flavour. As he chewed, he studied the man. From this close, he didn't look as old as Chris had first thought. It was just because his hair was a mess and his whole demeanour had appeared hunched and so miserable that he'd appeared old. Chris now thought the man was perhaps in his mid-thirties, although that was still really old to an eleven-year-old.

'The secret to good paste', Nemid said, 'is to make sure the seed heads are dry. Now, see here how I put it onto the stone? See how I put it in the middle and let the paste run out on its own?'

Although Nemid appeared to be concentrating on the fire, he used the opportunity to take a closer look at his new little friend. The boy leant forward to see, all the while chewing on the pancake.

'Flipping them is the hard part', Nemid said. 'You must use the right type of stick.' He held one up. 'Dead sticks, not green ones, or the sap will flavour the pancakes. See how I've snapped off the end to make it sharp?'

Nemid turned the stick for the boy to see. The boy shoved the last of the pancake into his mouth as he leant forward to examine the stick.

'This is so I can use it to get right under the pancake. Watch closely.' Again, he used the stick to pry the half-cooked pancake from the rock. 'To flip it, you must use two sticks, like this', he demonstrated.

Nemid slowly looked up to find the boy gazing intently at the food. Nemid placed a hand on his chest.

'This one is called Nemid', he said. 'What's your name?'

Chris was about to answer then stopped himself. He'd nearly fallen into the trap. If he told this man his name, in no time, Barry would come and drag him back home. Chris was never going back there again, ever. He took a wary step back. When Nemid raised his hand to scratch his head, Chris shied away and raised his spear into a defensive position. Nemid stood up, and Chris skipped back toward the trees. Nemid let out a frustrated breath. He removed the food from the fire and put it to one side.

'Do not eat this yet. It must cool.'

Picking up the little fern basket, Nemid removed the greens and went down to the river. He gave them a brisk wash, and when he turned to come back, he saw the boy was beside the fire, poking the pancake with his finger.

'Is it cool?' Nemid called out.

The boy gingerly picked up a pancake, nodded, then blew on it before taking a bite.

'These greens', Nemid said as he began walking back towards the campfire, 'can be eaten without cooking. They are good for us. Here, try some.' He held out a handful.

The boy stared at them hungrily but didn't take any. Nemid held up a green stalk and made a show of eating it. Then he shoved the rest of the greens back into the basket and tossed the basket to the boy, who caught it with one hand, though Nemid noticed him wince.

'Are you hurt?' Nemid said.

The boy glanced at him, slowly pulling out a green stalk and nibbling on it before eating the whole thing. Nemid returned to the fire and sniffed.

'Mmmm, these tubers smell like they are ready', he said pushing the cooking rock off. 'Again, you must use two sticks to get them out, but this time, use green ones as dried ones will burn. Watch.' Nemid demonstrated with two stout green sticks to flick the tubers out of the coals. They landed with a slight shushing sound on the sand.

'The outsides will be hard', he said. 'Throw me one, and I will show you how to peel it.'

Cautiously, the boy walked over to the small pile of tubers. He picked one up and dropped it immediately, blowing on his fingers.

Nemid chuckled. 'I said they would be hot.'

With a reproachful look, the boy picked up another and tossed it to Nemid. Nemid held the tuber, and the boy noticed callouses on Nemid's hands.

'Always start here', Nemid said pulling the rind from the middle. 'I know it seems like one should start at the top, but if you start here, you can do this.' He pulled back a few pieces using both hands to split it down the middle and open it out so all the flesh was exposed. He blew on the fluffy white interior and took a bite.

'Try one', he said, munching happily.

Nervously, the boy picked up a small tuber and started to pull at the middle. But the tuber was hot, and he had to drop it quickly, blowing on his fingers afterwards.

'Use the water to cool it down.'

The boy obeyed, walking to the river and dropping the tuber in. After a few moments, he pulled it out and plucked at the rind. Nemid joined him and pointed to the middle of the tuber.

'Pull here. Yes, that's right. Now hold it in both hands and press the middle while pulling it apart with your thumbs. There.' The tuber split open, and the flesh puffed out.

'I did it!' The boy cried in delight.

Nemid patted the child's shoulder. The boy winced in pain, dropped the tuber and squirmed away.

'What's wrong?' Nemid said, but the boy was running again.

Nemid glanced up at the afternoon sun. It was going to be a cold night, and he wondered if the boy knew how to make a shelter. He reminded himself that this boy was not his problem; he had enough troubles of his own. Returning to the fire, he pulled off his steel and flint necklace and hung it from one of the nearby branches so the boy would see it. He also left the cooked tubers and the fern basket of greens beside the wood. At least this way, the boy would always be able to make a fire to cook and stay warm.

'I have to be getting back to my village', he called out in the direction the boy had gone. 'Preshta millo. That means goodbye in Nahill.'

Hiding behind a tree not far away, two eyes watched as Nemid walked up the river bank. Chris was annoyed. It seemed grown-ups were everywhere, and he was sick of them. This river had been the perfect place to live, but now he would have to go deeper into the forest if he wanted to be left alone. He took some pride in the fact that he had not told the old guy anything. You could never tell why someone was being nice to you. He resolutely shouldered his bag and bit back a cry of pain. His back felt like it was on fire.

'Damn it', he hissed, pulling the bag off. 'Wrong shoulder.'

Chris sank to his knees and willed the pain to stop. A pang of fear ran through him as he realised that his injuries were getting worse by the day. The blood and gore he washed from his shirt each morning frightened him. He closed his eyes, hugging his knees to his chest, as he rocked back and forth. From now on, everything would get better, he silently chanted. He could do this. He could look after himself just fine, and no one would ever beat him again.

2

Nemid hummed to himself as he strode along a barely discernible forest path. The boy's spear had been pretty good, he mused. It was the wood that had let it down. He frowned and wondered if he still had that old spear he'd made for his eldest son. Tolmn had been a kind boy with bright eyes and a wide smile that lit up the whole room. And Evney, Tolmn's sister, found it hard to sit still and was always doing things. Friendly with almost everyone in Red Camp, she was the families' extra source of news. It occurred to Nemid that this was the first time he had thought of his dead family all afternoon. His pace slowed as a pang of loss ran through his heart.

He told himself he should get back to his mourning, but his mind returned to the boy. How could anyone not bring a jacket or even a blanket into the wilderness? Had he never been into the forest before? Nemid stopped walking, hands on hips and looked back in the direction he'd come. Was that why the boy was so ill-equipped?

'Fool', he muttered and began walking again.

What was it about white people, Nemid mused, that made them all think that every place they went was just like the white world? Not that Nemid had any real experience of the white world himself, but he'd seen pictures and heard stories. Unlike the Nahill, people who lived in the white world could have anything they wanted just by asking. The Nahill had to work hard for everything, whereas white people did not know the meaning of 'there is no more'. Just thinking of it made him angry, and he increased his pace. White people had no right to be on Jhunti land, he continued to himself. It would serve the boy right if he froze or starved to death. Whatever happened to him was no concern of Nemid's. Feeling better for having decided to leave the boy to his fate, he continued home, ready to return to his mourning.

The Jhunti reservation was home to a number of camps, some settled by their ancestors and others new. Nemid lived at Red Camp, which was between White Camp and Black Camp. Red Camp lay in a fertile river valley with mountains on either side. At the far end was what had been the original village. It consisted of European style cabins that had been built long ago. These dwellings were single storey and built of weatherboard with European style doors and windows. Inside them was one large room with a fireplace of river stones and two, sometimes three, smaller rooms used for bedrooms running off the main room.

These cabins were set out in grids of six with what used to be roads wide enough for a horse and cart running between them. Some of the cabins had fences, and many still had non-indigenous plants like roses, daisies and foreign trees in the gardens around them. At each crossroad were dilapidated signposts. The names on them were almost illegible with age, not that it mattered. Few at Red Camp could read English.

Over time, the Jhunti had lost the arts needed to build these cabins, or perhaps they just preferred the new design. The newer dwellings were round and made of adobe mud-bricks. The windows had wooden shutters over them as glassmaking was another lost skill.

Nemid passed through the adobe dwellings, following along the narrow dirt paths, ducking under low shrubs and skirting around the clumps of tall trees. Baked clay chimneys stuck out of shingle rooves, and the freshening wind grasped the smoke, throwing it towards the darkening sky. Here and there, groups of Nahill were completing their evening chores. Some were herding goats, pigs or chickens into their pens for the night. Others were taking in loads of wood. Here and there, children were being washed in buckets of cold water. Babies were crying, and everywhere was the smell of evening meals being cooked.

In the middle of the camp stood a huge meeting hall. Its strong stone walls were three feet thick. The windows were narrow slits, too thin for anyone to squeeze through. Each window had wooden shutters on the inside, and the roof was made of slate. At one end, a large fire burned in the hearth and wooden benches lined each wall. The floor was covered in a thick layer of coarse sand from the nearby river. A European might recognise the design as being styled on keeps of the Middle Ages, the slit windows being for archers, not ventilation. The iron wood doors had long ago fallen away, but the sturdy, hand-forged hinges remained.

This building was the heart of the camp, and the fire was never allowed to go out. It was where everyone congregated to catch up on news. It was also where the inhabitants gathered for tribal nights, council meetings and for festive or ceremonial occasions. Tonight a large group of children and adults were listening to a storyteller. They all chewed on the pancakes made from corn and bean meal, a staple of the Nahill diet. The story ended, and people thanked the storyteller as they stood up and stretched their legs.

'Hey Nemid!' a man called as Nemid trudged past the doorway with his head bowed.

Nemid looked up and gave the man a wave then changed direction. Although it was almost dark and Nemid was tired, he knew it would be rude not to stop. He went inside and in no time, his news of finding a white boy in the forest had spread, and a crowd had gathered around Nemid.

'A *white* boy?'

'Yes', Nemid said. 'I think he is hurt.'

'Whites have their own medicines', one of them scoffed.

'A *white* boy in *our* forest?'

'On *our* land?'

'What colour are his eyes?'

Nemid hesitated. Most Nahill had black hair and eyes the colour of the earth.

Occasionally, a Nahill was born with blue or green eyes. They were known as water-eyes and were considered unlucky by some.

Once in a very long while, a Nahill was born with grey eyes. Grey eyes were called sky-eyes, and the Nahill were wary of those with sky-eyes, as they believed that the Great Spirits could see directly through them. People with sky-eyes usually became Oracles. Nemid licked his lips.

'Green', he said.

'He's white and has water-eyes?'

'Water-eyes are bad luck.'

'Not everyone believes that', Nemid said defensively.

'Most here do.'

The hub-bub soon caught the attention of the Drekesh, the Nahill equivalent of peace keepers and soldiers. A small group of them – strong, agile men – made their way towards Nemid. He recognised them as being from Tree clan. Although Nemid was a Drekesh, he was from Water clan, and his clan, like most of the other clans, found those from Tree clan to be pompous and heavy-handed when it came to matters of territorial disputes. Nemid was beginning to regret having said anything as he pictured the child being confronted, dragged through the forest then thrown into the road by these warriors.

'What's this we hear about a white man trying to take our land?' the leader said.

'He's just a boy', Nemid said, 'and he's not trying to take anything. I think he's lost.'

The leader crossed his arms over his chest.

'White people have no business on Jhunti land!'

Another stepped forward. 'Where did you last see him?'

Nemid opened his mouth to say down near the slow bend in the river but closed it again. Their haughty stares suddenly made him reluctant to say anything.

'Why do you hesitate?' the leader said.

'Have you been somewhere you should not have been?' asked the other.

'Perhaps once again you are stirring up trouble for Tree clan?'

'What?' Nemid was indignant. 'No!' And because he was angry

with himself for reacting to their enquiries so personally, he did something childish. 'That way', he said, pointing in the opposite direction. 'He was heading towards Black Camp.'

'Thank you', the Drekesh leader said. 'We will leave at first light.'

They strode away, and Nemid felt a pang of guilt about misleading them. Why had he done that? He had been just as annoyed as the Drekesh to find a white person on Jhunti land and now … was he helping the boy? He set his jaw in a scowl and trudged through the pretty, well-kept part of camp and on to the old part, eventually turning onto a wide street that lead to the timber cabin where he lived.

The next morning Nemid was sitting on a rocky outcrop to one side of Red Camp watching the pink tendrils of dawn spread out across the sky. He had awoken from a bad dream. It had reminded him that he and Leath had argued the night before he had left. It had been about their eldest daughter, Evney. Leath had wanted him to take Evney to Big Camp and introduce her to his influential Big Camp contacts so she would marry well.

Most young Nahill began the claiming, or marriage process, once they reached eleven or twelve snows. Not that age was what mattered. To be available for claiming, a young person had to demonstrate that they were independent and able to care for themselves, their partners and their family. Some children were ready to claim after eleven snows, others not for sixteen or seventeen snows and some never claimed.

That night, Nemid had made it clear that Evney was still too young for matchmakers, and besides, he did not want any child of his involved in the politics of Big Camp. Leath had insisted that was a decision for Evney to make. He told Leath he wanted his children to have what he'd never had, a simple life here in Red Camp. When he'd left that last morning, Evney had accompanied him as far as the fork in the path. They'd laughed at the young rosellas hanging upside down from tree branches and engaged in a long discussion about the most recent council decisions. The walking time had flown by, and he'd found the parting heart-wrenchingly difficult. How he had wanted Evney to accompany him to Big Camp and to share the reasons for his many trips there. It suddenly occurred to him that this had been Leath's intention. She'd sent Evney on purpose. He shook his head. That was such a Leath thing to do, he mused, subtle but firm.

Nemid sighed and closed his eyes. He made believe that he was out hunting and that Leath and his family were all at home waiting for him. He pretended that, at any moment, Leath or one of his children, perhaps Tolmn, would come running up behind him and tell him to come home because breakfast was ready. For that short moment, everything felt like before the tragedy, back to when everything was normal, before his life had ended. He bowed his head and sighed sadly. If only, he thought, if only.

He raised his head and stared out at the swathes of pink and purple taking over the horizon. The dappled clouds told him that rain was on the way today or tomorrow. He studied the clouds more closely and tried to determine when the change would come.

When he had lived at Big Camp with his first wife, he had never had much time for sunrises or trying to divine the weather. It had been Leath who had forced him to slow down and stop living so much in his head.

'Not everything's about politics and intrigue', she'd scolded him. 'You have to learn to stop and watch the sunrise. Appreciate how insignificant we are and how small are our worries compared with the miracles our Earth Mother performs every day.'

He stared at the growing colours and thought of Leath, her long hair blowing in the morning breeze, the smile that was never far from her lips, the look of adoration that she kept just for him. When he and Leath had married, Nemid had found being apart from her difficult, especially after the birth of Tolmn. Understanding his inner struggle, Leath had made a suggestion:

'When you are missing us', Leath told him, 'find a place up high and wait for the first breeze of dawn. Close your eyes and imagine that same breeze blowing through our cabin, touching the children's cheeks before it makes its way to you.'

First one tear and then another ran down his face as he imagined the breeze tying him and his family together. He closed his eyes again, turning his cheek towards the dawn. The first warm kisses of the rising sun were like Leath's hand on his cheek. He leant into her soft caress.

'Guess what I heard, dad?' he could hear Evney's voice so clearly and picture her impish grin as she stared up at him, bursting with news.

Another tear ran down his sunburnt cheek as he imagined her face. He swallowed back a lump in his throat.

'I miss you all so much', he whispered in a choked voice to the wind.

A crow cried out in the distance. The Nahill believed that crows were the messengers of the Great Spirits. This crow was telling Nemid that his loved ones were safe in the garden of the Great Spirits with all those who had gone on ahead.

I have to stop this indulgent grieving, he told himself firmly, it isn't right. I am a Nahill, a Drekesh, and I should be setting an example. Nahill know the dead are happy and safe in the garden of the Great Spirits, free from all the ills and struggles of life. If anyone sees me...

With a sniff, he wiped the tears from his cheeks with the back of his hand. The sun was above the horizon, and the moment was gone. He went home, head down and shoulders hunched, not noticing the smoke coming from the chimneys around him or the chickens squawking as they bustled out of his way.

Nemid's cabin had four rooms, which, by Nahill standards, was palatial. He walked in off the veranda into a large room with a fireplace and wooden bench at one end. This was where the cooking was done. Wooden shelves along the walls were filled with pottery jars and wooden boxes.

Off this room were three bedrooms. In each bedroom, sleeping pallets made of linen stuffed with straw lined the floor. All the floors were wood, and the exposed beams above were hung with bags of drying beans, corn and items for hunting and fishing. The only two adornments were a large rug of Water Clan colours, dark blue and light green, which covered the floor in the main room and artwork made by little hands dipped in different coloured ochres, which adorned the walls.

Nemid went from one bedroom to the next. Everything was exactly as his family had left it that fateful day. In the first bedroom he touched the small items of clothing Leath had left in one corner ready for washing and hugged them to his chest, breathing deeply. The scent of Leath and his children was still strong here. Next he went to sit on the mattress in the second room and stared at the toys on the floor. His youngest children had been playing with them before they left. He was sure the game must have had a pattern and rules; and each day he tried to figure out what the game had been from the arrangement of the pieces. He tried to figure out which child had been sitting on which side and which one had placed which toy where. He imagined the looks on their faces, only today the face that kept coming to mind had green eyes not brown. Green eyes that held pain, hunger and fear. Green eyes that belonged to a lost boy.

Going back to the bedroom he'd shared with Leath, he lay down on her side of the mattress, closed his eyes and took in long, slow breaths, searching for the scent of her that used to be so strong but was now becoming faint. Like a starving man breathing in aromas from cooking, he moved his head back and forth until he identified it. A slight smile crossed his lips as he imagined her lying there, staring at him, a hint of mischief in her eyes.

'What're you thinking, Love?' he whispered.

He imagined her reply. Today it made him frown.

'What about the boy?' he said.

His frown deepened as he imagined her reply.

'But he's white… I know that but… I see your point; however, I don't think… Well if you'd let me finish… I see that but… And you are too soft.'

His eyes opened, and he sat up.

'Impossible woman', he said just as he had told her a thousand times when she was alive.

Deciding to take his mind off his troubles by doing some long overdue tidying, he went to the things Leath had piled in the corner and began sorting them. He came to an old frayed winter coat with holes in the sleeves. He knew he should have sent it over for animal bedding long ago, but it had been the first one Leath had made for him, and he was loath to get rid of it.

'If only I'd had this with me yesterday', he mused, 'I'd have given it to that boy. What kind of person allows himself to wander the forest without a winter coat?' His fingers ran down the length of the tattered sleave. He really should get rid of this. He knew he'd never wear it again, and the Nahill did not believe in cluttering up their living spaces with items that were not in everyday use. He put the coat over his arm, and then snatched up Leath's medical bag. He was unlikely to use it so would drop it in at the Healer's cabin on his way to the forest to resume his mourning rituals. Shoving a few meat rolls into his pocket and snatching up an old blanket, in case it got cold, he strode purposefully out of the cabin. But when he got to the edge of camp, instead of turning right, he turned left towards where he last saw the boy.

'Only you can talk me into doing such foolish things', he said aloud to Leath. 'What was that?'

He listened as Leath's words flowed through his mind. She was reminding him that he'd always been a passionate man who cared too much. His gruffness disappeared, and a soft smile ran across his face.

'Yes, my Love, and if it goes well, then I will know you are all watching over me.'

He continued, his footsteps taking on a determined spring that had been missing since the tragedy. He hadn't gone far when he heard footfalls behind him. A black mongrel dog cantered lazily past him.

'Chet Chet?' he said.

Chet Chet had thick black hair that bristled in every direction. She was a German Shepherd Husky mix possessed with boundless energy and a thick, bristly tail that could knock a child over with one sweep. This happened regularly when Chet Chet got excited, and Chet Chet was usually excited. Nemid turned to see a lithe figure approaching him. The girl had seen thirteen snows and had long straight black hair pulled back in a ponytail. Her large brown eyes flicked back and forth as she went, and Nemid knew she was scanning the forest for Healer herbs, a constant habit. She had a small nose and large bushy eyebrows that emphasised her brown eyes. Her easy, swinging gait spoke of someone used to doing a lot of walking. Her bare feet made little sound on the dirt path. She waved at Nemid with a flash of white teeth.

'Wait for me father', she called out.

Nemid waited as Healer Chani hurried along the path towards him, her Healer's bag thumping at her side with each step. In Nahill society, Healers were female and only had female children. They never married and only sought the company of men to procreate. To be chosen to sire a Healer child was considered an honour and a duty. Once a Healer was pregnant, the sire rarely got to see his daughter let alone have any kind of ongoing relationship with her. However, Chani's mother, Healer Deikter, wanted a daughter who would dedicate her life to a very special mission. To complete that mission, she would need the help of a special man, and it made sense for that man to be the girl's father.

Healer Deikter had chosen Nemid to sire her child because of his political leanings and reputation for being progressive. She'd been quite open with him about her plans, and he had agreed to do his part. Chani had lived up to all their expectations and more. She was intelligent, persuasive, courageous, diligent and strong. One day soon, Nemid and Healer Deikter would explain the plan to Chani. If she agreed to carry it out, she would be at odds with her sister Healers from that time on, which was another reason Nemid had remained close. Chani reached her father, slightly out of breath.

'This one comes to join you', she said. 'If someone's sick, we should help, even if he is white.'

Nemid patted her shoulder and smiled. 'Good girl', he said.

As they walked, Chani glanced at her father. She could sense his excitement and was pleased. This was the first time since the tragedy she had not seen him dwelling on the loss of his wife and children. Every day, she'd given offerings to the Great Spirits and asked them to help Nemid. She'd also placed amulets around Nemid's cabin to ward off the sadness, and it seemed as if her efforts were having some effect. She smiled to herself, pleased at her growing healer prowess.

'This boy', Nemid said, switching to English, 'he speaks the language of the whites.'

Chani smiled.

'Someone for me to practice on then.'

'That is why I am telling you now. I do not want you to show him you can understand English yet. I have a little test I wish you to help me with.'

Chet Chet let out a bark and raced off into the bushes.

'I want to know', Nemid continued, 'what the boy thinks of us. He knows that I understand English, but if he thinks you do not, he may speak his true thoughts about us. I want you to listen to him carefully and encourage him to speak to you when I am not around.'

She frowned slightly.

'What do you think he might say?'

Nemid didn't want to tell Chani some of the degrading slang white people used to refer to Jhunti even though she would find out soon enough.

'That is where the mystery lies. Do you understand what you are to do?'

'Yes father.'

'There's one other thing you should know. He has water-eyes.'

'I've seen water-eyes before. Several Nahill have them. I've even seen one babe with sky eyes, and I wasn't afraid one bit.'

They continued. Chani increased her pace, taking two steps for every one of Nemid's. She was pleased to get out of Red Camp. She wasn't treated the same as the other young Healers, and everyone said it was unusual for her to spend so much time with her sire. But to Chani, it seemed perfectly natural. The more others pointed out how odd it was, the more time Chani wanted to spend with Nemid. He always had interesting stories about the politics of the tribe and its history, and Leath had taught her to make baskets and weave material to make clothes and many useful things that no other Healer knew. Chani had loved playing with her half siblings and had spent many, many nights enmeshed in the merriment and excitement of Nemid and Leath's cabin. A lump came into her throat at the knowledge that those days were over. She slipped her hand into her father's. His skin was rough and calloused after many snows of physical toil.

'Have many in the tribe gone on ahead?' Nemid said.

Chani thought for a moment, trying to remember who had died recently.

'Wenet's new-tooth son from sour stomach and Ketal's most recently born daughter. Lalmis's family has farewelled a number of cousins, and old Rehet and her two friends Petri and Smort have all farewelled loved ones.'

Sad and yet heartened by this news, Nemid found a perverse comfort in knowing others were grieving too.

'I heard three babies have left us over at Black Camp', he said.

Chet Chet bounded back towards them with her tongue hanging out. She fell into step beside them, her panting all but drowning out the bird calls echoing through the forest.

'Do you ever think', Nemid said, 'of what happens to those after they go on ahead?'

'No', Chani said too quickly. 'It is not something we should think about. They go to the garden of the Great Spirits and are happy there.'

She spoke with a firmness she did not feel; however, it was the standard speech all Healers gave to the bereaved. Part of their job was to be impartial and firm so that people did not dwell on their pain. Everyone had to focus on staying alive.

'Let's say that is true', Nemid said, 'how do you think someone recognises those who've gone on ahead once they get there? Do you think a person looks the same as they did when they were alive?'

Chani frowned as she considered this.

'Yes.'

'So what if someone died from an injury or had lost a limb? Is this how they will live for eternity? Sick or disabled?'

Chani shook her head.

'Oh no, everyone in the garden is well and happy.'

'And how old are they?'

She turned her head to look up at her father.

'How old?'

'Yes. A baby can't live without her mother, the elderly would need help also, so how old are people in the garden?'

Chani opened her mouth then closed it again. She'd always imagined everyone looking just like they had while alive, only healthy.

'I'm not sure', she said. 'I've never thought about it.'

'Ah huh', he said, and she could tell they'd at last reached the point he was trying to get to. 'There are many parts of our heritage that do not hold up too well to scrutiny. I want you to always remember that.'

'Are you saying that our beliefs are lies?'

'I'm saying that we believe what we are told because it helps us make sense of the world, but that does not always mean that what we believe is true.'

They walked on for a little way more. The path narrowed. Chani released Nemid's hand and fell into step behind him.

'It upsets me', she said, 'to think that people in the garden are not happy and healthy.'

'I didn't say they weren't. I just said that we don't know.'

'I can't tell that to my patients. They seek answers.'

Sensing he might have used a bad example, Nemid changed tack.

'The point I was trying to make', he said, 'is that not everything we believe in is the truth.'

'But you're right', Chani mused. 'Who looks after the babies up there?'

Hearing her distress, Nemid stopped and crouched down so he could look Chani in the eyes.

'The Great Spirits look after them, just as they look after us', he said firmly. 'That is not just a belief; we know that for a fact. Yes?'

Her face cleared.

'Yes.'

'Good. But the reason I wanted you to think about this is that we are going to help a white boy. I want you to put aside all the bad things you've heard about white people and make up your own mind. Do you think you can do that?'

She nodded. He ruffled her hair before continuing on along the path.

The sun was high overhead by the time they reached the river bed. The boy was gone. His fire was cold. Nemid walked back and forth searching for fresh prints while Chani and Chet Chet drank from the river.

'This way', Nemid said.

Chani and Chet Chet trotted after him. The going was much slower now because the boy's footprints were faint, but Chet Chet helped by bounding ahead, her nose to the ground. They toiled on deeper and deeper into the forest. The shadows were long and the sun setting when they came to a clearing. The boy sat beside a spring, hugging his knees to his chest and staring at Chet Chet who stood a few feet away barking.

'Chet Chet, come!' Chani called in Nahill.

The dog stopped barking and obediently went to her side as Nemid strode forward smiling.

'Preshta', Nemid said jovially before switching to English. 'That is Nahill for hello.'

A cloud of flies took wing as the boy slowly raised his head. They could both see the flush of fever on his face. Nemid's flint and steel hung around the boy's neck, and his spear and knife lay beside him. He gave them a weak smile but did not get up. He was happy they'd come back but wondered if the old guy was going to yell at him again and tell him to piss off. If so, they were out of luck. He'd hardly slept because his body ached so badly, and this morning when he'd tried to get up, the pain was so unbearable, he began to cry. There was no way

he could shoulder his bag let alone hike up those gullies. All he wanted
to do was lie down and sleep. Nemid crouched before him.

'Not well?' he asked.

The boy slowly shook his head.

'This is Healer Chani', Nemid said.

The boy glanced up at her and his pain was apparent. Chani fought
to keep her face impassive as befitted a Healer. She'd never seen a
white person before. His blonde hair was extraordinary and his eyes!
His eyes reminded her of the colour of newly sprouted gum leaves.
Never had she seen eyes like this before.

'Preshta', Healer Chani said and inclined her head slightly.

'Show her what's wrong', Nemid said.

The boy dislodged another swarm of flies as he slowly removed his
jumper. He clenched his teeth as he eased his T-shirt from his bony
shoulders. The material was stuck in several spots, and he winced as
he pulled it free from the wounds. Nemid kept his face impassive
when he saw the boy's back. It was covered in bruises, and there were
several long red welts with infected broken skin. As Nemid neared,
he saw more and more marks on the boy that indicated sustained
cruelty and beatings. He took the blanket from his pack and unfurled
it on the ground.

'Lie down', he told the boy.

Chani placed Chet Chet next to the boy for warmth and to keep
the flies away. She and Nemid worked on cleaning his wounds and
applying their strongest remedies. The boy tried hard not to cry,
biting down on a stick between his teeth and clawing at the ground.
After a time, he fainted and both Chani and Nemid agreed this was
a good thing that made their job easier.

When the boy woke, there was a merry fire and appetising smells.
His back ached and stung, but it was feeling better. They'd covered
it with something that felt like jelly and then draped the blanket over
him. He tried to sit up, but Chani raised her hand.

'Dis nect retan', she called.

The boy glanced at Nemid.

'She asks you to lie still', Nemid said.

The boy turned his head towards the dog. Chet Chet lay beside him, and her warmth reassured him as her bright brown eyes watched the movement around the campfire. She had been digging, and the damp earth clung to her shaggy coat. The boy placed a tentative finger on the dog's paw. She licked his face.

'Awww, yuck!' he protested.

Chani regarded them.

'Chet Chet, dis nect!' she hissed.

Nemid watched as the boy wiped where the dog had licked him.

'Her name is Chet Chet', he said. 'And what's your name?'

The boy paused for a moment.

'Kal', he said finally, liking the sound of his new name.

'Kal?' Nemid repeated the name to himself.

Kal rested his cheek on his forearms and turned his head toward the dog. She was panting only a few inches from Kal's face. This close, he examined her teeth, which were white against her pink tongue. Her breath smelt of fish, which reminded Kal of his grandparent's dog Max.

Max was a little white terrier obsessed with tennis balls. Kal would throw the ball into the most difficult bushes, and Max would scrabble through every obstacle to retrieve it and drop it at Kal's feet. Kal swallowed back a lump in his throat. Leaving his grandparents and Max had been the hardest part of running away, but there had been no other choice.

'Hi, Chet Chet', Kal whispered.

The dog continued to keep watch while Chani and Nemid chattered in a language the boy couldn't understand. The sound of it was like the wind whispering through the trees, Kal thought. He found it relaxing and soothing. The reassuring warmth of Chet Chet beside him, the soft murmur of voices and feeling safe for the first time in many years lulled Kal off to sleep.

The next morning Chani was sitting by the small cooking fire alone. She was deep in thought as she stripped aromatic leaves from a branch and placed them into a linen bag in her lap. She was mulling over what Nemid had said. He had asked her to be open-minded about helping this white boy. Of course she'd heard of how horrible and dangerous white people were; however, the longer she spent with Kal, the more she wondered how much was true. It helped that the boy was in such a wretched state. She doubted he could wrestle a baby let alone hurt either herself or Nemid.

Kal awoke with a start. Chet Chet was lying beside him. He propped himself up on his elbow and looked around. Spying Chani, he gave her a weak smile.

'Hello?' he croaked.

She looked up and was about to ask if he was feeling better but remembered just in time that her father had asked her to pretend she did not speak English. She put her work aside and picked up two cups. She squatted down beside him and held one of the cups out to him.

Kal eyed it suspiciously. 'What is it?' he said.

She moved it closer. Kal smelt the delicious meat broth. Taking it in both hands, he gulped it down. When he finished, she handed him a bitter-tasting herbal infusion. He made a face then took a gulp.

'Awe yuck!' he spluttered and wiped his mouth with the back of his hand.

Chani indicated for him to finish. Holding his nose, he downed the last of it in three big swallows then coughed as he handed the cup back. She gave him a wry smile and returned to the fire. Kal glanced around then stood up uncertainly. Chani shot him a questioning glance.

'I gotta go', he said self-consciously and pointed to a clump of bushes.

She picked up a fresh branch and stripped the leaves into her bag. Kal flexed his shoulders. His back did not ache as badly as before. He walked a short distance from the camp till he was out of sight of Chani, dug a hole and relieved himself. When he came back, he sat beside Chani and studied her nimble fingers as they stripped the leaves.

'D'you speak English?' he asked.

She continued her work in silence. Kal interlaced his fingers and looked out at the huge trees that surrounded them. He took in a deep breath of the crisp air. It smelt moist and green and filled with unfamiliar scents. Chet Chet came to sit between the two of them. Kal stroked her warm fur and felt a deep sense of peace that he'd never felt before.

'Where I come from', he said, gazing out at the forest, 'we don't have trees like this. It's called the wheat belt, and it's hot there most of the year. But I like the smell of the air here.' He took in another deep breath. 'It smells real different. Nice, but cold.' He stifled a yawn. 'I don't miss home though', he looked at the dog. 'Well, I miss my grandparents. They were nice to me, but my dad…', a slight smile of satisfaction crossed his lips, 'I'd love to see his face when he realizes I'm gone for good. I'm gonna make sure he never finds me ever again, no matter how hard he tries. That's why I changed my name.'

Although his words were firm, there was a quiver of trepidation in Kal's voice. He hoped changing his name and hiding here would be enough to keep Barry away from him. Chet Chet stood, yawned and arched her back, bowing down as she did so. Over her back Kal found Chani staring at him. He blushed, suddenly self-conscious and glad she hadn't understood what he'd said. A sudden wave of lethargy overtook him, and he stifled another yawn.

'I might go lie down', he said, indicating the blanket. He curled up in it, Chet Chet coming to lie beside him. No sooner had he closed his eyes than he was asleep again.

Later he awoke to the sound of voices. From the look of the sun, it was late morning. Chani and Nemid sat beside the fire drinking from steaming cups. Chet Chet stood dutifully beside her mistress. Because his back was smarting, Kal carefully sat up and turned to face them.

'Preshta', he said.

They smiled.

'Preshta, Kal', Nemid said.

'Preshta, Kal', Chani said.

Nemid helped him put his arms into the old Nahill jacket that was soft from long use and several sizes too big.

'Warmer?' Nemid asked.

'How do I say yes in Nahill?'

'Hai.'

'Hai?'

Nemid smiled and handed Kal a cup of steaming meat broth, which he drank down, glancing about for more. Nemid gave him a pancake rolled up with something sweet in the middle. Kal took a bite and thought he had never tasted anything so wonderful in his life. Chet Chet was watching him and licked her lips. He pulled off a small piece and tossed it to her.

'Me nect des la', Chani said.

Kal glanced at Nemid.

'She said Chet Chet has had her breakfast.'

The boy nodded and did not give the dog any more despite feeling Chet Chet's eyes upon him.

Nemid studied Chani. The nagging thoughts about her future came again. Nemid was not a young man and had been grooming Evney, his eldest daughter, to help Chani when Nemid got too old. Since the tragedy, Nemid had realised that if something happened to him, it was doubtful Chani would be able to accomplish all that needed to be done, and then it would all be for nothing. The familiar ache of loss came back.

At that moment Chani nudged Kal and pointed. Nemid followed her finger. Chani and Kal were both looking up at some young rosellas on a nearby branch. Chani explained to Kal that they had seen some on the way that were hanging upside down. Kal regarded her closely, although Nemid knew he couldn't understand a word. But there was something in the way the boy regarded his daughter that brought a gentle smile to Nemid's lips. He knew Chani had been lonely in her own way since the tragedy, not that she'd said anything. It would have been most improper of her to do so, but he could tell.

'Perhaps', he said to Kal in English, 'it is time to take you home. Can you walk?'

Kal gave Nemid an appraising look. Maybe it would be smart to go with the old guy, just until he was feeling better. Besides, he liked being with Chani and Chet Chet, so he nodded. Chani stood then held out her pancake roll.

'Me nect des tweash. De hes?'

'She asks if you would like more', Nemid said.

'How do I say thank you?'

'Beecha tas.'

He turned towards Chani.

'Beecha tas', he said.

She handed him the roll. He tore it in half and handed half back to her. Chani smiled. Kal finished the last of his food then, using his spear as a staff to help him walk, they started their journey to Red Camp.

3

It had been dark for a long time, but Nemid insisted they continue. Wind swirled in the treetops, and the smell of rain was in the air. Kal had no idea how Nemid managed to find his way along tracks that Kal couldn't discern from the forest floor. After a while, they emerged from the forest into a clearing.

'We are here', Nemid said.

Kal looked about, expecting to see street lights and cars. Instead he noticed a series of black lumps. Were they houses, he wondered, huts, or even igloos?

Not one light shone as they walked through the village, and the air was thick with smoke coming from every chimney. A few camp dogs barked as they passed, and occasionally a goat bleated or a rooster crowed. A gust of wind swirled leaves around their feet and brought with them the strong, unmistakable odour of pigs.

Too tired to concentrate on anything more than walking, Kal lowered his head and shrugged deeper into the coat Nemid had loaned him. After a while, they veered to the right, and Chani said something in her language, waved goodbye and ran off with Chet Chet at her heels.

'We are just up here', Nemid said, pointing to a black lump that looked the same as all the other black lumps.

Nemid guided them to a set of wooden stairs. Kal put a hand on the rail and slowly made his way up onto a wooden veranda. He could see the night sky reflected in the glass pane of a single window. Nemid opened his front door, which, Kal noted, had no lock on it, and disappeared into the darkness. Kal glanced back the way they'd come and could just make out the 'street'. Or was it a path or a track they'd been following?

The first splat of rain made him start and look up. Another loud splat and another and soon the smell of damp earth rose as the dust turned to mud. Kal could just make out the drops of rain as they fell off the edge of the roof, past the veranda rail and onto the ground. There was a flare of light from inside as Nemid lit the fire, and suddenly everything around Kal was sheathed in an impenetrable blackness. Kal turned towards the light and squinted. His fingers tapped against his thigh.

Through the window he could see Nemid crouching before the hearth. He ran his fingers through his short hair and blew gently on the fledgling fire. Kal's gaze flicked back and forth as he assessed Nemid's house. It reminded Kal of something out of a history book. Everything was made of unpainted wooden boards. The eaves were round wooden boughs, and on top of them were lining boards with straw coming through the seams.

Another gust of wind blew a spray of rain onto Kal, and the fledgling flames faltered. Nemid looked up, annoyed that the door was still open because Kal was staring through the window.

'Come in and shut the door', he said, beckoning impatiently.

Kal reluctantly entered and shut the door behind him. The room smelt of damp earth, fish and wood resin. He stood uncertainly next to the door, still holding his spear firmly. Another gust of wind whistled underneath the crack at the bottom of the door, chilling his ankles. Nemid was leaning forward, still blowing on the fire and occasionally feeding it sticks. The yellow light cast shadows across his wrinkled face.

Nemid wondered why on earth he was bothering with lighting the fire at this time of night. The rest of the camp was asleep, and he wished he was too. Still, he'd seen the caution in Kal's eyes and knew that a fire always made things seem more cheerful. Besides, he reasoned, he wanted the boy to see there was nothing to fear in this house. He was just thinking about which room to put Kal in when he noticed Kal staring at the fishing spear leaning against the wall.

'That belonged to…' Nemid had been about to say Tolmn but stopped because it was bad luck to speak the name of those who've gone on ahead. 'It belonged to my eldest son.'

Nemid rose and took the spear, moving it so Kal could see the prongs as he ran a finger along the binding.

'See here?' he said. 'This is the tricky part. I will teach you how to make these knots so your next spear will stay strong. With each use, these knots get tighter.'

Kal studied the knots and the way the prongs had been fitted so neatly together. He lifted his own spear to compare them.

'Yours', Nemid said gently, 'is a very good effort, but the wood is wrong. Feel the weight in this one?'

Kal weighed them both in his hand and could tell right away that his was vastly inferior. Nemid took Kal's spear and tossed it towards the hearth.

'We'll use it to start the fire tomorrow.' He returned his attention to Tolmn's spear, running his fingers along it as he remembered. 'This spear has brought many fish to us. I remember one of the fish we caught. It was in the season of the Apples and…'

Kal stifled a yawn. Nemid suddenly noticed the boy's tired, dull eyes.

'Perhaps another time', he said leaning the spear against the wall. 'Let's get you settled for the night, and we'll talk tomorrow.'

He took a shell lamp from one of the shelves, lit it and led the way into one of the bedrooms. Against each wall was a child-sized mattress made from coarsely woven linen and stuffed with straw.

'You can sleep here', he said.

Kal glanced around and noticed toys and small clothes in woven baskets.

'Where are they?' Kal said in a soft voice.

Nemid followed his gaze to his children's few possessions.

'They are … gone', he said.

Kal felt his heartbeat quicken. Had they run away like him? Was this man just as mean as Barry? Again his big green eyes stared at Nemid.

How was it, Nemid wondered, that this boy could say so much with his silence?

'They died', he said in a crisp tone. 'It is not something I speak about.'

He briskly removed the clothes from the basket. Kal backed quietly away, and suddenly Nemid realised what the boy was thinking.

'They drowned last season', he said. 'All of them. I should have been with them, but I wasn't. I was…', he shook his head and clenched his jaw. 'They had gone to collect berries along the creek by the lake. The Trill told me that the three oldest made a raft.'

He cocked his head towards the spear.

'My eldest boy had forgotten to take that. He'd have wanted to catch some fish… I don't understand why they built that raft… It makes no sense.' He swallowed heavily and bowed his head. 'I was told the stream took them out into the lake and that my wife ran in after them. She had the baby with her. She was taken by the current. The boys managed to paddle the raft to her, but the extra weight…' he added more small clothes to the pile in his arms, 'it overturned. By now the others had come. In the confusion, my other children raced into the water to help… None survived.'

He swallowed the lump that was suddenly in his throat. What on earth had possessed them to do such a stupid thing? You should have been there, his conscience nagged at him. You should have been there, not down at Big Camp on your *mission*. If you had been there it would have made the difference.

'I blame myself', he said in almost a whisper. 'I should have been there.'

At first he had found it hard to breathe. He had lain down and asked the earth to take him too, but it had not. He reminded himself that Nahill agreed to be mortal so they could have children, but it was cold comfort now that he had no children and had vowed to never have children again. No, he was to be a bachelor till he died.

Never again did he want to feel like this. Never. Never. Now he had little purpose but to wait till the Great Spirits called him home.

'Is that why you were crying?' Kal said.

Nemid nodded but did not look up. Kal studied the emotions as they crossed Nemid's face. Sadness, anger, resolution, desolation. Now he understood what Nemid had been singing about. Nemid touched his short hair.

'I have this to show I am in mourning because I miss those who have gone on ahead. Not that a child would understand how I feel.'

Annoyed that Nemid dismissed him as a mere child, Kal's jaw muscles tensed. 'My mother died', he said, wanting to show he understood just fine. 'When I think of her I feel like something is eating my stomach from the inside.'

Nemid nodded, knowing that feeling all too well. He sighed and seemed about to say something but turned and left the room instead. Pressing the clothes to himself, he found comfort breathing in the familiar scent of his children. As he passed the second room, he saw more toys on the floor. On impulse he tossed the clothes towards the bucket of water near the door then dropped onto all fours and collected up the carved wooden figures his children had been playing with. Kal came to stand in the doorway, watching him.

'Did those belong to your kids?'

'Yes.'

Nemid found the linen bag the figures were kept in and put them away. Kal scratched his arm.

'My dad said my mother's damned in hell', Kal swallowed back a lump in his throat. 'I hate to think of her being down there.'

Nemid had an understanding of the white people's Heaven and Hell from his school days with the missionaries.

'Maybe', he said, 'your mother is in the Garden of the Great Spirits.'

'Where's that?'

Nemid continued to collect the carved figures. He remembered making every one and the delighted look on his children's faces as he handed them over.

'Our ancestors', Nemid said, 'they all sleep in this land, and the gardens all around remind us that they, too, are in a garden, the Garden of the Great Spirits. We believe that the earth is a constant reminder that we are all one, that none of us can live without the others who inhabit this world. Not just people but creatures', and he picked up a wooden carving of a wallaby, 'and birds', he picked up a carving of a kookaburra, 'those that live in water', he picked up a fish, 'and everything else', he indicated the carvings of flowers and trees and leaves and beetles and dragonflies.

He placed all the figures into the bag then stood. 'It is the earth that sustains us', he said, leading them out of the room. 'It gives us the air we breathe, the water we drink and the food we eat. We know that cultures which worship humans or human–like deities do not understand this way of thinking.'

He put the bag of toys near the clothes.

'While we believe that the Great Spirits created us and this wondrous world, it is not they who provide our everyday needs, it is the earth. They created the birds and animals who are our companions, and who help to keep us fed and healthy both in body and in mind. It is therefore our duty to care for them by only taking what we need and by using our actions to improve what is around us. When we hunt we take the weak and sick, when we find a barren place, we spread seeds, we clear streams and create waterholes. We do this not just for us, but because it is what is best for everything and because we know the Great Spirits made us to do these things. Every creature can do things that others cannot, and it is the sacred duty of every creature to play their part so that all can live well and prosper.'

They returned to Kal's bedroom, and Nemid looked around. He took two child-sized coats from the back of the door and put them over his arm.

'If you need anything', he said, 'I am in the room at the end.'

Kal smiled and Nemid straightened, feeling the weight on his own heart lighten.

'I'll see you in the morning', Nemid said, picking up the lamp.

'Door open or closed?'

'Open.'

Nemid walked out into the main room. Kal sat cross legged on the mattress and watched Nemid's shadow move about the room. He could hear the water sloshing as Nemid washed the clothes. He smelt the dampness of the wet material. The shadow moved again as Nemid hung the clothes up to dry. Kal could hear the drip-drip of water on bare floorboards. He saw the light flicker as Nemid banked the fire and heard Nemid's steps shuffle. Kal counted them: one, two, three, four, five. A door closed, and all went dark. Kal remained seated on the mattress, his every sense on high alert.

In his room, Nemid stared through the open doorway at the pile of clothes and toys. Why had he disturbed everything that helped him to remember his family for a boy who would soon be escorted off the reservation? What would would Leath think? Her reply was a warmth that spread through his heart. She had always been ready with a motherly cuddle for any distressed child. Thoughts of his wife's smile as she held their youngest brought back the raw sense of loss.

'Help me, Great Spirits', Nemid whispered into the darkness. 'Help me to accept your wishes without question. Help me to accept that I will never see my children grow up or have their comfort and laughter in my old age. Help me to accept my new life without them. Help me.'

He closed his eyes and allowed the warmth that came from talking to the creators wash over him.

Morning dawned grey and overcast. A light pattering of rain fell on the roof. Kal awoke with a start, feeling cold and cramped. At first he was confused about where he was but then remembered Nemid. He got up and went to the rain-smeared window and looked out. In the dim light, he could distinguish cabins similar to Nemid's scattered in every direction. A few of the chimneys already had smoke coming from them.

Kal had assumed that Nemid and Chani lived in a cabin in the woods like in the fairy tales he'd read. Now it dawned on him that he was surrounded by strangers, by men. A chill of fear ran down his spine, and butterflies awoke in the pit of his stomach. His fingers tapped against his thighs. It had felt alright while Chani and Chet Chet were with them, but now… Just how stupid are you, he thought? You are in the middle of nowhere and have followed a stranger to his house. How many talks had there been at school warning kids never to go anywhere with a stranger? Suddenly every one of his senses was on high alert, and he berated himself for giving Nemid his spear, which now lay in pieces amongst the kindling. At least he still had his knife, except now he remembered Nemid had taken his bag because Kal's back was still too sore to carry it. His knife was in that bag.

Kal went out into the main room and glanced about for his bag. He couldn't see it anywhere. His stomach gurgled and reminded him that they hadn't eaten last night. He searched for something but found only a sack of dried beans and another of dried corn. There were several earthenware jars on the shelves, but he didn't dare disturb anything in case the noise woke Nemid.

Resigning himself to an empty stomach, Kal turned to leave right as his eyes fell upon Nemid's fishing spear. With a real spear he'd be sure to catch a meal, he thought. But wouldn't that be stealing? He took two silent steps forward and put his ear to Nemid's door. Soft snores came from within. Reassured, he carefully took the spear from the wall and headed towards the front door. His eyes returned to the room where he'd slept. The coat Nemid had lent him was on the mattress. He considered taking it but decided it was too valuable so left it. Opening the door slowly so that the hinges did not squeak, he let himself out.

After the warmth of the cabin, a gust of wind made him shiver, and the sudden change in temperature almost hurt. He gritted his teeth and reminded himself that this was an adventure and he was ready for anything. A sound on the steps made him turn. His lips curled into a smile.

'Good morning', he whispered as Chet Chet came panting up to him. He patted her wet head and then threw up a hand to protect his face as she shook rain droplets from her fur. When she spotted the spear, her tail wagged and her ears pricked.

'You like fishing, huh?' Kal said. 'Well, OK then, you can come.'

Feeling reassured now that he had a companion, Kal walked along the veranda as quietly as he could with Chet Chet whining and dancing excitedly beside him.

'Shhhhh', he hissed, 'you'll wake everyone up.'

They went down the stairs, and as soon as Kal placed a foot onto the ground, his sneaker sank into the soft mud.

'Gross', he muttered.

He took another step forward, and his other foot sank too. His shoe made a sucking sound as he wrenched it free. The rain increased from gentle patter to a steady downpour. Kal's lightweight jumper and jeans became soaked through, and water ran from his hair down the back of his neck and under his collar. He bitterly wished he'd taken Nemid's coat. With dogged determination, he continued, reasoning that this muddy slush would ease up soon; it just had to.

Nemid groaned as he stretched. His muscles were sore, although they were always sore these days. He lay for a short time listening to the rain pattering on the roof. Kal should be feeling better today, and Nemid had planned to take him to the road. The rain changed things, he thought. Rain always brought out the leaches and ticks, which would climb all over an unsuspecting traveller. He and Chani had removed a handful from the boy yesterday while he slept. Kal's skin was soft as a newborn's and an easy target. Nemid did not fancy getting wet either. He had to remember he had short hair now, and until it grew back, he could not array his hair about him to repel the rain.

He yawned and began to replan his day. First breakfast, he thought, and then he would see what clothes he had that would fit Kal. He frowned knowing they would all be too small. He also wanted to find out how the boy came to be on Jhunti land. Yes, he thought, there was a lot to do today.

He rolled out of bed, pulled on his clothes and boots and walked into the main room. The fire had gone cold. Once he had it crackling, he went into the room where Kal slept. It was empty. For a moment he stared at the rumpled bedclothes not understanding what he was looking at. A chill of fear ran through him. The boy was gone. Had the Drekesh taken him in the middle of the night? Had he become sick and wandered off? Was he lost or dead? Perhaps he'd just gone outside to relieve himself.

Nemid went onto the veranda. The wind was cold and damp. Kal's footprints led away up the street. Seeing Chet Chet's paw prints made him think that maybe the boy had gone to visit Chani.

Nemid went inside, but suddenly the cabin felt empty just like it had after the tragedy. He clenched his jaw and reminded himself that he'd have to get used to it. He'd vowed no more wives and no more children. He poked the fire, accidentally making the carefully constructed log tower fall apart, scattering the coals and putting the new flames out.

There was a quick knock at the door before it opened. Nemid looked back and was not surprised to see Galith, the leader of the Water clan Drekesh standing before him. Knowing why he'd come, Nemid returned to rebuilding his fire, unrepentant.

'He can't stay', Galith said.

'He is not here. See for yourself', Nemid gestured around the cabin.

Galith's eyes quickly scanned the empty rooms then returned to Nemid.

'Where is he?'

'Gone.'

Galith pursed his lips.

'Don't play with me, Nemid. It's one thing to be less than forthcoming to Tree clan Drekesh, but you are Water clan, and it is your duty to be candid with me.'

Nemid sat back on his heels, his eyes on the infant flames.

'I don't know where he is', Nemid said. 'I awoke to empty rooms.'

Galith cocked his head towards the veranda steps.

'I saw tracks in the mud out there. Do they belong to him?'

'I don't know.'

Galith shot him a reproachful look, and Nemid shrugged.

'I suspect so. I thought he might have gone to relieve himself, but he's been gone a long time. I am starting to get worried.'

'About a white boy or about us?'

Nemid rose, turning his back to the fire so that he faced the young warrior, his expression impassive. Galith knew what was coming, another plea for tolerance. He took a step closer, irritated that Nemid did not understand.

'Tell me how', Galith said heatedly, 'we are expected to live when they will not leave us alone? They scare the animals away so our families go hungry. Our forests used to be home to us all. Already many species are remembered in legends only. They are extinct due to the White man's greed. Now which way did he go?'

Seeing the annoyance on Galith's face, Nemid suddenly felt like a child who was being chastised, and that irked him. He was a tribal elder and a senior Drekesh and, as such, should be shown some respect instead of this insolence. In this young man, he saw echoes of himself as a young man – so sure about everything, particularly about what was right and what was wrong. Nemid shrugged.

'White people PAH!' Galith spat. 'Listen to this. If you show them sympathy, they will swarm over us like ants on a dead fish and where will we be then?' He bowed slightly then strode from the cabin.

Nemid sighed and leant back against the fireplace. Where indeed?

<h1 style="text-align:center">4</h1>

Kal had been trudging along for what seemed like forever. First he passed cabins like Nemid's then dwellings made of mud, which looked like huge bee hives. These were grouped haphazardly along thinner paths that meandered around trees and clumps of bushes. Chet Chet galloped past him, her nose sniffing the ground. He envied her grace and ability to tread so lightly. The path started to climb upwards, and Kal had to use the spear as a walking stick. Instead of running lightly along, as he'd planned, each step was ponderous and his feet made noisy, sucking sounds as he wrenched each shoe out of the mud. When he glanced back, he saw the outline of every step he'd taken. So much for a stealthy exit, he mused. His thin jumper was wet through, and rain dripped down his face. A gust of wind made him shiver. His stomach rumbled, and he told it to shut up.

Once we get into the forest, he reassured himself, we'll be safe. They trudged past the last of the mud houses, and then the trees began to grow more thickly, closing over them like welcoming arms. They hadn't gone far when Chet Chet stopped and turned her head.

'What is it?' Kal whispered.

She stood still, ears pricked, nose sniffing the air, tail sticking straight up. Kal looked in that direction but saw only mist and clumps of dripping wet bushes. Chet Chet began to whine.

'What's the matter?'

Chet Chet glanced at him and wagged her tail a little before returning her steady gaze to the right. Kal squinted, trying to peer through the mist.

'I can't see anything.'

Suddenly, Chet Chet took off like a rocket.

'Hey', Kal called after her, 'I thought we were gonna fish.'

He waved his spear hopefully in the direction she'd gone, willing her to return, but she disappeared into the mist and bushes. Kal stood undecidedly for a few moments then continued on his way.

The daylight slowly brightened, but this only made everything look grey and muddy. Kal berated himself for letting Nemid persuade him to leave that clearing he'd found. It had been perfect with a spring not far away, plenty of trees for shelter and lots of droppings, which meant animals frequented it, so he'd have been able to catch something easily.

'Adults!' he muttered to himself. 'Come in and muck everything up. I was doin' just fine by myself when that old guy pretty much kidnapped me.'

He continued to plod along, no longer paying attention to where he was going as it didn't really matter. After a long while he stopped to rest against a tree root. He was soaked through and realised that he had badly miscalculated by not bringing so much as a water bottle with him. He sat, cold and shivering, his stomach rumbling with hunger and his throat dry with thirst.

'There's gotta be a stream around here somewhere', he said, scanning the sodden landscape.

All he saw were trees reaching up to the sky. Some had smooth, white bark, and others had rough, brown bark. Every now and again a gust of wind made the branches sway back and forth, and a fresh cascade of water droplets fell to the ground. He couldn't see far as the mist was too thick. When he'd first entered the forest, he'd thought of the trees as a welcoming cocoon to protect him from prying eyes. Now they loomed overhead like the clawing hands that he was so desperate to escape. The bushes obscured his way ahead, and the path he'd been following was no longer an arrow to freedom but had split like fractured glass. Was the forest trying to confuse him? He felt like a fly caught in a spider's web, and for the first time, he realised he might die here.

He lowered his forehead to rest on his knees and fought back a wave of loneliness and fear. For the first time since he'd run away, he questioned if he could carry out his plan to live on his own in the wilderness. This had been his fantasy for years now. He'd lie in his room at home, afraid of his father, and picture a forest like this and fantasise about being on his own. Somehow he'd thought he'd feel free and jubilant, not small and insignificant. He dragged his mind back.

'I'm a man now', he said sternly to himself, 'and sometimes a man has to do things on his own.'

Kal willed himself up and turned to continue but could no longer discern the path he'd been following. He looked back, but the rain had washed his footprints away, and he could no longer tell what was a track and what was just bare ground between the trees. With a chill, he realised everywhere looked the same. He fought off another wave of panic and, again reminded himself that it didn't matter which way he went. Picking a direction at random, he started out again. This time his cold muscles complained, and his feet squelched inside his sneakers. As he trudged along, it dawned on him that he wouldn't be able to return to the village and Nemid's cabin even if he wanted to. He was totally lost, and somehow, this realisation sent a surge of longing for Nemid's warm fire through him.

Now he understood how fragile life was out in the wilderness on your own. He could die and no one would know. It mattered nothing to the forest. In fact he realised that what Nemid had done for him was a very special thing. He'd shown kindness to a stranger for no apparent reason. He'd been good to him, fed him and given him a warm place to stay. And how had Kal repaid him? He'd taken off without a thank you and had stolen his fishing spear. It occurred to Kal that having people that cared about you was a very special thing. Instead of thinking bad things about Nemid, he should have marvelled that anyone cared about him at all.

Raindrops ran from his hair down onto his face. He felt very small and alone. Kal shoved his hands into his pockets and reminded himself of why he'd run, of what was waiting for him if Barry ever found him. His body ached at the memory.

'You failed Maths?' Barry had yelled. 'I told ya ta study!'

Barry had reached for a handful of hardcover encyclopaedias, and Kal threw his arms over his head, cowering in the corner.

'What's the point', Barry had yelled, throwing one volume at Kal, 'of having these…'

'Daddy, stop', Kal had begged, 'daddy, please stop.'

'…if you fail everything?'

Barry threw more of the heavy encyclopaedias at Kal. Why didn't anyone come, Kal wondered? Surely the whole street could hear Barry and the crashes and bangs.

'Because you're a useless…', another volume hit Kal's shoulder, 'stupid…', another volume, 'moronic… bastard!'

The corner of each encyclopaedia had stung as it dug into his skin and left a bruise. When all twenty-six volumes and the heavy dictionary had been thrown, Barry stormed off to get a beer and 'cool down'. Kal had cried in silence as he'd replaced the volumes on the book shelves and went to bed hungry. The kids had asked about the bruises when he'd changed for sport. Too ashamed to tell the truth, he'd said he had fallen out of a tree. They'd teased him and called him clumsy. Kal pulled his mind back, his jaw setting into a determined line. In his pockets, his fingers curled into fists as he strode along.

'I don't need anyone', he said firmly. 'I can do this on my own.'

He lowered his head so the rain drops fell off his face instead of into his eyes. He was concentrating so hard on walking that he didn't hear the group of Drekesh surround him.

'Hello', said a deep male voice.

Kal froze as his head whipped around. He gasped as he saw the men.

This particular group of Water clan Drekesh was led by a man of about twenty snows old named Ashekii. He was Nemid's favourite cousin. Like most Nahill men, Ashekii was about five feet six inches tall with powerful shoulders, an angular chin, dark brown eyes and hair that was black and shiny like a raven's wing. He was well-respected and had a reputation for being stern but fair. He was strong, courageous and a loyal friend. His only weakness was his wife, Hahina. He could deny her nothing and was constantly thinking of what would be best for her and her family. The rain ran down his long thick hair, which was arrayed about his shoulders to repel the droplets and give his back extra warmth.

Ashekii put a hand on his chest. 'I am Ashekii', he said in English. 'Call me Ashe', he pronounced it A-shee. 'I am cousin to Nemid. He asked me to find you. Come now, he is waiting.'

Kal felt a mixture of relief and annoyance that he'd been found so easily. The Drekesh turned back the way they'd come, and Kal obediently went with them. It never entered Kal's mind to refuse. His throat was parched with thirst, but he did not dare ask them for a drink. It was ironic, he thought, that the rain meant there was fresh water everywhere except in the place it was needed the most. Wiping the rain from his eyes, he stoically did his best to keep pace.

'Wanderer's gully', Ashekii said.

Kal looked up at him questioningly. The Drekesh wasn't even breathing hard.

'Where we found you', Ashekii said. 'It's called Wanderer's gully… I tell you this because Nem will ask how far you got.'

Ashekii waited for the boy to say something but he remained silent. That meant he was either being rude or was scared. Ashekii rightly guessed the latter was the truth.

'There's no need to be afraid of us', he said. 'No one will harm you while you are under the protection of a Water clan family.' Again he waited for a response. Kal searched his mind for something to say, but the murmur of gratitude he tried to make wouldn't come out because his throat was so dry.

'It's not a bad effort', Ashekii said in one last effort to cajole the child into speaking, 'particularly for a shorty like you', and he gave Kal a teasing nudge with his hand.

Kal swallowed then smiled up at him.

'Thank you', he managed to rasp out.

Ashekii frowned.

'Thirsty?'

Kal nodded. Ashekii chastised himself for not realising sooner.

This was a white child and white people knew nothing about how to survive in the bush. He said something to the others in Nahill, and they changed course, taking a slight detour along the side of the hill. After a moment, they stopped at a frothy rivulet that was coursing down the hill.

'Drink all you want', Ashekii said to Kal.

Kal dropped to his knees.

'Not like that', Ashekii said, hauling him up and sending a wave of pain through Kal. 'Here, like this.'

Ashekii went to a large leafed bush before them. Taking one of the leaves, he rolled the edges up slightly then tipped it so the water that had collected in the middle of the leaf ran into his mouth. Kal went to the bush and, after a few tries managed to get the water into his parched mouth. He felt so stupid for not having thought to do this in the first place. As Kal drank from leaf after leaf, the Drekesh drank from the higher up ones but were careful not to disturb the water in the ones at Kal's height. Once Kal was sated, he sighed with relief and licked his lips.

'Thank you', he said then glanced down at the ground water. 'What's wrong with that?'

'See the froth on the top? That means it has travelled through things that are bad for us to drink. The froth is a warning to us that it is only for the forest brothers and sisters. Hungry?'

Kal's eyes widened, reminding Ashekii of a baby bird when it's mother arrives with food. This child was so helpless, he thought. Ashekii could understand why Nemid had taken an interest in him. The whole party moved under the shelter of a large tree where the men removed small bundles from their belt pouches. Ashekii handed Kal a small linen bag of meat rolls. Kal gobbled them down so fast it made the men chuckle. Everyone had been that hungry at some time in their lives. They washed their meal down with more water from the leaves. Kal felt sated for the first time in a long while.

'Thank you', he said, handing Ashekii the empty bag back.

Ashekii took the bag and put it away, wishing he'd taken a few rolls for himself before handing the whole bag over to the boy. He reminded himself it wasn't the first time he'd gone hungry and mentally shrugged. Growing boys were like ravenous ravens. The rain had been growing steadily heavier, and now it pelted down. Ashekii shot his men a rueful glance.

'Looks like we're going to get wet.'

Blowing out a determined breath, they resumed their trek back to the camp. As they walked, Ashekii shot a sideways glance at this child that was causing such an outcry at Red Camp. He could see now what Nemid had meant by him being 'just a boy' and not capable of doing harm. Nemid had highlighted the urgency of finding Kal by saying it was too wet and cold for a child like that to be alone in the forest.

'And besides', Nemid had said, 'I brought him back here as my guest, and we did not eat last night. Now he has left with no food and that makes me a poor host. It is a matter of honour that he returns and I at least feed him.'

Ashekii had seen something else in his cousin's eyes as he spoke of the boy. It was something he'd not seen since the tragedy. It had been a glimmer of the old zest that Nemid used to exude. It was for this reason that Ashekii had reluctantly agreed to track the boy down, knowing his actions would irritate the already agitated Tree clan Drekesh who were still out searching in the wrong direction.

The door to Nemid's cabin opened. Nemid, who was crouched by the fire, looked up. He had been expecting either Ashekii or Kal but was surprised to see Healer Deikter enter. She was thirty snows old and her thick black hair was pulled back into a ponytail. She had a broad nose and the same intense brown eyes of her daughter Chani.

'This boy you've found', she said in hushed tones, quickly shutting the door, 'what're your plans for him?'

Nemid stood and leant one shoulder against the mantelpiece, regarding her steadily.

'Why do you ask?' he said.

She gave him a sharp look, unused to being questioned.

'I'd have thought that was obvious.'

'No, esteemed Healer, it is not.'

They stared at each other for a long moment; the usual tension between a woman of Healer clan and any man who was not a patient was all too evident. Healer Deikter stayed her rebuke and reminded herself that Nemid was her co-conspirator and the only man she trusted or gave a finger-snap about.

'I think only of my daughter and the task before her', she whispered. 'Now that your children have gone on ahead, we need to rethink things. Their deaths were obviously a part of the Great Spirit's plan. This boy must have been sent as a replacement. He may be of great use to us.'

Even though Nemid was used to the blunt way that Healers spoke, Healer Deikter's words still stung. To hide his true feelings, he outwardly frowned as if pondering her words.

'Maybe', he said, 'but there is much resentment afoot already about a white person in the camp, and the Drekesh seek to put him out.'

'You leave the Drekesh to me.'

'People won't like it.'

She waved a dismissive hand.

'Irrelevant. Chani said the boy seemed intelligent and pleasant. Do you think you can train him in time?'

Nemid considered. From what little he'd seen, Kal appeared to be a kind, bright and genuine boy. Nemid's eyes went to the bare patch on the wall where his fishing spear had been. Kal obviously had no qualms about stealing if it were necessary, which also bode well for their plans. But still, Nemid thought, even with all the training in the world, there was no getting around the fact that the boy was white.

'No one will listen to a white man', Nemid said.

'They will if he's adopted.'

'Adopted? Who'd be crazy enough to do that?'

Healer Deikter's gaze never left Nemid. Nahill tradition dictated that if a man or woman had no child to leave their titles and duties to, then they could adopt a child for this purpose. It was usually a niece, nephew or other blood kin; however, it was not unknown to adopt someone unrelated, particularly among the high born where blood feuds were rife and lasted generations. Nemid shook his head even though they both knew he would agree.

'Women's Council will never permit it', he said.

'We both know your first wife held great sway over Women's Council. Perhaps some of those old avenues of influence are open to you still, particularly if Healer clan raises no objection to the adoption.'

'I doubt even you could do that', Nemid scoffed.

'It is not just me', Healer Deikter said. 'Remember that this mission came to us from the Great Spirits, and so they will help us to do what needs to be done.'

Nemid opened his mouth then closed it again.

'And what if the boy doesn't want to stay and be adopted?'

Healer Deikter shrugged. 'Then we will know he was not sent to us by the Great Spirits.'

A part of Nemid wanted to protest further. He'd vowed no more children, no more wives, no more heartbreak, but there was no faulting Healer Deikter's reasoning.

'Very well', he said, 'I will do as you ask.'

'This is not what I ask, it is what the Great Spirits ask.'

Kal and Ashekii's small escort of Drekesh made their way back to Nemid's cabin. Kal clomped his way up Nemid's steps, leaving huge muddy prints to the door. Remembering that his grandmother had always taught him to remove his muddy shoes before entering a house, Kal unlaced his shoes and kicked them off with relief. Suddenly his feet felt weightless. He went inside to find Nemid crouched before the fire and the smell of something delicious cooking. After sending his men home, Ashekii followed the boy inside. The pair of them stood dripping water onto the bare floorboards.

'Anything else cousin?' Ashekii said in a long-suffering tone.

Nemid glanced back at them, his gaze stopping on the spear in the boy's hand. A fleeting look of annoyance crossed Nemid's face. He'd have given Kal the spear if he'd asked. Kal hung his head guiltily.

'I'm sorry', he said.

Nemid's gaze went to Ashekii. 'Thank you for finding him.'

'It wasn't hard. He left footprints the size of echidnas.'

Ashekii reached out a hand, and Kal steeled himself for the beating he knew was coming. Ashekii ruffled his hair.

'How about we get you some dry clothes?' he said in English then looked at Nemid. 'What've you got?'

While Ashekii shrugged off his jacket and hung it by the fire, Nemid went to a basket in the corner and rummaged through the clothing. He pulled out a little tunic, held it up against himself, and shook his head, folded it and put it aside. He did the same with pants. The clothes ranged in size from ones that would fit a toddler to others that would fit a child of eight snows. It wasn't long before he came to the bottom of the basket. He put them all back and went into his bedroom. A moment later he returned and handed Ashekii a dry jacket and Kal one of Leath's old tunics. The tunic had holes in it from many years of use. Kal ran his fingers over the material and found it very soft.

'Try it on, Eyas', Nemid said.

'What does Eyas mean?' Kal asked quietly.

'You should know this', Nemid chided him. 'It is the English word for a young hawk. I have decided you have the eyes of a hawk. You miss nothing.'

Kal smiled, liking the thought of that. He had the eyes of a hawk.

'Thank you sir.'

'Call him Grandfather', Ashekii said. 'It is how a Nahill shows respect.'

Kal looked back and forth between them, uncertain if he was in trouble. Sensing his discomfort, Nemid patted his arm. 'You do not have to call me Grandfather', Nemid said. 'What do you want to call me?'

Kal had meant to say Nemid, but the word got caught in his throat and came out as Nedda.

'Nedda it is then', Nemid smiled. 'Now let's get you out of those wet things.'

Kal pulled off his jumper and t-shirt. As he did, his back was turned towards Ashekii who saw the healing bruises and scars and took in a sharp breath. Kal knew that sound, and embarrassment clouded his face. The kids at school used to make fun of Kal's scars whenever he had to get changed for sport. They called him a freak and an alien.

Kal pulled the tunic over his head and let it fall lightly over his back, sucking in quick breaths as it brushed against his healing skin, sending stabs of pain through him. The tunic fell to his knees. Kal kicked off his jeans and socks. Nemid took Kal's wet clothes and hung them by the fire to dry then handed Kal a piece of leather to tie around his waist. Ashekii studied Kal for a few moments then crouched down so his eyes were at the same height as Kal's. He pulled his own tunic over his head and turned slightly so the boy could see the healed scars that covered his body.

'We call this history skin', Ashekii said, indicating scars on his shoulder and upper arm. 'A man isn't a real warrior until he has history skin. See? This one is very proud of his history skin.'

Ashekii beckoned for Kal to come closer. Kal took two steps forward and peered at the scars as Ashekii ran a finger down one that was a few inches long.

'This one?' Ashekii said. 'It was the season of the First Snow and very cold. I was only, oh, maybe not much older that you are. It was my first hunt, and my mother had made me new clothes. On the way home, I was carrying too much and slipped. Down I fell, splash into an icy stream! I nearly drowned; my new clothes got ripped, and I got this for my trouble. I saved all the meat, but never again did I try to carry that much. It taught me not to brag.'

Kal took another few steps forward until he was standing beside the warrior. He ran his fingers over the scar. Ashekii's skin was taut and his arm well-muscled. Ashekii pointed to another scar.

'This one', he said, 'was from my first fight with a big roo. He was as tall as that door and very strong. I got too close, and he gave me this for my trouble. See where his nails went?'

Kal ran his fingers along the dual lines sliced through Ashekii's skin.

'I was lucky he ran away because he could easily have killed me. This scar reminds me to be far more respectful of our forest brothers and sisters.'

Kal saw more scars on Ashekii's back and one on his face. As he studied them Ashekii told him the history of each one and the lessons he'd learnt. Eventually Ashekii pulled Kal's tunic up.

'With a history skin like you have', Ashekii said, 'you must be a great warrior.'

Kal frowned, puzzled.

'Yes', said Ashekii. 'Look at all the battles you have been in, and you must have won because you're still here, eh? Shows you're a great fighter. If I had history skin like that I'd show it to everyone.'

Kal stared at him for a long moment. History skin, he thought. A Nahill warrior had called him brave and strong. No one had ever said things like that to him before. His finger went to the scar on his chin. As if making a decision, Kal tilted his face so Ashekii could see it.

'This', he said in a quiet voice, 'came from a hairbrush that belonged to my mother.'

The two men listened quietly as Kal cleared his throat feeling the panic growing deep inside at the risk he was taking. He told them about how he'd been eight the day everything changed. He had been in the back shed rummaging through some old boxes. In one of them, he found an ornate lady's hairbrush with strands of long blonde hair snared in the bristles. The sturdy wooden handle had a silver emblem on the back. The silver emblem had glinted in the sunlight. Barry had smacked Kal across the face with the hairbrush, the silver emblem slicing through the skin and leaving this crescent shaped scar. As he spoke, the scar began to tingle. Kal gave it a gentle rub with his fingertip.

'I never found out what I did that made him so mad', Kal said, 'but from that moment on, he hated my guts.'

Kal swallowed heavily, unable to look the men in the eye. His heart was pounding, and he chastised himself for being so candid. What if they turned on him too?

'What that scar tells me', Ashekii said gently, 'is that your father had better stay away from here or the Drekesh will have some stern words for him. Yes?'

Kal looked up uncomprehendingly.

'What Ashe is trying to say', Nemid said, 'is that the fault was not yours but your father's. Perhaps the real lesson of that scar is that for some of us, our childhood ends more quickly than for others.'

Nemid drew Kal to him in a hug, tucking the boy's head under his jaw. Kal could feel the man's heart thudding beneath his cheek. It felt strange to be engulfed in strong warm arms. Nemid's chest vibrated against Kal's cheek as he spoke.

'Ashe', Nemid said, 'perhaps you could share with us the story of when you knew it was your time to become a man.'

Ashekii cocked his head towards Kal.

'Perhaps you should start, cousin.'

Nemid gently stroked Kal's hair as he began to tell a story about the day he'd lost his way in the forest. He'd spent his first night alone and went into detail about how frightening it had been, but Kal was only half listening. He closed his eyes and revelled in the warmth and security of the strong arms that encircled him and held him safe and snug. It was the first hug he'd had since his mother left, and it was wonderful. He didn't know when he fell asleep or who carried him into bed. Much later, he was roused by Chet Chet climbing onto his mattress and settling herself against his back. He took in a deep breath of the mattress and pillow. They smelt of straw and earth and were comfortable. Within a few minutes he was asleep again.

In the morning, Nemid awoke to the sound of childish laughter. He got out of bed and came out to find the fire burning merrily and the front door wide open. Chani and Kal were on the front veranda.

Curious to see why they were laughing, he went to the doorway. A cockatoo screeched as it swooped over the cabin. Both Chani and Kal's heads turned as they followed it. The bird landed on a nearby tree branch, which had half a dozen white birds on it. There were screeches from those already on the branch, and several raised their yellow combs.

'La', Chani said, pointing.

Kal moved his head, and both watched as the snow-white bird jumped up onto another branch to join two more. Three sulphur crests went up as the three squawked and chattered to each other. Chet Chet barked, wagging her tail.

'Marrrk, Marrrk', squawked Kal, mimicking the bird's call.

The birds chittered on.

'Baaaaahrg, Baaaaahrg', squawked Chani.

The birds stopped and turned to look in her direction.

'They understood!' Kal cried and turned towards Chani. 'Do it again.'

Not noticing that she understood him perfectly, he watched the way her mouth moved as Chani repeated her bird call.

'Baaak', Kal tried to imitate her.

'Eah', Chani said, shaking her head. 'Baaaahrg. Shez net.'

She indicated for Kal to try again.

'Baa....'

'Baaaah', Chani exaggerated her movements, 'baaaahrg, baaaahrg. Nes tas.'

'Baaaahg.'

'Hai', she said excitedly.

'Baaaaahrg, Baaaaahrg.'

'Hai!' Chani grinned at him.

They both laughed.

'Anyone hungry?' Nemid interrupted.

Chet Chet went inside followed by Chani.

'Preshta', she said with a smile.

Kal followed her.

'Preshta', he said.

'It is good to see these faces too', Nemid smiled.

For the first time, Kal was grinning, his eyes bright. Maybe Healer Deikter was right, Nemid thought absently, the two of them did seem to get along well. Nemid made pancakes and served them onto wooden plates. He ladled a heaped serving of fish paste and pumpkin relish onto each. The three of them sat on the floor and ate. Kal copied the way Nemid and Chani scooped up the runny toppings. Kal found the food tasty if a little gritty. The pancake had a distinct tang of wood smoke, which went well with the fish paste. Chet Chet watched every bite in case anything fell to the floor.

Nemid poured boiling water from an old blackened kettle into mugs. He added several pinches of dried herbs from a pouch next to the hearth then a good dollop of cold water from a wooden bucket. The air was infused with a sweet smell. He gave one mug to Chani, one to Kal and then sipped his own as he gazed at the fire, deep in thought.

Kal took an experimental sip. The brew was sweet and had a nutty flavour. It was refreshing and the exact thing to wash away the strong tastes of the fish and pumpkin relish. Chani rinsed off the dishes and fetched a linen bag. She upended it, spilling its contents of smooth river pebbles onto the floor. Chet Chet yawned, stretched and settled before the fire.

'Am I allowed to speak in the white tongue?' Chani said to her father.

'Not just yet.'

'Then can you explain to Kal how to play stones?'

Nemid indicated for Kal to move closer. 'Each player', Nemid said showing Kal the stones in his hand, 'can remove one, two or three stones. Whoever takes the last stone is 'out'.'

'You start', Chani said impatiently to Nemid.

Nemid took three stones, then Chani took three. Kal thought this the most childish game he'd ever heard of but said nothing as he removed three stones. Nemid took another three then Chani took two, Kal took three. Nemid leant forward, studying the small pile of stones that were left. After a moment, he removed two, leaving nine stones in the pile. Nemid sat back looking very pleased with himself.

Chani studied the remaining stones. Her fingers went to a single stone, but she stopped herself.

Kal stared at the stones trying to work out why it was so hard. If Chani took one, that would leave eight. Kal would then take three, leaving five, then Nemid would take three, leaving two, and that meant Chani would take one, leaving Kal with the last stone and he'd be out. No, he thought, wait a second. If Chani took one and then he only took two, and if Nemid took three, that would leave Chani with three, but then she'd only take two, and Kal would again get the last stone.

No! He didn't want to lose his first game. He let out a frustrated breath as he shot an impatient look at Chani, wishing she'd hurry up and make her move.

It was afternoon by the time they finished playing. Nemid had won all three games. He rose and stretched.

'Time to cook', he said.

'What are you making?' Chani said.

'Fish stew.'

Chani made a face.

'We can't stay', she said and stood up.

Kal looked back and forth, not understanding what they were saying.

'We have people to see', Chani said. 'Come, Chet Chet.'

Chet Chet reluctantly rose, stretched and yawned. She followed her mistress out the door as Kal gathered the stones and put them into the bag.

'You can help me', Nemid said in English, placing a pot half-filled with water onto the fire. 'Bring that bucket of water over here.'

Nemid showed Kal how to make fish stew using vegetables that were in the bags hanging from the roof and dried fish that was in a barrel in the corner. Together, they ground the beans and corn into the flour that he used to thicken the stew and to make more flat bread pancakes.

After their meal Nemid retrieved a shaft of wood that had been hardening in the rafters. He showed Kal how to cut grooves around one end where the binding would sit snuggly and then made divots where the prongs would go. He showed Kal how to fashion the prongs and removed some dried sinew from a bag.

'Chew', he instructed.

Kal put the sinew into his mouth and munched into it.

'Careful', Nemid said. 'Get it wet and limber in your mouth. Do not break it.'

Kal continued to chew as Nemid thrust the prongs into the fire.

'This will toughen them', he said.

Once he was satisfied, he held out his hand, and Kal put the moist ball of sinew into his palm. Nemid separated out a single strand and slowly wound the sinew around the end of the spear. After a time, he stopped and placed the prongs into place.

'You turn the spear', he directed. 'Slowly. Roll it along your leg.'

Kal chewed his bottom lip as he carefully moved the spear shaft, rotating it gently as he went. His eyes were on Nemid's movements as he carefully wound the sinew around the prongs, holding them firmly in place.

'You must be careful', Nemid said, 'not to break the sinew. When it is like this, it is pliable and easy to work but fragile. Once it dries, it will be strong and very tight.' They continued to fasten the sinew with the thread going up and back down to the base of the prongs.

'To finish', Nemid said, 'you do this.' He slipped an echidna quill under the last loop. 'Then around and around like this', he threaded the sinew into the loop again and again. 'Now', he said, 'carefully…', and he removed the echidna quill. The sinew snapped back into place. Nemid licked his finger and ran it along the join, pressing the end firmly into the coils. Satisfied, he placed the spear to one side.

'In a few days it will be ready.'

The look he gave Kal left Kal in no doubt that Nemid had made that spear for him.

'A boy always remembers his first spear', Nemid said. 'It is his first step towards being a man. It is special.'

Kal lowered his eyes, remembering how he'd stolen Nemid's spear with so little thought as to what that would mean to Nemid.

'I'm sorry for taking your spear', he said.

'Will you ever do it again?'

Kal shook his head, and they both knew he meant it.

'Then', Nemid said, 'that is a lesson well learnt.'

Kal glanced towards the window and was surprised to see it was dark outside. The only illumination came from the fire. Nemid got up and stretched. His eyes were sore, and he had a headache after all the fine work required to make a spear. His eyes were not what they used to be. Still, to teach a lesson well took time and patience, he reminded himself. Again, he wished he had young eyes to help, but alas all his children… He dragged his mind back to the present moment as quickly as he could and rotated his shoulders. All day he'd been expecting the Drekesh to burst in and demand that the boy be removed from the reservation, but was pleased that they hadn't. It seemed Healer Deikter had done her work.

'Time for bed', he yawned.

Over the next few days, Nemid taught Kal how to use the Nahill equivalent of a toilet and showed him how to wash. Reports back from Chani were that Kal never said a bad thing against either Nemid or the Jhunti in general, but seemed grateful to be here. Nemid's own observations concurred, and so he cleaned up a room for Kal and gave away most of the things that had belonged to his children. Chani and Chet Chet came every day to check on Kal's wounds and to give him bitter herbal tea. Finally, Nemid allowed Chani to speak to Kal in English, so she began to teach Kal Nahill words.

After a week of Nemid's tender care, Kal was feeling almost back to normal, and wherever Nemid went, there was Kal. The boy usually kept his head bowed, avoiding all but fleeting eye contact; however, those big green eyes drank in everything about the village, and his sharp ears picked up the nuances in people's tones. Every day, he was able to understand more Nahill words and made a habit of saying things in Nahill whenever he could. Nemid told Kal that right now everyone was getting ready for the first snowfall. Kal was excited as he'd never seen snow before. It never occurred to Kal that he no longer thought of living anywhere else.

5

One night a moon later, Kal sat at his bedroom window staring out at the falling snowflakes. Never had he seen anything so beautiful and delicate. He watched the fat flakes float down, hit the ground and disappear. It was so different here, he mused, not that Kal knew where *here* was. Where he came from, everything was hot and dry and flat. A flurry of snow dashed against the window, and Kal wished he could tell his Nan and Pop about this wonder. He missed them and wished he could write them a letter, but the Nahill had no post, no paper and no pens. Kal ached to brag about how he'd learnt to make fire, to grind seeds and beans and make paste and pancakes, to make a fishing spear and to sew using a bone needle and animal sinew. He was also pleased that he didn't need to shower and no one cared if he smelt because everything smelt.

There were many parts of the day that Kal enjoyed. One was combing Nemid's hair with a carved wooden comb and then having his own combed in return. They'd chat about little things as they did it. Nemid taught Kal new Nahill words, and there was always time for a story as they discussed their plans for the day. Kal also enjoyed meal times. There was no tension and very few rules for him to remember. Nemid told him that soon it would be tribal night when all the camp and council business was conducted and everyone caught up on the news.

On those nights, the hunters would bring back something for the fire pit. While sometimes it was meat, last time it was big red tubers that had a strong, earthy taste. Once roasted they'd been the perfect accompaniment to fish paste and greens. One time it had been nuts. Everyone sat around breaking the shells open between two rocks. Badly hit nuts shot away, landing on random people and making everyone laugh.

Kal also relished that time after the day was done when he and Nemid sat and stared at the flames of their fire in companionable silence. They listened to the cry of the night birds, the soft murmur of distant voices, an occasional baby crying or dog barking, all mixing in with the crickets and other sounds of the forest around them. Kal loved to watch the logs steam, hiss and then burst into flames. They'd sit watching until the flames died down to glowing red coals. The smoke, dotted with glowing red embers, would swirl and rise. It was very satisfying to sit after a long, hard day's work knowing the work provided for one's self and others. A body could ache, but it was a good kind of ache, and when it was time for bed, restful sleep came easily.

Another snow flurry hit the window. Not wanting to miss his first snowfall, Kal pulled his clothes on, dragged on his new fur-lined boots and winter coat and quietly opened his bedroom door. The cabin was empty as Nemid was out. Kal walked through the darkened living room, stopping for a moment to warm his hands by the fire. Opening the front door, he stepped outside onto the veranda.

The cold air made him take a sharp breath. All around, the fat flakes filled the air. He moved quietly along the front porch then out into the snow. Several large flakes landed on his face as he lifted his eyes skyward. They made an unmistakably dense hissing sound. Kal walked a little further, his boots crunching on the frozen mud. He held his hands out and tried to catch some of the falling snow, but it melted as soon as it hit his warm skin. He tilted his head and opened his mouth. Breath came out in white puffs. Sticking his tongue out, he managed to catch several flakes, which tasted strange and made his mouth feel funny. He closed his mouth and put his hands out again, determined to gather enough to taste properly.

Laughing at this game, Kal's way was lit by the lamps still burning in the front rooms of most of the cabins. He decided that the season of the First Snow was the best season ever. Rounding the corner, he heard angry voices coming from a nearby cabin that stopped him in his tracks. He was about to run away when he recognised Nemid's voice. Making out a few of the words, he wondered what had upset everyone until he heard his own name.

'Well you can't have it both ways', Nemid was saying. 'Either you think Kal is ill-mannered, in which case he must be taught how to fit in, or you accept him the way he is.'

'Teach him our ways?' an indignant male voice said. 'Are you mad?'

Kal moved closer. Inside, the man glaring at Nemid shook his head. It was better that Nemid heard this from his Water clan elders than from others. The white boy was being discussed everywhere. Most thought Nemid's attitude was a by-product of a too liberal upbringing. Others had assumed it was temporary, but it had been over one whole moon cycle now, and the white boy's continued presence was making people uncomfortable. Pressure was being brought to bear on the Water clan elders to *do* something. A baby started crying in the cabin next door. Kal moved closer still so he could hear.

'This cannot continue', said a new voice. 'Everywhere I go people are talking about him. You know as well as I do he should never have been allowed to stay.'

'We only survive while we remain separate from *them*.'

'He's just a boy', Nemid said.

'He's white scum!' said the angry male voice.

'He has to go and that's an end to it.'

'He means us no harm', Nemid said.

Again there was silence. Kal was oblivious to the snow catching in his hair now or how wet his coat was becoming.

'We know he brings you comfort', said a male voice. 'However, it must stop. Let us find you a new wife.'

'No! No more wives. No more children.'

'Then you must move. That cabin is needed for bigger families.'

There was a hiss of breath.

'We were not', a female voice said, 'going to raise that topic tonight.'

Kal quietly climbed up onto the veranda and peeped in the window. There were four men and one woman sitting on the floor with the fire at one end of the room. Nemid was sitting to one side, gaping at them in disbelief. He quickly schooled his features.

'If the cabin is needed, so be it', he said matter-of-factly. 'Kal and I can move into the single men's quarters.'

'Out of the question!'

'At the end of the day, the boy is not welcome here.'

'There is no cabin here that will take him', said another.

'He does not belong.'

'People have tolerated his presence only out of respect for you and our understanding that he helps you to recover from your loss.'

Kal watched Nemid's face flush and his fingers curl into fists.

'He is mine!' Nemid snapped. 'He was sent to me by the Great Spirits. His place is with me.'

'Maybe neither of you belongs at Red Camp', a man sneered.

'Now, now', said the woman shooting the other man a hostile glare. 'There is no need for that. We only want the boy to be returned to his people. It is the right thing to do. How would you feel if you lost one of your children?'

Although she'd meant it kindly, the others did not miss the pain that was suddenly on Nemid's face. He stood up.

'He is mine', Nemid said emphatically, 'and if we are no longer welcome at Red Camp then we shall go.'

One of the men hurriedly stood up and put a hand on his arm.

'Be at peace, old friend. We do not want you to go. Please, this is something that we know upsets people, so let us discuss it again with cooler heads. Do not feel you must leave Red Camp.'

Nemid was still for a moment then nodded.

'Very well. We shall talk of it more, but my answer will remain the same. Kal is mine, and I intend to keep him. If we are not welcome here, then we shall go.' He gave the man a brief hug then made for the door. Kal tiptoed silently back along the veranda, jumped down into the snow then started running. His heart raced, and he bitterly regretted his decision to stay. He knew what adults were like, and yet, he'd allowed himself to be lulled into feeling safe. He shook his head and again berated himself for being stupid. If he'd just stuck to his original plan, by now he'd be holed up in a nice, warm cave somewhere safely on his own.

He reached the cabin and, with practiced ease, pulled his clothes and boots off as he dove into his bed and buried himself under the covers. How many nights had he done just this when he'd heard Barry come home drunk and furious? Usually if he lay very still and didn't react, no matter what Barry said, he'd be left alone. Waiting now, he listened for steps along the boards, his heart thudding in his chest. When he heard Nemid's soft shuffling, he steeled himself by closing his eyes and pulling the blanket over his head. The front door opened. Kal's fingers curled into fists, vowing that when the first blow came, he'd not react. He knew the blanket was thick, which would lessen the impact, and he hoped that the beating didn't hurt too bad. The footsteps came to the bedroom, and the door opened. Kal shook with fear, and he prayed his movements weren't visible in the dark. Barry always got angrier when he knew Kal was feigning sleep. He wondered if it would be a belt or a stick or if he'd just hit him with his fists or kick him.

Nemid stood in the doorway staring at the small shape in the bed, one hand resting on the door jamb. Nemid knew he would not be able to keep Kal for much longer if things continued the way they were going. He sighed deeply, reluctant to approach Healer Deikter for more help because every time she showed him favours, it increased the likelihood of their plans being discovered and foiled before they had fully matured. He hoped the boy would be up to the task. It was a lot of responsibility to place on such small shoulders, but something deep down told Nemid that Kal would not let him down. Again he felt the presence of the Great Spirits on everything, and suddenly his conscience was allayed. If this was the way the Great

Spirits wished everything to be, then they would make it so.

Feeling reassured, he turned and went out of the cabin towards Healer Deikter's home. As soon as the front door closed, Kal sat up in bed, his eyes wide in disbelief. He glanced around the room, seeing all as it had been before. Nemid had taken nothing, smashed nothing and, best of all, had not laid a finger on him. Why? He jumped out of bed, tiptoed to the front window and pressed his nose against the glass as he spotted Nemid trudging through the snow along the path. Kal wondered where he was going. Part of Kal wanted to grab his things and run, but the other part knew Nemid would never harm him. He stood for a long while paralysed by indecision until he began to shiver. Deciding that it would be foolish to leave in the middle of the night when it was snowing, he went back to his mattress and snuggled into the welcome warmth of his blankets.

Unable to sleep, Nemid got up before dawn and restarted the fire. Taking up a cob of corn, he shucked the kernels into a basket. As he worked, he reviewed his life. He remembered that it had taken him many snows to confess to Leath that while he had loved his first wife, he had always regretted they had never been able to attract any baby spirits. Being sad that they were childless was something he had never told Trinuxa. But now that Leath was gone, he knew he would never confess that to anyone ever again.

The first grey of dawn came through the window. Nemid looked out at the thick mounds of snow that had settled around the village overnight. He moved his head from side to side watching the way the light sparkled. His children had always loved running out to play in the snow, he mused. He'd been planning to make them a new sled this season because the last one ended up in a bonfire. He smiled at the thought of that wonderful night, but then his smile faded and he dragged his thoughts back from the melancholy that beckoned to him. Tonight they would hold the first of the snow season feasts. In the great hall, there would be games, storytelling and contests.

Everyone would take something to share. He was pondering what to take as Kal emerged from his room, rubbing the sleep from his eyes.

'Morning', Nemid greeted Kal in Nahill.

'Morning', Kal yawned, also in Nahill.

Kal joined Nemid at the window and gazed out at the sparkling vista.

'More snow?' he said in English.

'Mmm.'

Kal stared out at the great expanses of white that he thought he'd never get tired of seeing. A flash of colour drew his attention. A group of young children were running in a circle, playing in the snow. Nemid followed Kal's gaze. All the children were Kal's age or younger. Their breath came out in white clouds, and he could hear a shriek of laughter as one of them fell over.

'Would you like to join them?' Nemid said in English.

Kal stared longingly at the children. Several were making snowballs and throwing them at a target, laughing when they missed.

'Go on.' Nemid gave Kal a nudge towards the door. Kal glanced at him and, seeing Nemid was serious, hurriedly dressed. Nemid watched him jump down into the snow and jog over to where the other children played. He hoped Kal would make some friends, as friends made all the difference when one had little family around.

When Kal reached the children, he stood awkwardly as some of the children spoke with him. After a brief pause, Kal made a snowball and threw it at the target. He missed and the children laughed before throwing their own snowballs at the target.

Nemid stepped away from the window to prepare breakfast. As a young man, he had wanted to make a difference to his tribe. He married into a powerful family and moved to Big Camp, the home of the Women's Council and the heart of tribal politics. Seen as somewhat of a rebel and once paired with the politically savvy and well-connected Trinuxa, he attained status and influence. But he lost all that when Trinuxa died, and he retreated into himself. Leath had lured him out into the land of the living again. He'd settled into his new marriage and parenthood as a battered ship finally drops anchor in a safe harbour. With her and his new family, he had been content to let others bring about change. To many it seemed as if after Leath died Nemid had returned to how he had been before he met her – withdrawn, quiet and preferring to keep his own company. But now Kal had given him a new purpose. Each day, he awoke keen to see that little face and ready for whatever life had to throw at them.

Angry shouts erupted from outside, and Nemid went back to the window. Some older children had joined the younger ones, and Kal was lying in the snow. He struggled to his feet and was pushed into the snow again by an older child. This child pointed at Kal and said something in an angry tone that Nemid could not make out. Kal scrambled onto all fours and crawled towards the cabin. The older children jeered and threw snowballs at him. One splattered into the back of Kal's head. Now the younger ones, who a moment ago had been happily playing with Kal, were also throwing snowballs at him. Nemid wanted to go out and yell at the children, but he knew this would just make things worse for Kal. Instead, he stood back from the window so no one could see him watching. Kal made it to his feet and ran towards the cabin, snowballs smashing into the ground around him. The rebel in Nemid stirred. Watching how these children were treating Kal awoke the old fire in him. It wasn't fair or just. It spoke of prejudice and was short-sighted, and on principal, he'd be damned if he was going to sit by and let it happen. A plan began to form in his mind.

Kal stomped up the stairs. He paused at the door to brush the snow from his clothes. He was angry and upset at what had happened. For a short time, he'd been having fun and thinking things would work out here, but then those older kids had arrived. It felt just like it did at school when he was teased for having messy hair, unwashed clothes or for being smelly. He put on a brave face as he didn't want Nemid to realise what a looser he was. Shoulders back, he went inside.

'Back so soon?' Nemid said.

'It's too cold.'

They prepared breakfast, and Nemid told Kal about the snow feast that night.

'I might stay here', Kal said.

'I would like…', Nemid began in Nahill.

'Too fast', Kal said, also in Nahill.

Nemid switched back to English.

'I would like you to come because you are a part of this community now, and besides, it will be fun.'

Kal remembered the expressions on the faces of the big kids, and didn't think it would be fun at all.

'Just do as I do', Nemid said, 'and all will be well.'

Somewhat reassured, they spent the day preparing a large pile of pancakes and, late in the afternoon, took them to the hall. Most of the camp had already gathered outside to watch a wrestling match between Water clan and Tree clan Drekesh. Nemid added his food to the piles left by others and led Kal to a vantage point at one side. He cheered on the Water clan Drekesh as the two men grasped each other and tried to fling their opponent to the ground. Kal couldn't see over those in front of him, but he didn't care. He'd seen enough fighting to last him a lifetime. Instead, he took a few steps back so he was out of the scrum around the contestants and studied those around him.

Nemid had told him that winter was the time the Nahill socialised. People would journey from every corner of the reservation to spend the snow season with friends and relatives in other camps and villages. During the long winter nights, they'd catch up on the news and gossip from other camps. This included much talk about the doings of family and friends, deeds of reservation favourites as well as decisions from the Women's Council. During the day they'd repair equipment, make new tools, create toys, clothes and other items they'd need for the seasons to come. There was also a lot of speculation about who would marry during the season of the New Leaves, also known as the claiming season.

A collective cry came from the gathered crowd, and Kal waited to see if the match was over. A moment later the cheering began again as two new combatants took the ground. Kal shoved his hands into his pockets and glanced towards the groups of people arriving. As they passed, most shot him looks – some curious, some hostile and occasionally there was a smile. It was hard to miss him, he thought, with his bright blonde hair, water-eyes and fair complexion. Kal could understand why they would not want to take in someone like him. He assumed that everyone somehow knew all the things Barry had said about him and thought he was lazy, a slut, useless and stupid.

A final cry from the crowd signalled the end of the wrestling. Kal saw Nemid making his way out of the throng and was quickly at his side.

'Who won?' he said in his stilted Nahill.

'Water clan and then Stone clan.'

'Not Tree clan?'

A smug smile crossed Nemid's lips as he shook his head once. Kal grinned and Nemid nudged his shoulder. A woman nearly twenty-five-snows old put a hand on Nemid's arm and said something to him that Kal didn't catch. Nemid put a hand on Kal's shoulder and steered him through the crowd and into the building. Nemid waved to a group of elderly onlookers sitting on a log against the wall. He let Kal go and went to join them.

Kal remembered that Nemid had told him to copy everything Nemid did, so Kal also gave a wave towards the group of elders and made to sit down. The elders exchanged offended looks, taken aback at the cheek of a young pup like Kal giving them the greeting of an equal. Nemid turned towards Kal.

'No', he said in English. 'Only I am entitled to greet the elders in that way and to sit with them.'

Kal looked crestfallen.

'But you told me to do everything you did', Kal hissed, hoping he hadn't upset everyone.

Nemid patted his arm and stood.

'You are right', he said. 'That was my fault. Please forgive me.'

Forgive him, Kal thought? Since when did an adult ask a kid to forgive them? Nemid walked towards a crowd of people gathered around another fire. Kal followed.

'Nem!' one of the revellers greeted him with a grin.

They embraced with hugs and pats on the back.

'So good to see this face', Nemid beamed. 'May I introduce Kal?' Nemid pulled him forward, and Kal felt eyes upon him. He bowed his head submissively, steeling himself for their anger, but it never came. When he glanced up he saw only curiosity in their kind eyes. Nemid sat next to one of his friends and indicated for Kal to sit close so they could all get a good look at him.

'Tell us how you came by him?' one of his friends said.

'Well...', Nemid began his story.

Deep down he was enjoying the notoriety Kal was bringing him. He felt like an invisible wall had been lifted and that he was once again a part of his community. When he'd finished his story, people enquired after his health and if he had noticed any omens or portents lately. Some asked his opinion, others watched the way he interacted with Kal. It reminded Nemid of when he had been married to Trinuxa.

She had been important, and it wasn't until tonight that Nemid realised he had missed the deference people showed him when he'd been married to a high-status woman. He felt alive and vibrant. His eyes scanned the faces, suddenly taking notice of the groupings and who was sitting with whom, just like Trinuxa had taught him. He pondered on the alliances and who appeared to have the most influence. He sent a silent thank you to Trinuxa for teaching him so much. She'd been so astute at political manoeuvrings.

If only he were Pac of Red Camp, he mused, he'd be a Pac who would be a true leader. Then Kal would never have to worry about being accepted. If he were Pac, what he said would go and that would be that. But he was so out of practice, he lamented. He'd allowed Leath and the children to distract him. He should have remained politically active and capitalised on his status when he'd come back from Big Camp instead of focusing only on Leath and their growing family. If he'd stayed more active, he may well have been able to challenge for the title of Pac by now. As it was, he had very little sway, so maybe it was time to change that, starting tonight.

Knowing Kal's shy, unassuming demeanour was his greatest

asset, Nemid sought out an influential elder and steered Kal over to make introductions. Kal understood a lot more Nahill words now, although he still only spoke a few. As Nemid introduced him to one elder after another, Kal stayed by Nemid's side. The older man occasionally placed a gentle hand on Kal's shoulder to pull him close. Kal felt like a chick under a mother hen's wing peeking out at the big wide world.

The air about them was festive and relaxed. People were eating, drinking and laughing. Ashekii saw Kal and Nemid and ushered his family over.

'It is good to see these faces', he said.

They embraced, and Ashekii introduced his wife Hahina to Kal. She eyed him dubiously. It was the first time she'd seen him up close. He didn't look particularly special, she thought, yet the Oracle herself had sent word via Healer clan that he was to stay. No one knew why, but if the Oracle decreed it was so, then so it would be. Ashekii introduced his children, starting with the oldest, an girl eight snows old named Poh. Hahina glanced at Nemid. He looked almost like he used to before the tragedy. His company was also in demand these days, as keeping this white boy had given him notoriety, though not everyone thought it was good for Water clan. Still, she thought, it was better than him sitting and crying in the forest. After a few moments, she made their excuses and ushered her family away. Kal watched them go.

Nemid strolled outside with a white-haired couple, deep in conversation, Kal never straying far from his elbow. Kal found it difficult to understand how everyone could be having such a good time. People actually seemed to be happy to see each other. They joked together, and young men bragged and competed for the attention of the pretty girls. The children ran around, and no one hit them or yelled at them. There were no tense faces, and no one seemed to be hiding or looking like they didn't want to be there.

In their turn, the Nahill openly studied the white boy, most with curiosity, some with hostility. Kal's attention was caught by a group outside of the meeting hall. They were playing a game with much hooting and laughter. At the end, the winner was put into a blanket then tossed up into the air, screaming with delight. Kal tugged at Nemid's sleeve.

'Mmm?' Nemid said, bowing his head so his ear was close to Kal's mouth.

'Where's Chani?' Kal said.

'Healers don't come to purely social events.'

Nemid returned to his conversation, and Kal sighed. He missed Chani and Chet Chet. He watched as another 'winner' was tossed up in the blanket. That looked like a lot of fun, he mused. What if he won? A thrill went through him at the thought. What would it be like to be tossed up into the air like that? As if reading his mind, Nemid pointed to the group.

'Would you like to play?'

Kal hesitated, tapping his fingers nervously against his hips as he stared at them.

'Come on', Nemid said, 'they're about to start Red Robin.'

He steered Kal over.

'Red Robin away!' someone shouted.

A stick painted with red ochre flew up into the air, and everyone in the group scrambled to catch it. A young woman yelled in delight and held the stick above her head in triumph. The rest of the group went to a pile of sticks to one side and each took one.

'Here', Nemid said, handing Kal a stick.

'But I don't know the rules', Kal said eyeing his stick uncertainly.

'Ready?' someone shouted.

Those with sticks formed a large circle in the snow, facing the centre. They put both hands behind them so no one could see their sticks. Nemid leant towards Kal.

'One person is holding a red stick', he said in hushed tones. 'The rest of us have normal coloured sticks. During the song, we pass our sticks on and when the music stops, the person with the red stick is out. Understand?'

Before Kal could answer, people began to sing. It was a fast ditty about a red robin's journey looking for sticks for her nest. The crowd did several quick steps left then wove back and forth between each other, mimicking the Robin as she wove her nest. Those watching also sang, and every so often, there was a pause in the tune. At that time the spectators clapped three times, and everyone in the circle turned towards the middle. Making sure they did not see the colour of the sticks, they passed their stick behind their backs to the person next to them for three heart beats and then the song and dance began again.

Kal's heart pounded as he tried to keep up with the fast pace of the game. He even started to sing along although he didn't understand most of the words. At each pause, he turned towards the middle and passed his stick to the next person, receiving a new stick in return. Suddenly there was the bang of the drum, and everyone stopped and held their sticks out in front of them.

A man to the right let out a cry of disappointment as he held up the red stick. People laughed as he exchanged his red stick with that of the person next to him and went to sit the rest of the game out. The singing and dancing started again. Nemid was out three turns later and gratefully went to sit down and watch. As the game continued, the stick-passing became faster and faster. The pace of the song increased as the numbers became fewer. In the song, the Robin knew a storm was coming and was hurrying to finish her nest before the wind blew her sticks away.

Soon the tempo was so fast that people tripped over each other and ran into each other, which made everyone laugh. Each of the players was breathing heavily, their breath coming out in white clouds. Even the onlookers were puffing as they clapped, sang and shouted encouragement. Kal lasted till there were ten people left in the circle. He was grinning as he went to join Nemid, who gave him a warm clap on the back.

'Well done', he said in Nahill. 'Well played.'

Kal understood what Nemid had said and basked in Nemid's affectionate praise.

When the stick game was over, the winner's prize was to be tossed in the air on a blanket amid screams of laughter. After this there was another dance, this one much slower. Everyone took part in it, stamping their cold feet and clapping their cold hands as they sang a song about an owl caught out in the snow and how he flew from one tree to another searching for a place to roost for the day. The dance was another simple series of steps, although this time with the feet turned out to imitate the feet of an owl. When they came to the chorus about the owl flying from tree to tree, people flapped their arms. When the owl had to clear the snow from the tree branch, people windmilled their arms. Everyone was warm and panting by the time the song finished, and all the 'owls' returned to their roost for a rest.

It was getting dark now, and Nemid ushered Kal back into the hall. Near the huge fireplace, bowls of stew were being served from a giant pot. Nemid placed a hand on Kal's back and steered him over to join the line.

'You are learning the dances well', Nemid said.

'You sure seem to have a lot.'

Nemid smiled. 'Dancing is very important to our culture. Dancing lightens the heart, rebalances the mind, helps us to focus. It makes us happy and shows the great Spirits we are thankful for their bounty.'

They shuffled forward.

'We have dances of joy and celebration, sadness and victory, courage, thankfulness and power gathering.'

They reached the pot, and each were handed a bowl of stew and a large pancake, still hot from the grill. Nemid ushered them over to one side then showed Kal how to slurp the stew from the bowl, using the pancake to mop up the leftovers.

'We have dances that celebrate the different animals and birds', Nemid said. 'We have dances that teach us their habits and ways and that venerate their cleverness and skills. Dancing is also a good way to get warm on a cold day.'

He smiled down at Kal, whose eyes were glistening with pleasure and alive with interest. Nemid ruffled Kal's hair. With their dinner finished, they rinsed their bowls in a pot of hot water then placed them upside down with the many others. To one side was a circle of men and women with baskets of corncobs. They were singing as they peeled away the squeaky husks and handfuls of silk.

'Hoy, Nem!' one of them called out and beckoned to Nemid. He smiled and steered Kal over to them.

'These are some of my Big Camp cousins', Nemid said to Kal.

He introduced Kal to each of them. As Nemid and Kal sat down, another woman began to sing. The song, which was sung first by one person and then responded to by the group, matched the slow rhythm of the corn peeling.

Look and see, she sang.
Ripe buds are calling, replied the others.
And can you hear? she continued.
The rain that's falling? sang the others.
And what does that mean?
Corn time is calling.

Nemid picked up two cobs of corn and handed one to Kal. Kal pressed his thumb into a kernel. It popped quickly from the cob and flew into the rafters. Kal laughed, and Nemid smiled and leaned toward him.

'Like this, Eyas', he whispered.

Nemid showed him how, with brief flicks of his thumb, he could separate the kernels from the cob. Kal mimicked the motion of Nemid's thumbs until he got the hang of it. The stripped cobs were tossed into a third basket.

'We dry those', Nemid whispered. 'They make excellent fire starters.'

When the basket was full of kernels, it was emptied into a hessian sack. The sack was taken to the front of the building near the fire and then suspended from the rafters. Kal remembered seeing sacks just like these hanging in Nemid's cabin. Nemid followed Kal's gaze.

'Once the kernels are dry', he said, 'they can be used for eating and planting.'

The women continued their singing. Kal had seen similar work circles for shelling beans. The pods, which dried on the vine, were placed into sacks, bashed and jumped on to reduce the pod cases to chaff. The chaff was discarded, and the beans were put into storage baskets. There were different songs for beans. As the song was repeated, Kal began to haltingly sing along. After many, many repetitions, they stopped singing and one of the women told a story. Nemid whispered the translation to Kal.

'This is the story of the three sisters. The three sisters are what we call our crops of corn, beans and pumpkin.'

The story was about three sisters who lived together in a field. Each sister was quite different. The first-born sister had been planted in the season of the Snow Thaw. She was very tall and watched over the other two. The second sister was planted in the season of the New Leaves. She was very thin and clung to the first sister in order to stand up. The third sister found soil in the season of the New Wings. She was always the baby who dressed all in yellow and who never left the ground. Kal stifled a yawn and leant against Nemid's shoulder, his eyes growing heavy as he listened.

Days passed, and the warm sun helped the sisters grow big and strong. Late in the season of the Dried Grass, the second sister decided it was time to leave. Her sisters mourned her until the season of the Apples when the third sister also said it was time for her to leave. The first sister was now on her own, tall and straight, but lonely. The days grew short and the nights cold. Just before the season of the Fungi, the first sister decided she no longer wanted to stay in the field. So she gathered herself up and went to the nearest house. Who should she find there but her other two sisters waiting for her? They were so happy to be united again that they celebrated for five days and nights.

'To stay healthy, we must always keep the three sisters together', Nemid explained. 'They like to be present at all our meals, and we must use them together in everything we eat.'

Kal woke with a start. He was lying on a mattress. It was dark and quiet, and his body tensed as he tried to work out where he was. Moonlight shone through the window and fell onto the bare wooden floorboards. Slowly he recognised his bedroom at Nemid's cabin. He had no idea how he had gotten here. The last thing he remembered was listening to the story of the three sisters. He wondered what had woken him when he heard a scratching at his bedroom door. Nemid's door opened and his footsteps approached. Kal's door opened and Chet Chet came in. The door closed again as Chet Chet came to stand beside him, her breath on his skin. He reached out and stroked her face. She licked his hand. She circled a few times then lay down, resting her head on his leg. Kal stroked her warm fur then put a hand over his mouth, yawning. In the distance, he could hear music and voices. He pictured the people dancing to the new tune. A slight smile ran across his lips. If anyone had told Kal he'd come to love dancing, he'd have said they were crazy.

Chet Chet yawned and rolled onto her side, her back running along his stomach. Kal put an arm around her and closed his eyes. There was something magical about dogs, he mused. He'd always wanted a pet, but had been afraid for its safety around Barry, knowing it would be an easy target, just like his beloved comic book. He swallowed back a lump in his throat as he remembered.

It had been after midnight on a Saturday. He was fast asleep when his bedroom door slammed open and the light snapped on. He'd started up, suddenly wide awake. Barry stood there, shaking his report card.

'When were you gonna tell me about this, you stupid slut?'

Kal smelt the alcohol on his breath.

'You got D's, you hopeless loser. Thought you could hide it from me, did ya?'

'But I showed it to you last...'

A smart smack across the face had whipped Kal's head back into the wall.

'Liar!' Barry yelled, and he grabbed the boy's shoulders. He shook him so hard Kal saw stars. Barry's thumbs left bruises in both Kal's shoulders. 'You're a useless, lying whore just like your mother. Time for your punishment.'

Barry snatched up Kal's favourite comic book.

'No!' Kal cried out, reaching for it. He didn't miss the smug smile on Barry's cruel lips as the sound of ripping brought tears to the boy's eyes. Stupid, stupid, Kal chastised himself, do not show emotion. As soon as Barry realised Kal loved something, it became a target. It was why Kal had never asked for a pet.

Small pieces of comic book began to rain down on him. Kal fought back more tears and lowered his eyes so Barry couldn't see how much it hurt to hear his beloved comic book being destroyed. He dug his fingernails into his palms, the fresh pain helping to stop the tears. Another confetti of comic book squares was thrown into his face, but Kal no longer cared. He'd taken his mind to a different place, a safe place where nothing Barry did or said could touch him or hurt him. He rocked back and forth, and the pain in his body eased as his mind took off like a bird from a burning tree.

When Kal returned to his body, he was alone, and the door was closed. Slowly, he got down on all fours and felt in the dark for the pieces, collecting them all. He put them into his school bag because his rubbish bin had already been emptied for the week, and he wasn't allowed to put anything into it until Friday. Tears silently ran down his cheeks.

Kal awoke again with a start, his face wet with tears. He hastily scrubbed them away and looked around the room to make sure no one had seen. Now it was light. Chet Chet raised her head from his leg. She turned to look at the door. A moment later Kal tensed as footsteps climbed the outside stairs. The front door opened and the footsteps came inside. Kal relaxed, knowing it was just Nemid. A shushing sound made him look out the window. Fresh flakes of snow were falling. It was odd, he mused, that snow seemed to soak up every sound and the air had a thick, soft quality to it. Everything was so bright now that everywhere was coated in white banks of snow. It made the few areas of Red Camp that Kal had become familiar with unrecognisable. Chet Chet went to scratch at the door. It opened, and she went out. Kal knew it was time to leave his warm blankets.

'It is good to see this face', Nemid said as Kal emerged.

'Preshta', Kal said.

Kal took an empty cup from those hanging on the wall and added a pinch of ground nut meal and a sprinkle of dried honeypot bush flowers to it. Removing the large kettle from the fireplace, he poured boiling water into his cup, releasing the spicy honey scent of the mix. It blended in with the general smells of damp earth, wood, corn silk and stew. Kal put it on the hearth then went outside to relieve himself.

Nemid took a sip of his own cup, letting the warm liquid slide down his throat. There was a lot to do today. Last night had reminded him of just how many people from Big Camp had come to Red Camp for the snow season. Nemid knew now was the perfect time to introduce Kal to them. If he wanted the adoption to go through with a minimum of fuss, he needed to start his campaign. He was still pondering who would be best to start with when Kal returned.

Nemid glanced at the boy. His hair was still tousled from sleep and his cheeks and skin pink from the cold. Kal kicked the snow from his boots. Tonight, Nemid thought, he would make the boy mittens. So much to do, Nemid mused, and never enough time. It didn't occur to him that just a few weeks ago, time had weighed so heavily on his hands that the only thing he'd welcomed was sleep.

6

During the season of the Snow Thaw the snow melted. Everywhere, things were dripping and beginning to awaken after their winter hibernation. The time keeper, one of the most important women in the camp, was charged with knowing when it was time for such things as ceremonies or when a new season had begun. She was skilled in reading both the stars and the winds and interpreting the subtle signs of nature. One day she decreed that the rest time of the snow-seasons was over. Tomorrow, she said, was the first day of the season of the Salmon and time to start work. Some were to go to the streams to fish salmon, which would be coming back from spawning in the thaw-fed streams, and others were to start preparing the fields.

Kal awoke to the welcome smell of breakfast. Chet Chet was standing in his doorway, her tail wagging in a way that told him Chani was close by. He got out of bed and quickly dressed. Chani was pouring porridge into bowls and raised her head as he came in.

'Morning', he greeted her in Nahill.

'Morning, Kal', she replied.

Chet Chet sat beside her mistress. The dog's eyes were alive, and her pink tongue was hanging out the side of her mouth. Chani was the only Healer to have a dog, but Chet Chet was special. She seemed to just know when someone needed company. Chani's mother, Healer Deikter, had encouraged Chani to train Chet Chet how she saw fit and to ignore the jibes of others. Healer Deikter had also told

Chani that the Great Spirits had not intended everyone to follow the same path and that a person only had to look around to see this in the many different types of birds, plants and trees. If one looked hard enough, they could see that no two were the same. Her mother and Nemid had continually told Chani that she must trust her own judgement and follow her instincts when it came to healing people. They said she should follow this even if others did not agree with her. It was advice that often put her at odds with her sister Healers. However, she always had Chet Chet if she needed company, and now she had Kal too.

Chani stroked Chet Chet's head and studied Kal. She liked spending time with him. Everyone said Kal was trouble and it was a disgrace that Nemid kept him, but Chani trusted her parents' judgement. She sensed they saw something in Kal that others did not. He seemed to be smart and eager to please. His body told her that he'd been mistreated in the past, but the Nahill believed that everything happened for a reason. Like the Nahill, Kal would come to accept that the past was the past and there was only now.

'Ground', she said quietly and Chet Chet lay down.

Nemid came to join them, rotating his shoulders.

'Feel ready to help in the fields today?' he said to Kal.

'Yes', Kal said.

'Good. It is time to plant the first of the three sisters.'

They ate a hearty meal together. Kal gave Chet Chet a secret spoonful of his porridge. Chani ruffled Kal's hair as she walked past.

'I saw that', she whispered and left.

Kal chuckled and finished his porridge. He and Nemid packed their midday meal and a flask of water and strode out into the crisp morning air. Outside was suddenly alive with vivid colours and new smells. It was as if all one's senses had been asleep and now had woken up with the melting of the snow. The fragrances ranged from damp earth and honey-scented acacia blossoms to the delicate perfume of the first tiny orchid blooms. Kal decided that the season of the Salmon was the best season ever.

The two made their way to the huge planting field. People were already at work creating mounds. Two men, each with a bucket of ash, were measuring out where each new mound was to go then marked the spots with the ash. Taking a spade and a hoe, Kal and Nemid walked out to the nearest marker. They chipped off the top layer of weeds and grass then turned over a circle about three feet wide before digging a moat around the new mound. They added several spades of rich, well-rotted compost and flattened the top. Using a stick, Kal poked a hole in four corners of the mound while Nemid added a kernel of corn to each and covered it over. After that, they moved on to the next ash marker. As the villagers worked, they sang songs about the harvest. Kal hummed along.

Make our mounds rich
So the sisters are happy
Give us rain, give us sunshine
Let the ground be warm and fertile
That our sisters may grow
We thank you for this bounty to come
Praise to the Great Spirits of the harvest

When they stopped at midday, Kal wiped his hands, which smarted from new blisters. They walked to the shade of the trees, and Kal wished they had a tractor. Most of the children from his school had come from farming families, including his best friend Stewie. On the few occasions when Kal's father had let him stay with Stewie, Kal loved riding on the tractor with Stewie's dad.

'Nedda?' he said, using his pet name for Nemid and switching to English. 'How come you don't use tractors?'

'What are tractors, Eyas?'

'They're like… D'you know what a car is?'

Nemid was thoughtful.

'Yes, I have seen a car. Most of the camps have a few cars, although very few know how to drive them and they are not used often.' He cocked his head towards Ashekii. 'He knows how to drive a car.'

'OK, so a tractor is like a car but bigger. They pull stuff behind them. They're real strong.'

'Oh? Strong like a horse?'

'Stronger. I've been in one, but I've never driven one. I can drive a car though… well, I can drive a paddock bomb.'

'Paah dock bomb?'

'Yeah, an old car, you know, one only fit for driving around paddocks. Paddock bomb.'

'Paddock bomb', Nemid repeated quietly to himself.

'So why don't you get tractors?' Kal said.

'Because it wouldn't be right.'

Kal raised a quizzical eyebrow.

'We believe', Nemid said, 'that the purpose of life is to work with the resources nature gave us.'

Kal cocked his head towards the hoe then looked back at Nemid. Nemid smiled.

'We believe that the greatest pleasures in life come from overcoming obstacles. Think about it yourself. If you think back to something you did that gave you a great sense of satisfaction, was it something that was given to you, or was it something you had to strive for?'

Kal thought for a moment, remembering the only race he'd ever won. He'd practice for ages and eventually became stronger and faster. He'd shown that ribbon to everyone. Seeing that Kal understood, Nemid continued.

'We believe that although we could try to rid ourselves of adversity, this would not be good for us. It is why we shun the white world. It is not the removal of hardship that brings happiness. Instead, we believe what brings happiness is learning to deal with adversity. If a person can do this, then they will find happiness no matter how things turn out for them. It may only be what we call small happiness, but it will be happiness.'

'Small happiness?' Kal said.

Nemid handed him the flask of water. Kal took a drink, enjoying the coolness of the water on his hot and dry throat.

'Did that bring happiness?' Nemid said.

Kal nodded and handed the flask back.

'That is small happiness.' He indicated their surroundings. 'A shady spot to rest on a hot day. A child's laughter. The smile of your beloved. Small happiness's are what make our lives rich. If we strive for perfection, then we will not be able to see them in life's grandeur. Better to live simply and take comfort in small happiness's.'

They ate meat rolls and drank cool water while staring out at the field and the hundred or so mounds that now peppered the corner closest to them. Kal stared at them and could feel what Nemid was saying. He felt a great sense of achievement knowing he had helped create many those mounds. He also felt the small happiness of resting with Nemid beside him. The feeling reminded Kal of when he'd have breakfast with Father Stevens. Father Stevens had befriended him when he'd found 9 year old Kal going through the bins after a baptism, hungrily searching for food scraps. From then on Father Stevens had invited Kal to share breakfast. Kal remembered the last breakfast they'd shared together. It had been a few days before he ran.

'What did you learn at school this week?' Father Stevens had said.

Despite always being hungry, Kal tried not to shovel his food down too quickly, silently counting the number of chews and making sure each mouthful got ten. He had swallowed his mouthful and placed his spoon back in his bowl. Out of habit he followed Barry's rule of making sure that the handle was pointing straight toward his chest.

'Bush craft', he had said quietly, his eyes still on the table.

'Bush craft? What's that?'

Kal frowned, wondering if the Father was being genuine or if he would accuse Kal of being a smart arse if he answered. He stole a glance at the Father and saw an encouraging smile.

'It's learning about plants and animals and things like trap making.'

'Is that a fact?' Father Stevens had said.

Kal had nodded.

'Sometimes', he had said quietly, 'I ride my bike out to the reserve and find bush tucker.'

'What's bush tucker?'

'Like fungi and grass seeds and stuff.'

'Well bless my soul. I've never heard of anyone doing that before. An unusual hobby.'

Kal was brought back to the present by the movement of the Nahill around him. They were standing up and returning to the field.

Nemid stretched. 'Enough rest', he said.

Kal stood in one fluid movement, but Nemid struggled to rise. Today he was feeling his age. Together they walked slowly back to the field to recommence their backbreaking work.

The next morning Chet Chet came panting through the door just after dawn. Kal had been picking at the blisters on his hands as Chani came in. She dropped her healer bag beside him.

'Any injuries?' she asked.

Kal held out his hands. She rummaged in her bag for ointment and came to sit beside him. He'd worked hard, she mused, and his efforts had not gone unnoticed. Most people said whites where all stupid and lazy, but Kal was proving to be neither. She gently smeared a little ointment on each blister and rubbed it in. Kal gritted his teeth. When she was done with his hands, she pushed his leggings up, examined his shins and rubbed several scratches with ointment.

'Done', she said and stood up. 'Come, Chet Chet.'

With that, the pair left. The whole camp spent the next moon out in the field continuing to make mounds and plant the first of the three sisters. Even though Kal's whole body ached, he enjoyed the rhythm of subsistence farming. He liked that he knew what would be happening from one day to the next, that his safety was not dependent on anyone's mood and that he didn't have to try to read anyone's behaviour to see if he could sleep at home or if he had to run.

Once the mounds were finished, Kal had hoped they would be able to rest, but it was time to repair the trenches. The trenches went from the river to the crops and would bring life-giving water during the short but hot growing season. Using a hoe, they created a small channel between each mound for the water to flow. This took many days.

Once the smaller channels had been made, the men cleared the big channel. This was cold, difficult work that was done wearing only a loin cloth. Kal and Nemid were both chilled to the bone as they helped pull the weeds blocking the flow. Most of the time their feet were so cold they could not feel them. The only saving grace was that it was easy to see the leaches and ticks on their skin.

Once the channel was cleared, they checked that the sluice gates were working and spent several more days getting the flow just right. After this, Chani and Chet Chet came to inspect both Kal and Nemid. Both were pronounced fit for the planting festival.

The planting festival was filled with ceremonies to call for the Great Spirits' blessings on the new life to come. There were stories at night, and every day there were prayer ceremonies followed by a feast and games and dancing. Everyone dressed in their best clothes and adorned their long black hair with feathers, flowers and figures woven from brightly coloured threads. When the dance songs started, Kal sat watching with wide eyes. Ashekii came over to him.

'Come and join us, Kal', he said.

Ashekii grabbed Kal's hand and pulled him into the circle. Someone took his other hand. Kal's heart pounded for fear he'd make a mistake. The dancers and those watching started to sing and were accompanied by drums and flutes. The dance steps were simple. Step to the right, step to the right, stomp one foot on the ground then repeat the movement to the left. Kal soon picked up the rhythm and the words to the song and sang and danced along with the rest of them.

By the time they got to the season of the New Leaves, the second sister was planted, and there was another feast of thanks. Nemid sat on one of the logs surrounding the fire, and Kal took up his place in the dirt at his feet. Kal was beginning to feel like this was where he was meant to be. He scanned the now familiar faces, searching for the new boy, Trindal. At last Kal saw him sitting to one side. The young man had prominent cheek bones, a slender nose and water-eyes of a deep steely blue framed by long lashes. His straight black hair was in plaits halfway down his back. His attractive features were enhanced by his impish grin and dimples.

Kal was surprised when a woman from Trindal's family came to sit in the storyteller's place, wearing a storytellers' scarf. Chani came to sit beside Kal, Chet Chet taking up her place between the two of them. Kal absently began to stroke her soft fur.

'What you doing here?' Kal whispered to Chani in Nahill, which he understood well enough now not to need an interpreter. 'I thought Healers not come to social things.'

She cocked her head towards to an elderly woman settling herself on a log close to the warm fire.

'I came with Hersal', she said, as if that explained everything. She turned her attention to the two storytellers. 'That one's name is Bidiziil', she said indicating the woman. 'She is a storyteller originally from Black Camp. The boy, Trindal, is…'

When she paused Kal looked at her.

'What?'

Chani frowned.

'They do not treat him well.'

'Oh?'

Chani cocked her head towards the storyteller.

'That is not his mother. She is his cousin. Their whole family is storytellers, which is why they travel so much. He has been sent to live with many in his family. They believe water-eyes are unlucky, so none wish to keep him.'

'Shh', the person beside them hissed, 'it begins.'

The stragglers hurried to take their places beside the fire. Kal settled in with anticipation. Storytime had become his favourite time of the day. He could picture each character in his mind and visualise the scenery as it was described, adding his own details and colours. Because of this, he liked it better than watching TV or going to the movies. Sometimes the tales seemed so real, he smelt the fragrances described, felt the cooling breeze on his skin, tasted the thirst from the dust and dry wind, or his skin raised up in goose bumps from a tale set in the snow.

The two storytellers clapped their hands, and an expectant quiet fell over those gathered. Bidiziil glanced at the white boy in their midst. Knowing he'd be here, she had selected her story with care. She cleared her throat and began.

'Before we came to this land', she said, 'the Jhunti were as many as the grass on the plains. We still remember the peoples we traded with. There were the Tamar, who fished and lived by the big waters. There were the Clovellagul, who lived on the plains and hunted the fast runners. There were the Shapterong, who lived near the dessert and were black like the night sky. There were the light-skinned Gunwilly, who lived in the cloud-filled lands, and we, the Nahill, who always lived in the great mountains.'

Bidiziil scanned the rapt expressions about her.

'Every season of the Dried Grass', she said, 'everyone would gather together to celebrate, trade and feast. For as far as the eye could see, there would be fires. Our feasts were a time when eyes would be opened to what others were doing. It was a time for swapping young blood so that all prospered. It was a time to meet old friends and relatives. There were special games of strength, skill and endurance for the Drekesh. It was a time for sharing and trade. It was a time of peace and happiness for all.'

She cleared her throat, her eyes glistening in the light.

'We had many clans back then. We had spirit clans to care for our laws, customs and holy people. Clans of the Fire, Water, Air, Sun, Spirit and the clan of the Star Sisters. Which of these spirit clans do we still have left?'

'Water clan', they chorused.

Bidiziil smiled in approval.

'We had clans who cared for our fellow living creatures: Plant clan, Fish clan, Bird clan, Animal clan, Insect clan. From these, only Fish and Bird clan are left. We had clans who cared for Mother Earth

– the Stones that made our homes, the Trees that kept us warm and cooked our food, the Earth clan that fed us with plants, the Makers who would clothe us and create wondrous things. Of these clans, which now remain?'

'Stone clan and Tree clan', the children said.

Bidiziil indicated their surroundings.

'While some chose the plains, it is here in the mountains where we, the Nahill, are most at home. In the heart of the mountains, we leave our dead. In the heart of the mountains, we keep our ancestral records. In the heart of the mountains are our dreaming cliffs.'

Bidiziil again looked at the children.

'Today we are fewer, but we remember the stories of our ancestors. We honour their ways and live as they lived.'

She took a sip of water.

'We owe our lives to the good will of the traditional owners of this land. We pay homage to all their elders past and present. Without their generosity, guidance and wisdom, we, the Jhunti, would have perished a few seasons after our arrival.'

She indicated that the story was over and was handed a platter of food. Kal turned around to peer up at his grandfather. Nemid was staring thoughtfully at the fire. There was something in Nemid's expression that disturbed Kal. He frowned.

'Alright?' he said quietly.

Nemid dragged his thoughts back and smiled at his little foundling.

'Yes, Eyas. Time for bed for this one.'

Kal stood and helped his grandfather up. As they walked back to the cabin, Kal thought about his grandparents. He wished they could visit. There were so many things he wanted to show them and people he wanted to introduce them to like Nemid, Chani and Ashekii. He wanted to tell them about surviving just fine without electric lights and about how when people moved from one room to the next, they'd take the small lamps with them because it was considered wasteful to leave lamps burning in unoccupied rooms. He wanted to show them how all the water was carried from a nearby river in wooden buckets. Nemid said these buckets were only made in Black

Camp. Kal missed some things like toast and ice cream, but he didn't miss cleaning his teeth or being made to mop Barry's floors. He was getting used to no flushing toilets and not washing, but he was finding the daily check of his body for leeches and ticks tiresome.

He was also getting used to not hearing any mechanical noises as there were no cars, chainsaws or lawn mowers, no TVs, ringing phones or constant hum of agricultural machinery. There were no clocks, no sirens, radios or stereos. He could easily believe that the modern world did not exist. One night as he and Nemid were walking along, an aeroplane flew overhead, its lights blinking in the dark sky. Kal tilted his head up to look at it, feeling a jolt at being reminded of his past. Nemid also looked for the source of the noise, but it never occurred to him to look up.

Just like any farming district, there was always a lot of discussion about the weather. The sunrise and sunset were studied every day. Nemid said the clouds and colours gave a clue about the weather to come. The wind was also consulted. There were many types of wind, each with a different meaning. There was the squeaky wind that came when things were ready to harvest, the sneaky wind where everyone got their tasks done early in the day then sought shelter as it would throw things about, and the wind of the dead that was so cold it was like having dead fingers go right through you. There was also attention paid to the habits of the insects, animals and birds, as well as the plants and trees. Their instincts were never wrong when it came to the weather.

Nemid taught Kal the Nahill seasons as the Nahill way of life revolved around them. Right now it was late spring in the white world, but to the Nahill, it was the season of New Wings when the baby birds were fledging. This was time to plant the other two sisters – a hardy variety of broad bean and a small bush pumpkin. Every man, woman and child was engaged in the planting from sun up to sun down. Even the toddlers were put to work. They were given branches to scare the birds away and stop them from digging up the freshly planted seeds.

After this it was summer in the white world, but to the Nahill, it was the season of the Butterflies when the air was alive with the colourful creatures. This was followed by the hottest part of the year. The season of the Dried Grass was when old bedding was thrown onto the compost heaps and replaced with fresh smelling sweet grass. The broad beans and pumpkins were harvested, and green beans were planted. These smaller beans matured in only two moons, although the Nahill constantly roamed the fields snacking on them from the moment the sweet tasting pods emerged. After this was the season of the Apples. This season was characterised by pleasantly sunny days and cold, crisp nights. This was when the corn, green beans and apples were harvested, and again the whole village took part. Great vats of apples were boiled on open fires, and the resulting mush spread out onto specially prepared racks to dry. This was eaten throughout the year by travellers or as a sweet treat. Sometimes wild berries or nuts were stirred into the mix. If any honey could be spared, this would be added.

The season of the Fungi, when Nemid had found Kal, started after the first of the big rains. The Nahill would take sacks out into the forest to collect edible varieties of fungi. After this was the season of the First Snow. In the white world, it was called winter. To the Nahill, this was a time when no one travelled, and the time was spent mending, making and talking with family and friends. Discussing where one was to spend this season was a favourite pastime. After the season of the First Snow was the season of the Snow Thaw. This was a time of rapid change. Guests would make their way home, and vendors would travel from camp to camp trading goods. In every camp, funerals would be held for those who had died over the snow seasons.

The snow storm damage was mended, and everything was cleaned and made ready for the season of the Salmon. This was a season of great joy for the Nahill. Not only did everyone enjoying getting out into the sunshine to celebrate the end of the snow and cold, but it was when they held the ghost ceremony, thanking death for passing them by and honouring those who had gone on ahead. Everyone ate their fill of fresh salmon. This was also claiming season when couples married.

Nemid's cough brought Kal back from his reveries. He sighed and hoped his grandparents were safe and well. While he missed them, he had no thoughts of going back to the hell that was Barry's house, not even for them. Firmly putting thoughts of home aside, he blew out the lights as Nemid went to bed. Kal took himself to his own mattress, wrapped himself tightly into his blankets and fell asleep.

7

Kal woke every day to clear blue skies and hot sunshine. He and Nemid would breakfast then head down to the fields to plant the third sister. The third sister was a voracious bush pumpkin that grew to just bigger than a man's clenched fist. She was bright yellow in colour, and her spiky leaves spread out over the bean and corn mounds smothering weeds, deterring predators and keeping the moisture in. It was hard work, and Kal often came home exhausted with a headache from being in the sun all day. On a deeper level, he was finding it relaxing. Each day was the same, and the routines were comforting.

At first, everyone said the fine weather was a good omen as it made the three sisters grow fast and strong, but after a while, people noticed the forest drying out. The ground became crisp underfoot. Even birds and animals were panting in the unrelenting heat. All over the reservation, the Nahill entwined fern fronds with their hair to make instant sun shades. Every morning, they made offerings to Thondara, the Great Spirit of rain, asking her to quench everyone's thirst. The morning and evening skies were eyed keenly for any hint of rain on the way. Still it remained dry.

On the next tribal night, which was always held on the full moon, there were two storytellers, Aloth and Trindal. Storyteller Aloth was Kal's favourite. Her missing teeth allowed her to make the most impossible noises to illustrate her stories. She had mastered many different voices and accents to bring the characters in her tales to life. Her ratty black hair was bestrewn with coloured feathers. Trindal took his place beside Aloth as he studied the crowd, noting with satisfaction a number of elders, council members and powerful Drekesh. He had learnt a long time ago that it was always beneficial to endear one's self whenever the opportunity arose. At nine snows old, his features were already pleasing to look at with the promise of a handsome appearance to come. He used his good looks and his finely honed, engaging manner to charm everyone he met. Always an astute boy, he'd quickly learnt that storytellers were always welcome around a fire.

Trindal had never known his parents. His father had been white, and both had died when he was young. Beside him, Aloth readied her storytelling bag, pulling out the items they would use that night. Trindal had quickly attached himself to Aloth as she was a genius when it came to making different voices. He'd also learnt many new stories from her and was hoping the family of cousins he was currently traveling with would stay in Red Camp for a while so he could learn more.

Trindal had always loved stories. The tales of their history and the lessons learnt by those gone before gave him a sense of belonging. He was a natural entertainer and loved holding his audience's attention. As he told stories, he revelled in his listeners' gasps of wonder or amazement, hisses of anger and howls of laughter as he drew them along the story's path with him. Together the tales took them to strange lands and introduced them to new situations and people. As a storyteller, he was supposed to value each tale equally, but of course he had his favourites, and this evening he was going to tell one of them. He loved telling any of the kinship tales because these allowed him to show off his growing prowess in different voices. Hearing an expectant hush fall over the crowd, Trindal smiled at those gathered, his deep blue eyes glinting in the firelight. Aloth began to speak.

'This is the story of the big drought', Aloth said. 'None of us were alive when this happened. At first everyone was happy with the sunshine, basking in the warmth after the cold snows. People shed their thick overclothes and watched as everything became lush and green. The smells of the forest returned. The flowers came up, and everywhere was vibrant and alive after its big sleep. The insects and birds returned, making the air alive with buzzing, bird songs and flying things.'

'But the heat grew', Trindal continued. 'The heat became oppressive like when one sits too long at the fire. At first the warmth is welcome, but then it becomes stifling.' Trindal pulled some fern leaves woven together and started to fan himself as if he were very hot. 'We sweat and wish for relief.' He wiped his forehead with the back of his hand. His actions were so convincing, those watching began to feel their own temperatures rising.

'And so it was', Aloth said, 'for the three sisters, who grew increasingly thirsty. The streams dried up and so did the water holes – even the ones that never dried up. It was terrible for everyone.'

Trindal put a cup to his lips, but it was empty. He shook it upside down. Several in the crowd reached for their own drinks.

'One day Kin Echidna says, I'm sick of all this heat.'

Trindal used the fingers of one hand to form the spikes that covered the small animal. He placed his other hand in front of his face to illustrate the long proboscis with which the Echidna probes ant nests and sucks up the ants. He shook his head.

'I can't get my snout into the bark or the dirt to get those ants for my dinner', he said. 'We must do something. Who's going to see the Great Spirits and find out what's wrong?'

'Back then', Aloth said, 'the Great Spirits still lived on earth with us because they hadn't gone up to live in their garden yet. Did I tell you why they went up there?'

The children shook their heads.

'Oh, well, back in the before times, the Great Spirits lived here on Earth with us, and we could visit them if we needed to. After a while they decided that things here were going so well, we didn't need them anymore. So they called everyone together and said they were going back to their home in the sky. People were sad, but the Great Spirits said there was no need for sadness. They said they'd be able to look down on all of us.' She took a sip of water.

'Of course', Trindal said, 'to help them keep an eye on things and to carry messages back and forth, they asked the crows to help. Back then, crows were brown, but they made them black so they'd blend in with the night sky. Now, when you see a crow watching, you know it's the Great Spirits. If you want to send a message up to the Great Spirits, you tell a crow.'

Using a classic storyteller ploy, both settled back as if they were finished. Trindal's gaze went to Chet Chet. She was sitting next to Chani and looking at him. When their eyes met, her tail thumped in the dirt. He smiled then moved his gaze to Chani. She was saying something to the man seated behind her. Trindal wasn't sure who he was. The white boy, Kal, was sitting beside Chani and was also speaking to the man now. Gossip about Kal was rife everywhere Trindal went. It seemed everyone had an opinion about him. Just the mention of him livened up a campfire discussion as people passionately expressed their views. Deep down, Trindal felt a kinship with Kal because of their shared white heritage. Trindal wished he could speak white words as he had many questions to ask about white people. He rarely saw Kal, however, as he always seemed to be in the fields, and Trindal spent all his time with the storytellers. Before them, several of the children exchanged concerned looks.

'What happened to Kin Echidna?' a little girl said.

Storyteller Aloth raised an eyebrow.

'Oh', she feigned surprise, 'didn't we finish that story?'

The children shook their heads.

'Just as well you reminded us then', she smiled. 'Let's see. Where were we?'

'Kin Echidna couldn't find food', one child offered.

'Kin Echidna wanted to know who was going to talk to the Great Spirits', said another.

Aloth nodded. 'That's right. Well, let's see now. It's true, Kin Echidna wanted someone to go and find out what had happened to the rain. Kin Ant said he'd do it, but everyone said he'd be too slow. Then Kin Kangaroo arrived.'

Trindal smoothed out the dirt before them and, with thumb and forefinger, made the footprint of the kangaroo. First, he made one long print for the big toe then a single hole a finger's width from the end of the big toe. This was the lethal toenail that could split a man in two. Trindal made two smaller toe impressions on either side.

'This', he said, 'is Kin Kangaroo. She said she'd do it, but everyone said she'd be too slow. What we need, Kin Echidna said, is someone who can fly there fast. All the eyes went to Kin Falcon, who flew the fastest of all.'

Aloth continued the tale. 'Alright,' Kin Falcon said, 'I'll go.' So off she flew towards the camp where some of the Great Spirits lived. Soon she came to the home of Great Spirit Mezeh. He had long grey hair and was in charge of dragging the night across the earth. His skin was black, and he was always tired with big bags under his bloodshot eyes. He lived with Great Spirit Larath, the mother of the dawn, who chose all the colours we see in the sky each morning. Her skin was light blue and she had red cheeks and sky blue eyes and hair of white clouds. Their daughter was Great Spirit Deti, the one who cared for fish and all things that lived in the water. Her skin was the colour of mud, and her eyes were black like a deep well. In the next dwelling was Great Spirit Merita, the one who brought on the new growth. Her skin was brown and looked like wallaby fur. She was young and vibrant and always moving. Her fingers were long and supple and she moved with a spring in her step. She lived with her father, Great Spirit Deema. He was the old man who collected the dead and took them to the garden of the Great Spirits. He was solid and his presence reassuring. He was dressed in brown like the fallow earth, ready for new things to grow. Last was Great Spirit Steppa, responsible for war and worry. He was red all over with black hair and eyes like grey thunderclouds. Great Spirit Steppa was the only one who lived alone.'

Trindal took up the story. 'When Kin Falcon arrived she found that the land around the Great Spirits was just as dry as everywhere else. Now the Great Spirits, even though they look like us, don't need food and water like we do, so they hadn't noticed. Kin Falcon asked if they could find out what was happening as soon everything would begin to die from thirst. The Great Spirits decided they would go and speak with the Rain Spirit to find out what was going on. They took Kin Falcon with them, up they went. Up, up, up into the sky. The Great Spirits helped Kin Falcon fly higher and faster than she'd ever flown before. Up, up, up. Eventually they came to the home of Thondara the Rain Spirit. Her skin was white and translucent like a newborn tadpole. Her hair was made of waterfalls with rainbows about her, and her eyes were the deep green of the ocean.'

'What's the ocean?' one of the children asked.

Aloth smiled and held up her hands.

'That's a place we used to know well but not these days. It is a place that consists only of water and very strange creatures.'

'Is it as big as Lake Meri Yallock?'

'Many, many times bigger. I will tell some stories of the ocean another night.'

Trindal felt a thrill of excitement course through him. He'd only heard a few stories about the ocean and was keen to hear more, particularly stories passed down from the ancients.

'Now', Aloth said, 'where were we?'

'Kin Falcon had just found Thondara', one of the children prompted.

'Ah yes, Kin Falcon was at the home of Thondara the Rain Spirit and there was water everywhere. Pools, rivers, lakes and rain fell in big fat drops. A fine mist fell sideways in a swirl. Dew sat on everything, and to one side were all the different types of snow and sleet and ice.'

Trindal again took up the story.

'You know those rainbows you see after rain?' All the children nodded. 'Well that's her hair as she bends over to check that the rain has fallen in the right place.' The children smiled. 'Anyway, the Great Spirits told Kin Falcon to tell her tale, and so she did. She talked about the lack of rain and the drying streams and rivers. She told Thondara about Kin Echidna not being able to stick her snout into the earth to get ants. When she was finished, she asked what they'd done to anger the Rain Spirit.

'The Rain Spirit was puzzled. 'I just sent rain a few days ago', she said. Then the Rain Spirit reached behind her and grabbed a cloud that was filled with rain. She gave it a shove towards earth. They all stood watching as the cloud made its way closer and closer, and then, suddenly, it wasn't there anymore.

'Send another one', Great Spirit Deti said, thinking of all the fish and water creatures who were suffering. Thondara selected a second cloud, bigger this time, and sent it towards the earth. Rain poured down and then suddenly, it too, disappeared.

'We have to go and see what is happening to the rain', Great Spirit Steppa said, his hands clenched into fists. 'Maybe it is an enemy that we must fight.'

'Thondara sent another cloud after the first two, but this time, Kin Falcon and the Great Spirits were hidden inside. They floated along, rain teaming down beneath them and then suddenly, they felt themselves being sucked away.

'What mischief is this?' Great Spirit Steppa said, casting his eyes about for someone to fight.

'The next thing they knew, they were floating above a new piece of ground. Below them, all the trees grew monstrously tall, and all around them, clouds dropped rain and made puddles. All the rivers and lakes were brimming full. There was so much water, the waterfalls flowed into waterfalls. The travellers all jumped out of the cloud together, and that's when they saw Yorath the trickster. He was small, and the colour of his skin and hair kept changing depending on what mood he was in. Sometimes he took human form; sometimes he was an animal, bird or fish. Sometimes he took on the guise of a tree, rock or even the wind. Right now, Yorath was in the form of a blue-skinned man. He was reclining in a river, blowing fountains of water from his mouth and splashing about happy as you please.

'Yorath!' the Rain Spirit yelled. 'What's the meaning of this?'

'Yorath!' Great Spirit Deti yelled. 'What're you doing to my rivers?'

'Yorath!' Great Spirit Steppa yelled. 'You thief! You've stolen all the water!'

'Now that Yorath', Aloth continued, 'he had the good grace to look ashamed, though we were never sure if this was because of what he'd done or because he'd been caught. Right away he changed shape into a little girl with big eyes who was much harder to be angry with. Yorath did not fool the spirits, who all yelled at him good and proper until he cried and said he was sorry for all the trouble he'd caused. He changed into a crippled old man as he promised not to steal the rain clouds any more. After that, Thondara and the Great Spirits released all the clouds and sent them to rain over every part of the world. They tipped up the ground that Yorath's water had settled on and sent all that water back into the streams and rivers and lakes where it belonged. Then they sent Yorath off into the desert to see what it was like to live without water for a while and to teach him a lesson. When Kin Falcon got back, everyone cheered. Even though they were wet, they were happy to be so. The people asked Kin Falcon for her story, and so she told them all about how Yorath had stolen the rain clouds and how he was now in the desert for a lesson.'

The children laughed, and everyone joked at how Yorath would have looked lounging about in the water and making plumes while everywhere else was so dry. Trindal smiled, glad that everyone was happy. Aloth patted his knee and said he'd done a good job and was pleased with him. He liked Aloth and hoped the family of cousins he was currently traveling with stayed in Red Camp long enough for him to spend many, many more evenings with Aloth.

As it was getting late, the children were taken home to bed. Nemid took Kal and Chani off. Chet Chet stood, arched her back then strolled over to Trindal. She circled a few times then lay down next to him. He began stroking her warm fur as he stifled a yawn and forced his eyes to stay open. He wanted to listen to the next story, which was the tale of a great battle, love and jealousy.

Right now, Trindal was in the middle of learning the story of Wiccs and Laxa. This was an epic tale of war and betrayal. It took place in the time of the ancients and had many words that Trindal did not know the meaning of as they had been lost over time – words like 'sword' and 'battleship' and 'archer.' Still, it was a tale that kept the listeners spellbound. It took many nights to complete, longer if the storyteller was skilled. Some wove intricate subplots into the general story or described the heroic deeds in greater detail. This story was usually told over the long nights when the snow was thick on the ground. So far Trindal knew about half of it by heart, but it would take a lot more practice until he knew it well enough to tell it on his own.

Meanwhile he practiced Aloth's speech patterns and the way she pronounced certain words, remembering which parts to linger over as they made the audience laugh or cry.

Aloth returned from the food tables, wiping her mouth on the back of her hand. 'I think', she said to Trindal, 'we shall tell the story of the fish who swam backwards first. Do you know that one?'

Trindal shook his head. She sat down and made herself comfortable.

'Then perhaps', she said, indicating a spot by the fire, 'you should sit over there and watch what I do as you listen.'

Trindal moved to where she indicated, Chet Chet following him.

They made themselves comfortable in their new spot as Aloth took a piece of storytellers' string and some different coloured stones from her storyteller's bag. Sadly for Trindal, he fell asleep a short time into her story, but his dreams were filled with images of leaping fish and streams of cold, clear water.

Kal awoke to loud wailing outside Nemid's cabin. Chani was crouched over Chet Chet. The dog was lying on her side, her tongue hanging out of lips caked with white froth. Her breath came and went in ragged pants. Tears streamed down Chani's cheeks. Kal vaulted the rail to crouch beside her.

'What happened?' he said.

'Snake', Chani sobbed and buried her face in the dog's fur.

'Will she be OK?' Kal said, but before Chani could answer, he saw the light fade from the dog's eyes as her laboured breathing ceased.

'No!' Chani wailed and held Chet Chet closer. What was the use of having all these healing powers when she couldn't even save the life of her best friend?

'Here', said a man, reaching for Chet Chet's body, 'let me...'

'No!' Kal cried, pushing the man's arm away. 'I'll take her.'

He gently gathered Chet Chet into his arms. Chani turned, wiping her tears, and the two of them strode off through the village. It wasn't until they were clear of the dwellings, that Kal became aware that Trindal had joined them. Kal was about to tell him to go away when he saw the sadness on Trindal's face and realized that Chet Chet must have been his friend too. The three of them walked on until they reached a set of waterfalls. To one side was a circle of stones with a large body-sized fire-blackened pit in the middle. Chani indicated for Kal to place Chet Chet's body into the pit.

They collected the special foliage and herbs for the farewell ceremony. Once the fire was burning, they all three sat watching it consume the body.

'She was my first friend here', said Kal.

'She was like a sister to me', said Trindal.

'She was very special', Chani sniffed and wiped the tears from her eyes. 'Healers do not usually have dogs, but Chet Chet helped me when I was ill, and since then, she stayed with me. She always knew when someone needed extra company. I will miss her dreadfully.'

She began to sing. Kal's head came up as he recognised the tune. It was the one Nemid had been singing that first day.

'Great Spirit Mezeh', she sang. 'Take our brave friend into your house.'

Chani's voice echoed around the rocks and mixed with the tinkling of the water as it ran between the stones.

'She has gone on ahead of us', sang Chani. 'She will be there to greet us when our time comes.'

Trindal picked up the branches with green leaves on them and tossed them into the fire. A tangy fragrance burst forth.

'Great Spirit Mezeh, take our beloved', sang Chani, 'keep her with you as we wish she could have stayed with us. She has lived a good life. She brought honour to her family and clan. She will be missed by us all. Please, Great Spirit Mezeh, care for her and take her with you.'

Trindal placed the last of the green branches onto the fire. All three watched it burn. Chani sang the verses again as the flames consumed Chet Chet's body. Smoke, dark and acrid, rose into the air. Kal felt his grief rise inside him and spill over. His throat became tight as he allowed his tears to flow.

Once the fire had burnt down to embers, Chani took a pouch from her bag. Inside it were black crow feathers used by the lately bereaved. The Nahill believed that by entwining the feathers in your hair, your thoughts went directly to the newly departed. Kal realised that always carrying grieving feathers would be standard practice for a Healer, and this thought gave Kal an even deeper respect for Chani.

Chani scraped the embers aside and collected a handful of Chet Chet's ashes. She mixed these with mud.

'We who came from the Mother Earth now return to the Mother Earth', she sang. 'Hear me, my beloved. I wish you a smooth journey to the garden of the Great Spirits. Go now to join your family. This one will see you again when my time comes.' She used a knife to make a small slice on the back of her left arm then held the bloodied blade aloft and began to sing again.

'With this blood of my body, I show my love for you. I join you and enter into mourning for you as our bodies become one forever.'

She allowed her blood to drip into the mixture of mud and Chet Chet's ashes. She rubbed some ashes into her new cut, making the skin raise up. This scar would remind her of the one she had lost forever. Kal remembered seeing just such scars on Nemid's arms that first day. First Trindal then Kal repeated the ceremony. Using a combination of mud and the flax string, they tied the black feathers into each other's hair. As they worked, the wind sighed in the trees, and the flies buzzed thickly about them, attracted by the blood. With the feathers in place, each smeared mud onto their faces.

It was dark by the time they returned to the village. Out of respect there was no story tonight. All was quiet. The few people who saw them bowed their heads and placed their hands on their hearts. Kal made to return to his cabin, but Chani took his hand and led him instead to the meeting hall. It was empty, but the fire was burning brightly and three blankets had been placed ready for them. They wrapped themselves up and were soon asleep.

The fire had reduced to wisps of smoke as the birds sang their morning chorus. Trindal woke first. He sat up, rubbed his eyes and gave the other two a shake. They also sat up, yawned and stretched. Food and an earthenware jug of water had been placed on the hearth for them.

As they silently ate their breakfast, Chani remembered when she had been sick and awoken to Chet Chet beside her. The dog had stuck with her until Chani had gotten well. She had never forgotten how comforting the dog's presence had been and from that day forward, Chani had not felt alone. Always there had been her smiling companion. Soon Chani became determined to encourage her sister healers to also use dogs to help with healing. None had agreed so far and now … well, Chani was unsure she'd ever find another dog like Chet Chet. A tear ran down her cheek, and she wished that Chet Chet would come and lick her face once again. She lowered her head and stared down at the ground.

Trindal thought of the night not long ago when he had arrived in camp. He'd tripped and had bloodied his toe. Chani had cleaned and dressed his wound. When she left, Chet Chet stayed that night and many more after. How his heart leapt with joy when her toenails clattered along the wooden boards as she came to him. He'd gladly let her in and curl up with her welcome warmth.

It wasn't that the people he was traveling with were unkind to him; they just didn't care much about him. He had been handed from family to family for as long as he could remember because of his water-eyes. They said water-eyes were unlucky, so he was never allowed to stay long in one place, or with one family. In this way, his bad luck could not accumulate. His training as a storyteller was so he could wander the reservation for the rest of his days. He was cross with himself for not singing the grieving song for Chet Chet. He had been too upset, and his throat hadn't wanted to work. He glanced at Chani then gently took one of her hands in his.

Kal's head was bowed as he swallowed back the lump in his throat. The pain inside was like when his mother had left. He remembered coming home from school and finding his mother crying. She said it was the onions, only there were no onions. Kal frowned. He'd forgotten about that. Sadly, Kal realised that as time went on, he was forgetting more and more about his mother. She'd left when he was seven, and his father had said they didn't need her fucking up their lives. Her abrupt departure had left a huge hole in his heart that nothing seemed to fill up.

He felt the familiar feeling of falling as his breath quickened and grief threatened to overtake him. He summoned a picture of his mother in his mind and felt a surge of panic as he realised he could no longer remember the sound of her voice. He dug his dirty fingernails into his palms as he closed his eyes and concentrated, picturing the last time he had seen her.

Her eyes were red and her cheeks were wet… He'd held up his new car. 'Look mum, see what Dad got me!' She was standing in the hallway wearing her going-to-church clothes and her special-occasion white hat. Her hands were full of papers. He ran towards her. Her arms went out to him. Barry's hand slammed into his chest and stopped him short. What!!??

'Not this time, boy!'

'But dad…'

She pulled at Barry's arm. 'Monster! Bastard!'

Barry pushed her to the ground.

'He's MY son, now get out!'

Kal struggled, but Barry held him firmly. She was on all fours then and crying. She collected her papers and spoke in a strange, tight voice.

'Goodbye, little soldier. You be good for Daddy.'

The front door opened, and Kal let out a blood-curdling scream.

'Don't go! … No! NOOOOOOO!'

Kal's jaw muscles tensed as he remembered. With her gone, nothing was the same.

A warm hand slipping into his brought him back. He blinked and sniffed as he raised his head. Trindal was holding one of his hands and Chani the other. He sniffed again and straightened his shoulders, telling himself to stop being such a baby.

Chani gave his hand a squeeze then stood up. The three of them went out to the fields, each imagining Chet Chet bounding after them, her tail wagging and her tongue hanging out. People were busy tending the three sisters.

The children set to work going from mound to mound weeding, planting and watering. No one tried to engage them in conversation as all could see they were in mourning. At the end of the day, hand in hand, they went to the cabin of Chani's mother, Healer Deikter. She came out, a slight breeze rustling her ceremonial gown. The children knelt before her, heads bowed.

'It has been a while', Healer Deikter said, 'since the keeper of your hearts left you to join the ones who have gone on ahead. Have you completed all the cleansing and honouring ceremonies?'

They nodded.

'Have you refused to speak of your friend and uttered only the song of death, so she knows she can no longer be seen by you?'

They nodded.

'And have you kept the talismans of mourning in plain sight at all times to stop other spirits trying to tempt you to join your friend?'

They nodded. One by one, she removed the black feathers from their hair.

'You have been good friends', she said. 'Care for her spirit no longer. She is safely with the ones who have gone ahead and looks down on you in peace. It is finished.'

'It is finished', the children said and got to their feet.

They walked to the river, threw off their clothes and jumped into the freezing water with a cry of joy. Spluttering and laughing, they emerged, splashing each other with water. Once clean, they climbed out and lay on the side of the bank, trying to catch their breath. Kal sat up and rested his arms on his knees. He eyed Chani, the question clear on his face. She laughed.

'We can speak now, Kal', she chided him.

Trindal leant towards Chani.

'He understands Nahill?' he whispered.

'Yes, and he'll speak it, too, if you do this.' She tickled Kal. He laughed, and soon the two were wrestling on the ground.

'I'm gonna get ya!' Kal threatened.

'No! Never!'

Kal managed to straddle Chani, pinning her arms to the ground. He stared down at her smugly.

'Gotcha', he gloated.

Chani and Kal tussled for a little while longer before Kal allowed her to toss him off. Trindal's expression was one of pent up eagerness.

'You speak Nahill?' he said to Kal.

'Yes', Kal said as they all got dressed again.

'Would you teach me white people's words?'

'Huh?'

Trindal pointed to his blue eyes.

'This is all I know of my father's people. I want to know more.'

Kal wondered if this kid had any idea how bad it was in the white world.

'Speak some white words', Trindal begged.

'OK', Kal said. 'You want...', he cleared his throat and started again, in English this time. 'You wanna hear white words, well here they are. White people are crap. Trust me on this.' He frowned, finding the sound of English jarring after so long only speaking and hearing Nahill.

'More', Trindal begged again.

Kal stared at Trindal. The rapt expression on the boy's face made him throw his head back and laugh.

'OK, OK', he said then swapped back to Nahill. 'I'll teach you English if you teach me Nahill swear words?'

Trindal laughed and nodded. They all solemnly embraced to seal the deal.

'Time we got home', Chani said.

They returned to the village then went off towards their respective lodgings. Kal had only just made Nemid and himself a hot drink when there was a knock at the door and Trindal walked in seeming confused.

'They've gone', Trindal announced with an odd look on his face.

'Yes', Nemid said. 'Your cousins had to leave. They could not interrupt your mourning ceremony. I told them you could live here.'

'For how long?'

'As long as you want. You are brothers now', he said then indicated Kal. 'As you can see, we do not mind living with water-eyes.'

The two boys studied each other for a moment then grinned.

Nemid pointed to Kal's room. 'Your mattress is in there.'

Trindal gave Nemid a formal bow.

'Thank you, Grandfather', he rejoiced, using the traditional salutation for a respected elder. 'Thank you.'

8

The moonlight broke through the heavy clouds that raced across the sky. In Nemid's cabin, three people were fast asleep in their beds under piles of blankets. Nemid was snoring. Trindal dreamt of flying and had a slight smile on his face, and Kal spoke softly in his sleep.

'I'm here', he whispered.

In his dream, he could smell the fragrance of flowers. His dream-self turned his head and spied a huge bunch of red roses in a crystal vase. He was in a hotel room with cream-coloured walls with gold trim and a blue carpet that was soft under his bare feet. He walked inside, and instantly his heart began to pound. His mother was sitting at the dressing table putting on her earrings. She wore a gold dress and her mousy brown hair was cut to a short bob. Her green eyes twinkled. She saw his reflection in the mirror and smiled. The dangling earrings sparkled as they caught the light.

'Hello darling', she said.

Kal swallowed back an ache in his throat. It had been so long since he'd seen her, and he missed her so. A tear ran down his cheek. Suddenly he was walking down a hallway. His mother was just ahead, her dress flowing around her. He increased his pace, trying to catch up to her, but no matter how fast he went, she was always just that bit further ahead. Then she was standing beside a stocky man. Kal instantly recognised his father. He took in a sharp breath and stopped. Barry had black hair combed flat against his head, and he was wearing a suit. Everything went into slow motion.

'Parasite!' Barry yelled. 'Spawn of the Devil!'

Kal tried to run, but his legs wouldn't work. He yelled for help, but no one came, no one ever came. Barry raised the riding crop. Kal gasped and sat up. The snoring in the other room ceased.

Kal's eyes wildly swept the room, and it took him a few moments to understand that it had been a dream and he was safe at the Nahill camp. A hand on his arm made him jump.

'You OK?' Trindal said.

'I'm fine!' Kal pushed it away and quickly wiped the tears from his cheeks as his heart pounded in his chest.

Trindal yawned and gave his brother an appraising look. He could see the light glistening off the thin layer of sweat on Kal's bare shoulders and face. Usually when Trindal had bad dreams, no one cared or comforted him either. He didn't want Kal to feel like that. They had each other now.

'I have bad dreams sometimes', he said. 'I once dreamt I went down a wombat hole and couldn't find my way out. That one made me cry.'

Kal lay down and covered himself in the warmth of the blankets.

'What was your dream about?' Trindal said.

Kal sniffed and rolled towards Trindal.

'It was about my dad… He was beating on me… I couldn't get away… I yelled for help, but no one came….'

'One of my aunts used to beat me… I never knew what I'd done wrong. For a while, I thought all grown-ups were mean.'

'I still do', Kal whispered.

Trindal yawned and resettled into his blankets.

'Where I used to live', Kal said quietly, 'no one gave a shit what was happening to me. They knew what he was doing, and they … they never stopped him or did anything.'

'One time when I was little', Trindal said, 'one of the families forgot me. I remember we were staying out in the forest, and I woke up and found they'd left without me. I had to follow their tracks to catch up. I was really scared. Is that what you're afraid of, being alone?'

'No. I'm afraid of being around people. I don't trust most of them. I don't feel safe.'

Trindal was silent for a moment then chuckled.

'What?' Kal said.

'We're the opposite of each other and so much alike because neither of us were wanted by our parents.'

Trindal took Kal's hand and held it. Something had been weighing heavily on his mind about the funeral they'd given Chet Chet.

'D'you think', he said, 'it was disrespectful for me not to cut my hair when we were grieving for … our friend?'

Kal frowned.

'Cut your hair?'

'Ah huh. When in mourning, we cut our hair as a sign of respect and so others know what's happened. But I didn't because Chani didn't, but then grandfather said Healers never cut their hair. He said if they cut their hair every time someone they knew died, they'd be doing it all the time, so they never do it. But by the time I found that out, it was too late. Do you think she thought I was being disrespectful towards her…? Our friend, I mean?'

'No', Kal said. 'I think we did everything just right.'

Trindal let out a sigh of relief then closed his eyes. An owl hooted in the distance, and a nightjar screeched. Trindal yawned and resettled his head. Soon his breathing steadied as he went back to sleep. For a long time, Kal stared out the little window at the night sky, comforted by the feel of Trindal's hand in his and the sound of Trindal's breaths. Kal's thoughts returned to his dream.

His memories of his mother had always confused him. His father had told him over and over that she had died when he was born, but if that was true, then how come he had memories of her? He was sure they were real memories not just something he'd made up. He remembered her at Christmases and birthdays. He had several really clear memories of her walking with him to school and of her waiting at the school gate to walk him home again. He had never understood this, and he guessed he never would. He was still mulling it over when he, too, fell asleep.

The next morning, he awoke to find Nemid in his room up on tiptoes fastening amulets made of sticks to the left-hand side of the window. When Nemid let them go, they hung down across the window. Kal sat up and rubbed the sleep from his eyes.

'What're you doing?' he said.

Nemid fastened another string of amulets to the right side of the window.

'We believe', Nemid said, 'that when we sleep, our souls leave our bodies. Sometimes they wander about aimlessly by themselves; sometimes they revisit places we have been or people we miss. Sometimes they are taken by Dream Spirits.' He finished tying the amulets to the window, went to the door and tied a string to each side.

'There are many different types of Dream Spirits', Nemid continued. 'Some are playful and take our souls flying, some make us happy and our bodies laugh out aloud in our sleep, and some are mean and take us bad places to frighten us.'

Kal followed him out into the main room. There were amulets over every door and hanging down every window.

'Our souls', Nemid said, 'will always leave during sleep and go to play with others. These amulets will stop the Dream Spirits with bad intentions taking our souls away forever or doing bad things with them while we sleep.'

Kal stared at Nemid in wonder. Usually Kal felt embarrassed that he had bad dreams, but now he smiled at Nemid, and Nemid smiled back. It occurred to Kal that this was what it felt like to have a parent who cared about you.

The moon was half way through its next cycle when Kal, Nemid and Trindal stood in the river. The water level was so low that it no longer reached the sluice gates to the fields. Each day the people of the village formed a bucket line. Those standing in the river filled buckets with water then passed them on. The bucket went from one person to the next until it reached those standing in the field. From there, each precious drop was taken to one of the mounds and carefully emptied right onto the three sisters so they all got a drink. The empty buckets were then passed back down the line. It took every man, woman and child the best part of the morning to water the crops in this way, but it was the village's most essential task.

After this, Trindal spent time with Aloth learning more stories. Kal and Nemid visited different members of the village. There was only one topic of conversation, when it might rain.

'I think we should get advice from the Oracle', said one woman.

'She has said rain will come soon', said another woman.

'How long is soon?'

The woman shrugged.

'I'm just telling you what I heard.'

'Maybe one of us should go and see the Oracle again.'

'It won't do any good. She's sending offerings and prayers daily.'

'Maybe she should do it day *and* night to interrupt Thondara's sleep. That might get her to send us some rain.'

There was general grumbling and nodding of heads.

'Maybe Thondara does not find our offerings pleasing', said a man.

'We are giving her our best', said another.

'What news from other villages?'

'The same as us.'

'It is dry everywhere.'

None of them spoke their greatest fear: what happened if the crops died?

'We need a dance to bring it on', said Nemid.

The others considered this.

'Do you think it is time?' asked one of the women.

'Yes', Nemid replied, his conviction growing the more he thought of it. 'I think it is time Water clan invoked the help of the other spirits.'

There was more thoughtful silence. Kal glanced around then leant towards Nemid.

'What kind of dance?' he whispered.

'A rain dance, of course', Nemid said. 'We don't like to do this dance often as we run the risk of upsetting Thondara. This dance is to alert the other Great Spirits that we are thirsty and that Thondara might need some help doing her job. If she is in a bad mood with us or just busy elsewhere, she might get angry at the interruption and not let anyone send us rain.'

One of the women let out a resigned sigh.

'I think it's a good idea', she said. 'Let's get the others together.'

Nemid held up a hand.

'The business of summoning rain is for Water clan alone.'

He stood and, with Kal in tow, ambled off.

'I've never heard of a rain dance', Kal said as they walked. 'Is it different to the one we did at harvest time?'

'Yes', Nemid said, 'it is quite different. It is our way of telling the others around us', and his gesture took in the birds, trees and animals of the forest, 'about the events in our lives. Every creature has a dance. The birds perform their dances in certain seasons, as do the insects and even the flowers. It is always good to dance; you just have to pick the right kind of dance.'

It didn't take long before every part of the camp began preparations for the rain dance. Groups of hunters went into the forest to collect ripe fruit, berries and nuts. Others were busy decorating every dwelling with clan colours and pictures of clan totems. In this way, when the Great Spirits looked down, they would see that this heartfelt plea came from everyone. The front of every house was painted with ochres in clan colours. Totems were drawn in the dirt in front of the houses. Each family had a special tree, and these were daubed with ochre and decorated so they could do their part. Once this was done, everyone prepared their ceremonial clothes. There was a heightened sense of excitement and community in the camp.

Word spread that there was to be a rain dance, and spectators from neighbouring villages began to arrive. Meanwhile, the whole of Water clan spent a day getting their costumes ready. The Nahill would be sending a plea for rain not just from themselves, but from all the living things of the forest.

Kal was going to be a dragonfly, and Nemid showed him how to hold his arms out and imitate dragonfly movements. Kal practiced darting back and forth with arms outspread, perfecting his swooping manoeuvres. Trindal was to play a frog. He practiced squatting, leaping and croaking.

At the ceremonial grounds, storytellers and artists prepared the ground. They used sticks to draw intricate patterns in the dirt to represent all life; plants, trees, fish, birds, insects and animals were etched in vivid detail then blessed. The drawings were very beautiful and lifelike. The Nahill believed that these drawings would channel the energy of those depicted into the people who walked on them.

Once the camp's preparations were complete, a group sang as they pounded beans and corn into mash. This they fashioned into balls that would be skewered and cooked over the flames. Others made a spicy soup of dried fish, dried mushrooms, greens, wild ginger and herbs, and another group made the sweet and sour dipping sauce of apples, pumpkin, berries and wild onions. The smells of cooking food permeated the camp with a spicy, sweet, delicious smell.

Meanwhile, all of Water clan fasted to focus their minds. Each pictured the creature or plant they were to portray and, in their minds, became that being. They sent their pleas to the Great Spirits, each adding why their species was desperate for rain. In his prayers, Kal silently described to the Great Spirits how dragonflies needed the ponds to be full so they could lay their eggs next to it. He pictured how the dragonfly larvae hatched and spent time in the water before becoming winged creatures and moving to the land. Only over ponds could the dragonflies do their mating dance.

Trindal's prayers centered on how frogs needed water to live, how they loved mud and how, without water, their tadpoles could not grow up to become frogs. He visualised the pleas of the frogs and tadpoles, all living in parched, dry ground instead of water.

'Please send us rain', he whispered, his eyes closed, a look of deep concentration on his face. 'Please send us rain.'

After a night of prayers, the dawn broke. Once more the sky was clear and cloudless, and all knew that it would be another hot dry day. The Water clan drummers walked once around the ceremonial ground before silently taking their places. They beat out a slow rhythm. The boom … boom … boom of the drums echoed about the valley. People emerged from their huts and cabins and assembled behind the drummers. The villagers sat and stood, watching quietly as the drummers continued to pound out a beat. At the first rays of sun, the drummers were joined by women with flutes made from kangaroo bones. For a moment, the drummers stopped, and all was still except for the morning chorus of the birds. Flies buzzed past the onlookers, and to the right, a kookaburra cackled a cackle that echoed around the valley. More kookaburras arrived, their cackles joining the first. The drummers smiled, pleased that the birds had come to help. It was only right as the outcome of this dance concerned all of them.

When an eagle was spotted soaring in the blue sky, the flute players played a soft tune. All played the same melody for a short time, and then one group played higher and the other lower. After a while, their tunes became different yet complimentary. Soon the melodies intertwined. Another group arrived leading an old woman. They settled her in a place of honour where she turned her ghost eyes towards the grounds. Several crows flew overhead, cawing to each other. Everyone looked up. The crows circled a few times then settled near the kookaburras. The presence of the crows and the Oracle meant the Great Spirits were watching. It was time. All heads turned towards the beautifully decorated path.

One by one, the members of Water clan filed onto the dance ground, their bare feet making footprints on the designs. Their steps kept time with the beat of the drums. Each body was decorated; some had feathers, some animal pelts, and others were clad with pieces of shrubbery or leaves from specific trees. As they entered the grounds, they took on the character of the thing they represented. Observers recognised the ant, koala, possum, fern, wattle, owl and many other living beings of the forest. Painted in orange ochre on every shoulder were three wavy lines, which was the symbol of Water clan.

After entering the grounds, they walked, swam, jumped, flew or crawled as their character dictated in a circle around the perimeter.

By the time everyone from Water clan had entered, half a dozen lines of people formed concentric circles, and Water clan began to sing. The song described how important water was to each creature and plant and the chorus was repeated.

Yellow for the morning sun
Which greets us every day
Black for the earth
From which we were made
White for the ash
From our cooking fires
Red for the blood in our veins.
Come now rain
Come now rain

By now the sun had risen, and the sky was a brilliant blue against the grey green of the eucalyptus gums. The smell of resin permeated the dry air. The first rays of the sun filtered through the leaves of the huge trees and hit the ceremonial ground. The tune changed and the beat became faster. The people of Water clan gathered at one end of the ground. Now it was time for individual voices to be heard.

One by one, each creature, plant or tree came forward and performed as the others sang and swayed back and forth in the background. When it was Trindal's turn, he leapt forward and used his arms to symbolise his opening and closing mouth. Around him, the clan sang the song of the frogs.

We hop, we swim
The water is without and within
Our skin is slick
With water and mud
Without mud, we can't survive
Hear our pleas
The plea of the frog
Come now rain
Come now rain

Trindal hopped back to his place beside Nemid, who was playing the part of a snow gum. When it was Kal's turn, he ran as fast as he could this way and that, his arms out rigidly looking just like a dragonfly while the others sang the song of the dragonfly.

Fly dragon fly
Faster, faster, fast
Skim the water
Which is home
To your young
Find your mate
Become one over the water
Come now rain
Come now rain

He resumed his place beside Nemid. The rain dance continued for the rest of the day. As darkness fell, those representing the creatures of the night commenced their dances. Out came the bats, the mice, owls, moths and many others. When all the players had done their part, everyone sang their entreaty to the Great Spirits.

As the sun rose the next day, the singing stopped, and the exhausted members of Water clan ate warm broth and bread. After this, they all found a cool place to lie down and slept as the rest of the villagers put the camp back to rights and all the visitors went home.

Early the next morning, black clouds formed on the horizon. They slowly floated across the sky until the sun was blocked out. The first splat of rain came just before mid-day. One drop was accompanied by another then another and down it came in big fat drops. The Nahill ran out into the streets and cried in delight, jumping up and down in the dust that soon turned to mud. Every member of Water clan was thanked profusely for bringing the rain. It continued to pour for the rest of the day and all night.

It was still raining the next morning. Water levels in the river were growing at an alarming rate. This was when the first concerns were raised. Had they angered Thondara? Was she punishing them? Was

Yorath playing a trick on them? Or was this amount of rain just the natural consequences of the unskilled hands of the other Great Spirits at work? As people speculated on when it would stop, water ran down the hills in rivulets, and the streams became frothing torrents.

Kal, Trindal and Nemid stood on their veranda staring out at the rain when someone running past shot Kal a dirty look. Nemid frowned.

'What was that for?' he said, more to himself than to anyone else.

'They think having Kal dance insulted the Great Spirits', Trindal said.

'They are blaming *him* for this?' Nemid said incredulously.

'Ah huh. They think Dragonfly clan has sent a protest to Thondara that a white man portrayed them in the dance. They say this is Thondara's way of trying to wash him from the world.'

Nemid shook his head in disbelief.

'That is foolish indeed', he said. 'Alright, so perhaps he was rather enthusiastic, but I can't see that Dragonfly clan would have any cause to complain. If anything, his performance brought great honour and accuracy to their plight.'

They all stared out at the rain, and Kal wondered if, indeed, this continuing downpour was because of him. Kal was convinced the dance had brought the rain, so he guessed it made sense that he could have made it rain just a little harder because of the energy and earnestness of his entreaties. Just in case, he spent the rest of the day asking Thondara to ease the rain off by saying he was sorry if he'd caused offense. That night, much to everyone's relief, the rain stopped.

All too soon, it was harvest time, and everyone pushed themselves to the point of exhaustion. Every man, woman and child worked from first light till well after dark. One day blended into the next of frantic activity. First it was the beans, then the pumpkins, then the corn, then the apples. But just as suddenly as it had started, the harvest was over, and the Nahill spent a day in quiet prayer thanking the Great Spirits for the bounty.

That night the fire pits were ablaze, and everywhere the stew pots and surrounding benches groaned with meat. Musicians played and people danced and ate. Nemid and Kal stood to one side, watching Trindal, who sat on the ground surrounded by a large group of children.

'This' he said, 'is the story of why frogs hop.'

As Trindal began his story, Nemid admired the way he created new accents and voices for each of the characters. Even though Trindal was young, he already spoke with confidence and skill that attested to many nights spent with the Red Camp storytellers, particularly Aloth. The night before, Trindal had breathlessly told Nemid and Kal that he was to take part in telling the Epic of Remesh this season. This saga had come from the ancients and took many, many nights to tell. When a camp had a group of storytellers, they would each take a character. For Trindal to be given one of these parts was a great honour. Yes, Nemid mused, Trindal was blossoming and becoming an accomplished storyteller in his own right. Nemid glanced at his empty plate and leant down so his mouth was close to Kal's ear.

'Are you still hungry?'

Kal shook his head and indicated he wanted to stay and listen to Trindal's story. Nemid walked over to the nearest stew pot and helped himself to more. Blowing on it as he went, he meandered over to a log near the dance grounds and sat down. His eyes ran over the crowd of people, taking note of who was sitting with whom, particularly where the councillors were seated. Towards the back, a small woman with a wrinkled face and fingers gnarled from weaving beckoned to him.

'Amsay', he smiled and rose. He picked his way through the onlookers until he reached her. With an effort, she stood and the two embraced as old friends, then sat down next to each other.

'Did you hear about Isol's chin?' she said.

Nemid shook his head, and Amsay launched into a long story about a mutual friend. Nemid listened as he ate. The fire kept them warm as the night sky darkened and the moon and stars came out. The moths circled the flames, and the night jars and owls hooted. As the night wore on both Amsay and Nemid fell silent. Their eyes began to grow heavy with sleep. Amsay patted Nemid's knee.

'Time we went to bed old friend', she said. They stood, bid each other good night as they embraced then parted, each walking happily off towards their homes.

The days grew shorter, and the nights turned cold. No sooner was the harvest in when suddenly all manner of fungi were springing up. Some clung to tree bark, and some pushed their way up through the leaf litter on the forest floor. Every colour, size and shape was accounted for. Every morning, people from Red Camp would head out into the forest with sacks to collect as many of the edible varieties as they could find. Fresh or dried, fungi were a welcome addition to the cooking pot.

As the season of the Fungi was the last one before the snows came, it was also the time when the Nahill had to decide where they would spend the snow seasons. While most would stay at home, a large number packed up their families and belongings and set off to visit family and friends all over the reservation. Red Camp was no different and soon experienced an influx of visitors. One day, Kal noticed a new family speaking with a group of Tree clan Drekesh.

'Who're they?' he asked Trindal.

Trindal followed Kal's gaze then smiled and waved. An older woman waved back.

'That's Leerth', he said. 'She's Stone clan and lately arrived from Big Camp. She has a hand of children and several are our age. Would you like me to introduce you to them?'

Kal was always amazed at how easily Trindal made friends. He had an affable manner that quickly endeared him to people. Kal envied him that skill as he had always felt uncomfortable around new people.

'No', Kal said shyly.

Nemid joined them, ushering the boys towards the field.

'Let us get to work', he said.

It was time to dig up the dried stalks and clump them into sheaths for animal food. They sang as they worked.

We send our thanks to you
Mother Earth who feeds us
Sleep well
Till next season
Good bye, good night
Sleep well beloved

Kal straightened his back, and Trindal wiped the sweat from his brow. Nemid arched and put his hands on his hips. He'd never admit it to anyone, but he was getting too old for this. He wondered why he continued to volunteer to work in the field instead of opting for the lighter work of hunting for tubers and fungi in the forest. But deep down, he knew why. This task was considered a job for the young. He'd noticed most of his contemporaries heading towards the forest this season. Poor old crocks, he thought as he determinedly headed for the fields with the younger ones. It appealed to Nemid's vanity that he was still able to take on this chore when others his age could not.

As darkness descended, appetising smells wafted over from the camp. Nemid indicated for the boys to follow the others heading towards the fire pits. While Nemid and Kal took their place in line for stew, Trindal raced off to speak with some friends.

'How was Black Camp?' Nemid said to the woman in front of him.

She glanced back and smiled.

'Hello, Nem. I didn't see you in the forest.'

'I was in the fields.'

Her admiring expression made him puff out his chest.

'Black Camp was fun', she said. 'I can't believe how much my cousins have grown, and all have expanded their families. So many new ones that I have not met before. Now I have just to remember all their names', she laughed. 'And what about you? Are you staying here for the snows or are you heading off?'

'We will stay.'

They moved forward a few steps.

'I must drop in to pay my respects to your lovely wife.'

Nemid's face fell.

'My wife and children … they died. The raft they were on capsized, and they drowned.'

The woman put a hand to her mouth and gasped.

'Oh, Nem, I'm so sorry. I hadn't heard. I've been away… But you said 'we', so I just assumed you meant…'

Nemid reached behind him and pulled Kal forward. The woman's eyes widened when she saw Kal's blonde hair and unlucky water-eyes.

'This is Kal.'

'But … but he's white', she said, aghast.

'Yes', Nemid said then pointed to Trindal. 'And that is my other son, Trindal.'

She saw the flash of another set of unlucky eyes and moved a bit further away from Nemid. He felt a degree of satisfaction at her discomfort.

'But…', she hissed, as if Kal couldn't hear her, 'they're … oh, Nem, how could you? You're Drekesh! You're supposed to protect us.'

Nemid's stance hardened although his expression remained friendly.

'The Drekesh protect', he said. 'Drekesh also guide through example. Drekesh encourage through actions. Drekesh remind others of what's important. This is what the Drekesh are trained to do. This is what I am doing.'

Suddenly the woman did not know which way to look. She opened her mouth then closed it again. At that moment, the line moved forward, and a serving of fish stew was ladled into her bowl.

'I must go', she said without looking back.

She strode off towards a crowd of people that Kal did not recognise. Nemid's bowl was filled, but the server paused when Kal stepped forward and held his bowl out. Nemid frowned at the woman with the ladle.

'Is there a problem?' he said.

She seemed about to refuse but then put a small serving into Kal's bowl. Nemid would have protested, but Kal nudged him forward.

'Don't make a fuss', Kal whispered. 'I'm used to it.'

'Used to what? Not being given a fair-sized meal?'

Kal didn't want to tell Nemid that getting a small meal was nothing. By now he was used to the taunts of 'white scum' and getting tripped and jostled in crowds. Trindal got pushed around and taunted too. The way Kal looked at it, at least with the Nahill, he knew what was wrong and that there was nothing he could do about it. Most of the time, he and Trindal didn't even take it personally. They just accepted it as part of the Jhunti lifestyle.

Kal and Nemid went to one of the tree trunks laid out for seating and made themselves comfortable. It wasn't long before a couple of newly arrived Drekesh came over to them. They stood before Kal, arms crossed over their chests, glowering down at him. Nemid looked up, recognising their leader Reshix, a Drekesh who was newly arrived from Big Camp. Nemid smiled.

'Hello, Resh. How's your mother?'

Reshix's gaze never left Kal.

'She is well. Thank you for asking. How is Leath?'

Nemid quickly kissed the scar on his left arm, whispering 'he didn't mean it', before replying to Reshix. 'She died, as did all my children … but the Great Spirits have sent me Kal in their stead.'

Reshix's eyes shifted, and he studied Nemid, wondering if Nemid was joking. Nemid took a mouthful of stew.

'I had not heard', Reshix said. 'Condolences from Tree clan.'

'Thank you', Nemid said and indicated the empty spaces around them. 'Come, join us.'

Reshix shook his head.

'I have family waiting for me', he said. 'I was asked to come and see the…', he'd been about to say 'White Rat' but thought better of it, 'white boy myself. His presence here upsets people.'

'I don't see why', Nemid said in what he hoped was a casual tone. 'He's not doing any harm, and he's a hard worker. He's been in the fields with me every day working just as hard as the others.'

Reshix's arms tightened over his chest, and that stubborn Tree clan chin stuck out. Why, Nemid thought, was Tree clan always such a stickler for rules and regulations?

'You know the law better than most', Reshix said. 'You're supposed to be setting an example.'

'I am!'

Their discussion was gaining attention, and several more from Big Camp walked over.

'So it's true?' one said, staring down at Kal. 'You have a white boy?'

'On our land?' said another.

'By the Great Spirits', said another, 'why'd you bring him here?'

Trindal arrived with several of his new friends. One look at the stern faces of the Drekesh and Trindal's friends melted away. But Trindal came over to Nemid and Kal, a full bowl of stew in his hand. He made a show of sitting right next to Kal and even swapped his full bowl with Kal's meagre portion.

'Eat up', he said to Kal. 'I can get more.'

Filthy looks were levelled at Trindal, but he stared back at them, unrepentant.

'Have you forgotten', a woman said, 'that when they came, the whites nearly killed us all!'

Kal glanced around as more people came towards them. He put his untouched bowl down.

'I'm going home', he whispered to Nemid.

Reshix's eyes widened.

'He speaks our language?' he said.

Kal stood, lightly jumped over the log, and ran back towards their cabin. As he went, loud, angry voices followed after him.

'Where's he going?' Reshix said.

Trindal took Kal's place and began to casually eat his meal.

'You frightened him', Nemid said to those surrounding them.

'He's gone home.'

'Back to the whites, I hope.'

'This is Nahill land, and whites are not welcome here!'

Trindal put his bowl aside and stood, glaring up at Reshix. Reshix raised a hand then thought it unseemly for a Drekesh to be hitting a child. Instead, he turned his attention to Nemid.

'You mark my words; he will be just like all the other whites', he spat before storming off.

The others walked away, muttering crudities. Nemid and Trindal finished their meal in silence, their buoyant mood gone.

9

One evening as Nemid passed the meeting hall, he heard voices coming from the inside. He recognised one as being Healer Deikter, and he knew the others belonged to camp elders and councillors. He would have continued on his way, but the mention of Kal's name made him stop and cock his head to one side, listening.

'…and I was told that all the babes who died were *girls*', said one of the male voices, an elder from Stone clan.

'I had not heard that', Healer Deikter said. 'A most unfortunate turn of events.'

'What about all those Tree clan pigs that died?' said a female voice, a camp councillor.

'They were neglected', Healer Deikter said, and Nemid could picture her waving a dismissive hand at the councillor.

'Well how do you explain all our eggs hatching out roosters?' the Stone clan elder said indignantly.

'Fat lot of good roosters', muttered another voice that Nemid didn't recognise.

'What we need are chickens', the Stone clan elder said, 'and yes we've been walking backwards and spitting over our shoulders at sunset, but it's not made a lick of difference. All roosters! Now how do you explain that if it's not because his presence has upset the Great Spirits?'

'It's not natural', said a female voice, who was a Water clan elder.

Nemid felt his heart sink at her next words. 'I'll say it again, it's that white boy who is to blame.'

He leant heavily against the side of the meeting hall, the stone cold against his shoulder. While the prejudice of others he could tolerate, hearing such condemnation from his own clan was heartbreaking.

'I believe it is having the two together', said a male voice that Nemid recognised as Reshix, the Big Camp Drekesh he'd met a few days ago. 'That's what's attracting the evil eye, you bear witness to my words.'

'You're talking nonsense', Healer Deikter said. 'We've had a wonderful harvest, and I've not seen any signs of the eye.'

'Begging your pardon, Healer', Reshix said, 'but perhaps you're not looking so hard.'

Nemid stiffened and wondered if he should go in but then came a new voice that he recognised as another Water clan elder.

'I blame Nem', said the male voice, 'it's him what's brought so much bad luck on us.'

'I agree', the Stone clan elder said. 'What was he thinking keeping two water-eyes together under one roof?'

'There's only one solution for it', Reshix said, 'it's time they leave. It's what's best for everyone.'

'Have you forgotten', Healer Deikter snapped, 'that it's almost snow season? Let's say they did leave; where would they go? If you spread it about that the evil eye follows them, none will take them, and their deaths will be on your hands.'

All were silent.

'Let that be an end to it', Healer Deikter said. 'Now it's time I was in bed. Goodnight to you all.'

Nemid moved into the shadows as Healer Deikter strode out the doorway and towards her cabin. He was relieved that she had managed to quell this unrest but wondered how many others thought the same way about his children? He had hoped that Trindal's acceptance by the storytellers and Kal's hard work in the fields would endear them and allay any fears or concerns. He had obviously been wrong. He decided that he would make it his mission this snow season to counter this attitude. Reshix spoke again.

'There is another solution. If one, or both boys, were to want to leave?'

'Why would they do that?'

'Shhhh', hushed one of the women, 'the Healers have ears everywhere, and everyone knows Nemid is a favourite of Healer Deikter.'

They whispered, and despite leaning as far forward as he dared, Nemid could not hear anything for some time.

'And so it will be', said the woman.

There was silence. Nemid pictured them all nodding in agreement. Their talk turned to more mundane topics and, as Nemid began his trek home, he pondered what they were up to and how best to keep his boys safe.

A few days later Nemid and the boys were at home, sitting in front of the fire. Both boys had outgrown their clothes, and Nemid was teaching them how to make warm tunics, waterproof jackets and snow boots that would keep their feet warm and dry in the harshest weather. He helped Trindal finish his jacket, then arched his aching back. It was getting dark, and it dawned on him that he'd been bent over this task all day. Trindal reached for the jacket.

'Can I try it on?' he said.

Nemid handed it to him and Trindal pushed his arms through the sleeves then pulled the flaps closed across his chest. His hands were lost in the fabric and Nemid turned up the cuffs.

'Room for you to grow into it', he said.

Trindal grinned.

'I've never had a coat made just for me before', he beamed. 'It feels … special. Can I go and show it to Aloth?'

He made to leave, but Nemid held up a hand.

'Tomorrow', he said. 'It's getting dark and time we went to bed.'

Kal held out the boot he'd been working on.

'How's this?' he said.

Nemid turned towards the light of the fire and ran his fingers along the stitching. It was rough and uneven, but there were no holes that would let the cold through. He handed it back.

'It looks fit.'

'Wait till I show Ashe', Kal crowed.

He shoved his feet into the new boots and jumped up and down in them. Trindal joined him, jumping up and down in his new jacket. They were both delighted to have new clothes that they'd made themselves. As the dust rose in the air, Nemid held up a hand.

'Enough boys. Tomorrow you can test your outfits.'

As Nemid put his hide, cloth and sewing materials away, the boys served stew. After their hearty meal, they went to bed. When Nemid looked in on them, Trindal was lying on his side, his arms wrapped around his new jacket, and Kal had put his new boots in pride of place beside his mattress.

'Sleep well', he said.

'You too', Kal said.

'Mmm hmm', Trindal yawned.

With a soft smile, Nemid left them and took himself to bed. In the morning, he awoke to silence. He yawned and stretched as he glanced out the window. The sun was already up. He must have slept in. Nemid threw back the covers and went out into the main room. All was eerily quiet.

'Trin?' he called. 'Kal?'

The boy's room was empty, and their new clothes were gone. With a feeling of dread, he went outside and looked up and down the road. It was a fine, crisp morning, and the sunlight was glistening off the frost. He immediately regretted not wearing his boots as his bare toes were bitten by the cold. He beckoned to a couple passing by.

'Have you seen Trindal or Kal?' he said.

The woman pointed back the way they'd come, towards Ashekii's cabin.

'You've just missed them', she said. 'They all went to search for fungi.'

Relief washed over Nemid as he knew Ashekii would not let anything happen to the boys. After thanking the couple, he went back inside. He made himself breakfast, noticing how quiet it was eating by himself without the other two swiping pieces of each other's food or chattering about their plans for the day. Again he reminded himself they were in good hands and busied himself on starting a new jacket for Kal. He was so absorbed in his task that he did not stop until it was too dark to see.

The boys should have returned by now, he thought as he arched his back. The sinking feeling of disaster, which was never far from Nemid, crept over him. He got to his feet and went out onto the veranda. A young man was walking along the path.

'Realth!' he called. 'Hi there Realth. Have you seen Kal or Trindal?'

The young man trotted over to Nemid and looked up at him.

'I saw Trin with Ashe and his family this morning. I think they went that way' he pointed to the right.

Nemid glanced towards Ashekii's cabin. No lights shone from the windows.

'They must be having a good day', he said, more to reassure himself than as a statement of fact. He felt Realth still looking up at him and remembered his manners. 'And how was your luck today?'

Realth showed Nemid his sack of fungi.

'Many hunters out?' Nemid said.

Realth grinned.

'A lot. It seems like everywhere I look there is another family. So many people have come from Big Camp this festive season. I think we're going to have a lively snow season', he laughed.

At that moment Nemid spotted Ashekii and his family walking along the path, each loaded down with a bulging sack.

'Here they come now', Nemid said. 'Looks like they've found plenty for the pot.'

Realth turned to look and waved at the approaching family. Trindal broke from the pack and jogged towards the cabin.

'Look how many I got!' he cried, holding his sack out.

Nemid scanned the family for a blonde head. When he could not see Kal, that sinking feeling returned.

'Where's Kal?' Nemid said.

Trindal shrugged.

'He wasn't with us', he said nonchalantly then reached into the sack. 'Wait till you see this one I found. I reckon it's the biggest one ever.'

Anger bubbled up in Nemid at the casual way Trindal dismissed his duty.

'You are supposed to look after your brother!' Nemid snapped. 'You know he needs protection! If you go out together, then you stay together!'

As Nemid glared down at the cringing boy, Ashekii handed his sacks to his wife and came towards Nemid.

'Something wrong?' he said.

Nemid let out a frustrated breath.

'Have you seen Kal?'

Ashekii cleared his throat, choosing his words. He told Nemid that Trindal and Kal had joined them, but Hahina had not wanted Kal to stay.

'When we left, he said he'd go fungi hunting with his friends.'

'Kal doesn't have any friends', Nemid said shortly.

Nemid beckoned to some passers-by. The two elders approached with a smile.

'It is good to see these faces', Nemid said respectfully. 'How was your hunt?'

'Better than expected', said one woman, showing them her basket of fungi. 'Have you ever seen so many?'

As custom dictated, Nemid politely inspected her haul, extolling its' vibrancy and quality before turning to the subject he wanted to discuss.

'Did you happen to see Kal in the forest today?' he said.

One of the women nodded.

'Yes', she said. 'He was going towards the river.'

The river, Nemid shuddered.

'When was that?'

'I had just started, so it was early.'

By now others were stopping to find out what was happening.

'I saw him heading towards the road', said a man.

'Let's hope he keeps going', someone muttered, and they both laughed.

'When was this?' Nemid said, ignoring the jibe.

'When the sun was high and the shadows were short.'

As they spoke, more people stopped on their way home and the picture slowly built. Almost all of them had seen Kal blundering about in the forest on his own. Some had reported seeing him down in a gully, others on a ridge, others saw him wade through a freezing stream. Not one of them had stopped to speak with him, help him or invite him to join them. Nemid was furious with the callousness of his people. This was a child who wasn't used to the forest left to fend for himself and probably too scared to ask anyone for help. Most of all, Nemid was angry with himself for thinking Kal would be accepted just because Nemid wanted people to accept him, and now Kal was paying the price. It made him fume and broke his heart.

'I had better go and find him', Nemid said. 'It will be a cold night, and he did not take a coat.'

There were some sniggers. Nemid knew that the others hoped the boy did not survive, or at least did not come back, as that would solve the disquiet his presence engendered.

'Are any of you able to help with the search?' Nemid said tightly.

Even though everyone knew it would be dark soon and a cold night for a child with no warm clothes, every set of eyes turned away from his hopeful gaze. Ashekii's lips set into a firm line. It was one thing to dislike white people, but to wish a child ill purely because of the colour of his skin was un-Drekesh.

'I'll get the others and meet you over near boulder pass', he said to Nemid.

He headed off at a run to fetch his Drekesh friends. Trindal dropped his sack onto the veranda and made ready to leave. Nemid stopped him.

'You stay here', Nemid said. 'If Kal returns, keep him here until Ashe and I return.'

Hopelessly lost in the forest, Kal looked down at the mushroom in his hand. His stomach rumbled with hunger, but he dared not eat it. He'd heard so many stories about people being poisoned by deadly mushrooms. When he'd set off this morning, he'd been filled with high hopes of learning which ones to collect, but with no one to teach him the good from the bad, they all looked similar. He'd snuck a peek into the baskets of others, but it became clear that he couldn't tell one from the next. The Nahill made it look so easy, spotting fungi in the trees and on the ground and even on fallen logs.

Disheartened, Kal had decided to go home to Nemid and confess his ineptitude, and that was when he'd realised he was lost. To his credit he hadn't panicked. He'd used some of the techniques Nemid had taught him, like getting his bearings from the tree moss. He'd also found water and drunk his fill, but as the shadows grew longer and the air became colder, he realised he needed to find a place to stay the night.

He remembered back to this time last year when he'd confidently run away thinking he could manage on his own. How naive he'd been. It took a lot of skills to live off the land, and he had only a fraction of the knowledge he needed. He tried to make a fire but everything was too wet, and after a few failed attempts, he gave up. Cursing himself for not being better prepared and vowing never again to go into the forest without a jacket and a basic survival kit, he climbed a tree and resolved to wait till morning.

When he heard voices calling his name, he almost cried with relief. Never had he been so glad to see anyone in his life.

When Nemid found Kal, the air was so cold that Nemid's breath came out in white clouds. Kal was shivering uncontrollably, and all of them knew that if he'd been left out for the whole night, he may well not have survived. Nemid pulled his own coat off and wrapped Kal up in it. Kal's teeth were chattering so hard he couldn't speak, but the muffled sobs melted Nemid's heart. Ashekii added his own coat over the top of Kal's then called out to the others that the boy had been found. The search party turned for home.

Chani was waiting and ushered Kal inside where she administered a hot herbal soup to him then put Kal to bed with warmed stones all around him. Outside, news spread that the boy had been found. Nemid was angry at how the day had gone and strode in the direction of the Water clan elders, determined to give them a piece of his mind. As he went he overheard snatches of several heated conversations. He stopped to listen to one.

'Water-Eyes are bad luck.'

'He nearly froze to death!'

'He shouldn't be here. Having a white in the camp is a disgrace.'

'You've never even spoken to him! Don't be so closed minded.'

'What would you know, you just got here.'

'So this is Red Camp hospitality is it?'

Nemid stood still, his chest rising and falling as his anger drained away. He'd been so focused on having Kal accepted, he had totally lost sight of the bigger impact Kal was having on the camp. He thanked the Great Spirits for helping him to open his eyes and returned to his cabin. When he got there, he sat and stared at the fire for a long time thinking. The door opened and Healer Deikter came in.

'Well this is a pretty mess you've stirred up', she scolded him as she warmed herself by the fire. 'If I didn't know it was all part of the Great Spirit's plan, I would be very cross with you. However, it is the Great Spirits who have caused all those Big Camp visitors to be here and make them take offence at the boy's presence. Now we just have to work out what they want us to do about it.'

As dawn approached, it was as if a fog lifted from Nemid's mind. He realised that there was nothing else either he or Kal could do to help the boy be accepted. He looked at Healer Deikter.

'We have fought a good battle here', he said, 'but a wise man knows when to withdraw to fight again another day.'

'What does that mean?' she said.

As he outlined his idea, a slow smile spread across her face. Relieved to have a new, better plan, they thanked the Great Spirits, and she left. At first light Trindal came out yawning. One look at Nemid and he knew.

'We're leaving aren't we?' he said, already knowing it was true.

'I think it is time to show you both my birthplace', Nemid said. 'We shall go to White Camp, and I will show you the wonders of the home of Water clan.'

It did not take them long to pack. Chani dropped by to see how Kal was. She said she and her mother would join them at White Camp when the snows melted. When Nemid merely nodded, Kal got the impression this news did not come as a surprise.

'Would you please ask Ashe to come and say goodbye?' he said to her.

A few moments after she'd left, the door opened and Ashekii walked in. His eyes widened as he took in the three of them putting their possessions into packs.

'So it's true? You're leaving?'

'It is time', Nemid replied.

Ashekii slowly nodded, knowing that as fond as they had all grown of Kal, it was best for him to be returned to his people.

'I will see you when you return then', he said to Nemid then ruffled Kal's hair. 'I'm sure your parents will be pleased to see you again. Look after yourself.'

'I am not taking Kal to the white world', Nemid said, 'the three of us are moving to White Camp.'

'What?' Ashekii bristled then lowered his voice. 'Word of last night is spreading fast. If people think he is staying, there will be trouble.' He gave Nemid a pointed look. Nemid placed the last of his tools into his pack then began tying it closed.

'Which is why we are going.'

Ashekii put his hands on his hips. He had already been feeling guilty for the part he'd played in yesterday's debacle and this feeling was compounded as he watched them finish packing. It made his decision easy.

'Unless you want company, you should be away swiftly. I will drive you.'

He gave Nemid a knowing look. Nemid understood what he was saying. If they dallied, there would be an angry mob to escort them unceremoniously from the camp and to make sure Kal was put off the reservation. Nemid's heart began to race at the thought of his first trip in a motorised vehicle.

'We go by car', he said proudly to the boys.

'Car?' Trindal let out a whoop of wide eyed delight. 'I've never been in a car before. I've never even seen one. Can we...'

'Shhhh!' Ashekii held up a warning finger. 'No one is to know', he hissed to the boy.

Trindal continued to jump around in silence while Nemid thanked the Great Spirits for his cousin's wisdom and Kal put his last few things into his pack. In a few moments, they all hefted their packs and strode quickly towards the seldom-used track to the Red Camp car park. Trindal glanced about as they walked, silently willing his friends to see him going in the direction of the car park. If they knew he was to ride in a car he would be the envy of every last one of them. All the windows and doors remained firmly, unwelcomingly closed and they saw no one as they strode quietly through the camp.

At only a three-day walk, Red Camp was geographically the closest Nahill settlement to White Camp. However, to drive there took two days because one had to head in the opposite direction around the reservation, then around the lake then back up into the mountains.

Kal, Trindal, Nemid and Ashekii emerged from the track that came from Red Camp and stopped in a small car park that was home to three old cars, all with keys in the ignition. Ashekii led them to the old four-wheel drive and pulled open the door. It made a loud creak as it swung on seldom used hinges.

'This hasn't been started in a while', he said. 'Let's hope it'll turn over.'

Trindal stood beside the vehicle, running his hand along the side.

'So smooth', he whispered.

Nemid heaved open one of the back doors and Kal clambered in. He sniffed and wrinkled his nose. The inside smelt of diesel, damp upholstery and mildew. He scrambled over to the seat on the other side as Trindal was bundled in. Trindal reverently ran his hands over the ceiling upholstery then down the sides then the seat, a look of awe on his face. The door slammed and he jumped. The cabin rocked as first Ashekii then Nemid climbed into the front seats. Trindal winced as both front doors slammed in unison, making the air inside compact and ring with a metallic crunch. Ashekii checked the rear vision mirror and wound down his window a hand span then leant forward. He said a silent prayer before turning the ignition. The starter motor whirred but did not catch. He stopped then gave it another try. This time the engine caught and spluttered a few times before humming happily to life. Ashekii let out a relieved breath and pulled on his seat belt. Grinding the gears, he jammed the car into first, then carefully drove them out of the car park and onto a rutted track. After a short time, he wound up his window then set the heaters to maximum and glanced at Nemid beside him.

'Seat belt', he instructed.

Nemid reluctantly pulled the seatbelt across himself. He'd already decided he hated car travel and was glad he did not have to do it very often. Ashekii glanced in the rear vision mirror at his other passengers.

'You too.'

Kal helped Trindal with his seatbelt then did his own as they bumped along the road at a sedate pace. This was an old forestry track that ran right along the northern boundary of the reservation. It was winding, bumpy and rose and fell steeply up and down the mountains. When the rains came the dirt turned to mud making travel difficult. After a heavy snow it was impossible. This track eventually did a sharp turn and skirted the eastern boundary of the reservation before joining the sealed roads of the white world.

'Where'd you learn to drive?' Kal asked.

Ashekii glanced at him in the mirror, a smug smile on his face.

'A few of us can drive.'

'So why don't you get tractors to help in the fields?'

Ashekii glanced questioningly at Nemid.

'Tractors are like cars but larger', Nemid explained authoritatively. 'I told you Eyas, we prefer the old ways.'

Kal fell silent after that, letting his head fall back against the seat. Trindal stared out the window wide eyed, watching the scenery fly past. This car travelled faster than he could run, faster even than anyone he knew could run. His fingers were gripping his seat belt so hard they were white. With the rapid motion, the constant rocking and the dank smell of the air inside the car, Trindal's stomach was feeling decidedly queasy.

Kal tried to remember the last time he'd not had to walk from one place to another. He decided it had been during the last harvest when a horse and cart had come to help take the grain to the shed. For a treat, all the children had been taken for a short ride through the camp. Kal had grinned so much his face had hurt.

As they wound their way through the mountains, all were lost in their private reveries. Trindal thought of how fast they were going and how although it was bumpy, it was marvellous fun. Ashekii hoped the road ahead hadn't been washed away in that last big storm and was annoyed for not checking to make sure they had an axe in case a tree had fallen across the track. Kal wished he'd grabbed a snack for the journey. Having had nothing but a bowl of broth yesterday, his stomach was rumbling with hunger. Nemid settled back in his seat and pictured White Camp in his mind. White Camp sat perched on the side of a mountain and was the smallest but most beautiful of the Drekesh camps.

He remembered tobogganing down the slope as a child with his brothers and sisters. In his mind, he could see the snow falling across the valley and eddies of snow during a blizzard that made one giddy as they swirled this way and that. Children's cries and laughter echoed in his mind as he remembered he and his little gang of friends climbing the huge trees or coming to a panting stop before stripping off to plunge into the crystal clear waters of the lake. That water was always so cold.

He imagined the fire pits that right now were probably burning brightly with huge steel pots of stew over them, bubbling away with the most appetising smells. He could remember so many story nights gathered around those pits with his cousins and friends and siblings, eyes wide as they listened to the tales of old. He remembered sliding down the waterfall and imagined his own boys learning about these joys. He wondered if a night spent alone in front of the haunted shack trying not to scream was still a part of a young man's rite of passage. He could clearly picture the old buildings, one was once a church and several storage sheds had the marvel of concrete floors. The missionaries had painted everything white, and on sunny days, the sun shone off the paint like bolts of lightning glaring out amongst the muted greens and browns of the rest of the structures, trees and shrubs.

He remembered one time he'd been helping to build a new house and had befriended a crow. She would bring him brightly coloured objects, and he would leave her food. The thought of seeing his childhood friends who may still be living there sent a thrill through him. He wondered why he hadn't gone home long ago. That night when they had stopped to rest and were all curled in their blankets by the fire, Nemid fell asleep filled with a head full of happy memories.

At first light, while Nemid and the boys ate breakfast and packed, Ashekii refuelled the car from two metal Jerry cans. As they travelled on, the trees became taller and the vegetation greener. About mid-morning the dirt track ended at a T intersection with a sealed road. To one side was a truck stop with a sign pointing towards the lake. Kal instantly recognised this as where his Nahill journey had begun. It occurred to him how different his life might have been if he'd gone left instead of right that fateful day. Ashekii checked for traffic then turned right. As he increased speed, Trindal dug his fingers into the seat rests, an expression of horrified fascination on his face. Suddenly the trees stopped, and Trindal gasped.

'What happened to the trees?' he cried pointing at the grassland.

'They cut them down to make a farm', Kal said. 'Farms are where they grow food.'

'But', Trindal said, puzzled, 'there's plenty of food in the forest.'

'They grow different food.'

'But', he said, 'where do the animals go when it snows? What about all the birds and … what about all the things that live in the forest?'

'None of them live out here', Ashekii answered the boy. 'They stay with us on the reservation.'

The children peered out at the large, shaggy black and white beasts in the fields.'

What are they?' Trindal said.

'Cows... Angus short horns, I think', Kal said.

Even stranger, Trindal thought.

As they continued, Kal explained things such as power lines, telephone lines, telephone poles, white lines, reflective road markers, bitumen, fences, gates and trucks.

'Funny picture', Trindal said, pointing at a road sign.

'That says, slow down there's a sharp turn ahead', Kal said.

'You understand that?'

Kal grinned and from then on made a point of explaining each one. The sun was above them when they came to a cross road, and this one had a written sign giving directions.

'What does that say?' Trindal said.

Kal pointed.

'That arrow says Lake Meri Yallock is ten clicks down the road.'

Ashekii glanced at him in the rear vision mirror.

'Clicks?' he said.

'Sorry. It's what we call kilometres', Kal looked at Trindal. 'A kilometre is the way we measure how far away things are. A metre is this much', he held his hands apart, 'and a kilometre is a thousand of them. Understand?'

From Trindal's expression, Kal could tell he didn't understand at all. Trindal pointed to another sign.

'What does that one say?'

'The arrow pointing straight ahead says that Lake View Waters is twenty kilometres away, and that arrow says a place called Haddleyville is one hundred and fifty kilometres that way.'

Trindal frowned.

'So white people have more than one camp too?' he said.

'Yes', Kal said.

They turned towards the lake and drove in silence studying the fields. In what seemed like no time, they'd reached another T intersection. One sign showed symbols for a boat ramp and picnic area straight ahead. To the left, the arrow had 'Lake View Waters scenic drive' written on it. Ashekii stopped and pointed.

'This road takes us past Blue Camp', he said. 'It's named Blue Camp because it sits on the shore of a really deep harbour and the water is always Blue.'

'Blue Camp has the best fishing', Nemid added casually.

Trindal's eyes widened.

'But Blue Camp is almost a moon's walk. How can we be there already?'

'Cars are really fast', Kal answered.

Trindal shook his head in amazement. They turned and drove past more farmland until they came to another intersection. A dirt road had a large sign with 'Jhunti Reservation. Permit required for entry' written in red. In between the trees, they could just make out several houses and cars.

'That's Blue Camp', Ashekii said. 'Should we drop past to say hello?'

'Perhaps another time', Nemid replied, anxious to be at his beloved White Camp.

They turned and started driving again. It was soon Kal's turn to stare in wonder as the road took them close to the lake.

'Wow!' he said.

All were silent as they stared at the vast body of water. After a while the road swung back inland, and the lake was again lost to view. They passed more farms, and soon they drove by a small cluster of shops and houses. The streets were deserted, although some of the houses had lights inside. A marina to the right had several luxury boats moored in it, and as they drove on, they passed many multi-storeyed buildings.

'Look at that', said Trindal. 'White people sure have funny looking cabins.'

A street sign pointed to the golf course. Neither Kal nor Ashekii knew what that was, so they didn't explain what it said. When they stopped for fuel, Ashekii pointed out that if they could throw a spear straight across the lake, it would land in Big Camp. Ashekii removed the hose from the pump and opened the tank. Trindal unclipped his seatbelt and turned around, kneeling on his seat to watch.

'What's he doing?' he said.

'Refuelling', Kal said, scrunching down in his seat so on one could see him.

'What's that mean?'

'This car runs on diesel fuel', Kal said in a long-suffering tone. 'If you don't fill it up you'll run out, and then it won't go anymore.'

Trindal watched, fascinated as the numbers on the fuel pump whirled around. Once the tank was full, Ashekii replaced the cap and filled the two metal jerry cans that were bolted to the back doors. Trindal hugged the seat rest, his knees on the seat as he watched every movement. After Ashekii hung up the pump, he opened the back doors and began tugging on a linen sack.

'What's in there?' Trindal said.

Ashekii opened the sack and Trindal saw the pottery jars of salmon relish and fish sauce, a bag of meat rolls, a pair of fur lined winter boots in a child's size and a matching coat.

'These', Ashekii said, 'are my trade for the fuel.'

He hefted the sack onto his shoulder and went inside.

'I need to pee', Trindal said and opened his door.

'Me too', Nemid said, climbing out of the car.

Kal opened his door and accompanied them. Instead of going to the restrooms, Nemid stopped at a patch of grass. When the others began to relieve themselves, Kal joined them.

Inside the service station, a man in a plaid shirt sat at the counter reading a paper. He looked up and smiled as Ashekii came towards him.

'Morning, Ash', he said. 'Where you headed today?'

'Out the other side of the lake.'

The man's eyes went to the sack, and he licked his lips.

'My wife was hoping you'd stop by', he said, 'we just ran out of that fish sauce.'

Ashekii placed the sack onto the counter, and the man opened it enthusiastically. He frowned at the clothes.

'Sorry, we don't sell clothes.'

'They are for your grandson', Ashekii said. 'He made a big fuss of mine last time, so I made these for him.'

The man took them out, running his fingers over the soft leather then peering down to examine the delicate stitching and beadwork.

'They're beautiful', he said then glanced reluctantly at the pots of food. 'But I can't take these and the pots too. The fuel's not worth that much.'

'The clothes are a gift', Ashekii said and started for the door.

'Thank you', the man said, accompanying Ashekii to the door. 'You can fill up for free next time.' He suddenly noticed what Nemid, Trindal and Kal were doing. 'Hey! You can't do that there! Damn it, Ash, this happens every time!'

'Sorry.'

Muttering to himself, the man went back inside. Ashekii climbed into the car, and they set off. They drove past signs for fishing and scenic tours, and just as suddenly as they'd started, the houses stopped and farmland returned. After a while the combination of excitement, an early start and the rhythmic rocking of the car put the boys and Nemid to sleep. When they awoke, the lake was still on their right, and they were again passing fields of cattle. Occasionally they would see a farmhouse surrounded by trees and bushes. They drove all afternoon.

Eventually Ashekii turned off the main road and onto a smaller road. Again farmland passed on either side until they came to a place where the road bent around to the left. An arrow pointed to the left with 'Freeway 18 km' on it. In the distance Kal could just make out a small group of shops. They turned right and drove on until they reached a dirt track surrounded by bush. They passed a small cabin with a wire gate. A short time after that, they passed a sign with 'Jhunti Reservation. Permit required for entry' written on it.

'Welcome to Water clan land', Ashekii said.

They drove up a steeply winding, muddy road until, at last, it ended in a large cleared area where several cars were haphazardly parked. Three showed signs of recent use. Ashekii pulled up beside a pink jeep and turned off the engine.

'We're here!' he exclaimed.

They all got out, and with an air of anticipation, Ashekii and Nemid pulled bundles from the back of the land rover.

'You first', Ashekii said to Nemid.

They had not gone three steps when Nemid stopped to pick something up. He stared at it curiously.

'What's this?' he said, turning the small brown cylinder towards Ashekii.

The Drekesh studied it for a moment then shrugged.

'It's a cigarette butt', Kal said.

'A what?'

'A cigarette butt, from people who smoke', and Kal mimed smoking.

Nemid put it to his nose. He took a sniff and quickly moved it away, a disgusted look on his face.

'You don't eat it', Kal grinned. 'You throw them away, see?' He pointed to the ground around them. 'They're all over the place.'

As Nemid looked, he saw more and more butts. As affronted as he was to do it, he tossed the butt to the ground with the others. They moved a few more steps forward, and he stopped again. This time he stared down at a pile of beer cans and bottles interspersed with plastic bags and fast food wrappers.

'It's just rubbish', Kal said, unperturbed. 'I guess they don't have any bins handy.'

'Bins?' Ashekii said.

'Yeah, rubbish bins. You put your rubbish into bins and it gets taken to the dump.'

'Dump?' Nemid said.

'Rubbish dump', Kal said. 'All the stuff that doesn't get used, like that', he cocked his head towards the cans, 'gets taken to the dump.'

When Nemid continued to look at him nonplussed, Kal continued.

'A rubbish dump is like this place where they dig a massive hole so they can fill it up with rubbish. When it's full they put dirt over the top of it then find a new spot and dig another one.' He frowned down at the pile of rubbish. 'Some of this could be recycled, but I guess no one round here does that.'

Nemid opened his mouth to ask what recycling was but changed his mind. Nahill did not create 'rubbish' and had no need for 'rubbish bins' or 'rubbish dumps'. This was white crap, and it was an insult to the Nahill that they were bringing it here, to this Nahill place where no white things should be. He pictured carloads of sightseers and tourists coming to gawk at the magnificent view. This would have to stop.

'They inter this', Ashekii said in disbelief, 'into the ground? This is how they feed Mother Earth? With filth? What kind of children will she bare when fed this?'

'If I had my way', Trindal muttered, 'I would teach them the right way to treat our mother.'

Determined not to have his homecoming spoilt, Nemid turned his back on this outrage and lead them towards the edge of the car park.

'We will drop our things at my family's home', Nemid said excitedly, a joyous smile on his face, 'and then I shall take you all on a tour.' He hurried them forward, eager to get to the edge so they could behold the wonder that was White Camp. As they approached the edge, he threw his arms out wide. 'Allow me to show you boys what paradise looks like. Welcome to White Camp.'

They stopped at the edge, and the smiles disappeared. The camp was totally overgrown, and most of the cabins were in varying stages of decay. There were piles of rubbish and cigarette butts everywhere. The smell was a mixture of animal manure, mould, damp and decaying garbage.

'P.U.', Kal gagged.

They all covered their noses. A cloud of flies took off as they walked down the hill. Nemid steadied himself and thanked the

Great Spirits that they had come in cold weather. In the heat this stench would be unbearable. Several mangy, underfed dogs barked at them, their shaggy brown coats sticking out in all directions. Soon a barefooted Jhunti boy several snows older than Kal sauntered towards them. He was dressed in wide baggy denim jeans, a dirt-smudged pastel yellow t-shirt with 'I hate this t-shirt' written on it in English and a padded camouflage vest. He had an open, honest face, small brown eyes and several missing teeth. His teeth were the first thing you noticed as, if he wasn't smiling or laughing, he had a habit of leaving his mouth ajar. Occasionally he'd breath in a fly but didn't seem to notice. In one hand, he held a half-plucked chicken. His face was smeared with dirt, and he shuffled along in rubber boots that were several sizes too big for him.

'Hello', he said with a grin. 'I'm Laughs a Lot. Who're you?'

Nemid stepped forward.

'I am Nemid, lately of Red Camp.'

The boy's mouth was slightly open as he stared up at Nemid, a thin stream of drool running from it. He hadn't expected the man to answer as most people didn't. They tended to yell at him to do chores and to scold him when he didn't do them to their satisfaction, but none of them talked with him. Not that he had a lot of time for chit chat as, being the only person in the camp now, he was very busy. Nemid regarded the boy, puzzled.

'Dog clan?' he said.

Laughs a Lot's grin widened.

'Yes, how did you know? Are you my cousin?'

'No. We are Water clan.'

The boy thought for a moment, scratching his head.

'Water clan?' he said in a mystified tone. 'I thought you were just in stories. You know, the ones they tell at night to scare children.'

'Scare children?' Nemid said.

'Yes, you know', and Laughs a Lot made claws out of his fingers, 'the monsters that will come and steal our houses out from underneath us. Wasn't it Water clan that punished Dog clan for surviving the whites?'

Ashekii and Nemid exchanged glances. The boy scrutinized Kal then Trindal.

'Hey', he said, 'you look like the white teacher that comes with picture books. Are you white?'

'Where is everyone?' Nemid said.

Laughs a Lot scratched his head again and frowned.

'My mother went into town. She took my sisters with her.'

'Into *town?*' Ashekii said. 'Into the land of white people?'

'Ah huh. My mother's name is Sindri, and my sisters are Wisha and Lemon. When the snow melts, Wisha is claiming Besna from Blue Camp. He's going to come and live with us. My mother said he's bringing a dowry of goats, chickens, pigs, a new pot and a table. My cousin Ravrah claimed Rightly a while ago, but he was no good so she sent him home. They have two babies, Tomma and Nes. Rightly took the babies with him 'cause they were both boys. I liked Rightly. He only brought chickens, but he gave us all woollen scarfs, except I dropped mine into the river and it got swept away. My father was no good either. He got sent home. Wisha had a different father. He was no good and got sent home. Lemon says all men are lazy. They went into town. My mother said she needed to buy some things.'

There was another silent exchange between Nemid and Ashekii, both puzzled how anyone could *buy* things when the Nahill had no money.

'When did she go?' Ashekii said. 'We saw no car tracks.'

Laughs a Lot shrugged.

'When's she due back?'

Laughs a Lot shrugged again.

'Who looks after you?' Nemid said.

'I'm old enough to look after myself.'

Laughs a Lot turned towards Trindal.

'My name's Laughs a Lot, but people call me Lal. What's your name?'

'I'm Trindal, but you can call me Trin. This is Kal.'

'Lal and Kal!' Laughs a Lot cried with delight singing it over and over. 'Lal and Kal, Lal and Kal.'

As Laughs a Lot continued, Trindal and Kal exchanged uncertain looks.

'Who else lives here?' Ashekii said, more to stop the singing than to make conversation.

Laughs a Lot pointed to one of the empty cabins on the right-hand side. 'My Aunt Talks Too Much and Uncle Mends Things and my cousins Hasty, Remmy, and Mash live in that one.' He pointed to the next one. 'My cousin Gilmore lives in that one. Gilmore and Mash are best friends, and Lemon and Remmy are best friends. Hasty has the dogs, Begup and Bug, and his chickens are named…'

His attention was caught by an eagle flying overhead. That eagle had better not be after my chickens again, Laughs a Lot thought. The others were still waiting for Laughs a Lot to finish his sentence, but instead, he wandered off, his eyes following the eagle, his half-plucked chicken trailing behind him. Ashekii indicated for them to start walking. Laughs a Lot fell into step beside them as they went down the path, dodging pot holes and piles of rubbish. They arrived at a cabin not far from the top of the hill.

'This', Nemid said, 'is where I grew up.'

They made to go inside, but Ashekii stopped them.

'The floor's gone', he said. 'Let's try the next one.'

They continued down the hill. As they went, Laughs a Lot resumed naming the Dog clan residents and their livestock. Occasionally Nemid would ask about a Water clan family.

'I think they left', Laughs a Lot would say each time.

When Laughs a Lot had given the details of all seven occupied cabins, the men again glanced at each other but did not comment. The entire population of White Camp was one large Dog clan family consisting of fifteen adults and ten children of varying ages. As they examined the camp, it became obvious that the Dogs had taken over the very best cabins, and instead of caring for the rest, they'd left them to decay. When they came to the sixth cabin, Nemid and Ashekii stopped. Nemid pointed to a barely visible Water clan symbol etched into the veranda pole.

'See that?' he said deferentially. 'This is the cabin where the Water clan Pac used to live. See how it is equally close to all the cabins?'

'The what?' Laughs a Lot said.

'The Pac … the chief of the village', Ashekii explained.

They climbed the stairs and trouped in, Laughs a Lot with his chicken bringing up the rear. The cabin was in good repair, the roof sound and the walls solid and windproof. Kal wrinkled his nose at the smell and the thick coating of animal manure on the floor.

'This's our goat shed', Laughs a Lot said. 'They're out in the field now, but I will bring them in soon.'

'You keep your goats in … in our…', Ashekii was so angry he could not finish his sentence.

Laughs a Lot wiped his nose on his sleeve and stared at Ashekii, a smile on his face.

'I have goats', he said. 'Dopsil is the boss, and her daughter Nod, she's the greedy one, and…'

As Laughs a Lot continued to name his goats, Ashekii's jaw muscles tensed. 'This is outrageous!' he hissed.

Nemid laid a hand on the warrior's arm.

'It's not the boy's fault', he said. 'It's Water clan's. We have obviously been gone too long. Besides, at least the goats have kept this cabin in reasonable order.'

Ashekii gave him an uncertain look. 'You can't seriously be thinking of staying?' he said. 'You are Drekesh!'

Nemid smiled. 'All the more reason', he said. 'The Drekesh protect. Drekesh guide through example. Drekesh encourage through actions. Drekesh remind others of what's important. This is what the Drekesh are trained to do.'

Laughs a Lot studied Nemid up and down. 'Are you Drekesh?' he said. 'My mother says Drekesh are the lapdog of the council… What's a lapdog?'

Ashekii's jaw muscles tensed, but Nemid glanced around.

'It's going to take some hard work to have accommodation fit for Healers.'

'I've heard of Healers', Laughs a Lot said. 'I didn't think they were real.'

'You've never seen a Healer?' Trindal said. 'What do you do when you get sick?'

'We go to the doctor in town.'

'A white doctor?'

Laughs a Lot nodded. The two men could stand no more and set everyone to work. They cleaned the cabin of the goat manure then scrubbed all the floors using sweet smelling herbs. Trindal and Kal were set to work bringing the rest of the things down from the car then to gathering firewood while Laughs a Lot was told to find a new place for his goats. It was getting dark by the time the tasks were completed. As Kal set to lighting the fire, Nemid put a hand on Ashekii's shoulder.

'You have a long drive ahead of you', he said. 'You had better go.'

Ashekii glanced towards the Dog clan cabins.

'I would like to have a word with those Dogs', he said.

'There will be plenty of time for that. Go now. You have already stayed much longer than we agreed.'

Ashekii sighed and nodded.

'Very well, but I will come back soon with more supplies.'

Nemid gave Ashekii a hug before the younger man left.

10

Two days later in the early morning light, Nemid leaned against the porch rail staring out at the breathtaking vista of forest trees and hills. The hills got smaller all the way down to the river valley where Big Camp was located. To the right, one could see the blue of the lake waters with more peaks rising on the opposite bank. Nemid dragged his gaze back from the mesmerising landscape and focused on the church hall, which was now the school room. The building had not changed since he himself had been a student, Nemid mused. The big hall was intact and in good order, and according to Laughs a Lot, the visiting teacher still used it for weekly classes. Nemid had many happy memories of school. His teacher, Mrs Williams, had been very fond of telling them stories of the white world. He had found the glimpses of the alien white culture fascinating, and they had helped him to be more understanding and tolerant. He had also loved reading, not that he'd kept it up, but the images he'd seen in picture books of strange creatures and foreign lands had stayed with him.

Nemid imagined Chani sitting in the school room surrounded by books. She had a great deal more white things to learn if she was to complete her mission. The problems they'd had with Kal at Red Camp had been a timely reminder of how difficult her path would be once people knew. For several snows, Nemid and Deikter had been trying to work out how to covertly get Chani to White Camp so she could attend school. The night before they had left Red Camp,

Healer Deikter said that she would smooth things over for them and after a time she and Chani would join them at White Camp. When Nemid had tried to argue, she had berated him. 'Can't you feel the hand of the Great Spirits? Can't you see how hard they are working to help us achieve our goals?'

Nemid glanced at the storage sheds knowing there was a large hole in the roof of one and a collapsed door in the other. Both were easy to fix. Most exciting had been the discovery of the large storage barrels for apples and grain all still in good repair. They'd also found a grinding wheel, and last night, he and the boys made bean and corn meal. Laughs a Lot, or Lal as he liked to be called, had been very friendly, giving them supplies, showing them around and giving them dry wood. Laughs a Lot told him that Dog clan bought all their food from town although he got eggs from the chickens and made cheese from goats' milk. He had given them some of each.

Nemid took in another deep breath of the frigid air. White Camp was much colder and wetter than he remembered from his youth. Where Red Camp was nestled in a sheltered valley, White Camp was perched on the exposed side of a mountain. The spectacular views were why the Nahill had permitted white people access to this site; the breathtaking vista left one with a feeling of awe and wonder.

Yes, Nemid thought, how could one not love this place, this beloved home of Water clan? He smiled, knowing that he and his children had at last found the place where they belonged. A flash of silver caught his attention, and he walked to the end of the veranda. Sitting on the handrail was a bottle cap. He picked it up and examined it closely then straightened. His eyes glistened as they darted from tree to tree.

'Where are you?' he called out.

A crow cawed from the right-hand side of the camp. Nemid turned, held up the bottle cap and waved.

'Is it really you, old friend?'

He could just make out the dark shape against the green of the leaves. How long had it been? He swallowed back a lump in his throat and then searched his pockets. Finding half a meat roll, he placed it where the bottle cap had been on the handrail.

'It is good to see you too', he said.

A crisp gust made him shiver, and he went back inside his cabin. He carefully placed the bottle cap onto the mantelpiece. The boys were up and squatting by the fire. In the distance, several goats bleated.

'That'll be Lal taking them to the fields for the day', Trindal said.

'Lal seems a good boy', Nemid said. 'A little slow, but all in all not bad for someone from Dog clan.'

Kal frowned.

'What's wrong with Dog clan? How come everyone hates them?'

'They're not Jhunti', Trindal said. 'They don't look like us, and they sure don't act like us.'

Kal had only met Laughs a Lot but had to admit the boy did look different with his wide nose and thick wavy hair. He'd thought it was just how Laughs a Lot looked.

'The current families of Dog clan', Nemid said, 'are the descendants of a long line of itinerant traders. They tell us their home is somewhere in the Northern Seas...'

'But no one *really* knows where they came from', Trindal interrupted.

'What is known', Nemid continued, 'is that they would trade between the islands....'

'Trade?' Trindal let out a mocking snort, his expression making it clear that any dealings with Dog clan were usually to the disadvantage of their customers.

'Over time', Nemid said, ignoring Trindal, 'they set up a few trading stations. When the whites arrived, most of Dog clan left.'

'Then they came here', Trindal said indignantly, 'and hid in *our* mountains.'

Not wanting to fan the flames of old feuds, Nemid held up a hand to quiet Trindal.

'They spoke our language, you see', Nemid said, 'and felt more comfortable with our ways than those of the whites. The Women's Council agreed that Dog clan could stay.'

'Thieves and liars', Trindal muttered under his breath.

'I've heard people talk about the Women's Council', Kal said. 'Who are they?'

Nemid pondered his answer. Usually he was candid with Kal; however, this was getting into knowledge that only Nahill should know.

'Women's Council is our highest law', he said. 'They are down in Big Camp, and those who sit on the council are very wise. You can always tell councillors because they dye their hair red. Under Women's Council are the clan councils, and under them are the camp Pacs.'

Nemid paused for a moment then allowed himself a self-deprecating smile. 'One could say that as the most senior member of Water clan here', and he laid a hand on his chest, 'this one is currently the Pac of White Camp.'

The boys grinned.

'Esteemed Pac', said Trindal, giving a small bow. 'Are there any more meat rolls?'

'Sadly, no.'

Both boys pouted, and Nemid filled a battered tin cup he'd found with water.

'Let's have a drink instead' he said. 'It will fill up our stomachs', and he took a long drink.

'Does Women's Council decide who will be Trill?' Trindal said.

Nemid lowered the cup.

'No. To be Trill, one must be born with the colour.'

'Who are Trill?' Kal whispered to Trindal.

'Trill watch over us.'

'Like Healer clan?' Kal said.

Nemid handed the cup to Trindal, who took a few swallows then handed it to Kal.

'Healer clan', Nemid said 'has always been separate from the rest of us. Their duty is to do whatever they need to keep us healthy. Only women are permitted to be Healers, and Healers only ever have female children. It is a Healer secret as to how they do this.'

Kal drank the last gulp of water and handed the empty cup back to Nemid who placed it on the floor.

'So women', Kal said slowly to make sure he understood Nemid correctly, 'are the ones on the council. They're the only ones allowed to be Healers...'

'...and Trill', Trindal said.

'...and Trill. Are the Season Keepers all women too?'

Nemid nodded.

'And there's History Women and Oracles. They can be male or female provided they have ghost eyes, so...', Kal pondered. 'What do men do?'

'Some men become Drekesh, the peace keepers.'

Kal frowned.

'So how come I see them doing combat training all the time?'

'Because in the old days', Trindal said, 'Drekesh were soldiers.'

'Yes', Nemid said, 'but now, instead of fighting, we are the ones who stop fights. We are the experts in Nahill law. That reminds me. Now we are here', Nemid looked at Kal and Trindal. 'I want you both to go to school and learn to read and write.'

Trindal felt excited at the thought of school. He wanted to see books like Kal spoke about and to hear white stories to see if they were different. Kal's fingers closed around the stick he was about to put onto the fire. He had no intention of going to school. He wanted to be like the Nahill and pretend the white world didn't exist. Deep down he was also afraid that the teacher would tell Barry about him and Barry would come and drag Kal home.

'But I already know how to read and write', Kal protested, 'and the Nahill don't use books... I thought I was supposed to act like a Nahill now. Besides, there's too much work to do.'

'Chani will need your help when she arrives in the thaw. She is going to school too.'

'But...'

Nemid held up a hand and Kal fell silent, but his jaw tightened.

'Once Trindal can read and write', Nemid said, 'I want him to record our stories so they won't ever be lost.'

Trindal frowned.

'But … isn't that what the Memory Women do?'

'They remember our history. I'm talking about our other stories, perhaps some of our songs too.'

Trindal grinned, liking the sound of that. He could picture himself going from village to village collecting stories. Word would get around and everyone would want him because he would know all the best stories. He might even become the greatest storyteller the Nahill had ever known. His chest swelled with pride.

Nemid contemplated the young storyteller. This was not to be Trindal's only task. Although Trindal already spoke rudimentary English, thanks to Kal and Chani, Nemid and Deikter wanted more from him. They had already decided that Kal was to be Chani's primary support, but it was prudent to have another support in place should anything happen to Kal, and it made sense that her other support person be Trindal.

Outside, the birds were in full song, and the pale sunlight filtered through the dirty window glass. Kal stood up.

'Where are you going?' Trindal said.

'To ask Lal for more wood.'

He was back in a short time with an armload of sticks and some bark in a dusty old bag.

'What've you got there?' Trindal said.

Kal dumped the wood beside the hearth then unslung the bag from his shoulder.

'Lal said he found a bunch of stuff in one of the cabins. He said it's really dry and makes great fire starters.'

Kal grabbed one of the longer sticks and was about to break it over his knee when Nemid's eye was caught by the flash of a carved figure.

'Wait a moment' he said, going over to Kal and taking the stick from him.

He rolled it between his fingers, studying it and then his face paled as he recognised what he was holding. He looked down at the other sticks at his feet, then at the bag. He could just make out Healer symbols on the outside of it. There was a large burn mark on one corner. He blew on one of the pieces of wood, rubbing the ingrained dirt from the carvings and suddenly realised these 'sticks' were all Elder staffs. In the old days, the bestowal of an Elder staff denoted a person's transition to a superior rank. An Elder Staff was a symbol of authority and cherished by the recipient and their family. They were proudly conferred by the Women's Council, and there were different staffs for tribal elders, clan chiefs, camp Pac's, Oracles, senior Healers, Season Keepers and History Women. Nemid felt his blood begin to pound as a fury swept through him.

'You say Laughs a Lot is burning these?' he said in a tight voice.

Kal looked up. The expression on Nemid's face made the hairs on the back of his neck rise. He backed away. Sensing trouble, Trindal turned to face them.

'What's wrong?' he said.

Nemid took a calming breath and carefully laid the Elder staff against the wall.

'It seems', he said, 'that our little friend has found a cache of sacred objects. This is the staff used by the Pac', he said then pointed to the bag now resting against the 'sticks' on the floor. 'That bag should be filled with the objects used in ceremonies that keep the Great Spirits happy and our lives in harmony with what is around us. By burning these things...'

He did not have words for the affront that showed to the Great Spirits and to the land. It was also a massive insult to the Jhunti. Unable to explain further because he was so angry, Nemid wheeled about and headed for the door.

'Burn nothing', he said as he went in search of Laughs a Lot.

It took a while, but Nemid finally got the full story. The boy had been exploring the other cabins, looking for a new home for his goats, and had come across human remains. Many snows ago, this Healer, obviously the last Nahill left at White Camp, had stayed and watched over her dying village until she too had died. Over time, her bones had been scattered about the cabin by rodents, and among what was left of her things, Laughs a Lot had found the cache of sacred objects.

Being from Dog clan, Laughs a Lot had no idea what they were and so had brought them back as amusements. The rhythm sticks, inlaid with mother of pearl symbols of all the Nahill clans, he'd used to prop up a wobbly kitchen shelf. A necklace of Echidna spines, which conferred on the wearer the mystical energies of the land, he'd pulled apart and made into forks. The metal bowl engraved with sacred symbols and used in ceremonies to burn the herbs that would attract the attention of the Great Spirits, he'd filled with food scraps for his chickens.

Nemid returned carrying what was left of the sacred objects. He said nothing, just cleaned them all then laid them carefully away. After that he and the boys collected and burnt the bones of the Healer. They made sure to observe the proper rights due her status.

In the dawn of the new day, the pink tendrils of the new sun spread out across the horizon as Nemid sat on the rocky outcrop that overlooked White Camp. Nemid drew in the crisp morning air, the fresh scent of the frost on the eucalypts and the moisture in the lingering fingers of mist. All around him the birds were finishing their morning chorus. A kookaburra laughed in the big tree to his left. Nemid could feel the first stirring of the morning breeze against his skin. How he wished Leath and his children were still alive. He closed his eyes and pictured the breeze running through their cabin then coming to him. For a short time, he could sense their presence around him, and for a moment, he actually believed that when he went down to his cabin, he'd find them all waiting for him. His imagination was so strong this morning, he could hear soft footfalls approaching. A lump came to his throat, and a tear ran down his cheek. He missed them all so much. There were times when he wanted to be with them so strongly, it was all he could do to stop himself making this happen. It would be simple, just a few extra steps and then…

'Nedda?' came a soft voice beside him.

Nemid started but didn't turn as only one person called him Nedda.

'Are you alright?' Kal said.

Nemid hastily wiped the tears from his cheeks.

'Of course… What are you doing here?'

'I saw you leave, and I figured you'd come here. When you're sad you always sit somewhere high.'

'What made you think I was sad?'

'Am I wrong?' Kal said.

Nemid looked away.

'Is it so obvious?' he said.

'To me it is … it's something I learnt when I was with my dad.'

'Why?'

Nemid could see the tension in the boy's shoulders. As Kal rarely spoke of his brutal past, Nemid was torn between wanting to know more and leaving the past where it belonged, in the past.

'It doesn't matter', Nemid said gently. 'Don't speak of it if it upsets you.'

'No, it's OK.'

Kal wondered how to explain that for him, being hyperaware of details, noticing even tiny changes in a person's mood, habits, facial expressions, had become a habit. Things like the way a person walked, the clothes they wore, the tone of their voice, all gave clues about someone's mood. Kal plucked a stalk of grass and began to pull the leaves off. He knew Nemid was curious and wanted to tell him how his safety often depended on whether he noticed the way Barry shut the gate. A loud slam meant run, a quiet shut meant things were OK, not shutting it meant hide. On top of that were the thousands of rules he used to live by. Like when Barry had a hangover, everything had to be quiet. In the morning Kal would carefully put a slice of bread into the toaster then place a finger on the button, stopping it from popping up when the toast was done so it didn't make any noise. He'd remove his toast silently then add thick layers of butter and Vegemite so the knife slid over the toast quietly. He'd then take quick, silent bites, putting a hand over his mouth to muffle his frantic chewing.

'You saw what happened to me when I got my dad's rules wrong', he said. 'Nahill rules are easy to remember and they don't change.

My dad's rules…', Kal began then stopped, reminded of the endless rituals Kal had to perform in order to follow the rules. For example, there were rules for washing and putting away the dishes; Barry would inspect the cupboards to make sure he'd done it right. One spoon the wrong way around and there was hell to pay.

'He liked things to be the same. I had to make sure everything was put back with the labels facing the front.' Kal bowed his head as he focused on the stalk of grass he was pulling to pieces. 'All the kitchen chairs had to be pushed up to the table … and the salt and pepper shakers had to sit in the middle in case guests came over but … we never had real guests.' He shrugged. 'Sometimes he'd bring one of his drinking mates home, but I'd never stick around when he did that… Not smart.'

Kal remembered cleaning his teeth using a trickle of water, replacing his brush into the holder with the bristles pointing to the left. Every time he'd wash his hands, he had to wipe the sink with his bath towel before neatly folding it and placing it back onto the rail with the fold pointing towards the door. Rules, rules and more rules. Nemid gave the boy's shoulder a squeeze then stood up.

'Let's go back', he said. They began to pick their way down the dirt path to the camp.

When the path levelled out and they approached the open space above the camp, Nemid looked over it and felt a surge of belonging mixed with exhilaration. Instead of being depressed at the state of his once magnificent White Camp, he found the desolation invigorating. The idea of proclaiming himself Pac was growing on him by the day. After all, he reasoned, if not him then who?

As he warmed to the idea, the possibilities of all he could achieve began to occur to him. He'd be able to shape White Camp to his liking. He hadn't realized how much he would enjoy the feeling of being a leader. Not that his life at Red Camp had been unpleasant; it was just that he'd settled into a life of peace and routines, a life of old age. There would be none of that here, he thought with relish. His body was already aching from all the strenuous activity, but his mind was full of things to do, make and find.

Yes, he thought, as Pac he would take this run-down camp and bring order and prosperity to it again. This camp was the place where white people came, and it should be a showcase not a dump. Instead of a people in decay, he wanted to show the whites that the Nahill were a strong and proud people. He gazed down at the weed-covered fields and could tell they had not seen the three sisters in a long time. His eyes went to the apple orchard. The tree branches grew wildly and desperately needed pruning. That was the job he and the boys would undertake today so the apple harvest was assured for next season.

Humming a jaunty tune, he led the way down into White Camp, into *his camp*.

11

People were fickle, Ashekii mused. Once again he found himself bouncing along the boundary track in the old four-wheel drive. When Ashekii had returned from White Camp, he'd told Hahina about the camp being in ruins thanks to Dog clan's laziness. She had been indignant that Dog clan had taken over a 'Jhunti' camp. It was outrageous!

Ashekii had always preferred for his wife to do the talking and had been very uncomfortable when he was forced to tell his tale again and again. He had also been asked many questions about the camp, but he hadn't paid that much attention. His inability to answer every question had annoyed many people. It particularly irked the elders who were 'trying to get to the bottom of this'.

Word quickly spread. Suddenly Nemid, who only a season ago had been called a traitor, was being portrayed as a hero. The same people who had been saying Nemid and the boys had been run out of Red Camp and good riddance were now saying that Wise Nemid mystically knew White Camp had fallen. He was Gallant Nemid answering the call of a desperate camp in need of a champion.

Ashekii had been dispatched to fetch his wayward cousin and bring him back to Red Camp. He glanced in the rear vision mirror at his two passengers. Councillor Gleris and her husband had been sent to see firsthand what was happening at White Camp so a proper report could be given. His passengers were looking a little green,

Ashekii mused, and they were holding grimly onto the door handles and keeping their gaze out the window. Ashekii allowed himself a slight smile and increased his speed, thankful it was a quiet trip. When they arrived at White Camp, Ashekii bounded out of the car and left the Councillor and her husband alone to recover.

Trindal was the first to see them.

'Ashe's here', he called out.

Nemid dropped the log he'd been dragging and went to greet him, wiping his hands on his pants as he went. Ashekii was immediately struck by how well Nemid appeared. He had a new spring to his step and an animation that had been missing at Red Camp. They gave each other a hug.

'It is good to see this face', they said to each other.

'You'll never guess what has happened', Ashekii beamed. 'News that White Camp has fallen to the Dogs has incensed everyone. Clans from everywhere are saying they will send people. You're a hero, Nem. It's why I've come to take you back!'

Instead of being jubilant and jumping at the chance to collect his things and return, Nemid stared out at the view, a pensive expression on his face. While Nemid was tempted to return to his pleasant life at Red Camp, he wondered how long it would be before things returned to how they had been for Kal. Here at White Camp they had total freedom to do as they pleased and an opportunity to do something truly special. Nemid's attention was caught by the couple slowly making their way down the hill, pointing at cabins as they went. The proprietorial air with which they were inspecting *his* camp made Nemid bristle.

'Is that Councillor Gleris?' he said.

Ashekii followed his gaze then nodded.

'Yes. Council asked her to come. She is to provide a firsthand account of how things stand.'

Nemid was instantly alert. Why had council sent someone to give a 'firsthand account'? What did that mean? Suddenly the reason became clear; they had offered her the Pacship, and she was here to see if that would suit her. All the thoughts Nemid had about wanting to lead White Camp back to health and the changes he wished to enact galvanised him into action.

'I wish to be made Pac', Nemid blurted out.

Ashekii turned to face his cousin.

'Pac?' he raised an eyebrow. 'You?'

'Yes. None is more qualified, don't you agree?'

Ashekii cocked his head to one side. 'Who will fight a challenger should there be one?' he said.

'Kal is my eldest, so that honour would go to him. I can teach him to be Drekesh so…'

Ashekii's smile vanished. 'No!' he said heatedly. 'Teaching him to hunt and plant crops is one thing, but teaching him our battle strategies and combat secrets? Giving him instruction in our laws and customs? What if he uses this knowledge against us? It goes against everything that we … what you are suggesting is … is … to even think it is … you just can't, and that's an end to it!'

Ashekii glanced around then dropped his voice. 'You haven't told anyone else of this madness, have you?'

'No.'

'Good. I implore you, cousin, do not. It will bring disgrace to our family. The repercussions for us all could be severe. As for the boy, if he is taught the ways of the Drekesh, he will be seen as a threat. A white Drekesh would be hated and feared by all. Is that what you want for him?'

The two men studied each other. Ashekii was the first to drop his eyes. 'I'm sorry', he said, 'but it just wouldn't be right.'

While Nemid firmly believed Kal becoming a Drekesh made sense, what Ashekii had said was also true. He sighed and nodded.

'This one thanks you for your wise council.'

Both were silent for a moment. Ashekii felt bad for quashing what had obviously been his cousin's dream and wanted to make him feel better. If Nemid wanted to be Pac of this dump then as far as Ashekii was concerned, he was welcome to it.

'Me Pect Drekesh Nemid of Water clan', he said, his tone formal. 'Son of Neskatpi of Water clan, White Camp, grandson of Chalish of Water clan, White Camp hear this: I, Ashekii, Me Pect Drekesh of Water clan, son of Merith, Water clan of Red Camp confer to you today the formal title of Pac of White Camp. Any challenger should come forward now.'

They both looked out at the deserted camp. Several chickens began pecking at the ground near their feet. Ashekii returned his attention to Nemid.

'As there are none who bring challenge, this one will let all know that you are now Pac of White Camp. You have the loyalty and allegiance of the Drekesh, and hopefully this will keep you out of trouble', he added with a roughish grin. They shared a knowing look. 'But sadly, I cannot recognise Kal as your defender. He is not a blood relation.'

'He will officially be mine once I adopt him.'

Ashekii's eyes widened.

'You plan to adopt him?'

'Of course.'

'But … adopting a child is only for when a family does not have a suitable heir.'

'This is my situation.'

'But you can't adopt a white man', Ashekii said.

'Why?'

'Because… because… the Healers will not allow it.'

'The Healers track family lineages and check bloodlines. As you have pointed out, we have no blood ties. Neither Chani nor her mother think the Healers will object.'

'Then the Oracle…'

'This one has already asked the Oracle if the portents for adoption are favourable, and I have been told they are.'

'Well, our laws certainly won't…'

'I checked the laws most thoroughly', Nemid assured him. 'There is nothing to say I cannot do this. The Oracle herself reminded me that there is the legend of the adoption of Bezredet as a precedent. Bezredet was not a Nahill either.'

'Yes, but Bezredet was a Jhunti … and that was for very special reasons.'

Nemid stuck out his chin. 'I see no difference here. I am going to announce it at the next clan meeting. There is just the matter of needing someone other than myself to speak on Kal's behalf about what a good boy he is and how he will bring honour to his new family.'

Nemid shot a questioning glance at Ashekii.

'Oh no', Ashekii said and held up his hands. 'You're not dragging me into this. Helping someone to adopt a white man? My wife will let ants pick my bones clean.'

'You're a senior Drekesh. A reference from you would count for much.'

Ashekii shook his head. 'No. I am not convinced this would be a good thing for any of us.'

'Before you decide', Nemid said, 'perhaps you could spend more time with him and then make up your mind?'

Ashekii was about to say no when he saw the pleading look in Nemid's eyes.

'Very well', he agreed in a long-suffering tone.

Nemid beamed at him.

'That is all I ask, a fair opinion.'

Ashekii put his hands on his hips.

'What will you do if my answer is still no?'

Nemid shot a glance towards Councillor Gleris and her husband. The couple were slowly approaching, stopping to inspect each cabin on the way.

'If you say no', Nemid said, 'then it will be up to Kal's bride and her family.'

'Bride?' said Ashekii. 'He can't be claimed. What does he know of caring for a family? Can he make fire or build a shelter? Can he find water?'

'He's learning fast', Nemid said defensively, 'and he can make fire. He's also learnt to find berries and greens and tubers. And he can make very good baskets, well, with a little help. And soon he'll be able to do a lot more.'

Ashekii rolled his eyes knowing that these skills took many snows to perfect. They were essential to survival and learning them was the Nahill way of knowing if a boy was ready to marry.

'And who's the lucky family?'

Nemid shrugged.

'We're still in negotiations.'

'But you've had an offer?'

'Not yet, but we will soon. Kal does not have much of a dowry. However, there is one thing that will make him more attractive to a prospective family.'

Ashekii gave Nemid a measured look.

'Which is?'

'Being the grandson of a camp Pac.'

Ashekii grinned.

'Cunning. I see.' Ashekii placed a hand on his heart and bowed. 'May you live long and well, esteemed Pac.'

At that moment Laughs a Lot came to a panting stop beside them.

'My goats …', he puffed, 'want to go in with the apple trees … but Kal says they're not allowed … My mother and Uncle Mends Things are … pulling the fence down … Kal and Mash are fighting … You better come.'

'Perhaps', Pac Nemid said to Ashekii, 'this goat situation needs the intervention of a senior Drekesh.'

'Yes, Pac Nemid', Ashekii placed his hand on his heart and again gave Nemid a slight bow.

'Thank you, Pac Nemid', Laughs a Lot said loudly. 'This way, Drekesh.' Laughs a Lot took Ashekii's arm, and together they hurried off towards the apple orchard.

'Pac?' said a female voice.

Pac Nemid turned to see the couple from Red Camp.

'Did I hear that correctly?' Councillor Gleris said. 'You are Pac of White Camp?'

'Yes, it is true.'

He gave the woman a formal bow.

'It is good to see this face Councillor. Your presence does us a great honour.'

'It is good to see this face also', she said and bowed back, as was right when addressing a camp Pac, who was of higher status than a camp councillor.

Pac Nemid gave her husband a nod of welcome.

'How was your journey?'

'That car ride!' she said with exaggerated theatrics. 'I can't believe how fast it goes and how quickly we got here. I had heard of them being fast, but I had no idea… Ohhh, my stomach! It is still in knots.' She fanned herself as she examined the camp. 'But I had to come. When Ashe told us about the state of things…', she shook her head in disgust. Her husband indicated the piles of rubbish.

'None of us thought it would be this bad', he said.

'You know', Councillor Gleris said, 'my great grandmother was from White Camp. We are hoping that you will permit us to move here when the snow melts.'

Pac Nemid gave her a puzzled look.

'Red Camp council wishes to have a representative at White Camp?'

'You misunderstand', she corrected him. 'I intend to retire from council. To be honest, I thought the way they treated you was abysmal. I now find Red Camp politics tiresome and wish to join you here. There will be us, our daughters and a few claiming prospects.'

Nemid's face lit up, remembering all her daughters were single. Her eyes went up and down the dilapidated cabins.

'We should continue our tour', she said. 'Ashe will want to leave soon.' She let out a quick breath, a determined set to her face. 'I assume we can have any cabin?' she said. 'I mean, you haven't promised them all yet have you?'

'Not all of them, no', Nemid said.

She pointed to one at the very end.

'I think that one seems alright. May we go and see?'

Without waiting for an answer, she and her husband went down the hill. Pac Nemid stared after them, a thoughtful look on his face.

The raised voices were audible before Ashekii could see what was going on. There were shouts of 'white scum' and 'filthy dogs'. Ashekii increased his pace and came around the corner just as a boy pushed Kal backwards into the mud. There was a cheer from those watching. The boy was younger and smaller than Kal. He was wearing army boots and camouflage fatigues.

'Well done Mash!' called Aunt Talks Too Much.

Aunt Talks Too Much was the matriarch of the Dog clan family at White Camp. She was a short, stocky woman with a generous bust. Her fingernails were painted metallic red and matched the sequins on her red jumpsuit, which would not have looked out of place in the wardrobe of an Elvis impersonator. Her unruly black hair was bundled into a top knot, the long tendrils spilling all about her head. She pulled a loose strand of hair from her homely, round face. Her brown eyes had a large dollop of blue eye shadow on them and were dark with mascara. Her red lips were pulled back into a snarl. Beside her stood her husband, a man of similar age named Uncle Mend's Things.

'Come on, white scum', he yelled in a mocking tone, 'get up and fight!'

Uncle Mends Things wore an evening jacket and cargo pants that only went to his shins. The colour of his socks matched Aunt Talks Too Much's nail polish. His cheeks had the ruddy appearance of one who drank too much, and his open mouth revealed several missing teeth; the rest were nicotine-stained.

Laughs a Lot's cousins Remmy and Hasty hooted with laughter. Both sturdy teenagers had thick, dark, wavy hair. Remmy was wearing torn jeans, a Nirvana t-shirt and a flannel over shirt with her Doc Martin boots. Young Hasty had a big nose and even bigger hands. His one joy in life was creating mayhem by putting his pet ferrets down the pants of his unsuspecting victims.

'Whites are so pathetic', jeered Remmy.

'Oh, poor baby', Hasty taunted. 'I think he's gonna cry!'

Mash laughed and waited for Kal to get up.

'You Dog clan pricks!' cried Trindal. 'Get off me!'

Trindal was sprawled face down in the dirt. Lemon, a solidly built girl of thirteen snows, who looked and acted just like her name, was sitting on his back.

'Shut up, pipsqueak', sneered Lemon as she bounced up and down on him.

Kal got up to hoots and jeers as Mash readied himself. Kal wiped the blood from under his nose, and windmilling his arms, rushed at the other boy who sidestepped and tripped him. Kal smashed into a low-hanging branch then fell to the ground. Ashekii mentally cringed at how badly Kal was fighting. It was embarrassing.

'Come on, you white scum!' Mash said as he strode towards Kal. 'Get up and fight.'

Kal rolled into a ball and put his hands over his head.

'Do you give up?' Mash said.

'No!' Kal yelled defiantly.

'Then get up!'

Mash's eyes sought his parents.

'This's stupid. Anyone can see that I've won. Let's just pull down the fence.'

'Wait', Ashekii said. 'You are not to pull down the fence. It is there to protect the apple trees.'

They all gathered around Ashekii.

'And who are you?' said Aunty Talks Too Much, hands on her hips, a gold front tooth flashing in the sun.

'This one is called Ashekii. I am a Me pect Drekesh from Red Camp.'

'This has nothing to do with Red Camp. This is Dog clan land.'

'It is?' Ashekii said, feigning surprise. 'Since when? Last I heard, this was Water clan land.'

'No one from Water clan has lived here for a long time.'

'Well, now Water clan is back', he said.

Ashekii reached out and grabbed Lemon by the scruff of the neck, pulling her from Trindal. The boy jumped to his feet and made to punch the girl. She raised her fists.

'Stop that', Ashekii said. 'Both of you.'

They reluctantly ceased, making faces at each other instead. Ashekii indicated for Trindal to see to Kal before returning his attention to the Dogs.

'One old man', said Remmy, 'does not mean that Water clan is back.'

Ashekii cocked his head towards Trindal and Kal.

'They are also Water clan.'

'White scum', Hasty muttered.

'I am Water clan too', Ashekii said. 'Now all of you go home and no more trouble.'

'They started it', said Lemon belligerently. She kicked a chunk of dirt at Trindal, who was helping Kal to his feet.

'Don't do that', Ashekii said.

'Or what, Drekesh?' She let out a derisive laugh, and suddenly, his left foot flicked out and Lemon was lying in the mud.

'Hey!' cried Remmy. 'You can't...'

Ashekii's right leg shot out in a sweep and Remmy was suddenly lying in the mud beside Lemon. Aunt Talks Too Much took a step back and narrowed her eyes.

'Who're you to...'

Ashekii jumped forward and suddenly his hands were on her shoulders. She toppled backwards, joining the children in the mud. Ashekii raised an eyebrow at Uncle Mends Things and Mash. They bowed their heads demurely.

'Better', Ashekii said in approval. 'Should there be any damage to this fence, I will know who is responsible, and there will be trouble. All of you, go home.'

Reluctantly, they left, all except Laughs a Lot, who ran down the hill after his scattered herd of goats. Kal limped over to Ashekii with Trindal beside him.

'Trindal', Ashekii said, 'go and help Laughs a Lot...'

'Everyone calls him Lal', Kal said.

'...help *Lal* with his goats.'

'But...'

Ashekii made a hissing noise, and Trindal took off after Laughs a Lot. Bending down, Ashekii scooped up a handful of wet grass and moss. Placing one hand behind Kal's head, he shoved the cold compress against Kal's bloody nose.

'Didn't anyone ever teach you to fight?' he said.

Kal dropped his gaze, and Ashekii shook his head.

'Are you hurt anywhere else?'

'My knee', Kal said thickly.

'Hold this.'

Ashekii put one of Kal's hands onto the compress then squatted and pulled Kal's pants down.

'Hey!' Kal protested.

'Shh.' Ashekii turned him back and forth, examining the rising bruise on the boy's knee. 'It's nothing', he said.

Kal dumped the compress from his nose and hastily pulled his pants up. As they walked up the path, Gleris came towards them to inspect the last cabin. Ashekii smiled at her.

'Hello again', he said. 'Have you met Kal?'

Gleris gave Kal a dismissive look and was about to say something before she saw Kal's face.

'What happened to him?'

'A slight disagreement with the Dogs', Ashekii said.

She rolled her eyes.

'It's the biggest problem here, having to live so close to … them.'

She lowered her voice and leant towards Ashekii.

'Can't the Drekesh get rid of them?' she whispered.

'That would not be right.'

She shook her head.

'Such a pity. Well, we'll just ascertain where our daughter's claiming will be held, and then we'll be ready to go. See you shortly.'

They walked off in the direction of what had once been tribal fire pits. Ashekii put an arm across Kal's shoulders, and the two of them went to Nemid's cabin. So, Ashekii thought, this is to be the defender of Pac Nemid's kingdom. In no time, the Dogs would have told everyone that the boy was as soft as a puppy, and the challengers would come thick and fast. It would only get worse when Nemid sought council approval to adopt. The tempers that had cooled since they had left Red Camp would be ignited again. His head began to spin at the thought of all that extra work for the Drekesh. No, he corrected himself, extra work for himself as he was Nemid's nearest blood kin. He sighed and put a hand on his hip. Someone had to teach Kal how to fight.

'Kal', Ashekii said, 'I want to talk to you about Nemid's crazy idea to adopt you.'

'He', Kal said slowly, 'wants to keep me? For real and always? Me?'

There was something so pathetically grateful in the boy's tone that Ashekii's disapproval of the idea dissipated.

'Yes', he said. 'Is that what you want?'

Kal's face was one huge smile of relief and gratitude.

'I thought', he said quietly, 'that he was gonna have to throw me away. Everyone says he will. I … I didn't know where I would go.'

'Well', Ashekii said, 'I have a feeling we may have some trouble with the Dogs. It might sometimes be up to you to keep them in line.' He didn't miss the fear on the boys' face. 'So I think it would be smart for us … well, for me, to teach you some basic combat techniques.'

He glanced at the cabins then back at Kal, lowering his voice. 'But we have to keep this between ourselves. You can't tell anyone, not even Nemid, do you understand?'

The boy nodded.

'Good. I want you to start doing some exercises.'

Kal followed him to a pile of dirt. Ashekii glanced around to make sure no one was watching then sank into a half crouch.

'Punching is an excellent way to toughen up the fingers and wrists. Like this.'

He punched his fists into the soft dirt. Kal mimicked his stance and began to punch. After a few seconds, Kal's leg muscles were smarting. Ashekii straightened.

'Don't stop', he said as Kal made to stand. 'Feel that sting in your legs? That's your muscles getting stronger. I want you to be able to hold that shape for as long as you do this exercise. Eventually it won't hurt. Ashekii stood for a while longer, watching Kal and making a couple of corrections as Kal continued to punch.

'Stop.'

Kal collapsed onto the ground.

'I want you to do that exercise every day', Ashekii instructed. 'I'll know if you haven't. Understand?'

Kal nodded. Ashekii put an arm over Kal's shoulder and noticed that Kal's clothes were damp from being thrown in the mud.

'You go dry off and get changed', he said. 'I'll try and get back again soon so I can show you some more techniques.'

Kal walked back to his cabin. He knew he had no spare clothes and no fire as they were out of wood, again. Instead, he did the exercises Ashekii had shown him. Soon his face was red, and he was warm all over.

Trindal entered, covered in mud and smelling bad. 'Stupid goats', he said. 'Why did I have to go help chase 'em? What?'

Kal was grinning. 'You look about ready to be a planted bean pole', Kal teased.

'Shut up, Ox.'

They tussled with each other on the floor.

12

A mud-splattered white four-wheel drive with 'Education Department Special Needs Program' written on the side drove along the city streets. Inside, a young white woman named Karen Davis watched the road. Her long brown hair was clasped back from her face, and her blue eyes were bright and eager. She wore floral cotton pants and a silk long-sleeved button-up shirt in neon yellow. She'd deliberately picked something bright and cheerful the children at her primary school would find colourful and fun. She assumed they would all be wearing something similar as this was what everyone was wearing at the moment … unless they were into rap, she suddenly worried. Glancing down at her outfit, she wondered if she should have gone with her more conservative grey pinafore, black shoes and white shirt. She mentally shrugged. There was no changing it now. She checked her watch.

'Late already', she muttered to herself.

When she had been assigned to teach the Jhunti, she was given a file with a red sticker on the front cover that read 'Class A Environment'. This meant that her students had likely never had any immunisations and would be particularly susceptible to white people's diseases. Karen had been required to submit documentation that all her shots were up to date. The nurse had told her about a class A population that had been decimated by someone with a common cold. Karen wasn't sure if that was true, but it did worry her.

In addition to the red sticker, a note had also been clipped to the front of the folder from a previous teacher. 'Congratulations', the note read, 'this is the worst teaching assignment on the books. Most can't speak English and don't want to learn. Dress warm, take lunch, toilet paper, soap and a good book to read.'

As she had turned the pages, Karen had been taken aback by how many teachers had been assigned to this school. Most had only lasted a few weeks, some had stayed two months and three had lasted a whole term. Now her name was on the file, and instead of dread, she felt a rush of pride. This was her very own school, and she had big plans for it. The file also noted that the facilities were primitive but the library was sufficient for Jhunti needs. She stopped at a set of lights and glanced at her map. She had to continue until she came to the freeway, follow that for… Someone tooted, and she put the map down, thrust the car into first gear and lurched forward.

It was Karen's first day of teaching unsupervised since graduating from the university. She was desperate to make a good impression, and like all new teachers, she was on probation for the first few months. She was still amazed and humbled by the amount of trust the department was putting in her. According to the file, her class had thirty students ranging from five to fifteen-years-old.

Because of the age range, she'd spent the last week putting together her lesson plans and silently rehearsed them as she drove. She'd start by asking the children what they had done during the school holidays. This would be a good opportunity for her to learn names. After this it would be puzzle blocks for the younger ones, and the older ones would do some reading practice followed by multiplication tables for everyone till lunch. Afterwards the younger ones would go home, and the older ones would do some Maths and English comprehension tests so she could assess what levels they were on. A shiver of excitement ran through her. She was so looking forward to putting all her teaching knowledge into practice in her very own class in her very own school. Although it was only one day a week *if*, and she stressed that word in her head, the department liked how she ran things at the Jhunti school, then she might get other classes in other schools, and in no time, she'd be a full-time teacher. She sighed longingly as she raced along the freeway, climbing steadily up into the mountains. When the suburbs became farmland, she searched for the turn-off to the lake. As soon as she saw the lake sign, she took the off-ramp and continued along the well-kept road.

'Find the shops then turn left', she said to herself.

She came to a group of shops. One was a petrol station-come-general store, the second was a run-down marine supply shop that also sold bait, fishing and camping wares and the last one was a small real estate agent with faded ads in the window for lakeside holiday lets. She slowed and saw an old sign pointing to 'Mount Disappointment'. Checking her directions one last time, she turned left and continued to drive. After two kilometres, she came to another sign: 'Jhunti Reservation. Permit required for entry'. With a thump, the paved road ended, and she was suddenly on a corrugated dirt road. As she slowed she peered through the windshield. The road ahead was a muddy, slushy mess and climbed steeply up the side of the mountain. She stopped the car and got out, her breath catching at the sudden coldness of the air. Wishing she was wearing gloves, she quickly locked the wheels into four-wheel drive then got back into the warmth of the cabin. The dirt road wound its way up the side of Mount Disappointment and along the side of the Jhunti reservation. It was a slow, treacherous route, and her fingers were white as she gripped the steering wheel.

At 10.30 am Laughs a Lot came flying in Nemid's cabin door.

'There's school today!' he cried excitedly.

Having been working since dawn, Nemid, Trindal and Kal were sitting on the floor eating bean meal. Nemid swallowed his mouthful.

'How do you know that?' he said.

Laughs a Lot pointed towards the door.

'Listen.'

In the distance, they heard a car engine as it slowly wound its way up the rutted mountain road.

'The teacher will be here soon', Laughs a Lot said. 'I usually wait up at the car park. It's my job. I'm caretaker!'

'What's the name of the teacher?' Nemid said. 'Who are her people?'

Laughs a Lot frowned as he thought then began to count off on his fingers.

'Well, last moon it was Miz Roberts. The moon before that, it was Cita. We also had um … Mr Mosard and Mr Ngyen and Miz Wendy and Mohamad and um … I can't remember the others. Wanna come?'

'No', Kal said

'Yes', Nemid said firmly.

Kal turned to Nemid in silent appeal.

'You are going', Nemid said firmly.

'Yay!' Laughs a Lot rejoiced and ran off.

Kal moodily pushed around his food with a finger.

'But what if … what if the teacher realizes I'm white? They might … tell.'

'I will put your hair up in a scarf. With that out of the way, you and Trin look like brothers.'

The two boys glanced at each other. Their silent exchange ran along the lines of: 'What Nemid says is true, we are like brothers.' 'You really think they'll believe it?' 'Yes, besides it will be fun.' 'Alright then, if I have to.'

Kal put his boring mash aside and fetched his traditional Nahill sweat cloth. With Nemid's help, they wrapped his shoulder length blonde hair into it.

'There', Nemid said, 'but for your eyes, you will be the same as the others.'

The three looked out the window as they waited for the teacher to arrive. Smoke rose from most of the Dog clan chimneys in the camp, but no one came out to speak with them.

'Looks like all the Dogs have returned', Nemid said.

'Thieves and liars', Trindal muttered.

The sun was well above the trees by the time the four-wheel drive edged its way cautiously into the paddock, which doubled as a car park and was home to the collection of dilapidated camp vehicles as well as several huge piles of rubbish. Miss Davis stopped and peered over the steering wheel, wondering if this was the Nahill camp or if she'd taken a wrong turn and ended up in their rubbish dump. She glanced at her watch and pursed her lips. School was supposed to start at 9.30 am and it was nearly 11. Thinking she had taken the wrong road, she was about to turn around when she saw a boy coming towards her. In one hand, he held a plastic supermarket bag filled with rubbish. He tossed it onto one of the piles of garbage before proceeding towards her. The boy was about fifteen with ill-kempt thick wavy hair cut to just below his ears. He was wearing well-worn blue jeans, a black t-shirt and a puffy blue vest, all liberally smudged with dirt. His face also needed a wash, and when he smiled, his pink tongue showed through the gaps of several missing teeth. She glanced down and noticed he was bare footed. The sight of his skin against the freezing cold muddy ground made her shiver. With bear arms, he pointed to a parking spot next to an old brown station wagon. She gave him a wave of thanks, put the car into reverse and eased back into the spot the boy indicated.

'What I need', she muttered to herself, 'is a nice cup of tea. That drive was horrendous.'

'Welcome to White Camp. I am Laughs a Lot', he said in careful English.

He smiled at her, again giving her a flash of his missing teeth. She turned off the engine and smiled back. Special needs, she thought, and vaguely recalled someone telling her there was a picture book for the special needs child in her class.

'People call me Lal', he said as he pulled the door open. 'What's your name?'

The smell of rotting garbage hit her, and she only just managed to stop herself from gagging.

'I'm Miss Davis, the teacher', she said. She pulled on a thick coat, fumbled in her bag and took out her permit. 'Who do I give this to?'

Laughs a Lot took the piece of paper and, without looking at it, crammed it into his back pocket.

'I am caretaker. Preshta. That means hello', he laughed.

She glanced at the muddy track and back at her new suede shoes. Taking the Government Issue black rubber gumboots from the back seat, she was surprised when the boy began tugging at one of her shoes.

'Me help you', he said jerking it free.

Placing her shoe carefully into the car, Laughs a Lot took one of the gumboots from her hand. She pointed her toes, and he pushed the boot onto her foot. He then pulled off her other shoe and replaced it with a gumboot.

'Thank you', she smiled.

'We say beecha tas.'

'Beecha tas then.'

He grinned and held out a hand to help her down. She took one look at how filthy it was and shook her head.

'I can manage, but thank you.'

Laughs a Lot tucked her suede shoes under his arm, opened the back door and removed her heavy briefcase.

'Oh', she said uncertainly, 'I think I should…'

'This way', Laughs a Lot said.

The two walked toward the schoolhouse with Laughs a Lot leading the way. Karen held her breath as they passed by the closest pile of garbage then took in a deep breath as they started down the hill. On either side of the central path were a ramshackle collection of cabins. A motley assortment of shaggy, mongrel dogs snarled and barked as they charged out from underneath the cabins towards them.

'Back!' Laughs a Lot commanded in a fierce tone. 'Down!'

The dogs stopped a few feet from the slight white woman and eyed her suspiciously, growling as she passed, heckles raised and teeth exposed. Laughs a Lot strolled on undeterred. A flock of black chickens squawked as he shooed them from the path then pointed to a large puddle.

'Slippery', he said, skirting around it, his bare feet leaving large footprints in the inky black, smelly mire.

She stepped to the side, determinedly trying to avoid the mud and piles of animal dung. She took only small breaths through her mouth and tried to ignore the stench of rotten food, dog, chicken and who knew what other faeces, decay and mildew. It was horrendous! She picked her way carefully until they reached the large building that looked like an old church.

'This school room', he said.

She looked up at the white building.

'It's very old', she said. 'Who built it?'

Laughs a Lot shrugged.

'And those ones?' she pointed to the storage sheds.

'We use them for parties, except Lemon fell through the roof and the door on the other one got broken in a fight. This way to school.'

She followed him inside the hall. It was austerely furnished and bitterly cold despite a fire burning at one end. There was a single wooden table and chair close to the fire. A dozen straight-backed wooden chairs and two wooden pews were pushed against one wall. A single bookshelf was the only other furniture. Miss Davis removed her muddy gumboots at the door, put her shoes back on and went to the door with 'staff only' written on it. It was locked. Removing the ring of ancient keys from her pocket, she tried several before she found the one that fit. Inside, an ancient toilet stood beside a stained wash basin with a single tap. A candle stump but no matches rested where the soap should sit, and a note scrawled on the wall read 'Water not fit for human consumption'.

The room was very dark, and there was no toilet paper or hand towel. She closed the door and went to the bookshelf. Three sets of books stared back at her from the shelves: one row with blue covers, one with red covers and one with black covers. She picked up one with a blue cover. It was a beginner reader that had not been used in white schools for thirty years. The ones with red covers turned out to be prayer books with hymns at the back. She picked up a black-covered book and found it was a child's bible with pictures and large print scripture passages. On the bottom shelf was a pile of well-used picture books. Hanging on the wall beside the bookshelf was a calendar that was turned to September 1965.

A clanging caught her attention. Laughs a Lot had the school bell in his hand and was heading towards the door.

'Just a moment', she called, 'I'm not ready yet.'

He continued out the door and was soon ringing for all he was worth. Miss Davis shoved the bible back into the shelf and hurried over to the table. She opened the briefcase and found the school roll and a pen. Her supervisor had told her this was her most important task, to make a note of all those who attended and hand out the student allowances to their parents.

Kal strode along the muddy path, a load of wood in his arms. They all knew it wouldn't burn right as it was too damp, but it was better than nothing. Hearing the bell, he dropped the wood onto the veranda and beckoned to Trindal.

'That's the school bell', he called.

Trindal looked up at him.

'The what?'

'The school bell. It means time to go.'

Trindal hastily deposited his own pile of damp wood onto the veranda and ran after Kal.

'D'you think they'll show us books?' Trindal said with excitement. 'I can't wait to see books!'

Miss Davis gestured to Laughs a Lot who was ringing the bell fit to burst. This was what he loved most. The sound of the bell was crisp and loud. When he rang it, everyone could hear and knew he was doing his job.

'You can stop that now', she called. 'Lal? Please stop. I SAID STOP!'

The bell continued to ring. A look of annoyance crossed Miss Davis's young face as she wrenched off her shoes, shoved her feet into her gumboots and strode out then took the bell from him.

'That's enough', she said and went back inside.

She changed out of her gumboots and back into her good shoes then put the bell safely onto the top of the bookshelf. As she did this, two more boys of about thirteen and ten walked in. Both were barefoot and wearing brown linen leggings and handmade tunics. Their clothes were smudged with dirt, but not as filthy as Laughs a Lot's. One of the boys had a length of linen wrapped around his head, and Miss Davis wondered if this was for religious reasons. Laughs a Lot ran to them and took their hands.

'See?' he said. 'Now is school time.'

He laughed and dragged them forward. Kal regarded the young teacher warily. She had that startled yet determined expression that reminded Kal of the substitute teachers he'd had sometimes. In front of her was a large exercise book with blue lines marked on it. Kal's eyes ran down the list of names: Sindri, Wisha, Lemon, Ravrah, Laughs a Lot, Besna, Rightly, Tomma, Nes, Talks too Much, Mends Things, Hasty, Remmy, Mash, Dopsil, Nod. He recognized the names of the entire village and their goats and a few of Laughs a Lot's chickens.

'What're your names?' Miss Davis said, pen poised.

'Trindal and Kal', Trindal said.

She ran her finger down the list.

'You're not on here.'

'This Trin and Kal', Laughs a Lot butted in. 'They new here. Lal and Kal, Lal and Kal.'

She added their names to her list. She spelt Kal's name with a K instead of a C. It was the first time he'd seen it written and decided he liked it. Miss Davis handed each of them a dog-eared book and indicated the floor.

'Have a seat', she said. 'When will the others get here?'

'Soon', Laughs a Lot said in a well-rehearsed tone. 'They milk goats.'

Kal wondered if he should mention that none of the goats had any milk right now. Miss Davis glanced at her watch and frowned. It was well after eleven.

'I suppose we'll have to start without them', she said and squared her shoulders. 'Now children, I hope you are all well rested after the term holidays. My name is Miss Davis. Repeat after me, Miss Davis.'

'Miz Daviz', Laughs a Lot and Trindal said, slurring the foreign sounding ess as the Nahill did.

'Miss', she said, emphasising the crisp ess, 'Davis. Again.'

'Mizzz Davizzz.'

A slight frown ran across her brows. She decided to let it go.

'Very good. First up, class, I'd like you to tell me what you did in your holidays.'

Trindal leant towards Kal.

'What's that?' he whispered.

'Raise your hand if you have a question', Miss Davis said, leaning a hip against her table.

Trindal put his hand up.

'Yes?'

'What's hol-ee-day?'

'It's when you have time off, you know, to go away or to get things done before you have to go back to work.'

Trindal's puzzled look remained and Laughs a Lot walked over to the shelves and took out a child's picture book. The only sound was him flipping through the pages.

'Never mind', Miss Davis said.

Laughs a Lot held his book up.

'I know all these.'

Miss Davis took a new picture book from her bag and handed it to him.

'I guess this is for you then.'

Laughs a Lot grinned and took the book. He flipped it open.

'I get special book', he said tapping the first page. 'What's this?'

'A banana. It's a piece of fruit. Now Trindal and Kal, please turn to page four and…'

'What's fruit?' Laughs a Lot asked inquisitively.

Kal began to flick through his book. He recognised the big writing and pictures from when he was in first grade. He remembered the teachers all complaining that his little country school was the worst equipped they'd ever seen. With a long-suffering sigh, he turned to page four and waited, staring down at Betty and Bob who'd lost their stupid dog.

'Look', Trindal said, 'this's a funny hat!'

Kal glanced at Trindal, who was holding his book upside down and running his fingers along the middle pages, feeling the paper and tracing a picture of an ice cream cone.

'You can read Kal?' Miss Davis said.

'Huh?'

Miss Davis glanced at the book in his lap.

'You're on page four', she said.

Kal opened his mouth then closed it again. Stupid, stupid, he chastised himself. If she guessed he was white, she'd tell!

'No need to be frightened', Miss Davis said gently. 'You haven't done anything wrong. If you know your letters and numbers, then go and check the shelves to see if there's anything more advanced.'

Kal went to the book shelves and ran his finger along the ancient readers. On the bottom shelf were picture books of animals, some native, some farm animals and some zoo animals. He flicked through one that proclaimed to be about science, but it was filled with pictures of cartoon professors doing whacky experiments. Miss Davis came to stand beside him.

'Science?' she said.

'No.'

He put it back.

'You like science?' she said.

He shrugged.

'I like human studies more.'

He missed the way her eyes widened before she quickly schooled her features.

'Let's see what's in the bag', she said.

They went back to her desk, and she opened her briefcase.

'I'm new, you see', she said, 'so I'm not sure what they have given us.'

Inside the briefcase was a stack of envelopes, several more old readers, her lunch and a novel. He pulled out the novel. It was 'War of the Worlds' by H G Wells.

'Can I have this?' he said eagerly.

She blushed.

'Oh, that's mine. I just borrowed it from the library. You like science fiction?'

He nodded, his eyes shining.

'Alright then', she said, 'but give it back to me next week.'

Kal smiled and took the book back to his place beside Trindal. Trindal leant over to see Kal's book and frowned.

'That doesn't have any pictures in it', he said. 'How d'you know what it's about?'

Kal showed him the dust cover.

'It's a science fiction book', he whispered. 'It's about aliens from mars that come in space ships and invade the earth. I liked the movie.'

Trindal was about to tell Kal that he had not understood the words *science fiction, aliens, Mars, space ships, or movie* when two more children arrived. Miss Davis ticked their names off the list and gave them beginner readers. As Miss Davis started to sound out the alphabet, Kal was unable to resist. He opened his book and began to read. He was up to chapter 7 when a group of children erupted through the door followed by a much larger crowd of adults.

'Dog clan', Trindal whispered to Kal.

Kal studied the whirling gaggle and frowned at the clash of colours, textures and clothing styles. Their fashion sense reminded him of one time when he'd gone into the opportunity shop and the ladies were going through the racks, tossing the clothes that no one wanted into a large pile on the floor. The only difference was that this pile of sequins, suede, polka dots, paisley and tweed was moving. One thing that stood out to Kal was that unlike the Nahill, every one of them was either pudgy or overweight. Some of the men wore their hair short in the back and sides while some of the women had bob cuts and others had stripes of purple, blue and orange in their hair. Several of the women had painted their fingernails.

Miss Davis was swept back to her desk as they all spoke at once. The adults would thrust a child forward and tell Miss Davis to tick their child as having attended then hold out their hand for their envelope. From what Kal could understand, most were saying their child would not be able to stay due to some weak excuse. He also noticed that the same children kept being passed from one adult to the next as Miss Davis frantically tried to write things down and tick names. As the crowd shouted over each other, she gave up writing and just pulled out the stack of envelopes. They quietened as she began to call out the names. Hands reached forward and took each envelope until there were only a few left.

'I have one for the caretaker?' she said.

Laughs a Lot's mother, Sindri, who was wearing a fetching floral frock and army boots, held out her hand. 'Here!' she said. Miss Davis gave it to her.

'One for a delivery of wood?'

Aunt Talks Too Much held her hand out. She was wearing olive green slacks with grass stains on the knees and bottom, a powder-pink golf shirt and a thick gold chain around her neck. As her fingers closed on the envelope, she smiled, flashing her gold front tooth.

'So kind', she said.

Miss Davis moved back as a stench of garlic enveloped her.

'And one for cleaning?' Miss Davis said.

Uncle Mends Things, who was wearing a cheap sports coat over a pair of powder blue bell bottoms with highly polished black leather shoes took it.

'Rent and water rates?' said Miss Davis.

A man stepped forward. He wore tight beige cotton pants and a shirt striped with blue, white and pink. The first three buttons of his shirt were undone showing his stained undershirt. He reached for the cheque, but she was staring at it in puzzlement.

'Really? You get charged water rates out here?'

'Yes' he said and took the envelope. 'The whites charge us for everything!'

'It's outrageous', Aunt Talks Too Much grumbled. 'Us with nothing and starving.'

'It's a disgrace' another woman agreed.

Miss Davis opened her mouth as if to argue but changed her mind.

She took out the next cheque.

'Electricity… Electricity? Now just a minute, there isn't any electricity here.'

Uncle Mends Things pointed to the roof. Miss Davis squinted up and saw a single wire hanging from the ceiling. A clear light bulb was attached to it.

'Does that work?' she said.

'Needs new bulb', Uncle Mends Things said.

He snatched the envelope from her hand and then, as quickly as they'd arrived, the riot of clothes left. Miss Davis's eyes swept the room then she raced to the door.

'Hey!' she called after them. 'Where's the light switch?'

They all headed towards the car park without a backwards glance. She shook her head and walked inside to the only students she had left, Kal and Trindal.

'What's in the envelopes?' Kal asked.

'Cheques', she said, 'from the government. Each child that is enrolled gets a weekly allowance, and there were some other expenses by the look of things', Miss Davis sighed heavily and sat down.

'Tell your parents', she said, 'that I'll bring your cheques next week. Of course, you'll get two weeks' worth. But', she stressed, 'you have to come to school. You tell your parents that you only get the allowance if you come to school regularly.'

She glanced at her watch. It was just after one pm, though it felt much later.

'Well', she said, 'I supposed you can go as well unless we all just sit here.'

She made a silly face. The three of them laughed, and Kal decided then and there that he liked Miss Davis. She wasn't like the other teachers he'd met. When she smiled, her cheeks went a pretty pink colour. Kal ducked his head bashfully. Trindal stepped forward.

'Can you teach me to read?' he said.

'You want to learn to read?'

Trindal nodded. She stared at Trindal, and the light began to glisten off her eyes.

'I would love to teach you how to read. Come and sit beside me, and we'll start at the beginning.'

It was just after midday and White Camp resembled its name as the first snow was on the ground. In Nemid's cabin, the ceiling beams and most of the walls had frozen white crystals on them. Trindal sat beside a feeble fire feeding it bits of damp stick that hissed and crackled. As he laid them on the flames, he was careful not to put the tentative flames out. Search as they might, they had not been able to find any dry wood and were still trying to make do with wood that was damp and soggy. Fire from this kind of wood had precious little warmth in it.

Beside him, Kal ground corn kernels into flour with the grinding wheel. To the side, Nemid was pulling sacred objects from the bag Laughs a Lot had found and laying them out for the snow ceremony. All Pacs performed this as soon as the first snowfall ended. He knew that all over the reservation the other Pacs were doing exactly the same thing. It made him feel a bit less isolated.

At the far end of the room, three brown and white goats chewed their feed, their ears flicking back and forth, a bemused expression on their long faces. One raised its tail and added to the pile of droppings on the floor. Trindal shot an annoyed glance at it.

'Nod just did another poo', he said.

'So clean it up if it annoys you', Kal said.

Trindal glanced at Nemid, and Nemid shook his head.

'They are here for a reason', Nemid said. 'We need the extra heat from their bodies to keep us warm.'

Trindal sat back in frustration, tossing his flint and steel noisily onto the hearth. Kal looked at Nemid.

'Want me to ask Lal for more dry wood?' Kal said.

'His mother was very clear', Nemid said, 'that he should not have given us any. We are fortunate that they do not charge us for the loan of their goats.'

'Lal said he wasn't going to tell them', Kal said.

Trindal shook his head.

'Thieves and liars', he muttered in disgust.

Trindal continued to mutter curses about goats and Dog clan as he returned his attention to the fire. Nemid placed the restrung echidna spine necklace into the ceremonial metal bowl. Perhaps, he thought, it wouldn't hurt to teach Kal some etiquette. After all, Nemid reasoned, he and Trindal were now the grandsons of a Pac and it was important they knew how to be polite and well-mannered. It would also stop Kal from offending people unknowingly or causing them to think he was rude or did not know how to behave. Nemid indicated the rest of his ceremonial clothes. 'Pack these things up for me would you, Eyas?'

As Kal began tidying the things away, Nemid gave him an appraising look.

'Tell me', he said to Kal, 'what do you know about etiquette and diplomacy?'

Kal made a face.

'I don't really know what they are.'

'Let us say that we get a visit from the Pac of another camp. How would you welcome them?'

Kal shrugged and shook his head.

'How about if a Healer or a Drekesh came to visit?'

The matriarch of the goats raised her tail and let out a loud fart.

'Dopsil just farted', Trindal said and waved his hand back and forth in front of his nose.

Kal studied Nemid warily.

'Have I upset you?' he said.

'No, I was just thinking that it's time you learnt some manners.'

Kal's heart began to race. He knew what that meant and took a step away.

'When the Pac of another village comes to visit', Nemid began, 'proper etiquette dictates that … where are you going?'

Kal was nearly at the door. Nemid let out a frustrated breath.

'You think I am going to beat you?' he said heatedly. 'After all this time without me so much as lifting a hand in anger towards you? What will people think of me if they see you cringing like that? If you really think I am going to beat you, then leave. I am sick of it.'

He turned his back on the boy and continued to get ready for his ceremony. Kal stood there, watching and thinking. Trindal's gaze went back and forth from one to the other, willing Kal to apologise and stay. Nemid dusted off his robes and stood up. He turned and saw Kal.

'Why are you still here?' he said. 'I thought you were afraid of me. Don't you think I'm going to beat you over nothing?'

Kal swallowed heavily and stared into Nemid's dark brown eyes.

'I don't wanna go', he said softly.

'What was that?'

'I wanna stay.'

'Louder.'

'I want to stay!' Kal yelled.

'Better. Now stand up straight, head high. This is the cabin of the Pac of this camp. We are proud Nahill men, not cringing dogs. Do you really believe I would beat you?'

Kal hesitated only a moment before shaking his head.

'Say it.'

'I don't think you will beat me.'

'Very good. Now come, we have a ceremony to perform.'

Trindal reached for his boots.

'No', Nemid said, holding up a hand to stop Trindal, 'you have to stay and keep the goats quiet. We don't want Dog clan to find out that we have them.'

Trindal grumbled about what he'd like to do to the goats and to Dog clan while Nemid ushered Kal out the front door. Trindal stared at the goats malevolently. He picked up a small stick and tossed it at one. It bounced off her shaggy rump and fell to the floor. Her short hairy tail flicked back and forth, and she turned her head, her eyes fixing Trindal with a bright-eyed stare as she chewed her cud. Muttering curses, Trindal turned his back on them and poked the fire.

13

It had snowed again, and there was a freezing brightness to the air in White Camp. All the puddles had a frozen crust of ice on them. Inside the school hall, Laughs a Lot's picture book was sitting abandoned on the floor. The only remaining occupants were Trindal, Kal and Miss Davis. Kal wore a pair of headphones, which were plugged into a cassette recorder. He was lying on his stomach beside the fire. His legs were crossed at the ankles slowly swaying back and forth as he listened to the cassette and wrote down his answers in an exercise book with 'Maths' written on it. Beside him were more cassettes and exercise books from the departments' correspondence school. On the spine of each was printed the subject. The three remaining ones were English, biology and music.

Affixed to one wall was a map of the world, and next to it was a small fire extinguisher and a poster of the telephone numbers to call in case of emergency. Trindal and Miss Davis sat up at her table, a new story book before them. She had a brightly coloured blanket draped across her legs, and beside her was a china tea cup with little blue daisies on it. She picked up a shiny new thermos and poured tea into her cup.

'Try again', she said to Trindal.

He rocked forward on his elbows, head bowed over the book.

'Eee', he spelt slowly, 'tee, zzz.'

'Ess.'

'Ezzz.'

'Close enough, go on.'

She glanced up at the ceiling. The 'electric light' was still broken. She'd complained again last week, saying it was so dark she couldn't see and threatened to withhold the electricity cheques until it was fixed. This week there had been two oil lamps for her. When she'd asked for a definite date for it to be fixed, Uncle Mends Things had apologised for the delay saying that they had to borrow a special ladder and may have to wait till the snow thawed. Miss Davis did not believe Uncle Mends Things, and despite a thorough inspection of the hall, she could find no light switch. She was beginning to think there was no electricity connected at all as there were no poles outside. She gave the lightbulb one last malevolent scowl and returned her attention to her student.

'A?' Trindal said uncertainly.

'Yes! Next one?'

Trindal frowned and ran his finger along the page, mouthing the word silently.

'Um, what's that letter?'

Miss Davis made a 'C' with her fingers.

'This is a Cee, but when it's written like this, the sound it makes is Kaah. Right in the back of your throat. Now the book is trying to help you with this word. What's that a picture of?' she pointed to the fluffy cat on the page. Trindal stared at it and frowned.

'Um, is it a dog?'

'No, try again.'

Trindal scratched his head. 'Is it um … some kinda little wombat?'

'Now you're being silly. What is it really?'

Trindal picked up the book and walked over to Kal. Kal pressed pause on the cassette player, pulled off his headphones and raised his head.

'Mmm?'

Trindal squatted down next to him and tapped on the picture.

'What's this?'

'It's a cat', Kal whispered.

'A what?'

'A cat. We don't have 'em here.'

'Cat?' Trindal pronounced the new word slowly.

'Yeah', Kal whispered. 'White people have 'em as pets.'

Kal shot a worried glance towards Miss Davis, but she seemed to be busy reviewing something on her desk. Miss Davis strained her ears, listening to their quiet exchange. Although she couldn't quite make out the words, she could understand the context from their intonations. Kal was explaining the word cat.

'She's waiting', Kal whispered. 'Go back.'

Trindal walked back to Miss Davis, who pretended she hadn't been eavesdropping.

'It's a cat', Trindal said sitting down and thumping the book back onto the table. 'We don't have 'em here.'

'You don't?'

Trindal shook his head.

'White people have 'em as pets. What's a pet?'

'A pet? Oh, it's um, well it's something that keeps you company. It's usually a cat or a dog. Some people have birds or fish or even reptiles for company.'

Trindal was thoughtful for a few moments then scratched his head.

'Kaaaaaal?' he called.

Kal pressed pause again and pulled off his headphones, letting out a sigh. Trindal pointed to Miss Davis. Kal glanced at her questioningly.

'I was trying to explain what a pet is', she said. 'I told him you keep them as company. He doesn't understand.'

Kal frowned thoughtfully then looked at Trindal.

'Keeping something as company', he said in Nahill, 'means to keep an animal as a friend, you know, so you can play and do stuff together. A pet is an animal that lives with you and goes places where you go. I guess the whites would say that Chet Chet was Chani's pet.'

Trindal caught his breath and his eyes went wide.

'Quick', he said. 'Do this.'

He made a number of signs with his hands then kissed the scar on his wrist, all the while muttering 'we didn't mean it, we didn't mean it.' Kal frowned but mimicked Trindal's words and movements then kissed the scar on his own wrist.

'What was that for?' he said.

'You spoke the name of someone who's gone on ahead.'

'Huh?'

'Chani's … pet.'

'Is everything alright?' Miss Davis said.

Trindal switched back to English.

'Yeah, Kal said a bad thing.'

Miss Davis gave Kal a reproachful look, ready to scold him for swearing.

'What did he say?'

'He spoke of someone who's gone on ahead. We must never do that.'

'Why?'

Trindal tapped the scar on his wrist. ''Cause we vowed not to call her back to us as a spirit. It's very bad luck.'

The two boys stared at each other for a long moment then Kal put his headphones back on while Trindal returned to his book.

'Cat', Trindal said.

Miss Davis opened her mouth to ask more but changed her mind.

'That's right', she said. 'Now let's go through the letters again.'

It was a full moon on a cold, clear night at White Camp. The only sounds were the night jar screeches and an occasional owl. The sound of car engines coming up the mountain started as a faint purring then became louder and louder until the roar echoed around the silent valley. With a final rev, the engines stopped. When the car doors slammed, the goats in Nemid's cabin raised their heads, their ears flicking back and forth, their noses twitching and their eyes gleaming in the moonlight coming through the window. The voices of men and women came closer – some laughing and some calling out in slurring drunken voices. Suddenly there was a blaze of light as the revellers got the bonfire going.

At the bonfire, Aunt Talks Too Much put the beer bottle to her lips and took another long drink as Uncle Mends Things and several other members of Dog clan got ready for their monthly game of Two Up. Two Up was a very old game where two heavy penny coins are tossed into the air while people bet on how the coins will land, face up or face down. Dog clan loved Two Up because the rules were simple and it required nothing more than the two old coins to play. What made this all the sweeter was that Two Up was illegal in the white world, but just like everything else, out here on the reservation, the white laws did not apply.

More cars pulled into the car park, their headlights making a wide sweep of the tallest trees as they rounded the last bend. The white men coming down the path laughed and jested with each other.

'Good, good', Aunt Talks Too Much said to her husband, 'more punters mean more cash for us. Let's get some drinks for our friends.'

Aunt Talks Too Much called as the new arrivals came down the slope to the bonfire. 'Only $5 a stubby.'

Lemon and Wisha had an esky filled with ice and alcoholic drinks between them. They went from man to man, Lemon collecting the money and Wisha handing out the cans and bottles. The coins clinked into a purse tied around her neck by a piece of string. A flat rock situated on one side of the grounds where a storyteller would normally sit was now Uncle Mends Things podium, and he was busy clearing it of sticks and debris ready for the game.

'Get your bets ready gents', said Aunt Talks Too Much. 'Cash only and all the best of luck. My husband there is our Spinner. Which of you wants to be the Ringy?' she called out, knowing that the white punters all felt better with one of their own in charge of calling the toss. It didn't matter to her. The end result was always that Dog clan made a killing. One of the men raised his hand and stepped forward.

'Nice to see you again, George', she said then turned towards Mash and his teenage cousin Gilmore. 'How're those snags going?'

Gilmore's job was to tend the fire as Mash readied the grill with sausages. Aunt Talks Too Much always said a well fed drunk lasted longer than a hungry drunk. Several portable gas lamps were ignited, and suddenly the area was awash with light. More cars arrived full of members of Dog clan who lived at Blue Camp. Most of them were burly young men whose job was to take people's wagers, make sure people paid their gambling debts and to mind the money.

'The bank has arrived', Uncle Mends Things called, and there was a scrabble of people making their wagers.

Aunt Talks Too Much finished her beer and tossed the bottle over her shoulder into the darkness.

'Are all bets in?' Uncle Mends Things called. 'The spinner is loading the kip.' He took out the two old pennies and placed one heads up and one heads down on the small piece of wood called the kip. 'Are we ready for the first toss of the night?'

George grabbed his beer and moved forward so he could oversee the toss.

'Ready', he said.

'Up they go!'

There was a cheer as the coins flew into the air. Kal sat up, pulling his blanket around him. He could hear voices and some had that drunken slur that made the hair on the back of his neck rise. There was another shout followed by drunken laughter. Kal got up and went to the window to peer out. He could see a large group of men standing over near the bonfire. They were drinking and some were eating. Aunt Talks Too Much looked up the hill as a car engine revved and a horn tooted. It woke Nemid. The goats bleated and scrambled to their feet. Kal hugged himself in fear. He knew all about drunken men and what happened when they got angry.

'Who's making all that noise?' Nemid said, getting to his feet. 'It's the middle of the night, and they've upset the goats.'

'Shhh', Kal hissed and put a finger to his lips. 'They're drunk.'

Trindal sat up, confused.

'What's going on?' he said sleepily.

At that moment, a bottle smashed against the side of their cabin, and loud men's voices yelled obscenities, laughing as they cheered.

'Alcohol is not permitted on this reservation', Nemid said, reaching for his boots.

'No!' Kal cried, throwing his arms out to stop Nemid from leaving. 'You can't go out there; it's not safe.'

There were more shouts. A baby in one of the other cabins started to cry. Dogs barked, and another car horn tooted. There were more shouts and laughter. Kal stared pleadingly at Nemid in the dimly lit cabin. Nemid could see the fear in the boy's eyes, and with a resigned sigh, put his boots down.

'Very well', he said, 'I will stay here.'

At that moment, a banging on the front door made them all jump. The goats jostled each other, their ears flicking back and forth nervously. Nemid moved Kal aside, squared his shoulders and opened the door. A boy stood before them.

'I'm sorry for waking you', Laughs a Lot said, nervously playing with his fingers, 'but I'm scared. Can I come in?'

Nemid stood back and let him in. Laughs a Lot sniffed and wiped the tears from his cheeks. Nemid shut the door.

'Who's making all that noise?' Nemid said.

'It's Two Up night', Laughs a Lot said, going to the nearly extinguished fire and holding his hands out to it. 'My Aunt invites her white friends back from town. They talk funny and fall over.'

Nemid went to the fire and threw on a few sticks.

'Has this happened before?' Nemid said.

Laughs a Lot nodded and rubbed his hands together.

'Every Two Up night, I come here to sleep with my goats.'

Nemid's lips set into a firm line. Dog clan were gambling here? He chastised himself. Of course Dog clan would be into gambling. The only thing that surprised him about this new outrage was that he had been surprised.

'Let's try to get back to sleep', Nemid said.

He and Laughs a Lot settled the goats and got them to lie down again. Nemid then made room under the blankets for Laughs a Lot. Laughs a Lot and Trindal were both soon asleep, but Nemid remained awake and vigilant. He could feel Kal shivering with fright as the drunken voices got louder.

'Eyas?' he whispered.

'I'm OK.'

There were so many of them, Nemid thought, and for the first time, he felt afraid with so many Dogs in the camp. Perhaps it was not safe to live here while there were so few Nahill. He determined to discuss this with Ashekii the next time he came to visit. He berated himself for leaving Red Camp so ill-prepared. For some reason, he had expected to find White Camp as it used to be, and when confronted by the realities, instead of being sensible and going back, he'd stayed, too stubborn to admit to Ashekii that coming had been a mistake. He told himself to stop thinking badly. He was Pac now. If he left, others would claim it. He suddenly imagined all he could do here. His camp could become a model for others. There would be no impediment to Chani's mission. In fact, as Pac he may even be able to sway the Women's Council to hear their cause, perhaps even to agree to support it. Now that would be something. Buoyed by these thoughts, he focused on the endless list of things he had to do if he were to make White Camp into a shining example of how a camp should be run. He had to get the storage sheds fixed, clean out the storage barrels, fix the fences before planting season to keep the goats out of the three sisters, revive the compost heap, check the dam and sluice gates; it just went on and on. Eventually, he fell into a restless sleep.

Time passed slowly and again the moon shone brightly down on the ground, making the fresh mounds of snow glitter. Peals of boyish laughter came from the Pac of White Camp's cabin. Inside, three figures were wrapped in blankets and wearing every piece of clothing they had. The room was lit by a single lamp made from half a gourd filled with grease, a single wick supplied the tiny flame. They'd brought in the last of Laughs a Lot's small herd of goats, and the air was thick with the reek of goats and manure. The six nannies were lying on a bed of tree fern fronds. Although the boards were soaked with goat urine, Nemid and the boys were so used to the stench by now that they no longer noticed it. Nemid was at the opposite end of the cabin making a manger, which he hoped would get the goat feed up off the floor and discourage the constant stream of thieving mice and bush rats. Trindal and Kal were searching the walls, their breath coming out in white clouds. The wood they'd gathered was still too wet to burn properly, which meant they couldn't cook, so they were living on raw bean mush mixed with salmon paste.

'It has to be here somewhere', Trindal said, his eyes alight with excitement.

Kal strode into the herd of goats. They bleated and turned to face him. Pulling off his gloves, he went to Dopsil, the shaggy brown matriarch. She had pale blue eyes and udders like a pair of carrots.

'Is it here?' he said, running his hands through her fur, soaking up the warmth.

Trindal pointed to a white one.

'I reckon Nod ate it', Trindal said. 'She's a complete guts.'

Kal leant against Dopsil's warm side, putting his cold cheeks against her rough fur.

'You saw where Nedda hid it, didn't you, girl?' he said. 'Why don't you whisper it to me?'

He placed his ear close to her mouth. Dopsil's rubbery lips ran over his skin, her stiff whiskers tickling his chin. He laughed and pulled back, shoving his hands into his gloves as he went.

'You're getting closer', Nemid said.

The boys renewed their efforts, searching for the dried bean that Nemid had hidden somewhere in the room. The boys slowly made their way along the wall peering into every crack and join.

'Maybe it's on the floor?' Kal said.

He dropped to his knees and crawled along as he searched the boards. Several of the goats came to join him. Kal laughed as he shoved a black one with half an ear missing aside.

'I can't see, Katil', he said.

'I told you to follow Nod', Trindal teased.

At the sound of her name, Nod swung her brown eyes towards Trindal and flicked her ears back and forth. Trindal gave her a quick pat before continuing his search.

Kal crawled along on all fours, sweeping the pellets of goat manure aside. 'Is it down here?' Kal said to Dopsil, who was sniffing along the boards beside him.

Katil came to join her mother.

'Owww', Kal said, shoving Katil away, 'you're on my glove, you big fucking turd.'

Nemid frowned.

'Kal?' he said sharply. 'Where'd you learn those words?'

Kal deliberately didn't look at Trindal, who was suddenly very busy searching. Nemid pursed his lips.

'I do not want that sort of language in my house', Nemid scolded.

'Yes sir.'

They were silent for a short time before Katil moved forward, pushing Kal over.

'Doppy help!' he cried to the old matriarch.

She nudged his stomach, making him laugh, and the tension eased.

'Is it on the wall behind one of you?' Trindal said to the rest of the goats.

Nemid's eyes went to the bean wedged in the window frame and wondered which of the boys would find it first this time. Not that it mattered; what was important was that they remained active to keep warm. In desperation, they had sneaked over to the Dog clan cabins to steal wood only to find every wood store empty because they'd hidden it. Nemid looked at Dopsil. Eating the goats was something he had also considered and would do if he had to. Eating raw goat meat was better than starving, but their greatest enemy was the cold. Because they needed every last bit of body heat, all the animals were safe, for now. He sent a silent prayer to the Great Spirits to help them.

'Ha!' cried Kal pulling a stone out from a crack in the floorboards. 'Oh', his face fell when he saw it wasn't the bean. With a sigh coming out in a white puff, he tossed it to one side and jumped to his feet.

'It's not down here', he said to Trindal. 'What about you?'

'Let's try up there', Trindal suggested, pointing to the top of the door jamb.

Both boys jumped to touch the top of the door, but only Kal was tall enough to reach it and feel his way along. The goats moved out of the way. Nemid chuckled as they increased their efforts, wondering if the thumping would shake the bean loose. After this game, he mused, it would have been nice to play a round of catch with the ball he'd made from dried grass, except Nod had eaten the ball.

14

It had been snowing heavily all day. Karen Davis stared out the window, studying the fat flakes. She wondered if she'd have to get someone to help dig her car out. Fortunately, the path down to the school was always freshly cleared when she arrived, which she assumed was one of Laughs a Lot's tasks. The fire was blazing in the grate, and there was a new set of fire pokers and an ash pan beside it that she'd bought at a garage sale. Along one wall, she'd hung the colourful posters she'd been collecting. They brightened the room. Several came from the department and illustrated how to wash your hands, what to do in case of fire and showed a set of rules for a respectful classroom. Next to these was a poster of the alphabet featuring big and little letters with fun pictures of wild animals from around the world. As obesity was a problem for most of the Western world, she'd included a poster about the food pyramid. Each food group was colour coded to show the importance of eating fresh fruit and vegetables for a balanced meal. There were reminders down the side about how exercise was an important part of a healthy lifestyle.

Miss Davis always smiled as she admired her poster collection. The splashes of colour against the drab beige walls were uplifting. Low down was a sheet of paper with columns. A number of the columns had star stickers in them to indicate the completion of a task such as saying the alphabet, counting to ten, multiplying to twelve and knowing shapes. On the mantelpiece was an empty vase that Miss

Davis couldn't wait to fill with fresh mountain flowers once spring arrived. She sighed happily and settled back into the cushions on her chair. Yes, she thought, this hall was beginning to get a homey feel to it. Trindal approached her with his workbook.

'Finished?' she said.

He nodded and showed it to her. After leafing through, she smiled.

'This is excellent', she said and handed him a red star sticker. 'Go and put this and your name in the column that says 'I know my shapes'.'

Trindal went to the wallchart. Kal and Trindal were still the only students to remain for longer than the first hour. Kal sat by the fire listening to a foreign language cassette called *Let's speak German.*

'Guten Tag', he said to the recorder. 'How do you do? Welcher weg zur post? Which way to the post office?'

Trindal proudly put the star and printed his name in the row. He stood for a moment admiring the bright colour of the star, the sharp, pointy edges of it and the miracle that allowed you to stick something to a vertical surface. Kal shot him an envious glance. Kal's name wasn't on the chart as it was only for baby stuff like letters and numbers. Even though Miss Davis had said Kal was too old for stars, Kal still wished Miss Davis would give him one for something. With a longing sigh, he returned his attention to his cassette. Trindal returned to Miss Davis and sat next to her as she turned his workbook to a fresh page filled with different coloured shapes.

'Something a bit harder', she said. 'Now we're going to revise our colours and the shapes are going to help us.'

She tapped a blue triangle. 'Tell me what shape this is?' she said.

'Tria Gle?' Trindal said.

'Yes. Now can you tell me what colour this is?'

He chewed his bottom lip as he stared at it.

'I'll give you a hint', she said, 'this is the same colour as the ocean.'

'What's the ocean?'

She pointed to the world map.

'Remember when I showed you all the different land masses? The ocean is what's around them. What colour is that?'

Trindal looked at the picture of different shapes on the wall. He still didn't understand what it was a picture of, not understanding the concept of maps. He knew the colour he was looking at, but couldn't remember the English word for it.

'Blue', Miss Davis said. 'Say it for me.'

'Blooo.'

'Blue.'

'Blue.'

'Yes. What colour's this square?'

She tapped the green square. Trindal drummed his fingers on the table.

'I'll give you a hint', she said, 'it starts with the sound a lion makes.' She pointed to the poster of wild animals. Trindal followed her gaze and was able to identify the picture of the lion, but he had no idea what sound it made.

'Grrrrr…?' she said.

He chewed his bottom lip.

'Green', she said. 'This's the colour green.'

'Gree.'

'Green.'

'Greeeeen.'

'Yes, and the next one is…?'

When school finished, Kal stayed behind as usual. He helped Miss Davis put the books away and tidy the room. This had become his favourite time of the week. He brought his assignments to her table and pulled up a chair. He smiled secretly to himself and wished he had the courage to call her by her first name. Karen. It was such a pretty name. Kal and Karen. Karen and Kal. He started as her pencil dropped onto the table.

'Now', she said pulling up her chair, 'let's see how you got on this week.'

She took one of his exercise books from the neat pile before her and began to read. He took a deep breath of her perfume. Today it was different from her normal one. He liked it. He leant towards her, watching the way her deep blue eyes flitted back and forth over his work. As usual, she was wearing mascara and eye liner. He studied her eyes. She must have been in a hurry today as the lines didn't quite meet at the corners of her eyes. Usually she was very careful about that.

'This's really good', she said.

She turned the page and continued to read. He blushed and ducked his head at her praise. To impress her, he'd tried extra hard on this one. Picking up her pencil, she made a correction. He leant further forward to see what he'd done wrong. Oh, he thought, he'd missed an apostrophe. He relaxed and drank in the smell of the shampoo she'd used on her pretty brown hair, which was pulled back into a ponytail today, another sign that she had been in a hurry. Sometimes she put curls in it, but he liked it best when she left it down. He rested his arms on the table, interlaced his fingers, then frowned at how much dirt was in the pores of his skin and under his nails. He studied her hands; they were milky white and spotlessly clean. Her nails were pink with white ends. He unlaced his fingers and refolded them so his nails were not visible.

The fire crackled in the fireplace, and outside he could hear crows cawing. Straight after school he would do another set of the combat exercises Ashekii had shown him. He practiced them in secret every morning and night, just like Ashekii had told him to. He knew that one day soon Ashekii would come back and then he'd show him how much he'd improved. He returned his attention to Karen. Her eyes were running quickly back and forth across his words. He had been trying to improve his penmanship to match her lovely cursive script. His most precious possession was a note she'd given him which read 'Dear Kal, this is a list of subjects available on cassettes. Please have a look and tell me if any of these subjects interest you. I will talk to you about them next week. Karen'.

When he returned from his thoughts, he found her staring at him.
'Huh?'
'Nothing', she said trying to recover from her own surprise at his closeness.

She did her best to ignore the strong smell of sweat, grime and body odour emanating from him. All the children had incredibly poor personal hygiene, but she had almost become accustomed to it, almost. She'd found wearing strong perfume helped to mask the worst of it. Keen to make him sit back a little, she pointed to her bag.

'Could you do me a favour?' she said. 'Get the fruit out of my bag? I'm hungry, and I bet you are too.'

'Sure', he said.

He smiled, and she caught a whiff of his bad breath and a close-up view of teeth that had not seen a toothbrush or a dentist in a long time, if ever. She wondered if she should set Kal an assignment on dental hygiene and glanced at the poster of how to brush properly. He got up and went to rummage in her briefcase, savouring the privilege of rifling through her things. There were her car keys and a handbag, which he ached to peek inside of so he could find out more about her. There were the crusts from her sandwiches wrapped up in plastic wrap. He wondered if she'd notice if he took them. His mouth was salivating just looking at them. He determinedly dragged his eyes away and continued to rummage. At the bottom of her bag was a yellow lunch box and an envelope with his name on it. He took it out.

'What's this?' he said holding up the envelope.

She glanced at it.

'Oh, sorry, that's your education allowance. I thought I gave your brother both of them. Put it in your pocket and give it to your mother. That reminds me, I've been meaning to ask if you'd like to enrol in correspondence school. Then you could get a high school diploma at the end.'

'How would I do that?'

'It's easy. We just fill out some forms and...'

His face paled. Paperwork always led to questions, and then Barry would find him and the hell would start again.

'No', he said.

'But...'

'The stuff we're doing's fine.'

'But you're so bright, Kal. You could go on to university if you wanted. They'd send you the material in the post and…'

'We don't have post.'

'I'm sure we could work out something.'

His jaw muscles tensed. 'I said no.'

He shoved the envelope up his sleeve, took out the lunch box and brought it over to the table. Cracking open the lid, he was overwhelmed by the delicious fragrance of orange, strawberries and pears inside. His mouth began to water. Instead of gorging on them, he held it out to her.

'Ladies first', he said.

She smiled. There it was again, she thought, manners that could only have come from a white upbringing.

'Thank you', she said.

She took two pieces then handed one to him, keen to keep those filthy little fingers away from her food. He blushed and took the proffered fruit. Now he was convinced she must like him too. He wondered what they would do next. Maybe he should show her that new wombat hole. She finished his assignment and put an A at the top then circled it.

'Excellent', she said. 'Let's see how you went with maths.'

She pulled the next exercise book towards her and began to read. Every now and again, she would nibble her piece of strawberry. He'd finished his segment in two bites, and his stomach was rumbling for more. He chewed his thumbnail as his stomach rumbled again, and he was torn between wanting time to speed up so he could have more food and wanting it to slow down so they had more time together. She put the last piece into her mouth, and he instantly picked up the box and offered it to her.

'Would you like another?' he said.

He reached for them, but she stopped him. 'No don't!' she said then smiled to soften her words. 'I'll do it.'

She took out two pieces and held them out on her palm. Kal took a piece of pear, and she saw the dirt smears from his fingers on the white sides of the fruit. As she returned to her reading, Kal took another bite and only just stopped himself from moaning in delight. Never had fruit tasted so good. The pear was sweet and juicy and crisp. He sucked rather than chewed to make it last as long as possible. She wrote an A on his work then glanced at her watch.

'I might have to take these ones home with me', she said. 'It'll be dark soon, and that trip down the mountain is not something to be done at night.'

She handed his two corrected pieces back then gathered up the rest. As she put the lid back onto her fruit box, she noticed him staring at the box longingly.

'Would you like these?' she asked him.

His eyes widened, and his expression reminded her of a game show contestant who had just won the jackpot.

'All of them?'

'Of course. I'll need the box back though. Do you have anything to put them in?'

He cupped his hands, but she took one look at how filthy they were and shook her head.

'Let's stop past your place, and we'll drop them into a bowl. Come on.'

He didn't want to tell her they had no bowls in case she changed her mind and didn't give him the fruit. They quickly packed, and as Kal pulled on his jacket, he sighed longingly at the beautiful warm fire being left to burn itself out in the grate.

'You first', she said as she locked up.

He shoved his hands into his pockets and went outside. She stomped into her boots then hurried after him, briefcase in one hand and the yellow plastic lunchbox in the other. Kal strode through the snow up the central path, his breath coming out in white clouds. He could hear her following him in quick footsteps and wondered if anyone was watching. Did they see that he and Karen were going to his cabin together? His cheeks went red, and he slackened his pace so they were walking side by side. It was satisfying to find that they were almost the same height. As they walked along, he felt very grown up and as if they were on a date.

'Would you like to see a wombat hole?' he asked excitedly.

'A what?'

'A wombat hole. It's new, and you can see her claws in the mud and everything.'

'You know it's a she?'

He nodded. 'Ah huh. The tracks going in and out show that she's got a baby in her pouch. Wanna see it?'

She glanced at the overcast sky and frowned.

'It's getting late', she said. 'Maybe another time?'

He bowed his head and stared down at the path feeling foolish. Karen was a woman, not a kid. Of course she didn't want to see a stupid wombat hole. He quickened his pace. Karen glanced about and wondered which of these decrepit hovels they were going to. She was curious to see inside a Nahill home. But they all appeared so run down, she was a little concerned she might pick up something like lice or fleas. Her boyfriend Raj had told her that they probably just looked bad on the outside and were most likely quite comfortable on the inside. As they walked, she became aware of the difference in Kal's manner. He seemed nervous. She put it down to having to explain to his friends why the teacher wanted to meet his parents.

'So Kal', she said to try to ease the tension, 'where did you grow up?'

'Here.'

'Oh, but I thought you moved to White Camp recently.'

'We did, I meant … I um, I grew up here on the reservation.'

'There are other camps?'

He opened his mouth to say yes then remembered how his grandfather had forbidden them to speak of such things to white people.

'I meant we lived out of camp a little', he said.

'I see. And how many brothers and sisters do you have?'

'None', he said without thinking.

'But I thought Trindal was your brother.'

His cheeks went scarlet.

'Watch your step', he said and briskly trotted up the stairs, 'and your head.'

Karen ducked to get under the low hanging beam that needed to be nailed back into place. Kal stamped his feet to get the snow off then opened the door and walked in. Two things struck Karen as she entered. First was the almost overpowering stench of animal manure and second was how little light was coming through the filthy windows. Reluctantly, she stepped inside and closed the door. She caught her breath as she noticed the flock of goats staring silently at her.

At the far end was a fireplace with a feeble fire that was smoking heavily. Trindal and an old man sat as close to the fire as they could. Neither of them looked up. On the floor beside them was a stone grinding wheel. White finger marks of flour had been left on the stone basin underneath. Trindal had a small bowl in his hand and was pouring a white paste carefully onto a flat rock next to the fire. As Karen watched, the paste oozed over the side of the rock and dripped onto the hearth. Beside it she could see the burnt remains of their welfare cheque. They'd used it to start the fire, she realised.

'The wood's still too wet', Nemid said in frustration.

'I told you it wasn't hot enough', Trindal grizzled irritably. His tone took on the whining quality of a hungry child. 'I'm sick of eating it uncooked. Why can't you ever get it hot enough?!'

Miss Davis's smiled became fixed, and she seemed flustered by seeing the realities of survival in the flesh. Kal sensed her discomfort.

'Trindal!' Kal said firmly in Nahill. 'Do not criticise a Drekesh!'

Trindal turned, about to give a sharp retort, when he saw their visitor. He nudged Nemid, who turned and sat back on his heels.

'Don't get up', she said even though he hadn't moved, 'I was just dropping off this fruit.'

Kal squared his shoulders, keen to demonstrate his new etiquette prowess.

'Honoured Pac', Kal said in English, 'may I present our teacher Miz Karen Daviz. Miz Daviz, this is my grandfather Me Pect Drekesh Nemid, most esteemed Pac of White Camp.'

Nemid smiled at Kal's accompanying formal bow. He was so quick at learning, he mused with pride then waited for the young woman to bow, as she now knew he was an elder, a Drekesh and the camp Pac. When she rudely remained upright, he decided to be the bigger man.

'Welcome to our home', he said.

Karen looked at him uncertainly.

'You speak English?'

Taken aback by her abruptness, Nemid reminded himself to make allowances for her ignorance and lack of manners.

'Yes', he said. 'I grew up in White Camp, so I, too, went to school. Please, join us.'

She took one look at the filthy floor and shook her head.

'I can't stay', she said. 'I just came to give you these', and she waved the lunch box. Her eyes swept the cabin for a container but saw nothing suitable. 'You know what? How about you keep the box, I have more at home.'

She searched for somewhere to put the box, but there was not a scrap of furniture. In desperation, she handed it to Kal. Kal took the box over to the others.

'Look!' he said, opening it to reveal treasure.

'Wow!' Trindal cried and instantly grabbed two pieces.

The goats had also smelt the bounty and drew closer.

'I should go', Karen said backing towards the door.

'Please stay', Kal blurted out. 'I could make you something. We have … Fruit!'

He held up the box and smiled. With a determined bleat, Dopsil strode forward, ears back and a single-minded glint in her eye. Kal shoved her back, holding the container up high.

'Doppy, no!' he snapped at the goat.

Miss Davis reached for the door.

'It's getting late. Perhaps another time?'

Kal tried to hide his disappointment, not understanding why she didn't want to stay. Nemid knew why. He'd seen that expression before and knew it all too well. It was the look of disgust that white people had when they saw the Jhunti way of life. His lips set into a firm line. She felt behind her for the handle.

'Nice meeting you all', she said. 'Kal, can you see me to my car?'

Kal instantly brightened.

'Sure', he said.

He grabbed a piece of fruit and shoved it into his mouth then thrust the box into his grandfather's hands. She gave them all a tight smile, turned and all but ran out the door. The goats were bleating and closing in on the box of fruit as Kal ran after her. She took several huge breaths of fresh air to clear her lungs as they strode up the centre of the camp to the car park. She opened her car door and tossed her briefcase into the back seat.

'Kal? I'm going to ask you something, and I want you to be honest with me alright?'

He shoved his hands into his pockets and stared down at the ground. Here we go, he thought, she's going to ask about my parents. He mentally readied his story.

'Are you getting enough to eat at home?' she said.

His head jerked up.

'Huh?'

'Does your family have enough food?'

Relief washed over him.

'Oh', he stammered, 'yeah, of course but we just have trouble cooking it. No heat in wet wood as they say.'

She gave him a puzzled look. He didn't want to say they'd arrived too late in the season to gather dry wood or she'd know they'd come from far away. After all, who wouldn't have dry wood?

'Our wood is too wet to burn properly', he said.

'But surely if you brought it inside…?'

He let out a frustrated breath.

'You need heat to dry it. When the room stays cold all the time, nothing dries and it just makes everything mouldy.'

She pointed to the Dog clan cabins. All had smoke coming from their chimneys.

'Why don't you get some from them?'

He made a face.

'They're all Dog clan. They offered to sell us some, but we don't have any money.'

'You've got your education allowance, haven't you?'

She pointed to his sleeve, and Kal pulled the envelope out. She opened it.

'It's a cheque', she said and held it up. 'You know what a cheque is don't you?' He shook his head. 'You put it in your bank account.'

'I don't think we have a bank account.'

'Alright, then you can do what the others do. Take it down to the general store. They'll put it on the book for you.'

'Huh?'

She opened her mouth to explain then closed it again.

'Come with me', she said.

They both climbed into the four-wheel drive. She started the engine and put the heater on full then followed the other car tracks out of the camp car park and down the mountain. They crawled along the treacherous road in silence. When they got to the bitumen, she let out a breath she didn't know she'd been holding and accelerated.

'Have you ever been to the general store?' she said.

'No.'

'But you have been to a shop before, haven't you?'

He was about to say 'of course he had' but stopped himself. If he really had grown up on the reservation, would he have gone to the shops? She mistook his indecision for embarrassment and decided to change the subject.

'So the other allowance cheques I gave you, has he burnt them all?'

Kal nodded.

'They burn real good.'

She pursed her lips but said nothing as they got to an intersection. She turned right toward the small collection of shops. Several of the camp cars were parked outside.

'Come on', Miss Davis said.

They got out of the car, and she led him inside. He instantly recognised the members of Dog clan loading things into wire baskets. Miss Davis went to the counter. The elderly shop keeper was a slim Asian woman. Her greying hair was cut short about her head.

'Good afternoon, Miss Karen', she said.

'Hi', Miss Davis said. 'Mrs Li, this is Kal. Kal, this is Mrs Li. She runs this shop. Kal would like to start an account please.'

Mrs Li pulled a dog-eared ledger from under the counter. She flicked to a new page and wrote 'Cal' on the top of the page.

'It's spelt with a K', Miss Davis said.

'Sorry.'

Mrs Li made the correction and handed Kal a pen. He stared at the pen not knowing what to do with it. Mrs Li took his cheque out of the envelope and pointed to the dotted line at the bottom.

'Just sign it', Miss Davis said.

Kal leant forward and stared down at the cheque. It was made out to 'Custodian of Kal'. He gripped the pen between his fingers until they went white as he wondered what to write. He'd never signed anything and wasn't sure what signing was.

Mrs Li tapped the dotted line. 'Just put your mark there', she said.

Kal mentally shrugged and made a squiggle of nonsense.

'Thank you', Mrs Li said and took the cheque and pen from his hand. She stamped the back of the cheque then wrote the date on it. 'That's OK now. Bring what you wanna buy to the counter.'

Miss Davis picked up one of the wire baskets, gave Kal another and they started walking around the shop.

'From now on', she said, 'this is what you'll use.'

She put a bag of barbeque briquettes and a box of fire starters beside the counter. Next, they placed six loaves of bread into Kal's basket adding some butter, jam and several savoury spreads.

'When you're done with these jars', she said holding up the spreads, 'give them a good wash, and they can be used as drinking glasses or storage containers.'

Going to the dairy section, she put in one large container of milk, some salami and cheese. Last they went to the fresh produce section, and she loaded her basket with fruit and vegetables, which could be eaten raw. She showed him how to weigh things on the scales and told him how things in season were cheaper.

'Alright', she said, 'I think that's about all we can afford this week.'

They went to the counter, and Mrs Li put everything into plastic bags, ringing them up on the till as she went.

'You got $1.14 left', she said. 'You wanna buy some lollies?'

Kal grinned and nodded. There it was again, Miss Davis thought. He says he's never been to a shop, yet he knows about lollies. She had also noticed that Kal did not speak English with the same slight accent that the other Nahill did. Mrs Li added two large bags of sweets to Kal's purchases.

'OK', she said, 'I put the left over in the book for next time. See you next week Kal.'

Kal and Miss Davis took his bags outside. She peered hopefully up and down the street, but the other camp cars were gone. With a weary sigh, Miss Davis began to walk to her car.

'I'll give you a lift back', she said.

Her reluctance was obvious.

'No', Kal said, 'it's OK. I'll walk. I know a short cut.'

She looked at the dozen heavy bags then smiled.

'It's fine', she said. 'I don't mind. Come on.'

She followed the vehicle tracks back up the mountain and then waved him goodbye as he struggled down the path with his bounty.

Life at White Camp was finally looking up. It was too cold for the gamblers now, so Two Up nights had been cancelled, and all was quiet again. Every day, except Tuesdays, the boys and Nemid worked around the camp. At night, they got their fire going using briquettes, which Mrs Li had shown Kal how to use and now ordered in by the 50-kilogram bag for him. With a warm fire, they were at last able to cook their food, but they only used the expensive briquettes sparingly, and still slept amongst the goats. Although none would admit it, their weeks were now centred around Tuesdays.

Miss Davis was also settling in. Some days she caught herself looking at Kal sitting cross legged with his headphones on and his exercise book in his lap, occasionally repeating a phrase from the lesson. He remained a mystery to her. There was so much about Kal's manner and familiarity with white people that convinced her that he had been raised by whites. Several times she'd tried to draw Kal into a conversation about his childhood, but he'd remained elusive.

As school finished, Kal and Trindal ran up to the car park. Kal was glad he'd learnt to drive on Stewie's farm. At thirteen, he was way too young to get a driver's license and could only just see over the wheel and reach the floor pedals.

'Don't forget we need butter!' Trindal called out as Kal jumped into the only car Dog clan ever left. It was an ancient, blue Valiant with a dead battery. Trindal went to the back of the car as Kal put it into neutral and fastened his seatbelt.

'Ready?' Trindal called out.

Kal gave him a wave and turned the key in the ignition. Trindal put his shoulder to the back of the car and began to push. The car moved, slowly at first then faster until Trindal could no longer keep up, and the car careered down the hill. The first few bends were a hair-raising free-for-all as Kal waited for the car to get up to speed. Eventually he let the clutch out, and the car shuddered and almost stopped before the engine spluttered into life.

When he got to the shops, he parked behind a group of trees, leaving the motor running and jogging the half a block to the general store. He knew he could get much better value for his money by going to one of the supermarkets Dog clan talked about, but that would lead to questions. So he always shopped at Mrs Li's store with no mention of her outrageous prices, and she ignored the fact that a child was driving a car. As he pushed through the door, the little bell dinged.

'Hi, Mrs Li.'

'Hey there, Kally', Mrs Li called back. 'You need petrol today?'

Kal never drove the car to the bowser because if he turned the engine off, he would never get it started again. When he needed fuel, he would fill up a ten litre container and take it back with him, refuelling the car at the carpark.

'No thanks.'

He gave her a wave. Mrs Li put a bundle of old newspapers and cardboard boxes beside the counter. These were for Kal to take home to burn. Kal collected one of the wire baskets and went to the back of the store. He loaded his first basket with three cartons of milk, six loaves of bread and two packets of the sweet biscuits that Nemid had become addicted to. He filled his second basket with tins of sausages, Irish stew and spaghetti. Knowing that was one third of his two-cheque budget gone, he left that basket at the counter and picked up basket number three. Mrs Li reached under the counter and pulled out a 3-kilogram bag of oranges. Some had a light dusting of mould on them. Kal licked his lips.

'I got these oranges on special', she said. 'They're still good.'

'How much?' he asked.

'They were $6 a kilo. For you, half price.'

Kal shook his head.

'I'll give you 50 cents for the whole bag.'

Her eyes widened.

'Are you trying to rob an old woman? $4.25 a kilo.'

Kal studied the oranges. He wanted them but not for that price.

'I'll give you $1 for the bag.'

She put a hand on her chest, her expression one of pain.

'Are you trying to kill me? $1 is an insult. They cost me more than that.'

'And you're gonna throw 'em out if I don't take 'em. $1.25 for the whole bag, and that's my final offer.'

Grumbling to herself about ingrates robbing her blind, Mrs Li put the bag of oranges with his other baskets. Smiling, Kal went to the fresh food section. He had to get enough to feed the three of them and Laughs a Lot for a week, so he selected with care. All the while, he kept a running tally in his head, so he wouldn't overspend. Not that Mrs Li minded putting items in the book, but he'd learnt the hard way that on such a tight budget paying off a debt meant going without.

With his food items selected, he put his basket by the others and a thrill of excitement ran through him. It was time. Each week he allowed himself one luxury item, and for days, he had been day dreaming about what it would be this time. At first his luxuries had been lollies and cakes and, once, a packet of beef steaks. But over time, he'd become more practical. Eyes glittering, he went to his favourite part of the shop, the small camping and hardware section. His eyes went from the metal cookware to packets of nails, hammers and other tools. He eyed the thick woollen coats and waterproof jackets. At last he reached out and took what he had decided would be their luxury this week. It was a glass and metal hurricane lamp.

At $22.14, it was a big investment, but Kal knew they would use it constantly. Just the thought of having light as he cut up vegetables made him smile. No more nicking his fingers with the knife or burning food because he couldn't see what he was doing. His eyes went longingly to a large metal frying pan, but he told himself that would have to wait. Perhaps next week. He did the figures in his head and worked out that with this lamp, he would have $2.13 left. Perhaps he'd buy some bags of lollies. Cradling the lamp to his chest, he went to the counter. Mrs Li looked up from her magazine.

'Ready?' she said.

He nodded. She pointed to the lamp.

'You know how to use that?' she said.

He shook his head. She took it from the box then showed him how to raise and lower the glass, and the cloth wick.

'We sell new wicks', she said, 'for when this one burns out.'

She inserted the wick then twirled the wheel so that the wick poked up above the metal guide.

'You lift the glass and put the match in here', she said, showing him.

'We don't have matches', Kal said.

She took a packet from the cigarette counter and added them to his basket. He peered behind her to see the price. 10 cents. He had $2.03 left.

'Now when the wick gets ragged', Mrs Li said, 'you'll need to trim it with a pair of scissors. If you don't do that it will burn unevenly and it will blacken the glass. You got a pair of scissors?'

Kal shook his head. Mrs Li reached up behind her to the small collection of medical supplies and added a pair of nail scissors to his basket.

'How much are they?' Kal said.

She looked at the packet.

'$1.90. That OK?'

He nodded. No sweets this week, but they'd have light any time they needed it.

'And this', she said, unscrewing the metal lid on the belly of the lamp, 'is where the kero goes.'

She put it back on. 'OK buddy', she said, 'you're all set.'

She put the lamp down then paused.

'You've got kerosene, don't you?' she said.

He slowly shook his head.

'We sell it in 50 litre containers. $35 and that should last two months.'

Kal's heart sank. '$35 for two months?' he said.

'Ah huh.'

He stared down at the lamp undecidedly. It had never occurred to him that the lamp would have an ongoing cost. He'd thought it would be like electric lights that were just always on when you flicked the switch. $35 was a huge chunk out of their already tight budget.

'Want me to put it in the book for you?' she said, reaching for her accounts book.

Kal shook his head, knowing he'd have to buy petrol next week, so his budget would already be stretched. He contemplated the lamp, weighing up all the good things about having it against the things they'd have to do without to buy the kerosene. Reluctantly he put it back into its box.

'I've changed my mind', he said.

'I could maybe do the 50-litre container for $30.'

'No, it's OK. We'll go with a frying pan.'

She helped him put the lamp back into the box then went with him to the camping section. While she put the lamp back onto the shelf, he selected the largest frying pan. It cost $15.00. When they returned to his baskets, he kept the nail scissors and signed the back of his and Trindal's cheques.

Later that night as they lay on the floor amongst the goats, Nemid listened to the steady breathing around him. He stared at the remains of the charcoal briquette fire, the embers of which glowed red in the hearth. He absently rubbed his full stomach. Kal had shown them how to toast cheese sandwiches in their new metal frying pan, and they were delicious but far too rich for his old stomach.

When Nemid had seen the frying pan, he'd recognised it as one that was in common use at Red Camp. For some reason, he'd always assumed one of the clans made them, but now it dawned on him that Dog clan must buy them from the whites then trade them. Why had he not realised this before, he wondered? Everyone went on and on about how the Nahill were living the same traditional lifestyle as their ancestors, and yet so much of it was no longer traditional; it was a hybrid of cultures. He wished he'd realised all this before. He had imaginary conversations with those detractors who said Kal did not belong because having a white man on the reservation did not conform to traditional ways. He pictured himself holding up one of the iron kettles that were in every cabin and asking if they planned to throw these out too. He derived a smug satisfaction at imagining their indignation. For the first time in his life, Nemid felt grateful to the whites.

15

Over the next few weeks, Miss Davis noticed a difference in the camp. The piles of rubbish, which were such an eyesore, seemed to be getting smaller. She wasn't sure if that was her imagination or guilt because she kept meaning to get the council to come and remove them. Then one day, Trindal and Kal arrived with their boots wrapped in sheets of puffy plastic.

'What're you wearing?' she said.

Trindal grinned and held his foot out.

'We made 'em', he said. 'They're woven out of shredded plastic. This outer covering makes our boots waterproof.'

'And', said Kal, 'it provides insulation, which keeps our feet warm.'

'We've also got these', Trindal said turning his back to her.

She studied his new raincoat, which had been created from a patchwork of pieces of plastic and sown together with thread made of strips of plastic.

'Wow', she said. 'They're amazing.'

Both boys glowed at her praise.

'You got us started on it', Kal said. 'You told me to wash out the jam jars to use as drinking glasses. When I told Nedda, he wondered what else we could reuse. Now we spend every day at the dump finding stuff and cleaning it up.'

'Wanna see?' Trindal said.

The eagerness on both their faces made it impossible to say no, and so after school, Miss Davis followed Trindal and Kal back to their cabin. Kal pointed to their roof.

'See up there?' he said.

For the first time, she noticed flattened beer cans nailed to the roof.

'They make great tiles', Kal said. 'I bought some nails and a hammer at the store.'

As they mounted the stairs, she noticed rows of upturned metal bottle caps nailed to each of the treads.

'These stop you from slipping as you go up the stairs', Kal said.

'At first', Trindal said, 'we just nailed 'em on whole, but then they filled up with water and that froze.'

Kal laughed.

'We wound up flat on our arses', he said.

'Then', Trindal said, 'we found that if you flatten just one side it lets the water out and then your feet grip on it real good.'

She stared down at the caps and then imagined bare feet in summer being shredded by them.

'How will you take them off in summer?' she said.

Kal grinned.

'We won't. We just take the tread out and put it up the other way. One for each season. Smart huh?'

She smiled back.

'Yes, very innovative.'

'Wait till you see this', Trindal said.

She looked to where he was pointing. Along the edge of the roof, a gutter had been made of halved metal food tins. It ended in a downpipe of tin cans, which channelled the snow melt into a large plastic tomato sauce bottle which had drink straws coming out of the bottom. Each straw went into a clean beer bottle; the snow melt slowly filling the bottles with water.

'No more having to go get clean snow when we're thirsty', Trindal said.

'And when it's raining', Kal enthused, 'no getting wet!'

'You don't have running water?'

'Yeah', Trindal laughed, 'but it's all frozen over now' and he pointed towards the creek.

Karen was afraid to ask about their bathroom situation.

'These are great for clearing snow', Trindal said.

He pointed to three shovels resting against the wall of the cabin. They were made from a stout wooden handle with several flattened food tins nailed to it.

'And they'll be real useful come planting time', said Kal. He pointed to a scraper made of more upturned bottle caps. 'Use that to wipe your boots.'

As she wiped the snow from her boots, the boys peeled off their plastic outer layers to reveal their leather boots underneath. The three of them entered, and she was taken aback at the change inside. The room was lit by a dozen lamps made from oil with a linen wick in the middle of a glass jam jar. On the floor was a thick rug that had been made from discarded clothes that had been washed then shredded and woven together. There were sets of bowls made from flattened beer cans. Tin cans had been nailed to the walls and were filled with different grains.

'No more mouse poo in our food', Kal grinned proudly.

Suspended from a piece of wire over a roaring fire was a large tin in which stew was bubbling. On closer inspection, she saw that the wire had been made from a finely cut aluminium can. Nemid was sitting in front of a large stone before the fire. On one side of him were bags filled with empty beer cans. On the other side was a neat pile of flattened beer can tiles. He was busily pounding his latest can. The goats stared back at her from their beds of shredded paper. They were munching their bean mash out of buckets made from plastic containers.

'Grandfather', Kal said loudly over the banging, 'Miz Daviz is here.'

Nemid stopped and looked up.

'Hello', he said but again did not stand.

'Hi', Miss Davis said, her eyes darting about. 'I wanted to check that you weren't having any problems getting your allowance, but this is just incredible. You made all this from garbage?'

'It is not garbage', Nemid said, 'it is bounty.'

Kal held out a piece of wood with flattened bottle caps embedded into it.

'This is a really good serrated knife', he said.

'And we have spoons' Trindal said holding up one fashioned from a plastic drink bottle.

'And we've got cooking pots', Kal said pointing to the collection of large, blackened tins near the fire.

'And a way to keep tubers fresh', Trindal said pointing to a stack of old dog food bags that had soil inside with a few potatoes sticking out the top.

'That was my idea', Kal said proudly.

'More fuel, boys', Nemid said.

Kal opened the bedroom door, and the air was suddenly filled with the smell of damp and mildew. Inside were piles of old cardboard boxes and different types of paper from fast food wrappers to newspapers. Hanging from the wall was another of Nemid's bottle-top knives, and on the other side, were neat stacks of cardboard, each cut into single sheets. Beside them were papers flattened out so they could dry. Kal emerged with an armload, knelt beside the fire and tossed on a selection. They steamed for a moment, smoked and suddenly burst into flames. Miss Davis took a step towards the door as the air in the room became humid and fetid.

'Would you like a drink?' Kal said to her, holding out a beer bottle of water.

She smiled and shook her head.

'No, thank you. I should be going. It was lovely to see you again, Nemid.'

She gave him a slight wave then hurried out the door.

Nemid stared after her for a long moment. He was secretly pleased that she could not stand the smell of the goat manure or the reality of the garbage and waste that her lifestyle generated. Miz Daviz exemplified everything he both envied and hated about the white world. He envied that her body was pain free, well fed, warm and clean and that her hands were soft and unsoiled. But the waste generated by the Nahill and their goats would fertilize the soil and grow strong, healthy plants. The waste of the whites would kill and lay the earth barren. Nahill knew which type they preferred, even though it was harder on their bodies. He also knew there was no place for his kind of thinking in her perfectly clean world, only in the Nahill world.

'Nedda?' Kal said.

Nemid gave himself a little shake and picked up his hammer.

'Mmm?'

'What do you want us to do now?'

'More boxes', Nemid said, indicating his paper room, 'and Trin, you can refill the animals' buckets with some corn for their dinner.'

'What're we having?' Trindal said to Kal, his eyes gleaming.

'Hamburgers.'

Trindal did a little happy dance then went to fill the animal containers from the last of the sacks of grain they had brought with them from Red Camp.

It was another clear night with the stars burning brightly in the jet black sky. Everyone on the reservation knew that snowfalls kept the temperature up, and without them, everything froze. No clouds or snow meant that it would be frigidly cold tonight. Laughs a Lot sat in his cabin luxuriating in his roaring fire. His bare feet turned towards the flames, and the rest of him enfolded in his overstuffed armchair. He was engaged in one of his many pastimes, tossing pieces of bread and cheese to the floor and watching the mice run about the cabin eating the scraps of food. When the mice weren't amusing him, he mulled over what to do about his goats. At this time of the year, they always moved them to town until the snows melted. His mother had arranged to borrow a billy goat, and had said that any goat who did not deliver a live kid was going into the pot. Laughs a Lot was afraid that Dopsil was now too old to have babies. The mice suddenly scattered, and a moment later, there were footsteps on the wooden veranda. The door burst open and Sindri, Aunt Talks Too Much, Uncle Mends Things and Remmy came in. All of them were wearing puffy snow suits and carrying plastic bags full of take-away food containers.

'Ohhhh, it's freezing out there', Remmy said as she dumped her bags on to the table then headed for Laughs a Lot's fire.

'Warm in here though', Uncle Mends Things said.

They all stripped off their thick jackets, beanies, scarves and gloves. Remmy shoved Laughs a Lot's feet off the stool.

'Move over, Shrimp.'

She plonked herself down and warmed her hands. Laughs a Lot sat up. He could smell the alcohol on her breath. He didn't like it when they drank. They talked too loudly, argued with each other and called him stupid. Sometimes they made him do things he didn't want to do, like go to Nemid's to beg for food, which they all thought was hilarious.

'Have you eaten?' Sindri said to Laughs a Lot, warming her back at the fire.

'Ah huh.'

'At Nemid's?' Aunt Talks Too Much said hopefully.

Laughs a Lot nodded. Aunt Talks Too Much smiled. Her nephew was a moron and had no idea that he was deliberately being sent over to eat at the Nahill's to drain their supplies. It was petty, but it amused them all and was way cheaper than having to leave the brat food. She started to hum 'Take it to the Limit'. Uncle Mends Things put the takeaway containers onto the table while Sindri fetched plates and spoons. Laughs a Lot gave the food a cursory glance. It was that spicy stuff he didn't like. He returned his attention to his fire.

'Look what I got', Sindri said, pulling up her sleeve and showing Laughs a Lot her new tattoo.

He bent forward and examined the picture of a heart with blue birds flying around it.

'Like it?' she said. 'It was a present from Simon.'

'Who's Simon?'

'Someone special. You'll meet him in a day or two when we get to the house.'

Laughs a Lot sank back into his chair. He didn't want to go to the house in town. It was always crowded and noisy and his cousins teased him. He liked it here in the quiet where he could do as he pleased, but his mother refused to let him stay on his own over the worst of the winter months. She said soon the snow would be so deep, they'd not be able to get the cars up the hill for at least three moons. She said she'd miss him too much. Uncle Mends Things pulled a six-pack of beer from his bag, and put one can in front of each place at the table.

'Dinner is served', he said.

Sindri and Uncle Mends Things handed the plates around as everyone came to sit up, except Laughs a Lot. He remained far away from the spicy smells, sinking lower into his arm chair and pulling the neck of his jumper up over his nose. The others began to eat.

'You know', Remmy said, 'I saw them rummaging through the garbage the other day.'

Uncle Mends Things stopped serving and looked up.

'What garbage?'

'Our garbage', Remmy said.

'Oh this is just too funny', Sindri gloated. 'The proud and noble Nahill, one of them the supposed', and she made air quotes, 'Pac of White Camp, is reduced to living off the scraps that Dog clan has thrown away. Maybe we should call him the Pac of garbage?'

They all laughed. Aunt Talks Too Much opened her beer and took a swig. Her eyes went to Laughs a Lot.

'You didn't give them any more wood, did you?' she snapped.

He shook his head.

'You said not to. But I felt mean. There's holes in their cabin walls, and it gets really cold.'

'I've always said I'd be happy to sell them wood', Sindri said.

'They should not have come at this time of the year', Aunt Talks Too Much said. 'If they are struggling now, then how will they manage when winter really sets in?'

Uncle Mends Things nodded.

'It's been so long since any Nahill lived here', he said, 'that they have forgotten it is the coldest, highest and most exposed of the camps. It has none of the shelter or more temperate climates of the other camps.'

They all ate in silence for a short time, and Laughs a Lot was glad he had not told his family the goats were living with Nemid. He hadn't lied to them; it was just that no one had asked where they were. Sindri put the last spoon of food into her mouth and ran through her mental to-do list. Tomorrow all of Dog clan were packing up their belongings, and as soon as they got their education cheques, they would move to their winter residence in town. She knew Laughs a Lot didn't like it there, but she was not leaving him to fend for himself for three months. Any day, there'd be another blizzard five times worse than the last one. After that, the snow drifts would be as tall as the cabins, and no one would be able to get in or out of White Camp till the thaw.

'I want you up early tomorrow', she said to her son. 'It's moving day.'

'Tomorrow? But...'

She held up a hand. Every year it was the same argument. He didn't want to go. Dog house was too noisy. He could look after himself.

'You're coming', she said firmly. 'Straight after school, I want you to take the goats down the hill. Your cousins will be waiting there and will help you load them into the trailer.'

'Don't forget tomorrow's the last day of term', Remmy said. 'I recon they should pay us for holidays.'

'Cheap bastards', Aunt Talks Too Much agreed.

Laughs a Lot stared at the fire and thought about his poor Dopsil. He didn't want to have to eat her. He wondered if he could hide her somewhere.

Aunt Talks Too Much glanced around the cabin, noting items here and there that they should pack. She was glad they were going. When winter really set in, it scared her, especially that merciless wind that went right through you no matter how many layers you wore. On freezing nights, it got so cold whole trees exploded. Even walking was hard as the ice made every path into a slick death trap just waiting to put you flat on your back.

Dog clan had been spending winters at the Dog house in town ever since she could remember. Each year when they'd come back, there had been less and less Nahill until there were none. Aunt Talks Too Much had been only a child, but she still remembered the celebrations that night. A nasty smile crossed Aunt Talks Too Much's lips. Wouldn't it be wonderful if they returned this spring to find no Nahill?

Miss Davis finished packing up the last of her things into her briefcase and looked around the classroom. The new vase of dried flowers, colourful pots of crayons, pencils and pens had at last succeeded in turning the room into something that resembled a comfortable and inviting space for both herself and the children. What would be fun, she mused, was if they had a class pet like a fish, a rabbit or perhaps a budgie. Having a pet in the teaching environment allowed for many new experiences like shouldering responsibility instead of always being looked after. Some teachers had used pets to introduce the subject of how important it was to care for the environment by recycling and buying responsibly. She draped her lap rug over the back of her chair and pushed it up to the table.

'Maybe next term', she said aloud.

She picked up her briefcase, and her eyes ran over the tidy room. She was going to miss it. But all too soon, the winter holidays would be over, and they'd all be back at it again. She tsked and shook her head.

'I forgot', she said then went to the door and stuck her head out. 'Lal? Are you there, Lal?'

A few moments later, Laughs a Lot trotted up to her, his breath making white clouds in the cold air.

'Yes, Miz Daviz?' He followed her back to her desk, and she hastily took out a sheet of paper.

'I'm going to be away for a little while', she said as she wrote. 'These are the dates. I want you to give them to your mother. Ask her to tell the others. Please note that as well as the normal two-week holiday period, there will be no school for an extra three weeks. I have to do curriculum planning and attend some training', she checked her diary then tut-tutted. 'And the week after that, I have a dental appointment.'

She turned the note towards Laughs a Lot. He stared at the squiggles on the page and hoped she didn't expect him to remember any of this.

'As you can see', she said, pointing to the dates, 'there will be no school on the following dates; Tuesday 30th June 1998, Tuesday 7 July 1998, (regular school holidays), Tuesday 14th July and Tuesday 21 July 1998 (I have planning days), Tuesday 4th August 1998 (I will be on sick leave). That's a nice long break for you', she smiled. 'You can thank me later.' She handed him the page then raised a finger. 'I almost forgot', she said, reaching into her bag. 'I'd meant to give these to Kal. Can you please ensure he gets them?'

She handed Laughs a Lot a plastic bag. He peered inside, hoping there was food, but it was only the cassette recorder and a box of lesson tapes. 'And he'll need these', she said, dropping a pack of spare batteries into the bag. 'That's it. See you after the holidays.'

Laughs a Lot stared at her balefully. All the teachers said that, but they never came back. Miss Davis gathered up her things and headed for the door, humming to herself as she went.

Later that day, when Kal arrived back from Mrs Li's store with their weekly groceries, Trindal was waiting for him in the car park as usual. Kal carefully parked the old car so that it faced down the hill ready for next week. Trindal gathered up the bags of groceries, and Kal shouldered the essential sack of precious briquettes, snatched up the sack of spoilt vegetables and green waste Mrs Li set aside for Kal's goats, and the pair of them made their way down to the cabin.

'Lal dropped by after you'd gone', Trindal said. 'He took the goats.'

Kal's eyes widened.

'But we need them!'

'Grandfather said it's OK now we have the briquettes. Besides, Lal said he had to take them. He also left a bag and a piece of paper with a bunch of numbers on it that we don't understand.'

Kal frowned, wondering if it was extra homework. When they got to the cabin, they found Nemid busy making a rug out of shredded plastic bags, the last rug having melted from getting too close to the fire. The boys put the groceries away, and the rest of the Tuesday ritual began. First they cracked open the new bag of briquettes and refilled the wood box next to the fire. Then they sorted through the veggie scraps from Mrs Li. With no livestock, they put most of it straight into their stew pot. The rest they kept for eating fresh. Meanwhile, Nemid ate soup while the boys toasted cheese sandwiches. This was always followed by a piece of fruit each, even for the goats. This week it was a pineapple. Each of them sucked on the juice and savoured every morsel until all was gone. Replete, they all sat back, their feet turned towards the glowing briquettes in the fireplace.

Kal looked through the bag of cassettes Miz Daviz had left for him. There were ones on maths, English, history and the rest of the course of *Let's speak German*. He put them back, burped and crossed his legs at the ankle, grateful to be warm and well-fed. The new mats Nemid was making from plastic were perfect for keeping them up off the freezing cold floor. Nemid yawned and stretched.

'Time for us all to go to bed', he said.

'Shame to waste that', Kal said, indicating the fire.

Nemid patted the newly refilled briquette box.

'There will be more warm fires to come.'

Trindal yawned and dragged his new blanket made from a mixture of plastic and rags and goat fur over himself.

'I miss them', Kal said, cocking his head towards where the goats used to sleep.

'We will see them again', Nemid said.

He blew out the little oil lamps, and he and Kal settled in. Soon they were all asleep as the briquettes' glow dimmed and went out. The temperature in the cabin plummeted, not that they noticed with their new blankets.

The days passed, and as the supplies began to dwindle, Kal wondered when the next school day was going to be. It felt like more than a week had passed since Dog clan had left, taking bags of possessions and all the camp dogs and chickens with them. Kal and Trindal missed Laughs a Lot and the goats. At first, having the place to themselves had been a novelty, but now, seeing no other footprints in the snow but your own and hearing no evidence of another living being felt eerie and lonely. As they started the fire that night, Kal checked the briquettes and frowned at how few were left.

'Trin?' he said. 'Do you think we somehow missed school this week?'

Trindal shook his head.

'Nope. I've been listening for Miz Daviz's car. I'm gonna get my additions sticker this week.'

Kal sat back on his heels and shrugged.

'I guess it must be tomorrow. I'm sure she'd have told us if there was no school.'

Nemid rummaged in his pocket and pulled out the piece of paper, handing it to Kal. He read the note then grinned.

'Holidays?' he said. 'Oh, that explains it.'

He looked at his grandfather.

'It's alright Nedda, school holidays are a regular thing. I can't believe I forgot about them.'

'What's holidays?' Trindal said.

'It means we get to do whatever we want.'

Trindal turned towards Nemid hopefully.

'Can we?'

'Of course', Nemid said, 'provided what you want to do is help repair the roof on the storage shed. We will need to pound out a few more cans.'

Trindal groaned and rolled his eyes.

'How is it', Kal teased, 'that you can always read our minds?'

Nemid swatted Kal's leg and grinned. 'Cheeky brat.'

Kal laughed and ducked away. Nemid's gaze went to the briquette box then back to the paper in Kal's hand.

'So this holiday thing', he said, 'when does it end?'

Kal shrugged.

'It says the 28th of July. Does anyone know what today's date is?'

Both Nemid and Trindal shook their heads. Nemid's smile faded as a horrible thought struck him. Did this holiday thing mean they would have no cheques? They were totally dependent on the briquettes for warming the cabin and cooking. Nemid decided to put that thought to the back of his mind. He was probably wrong, and if he wasn't then … well, they were Nahill – they would manage.

Five days later, despite rationing everything, they had run out of briquettes, cardboard and paper and were back to partially cooked corn meal. The bottles of water remained frozen and the beans they put in to soak stayed hard. White frost appeared on the ceiling poles and went down the walls. The floorboards were also white with frost under the plastic rug. Their breath came out in white clouds. They had all slowed down, not having the energy to get on with their normal routines, preferring to stay snuggled up in their blankets day and night. Their faces became pinched, and despite spending long periods asleep, there were dark circles under their eyes.

There was nothing for it, Pac Nemid told the boys, but to endure. Soon, he said, they'd have their cheques, and all would be well again. Meanwhile, they would just have to conserve their strength as best they could. Even to himself, he was unconvinced as to how they would survive. He cursed the whites for not telling him that there were things called holidays. Their current predicament was entirely the fault of the whites. He would never trust them again! How were they to survive, he lamented? It didn't occur to him that, not so long ago, he had faced the exact same situation, except back then, he'd had a completely different outlook.

16

The mud-splattered four-wheel drive from the special education unit made its way speedily up the highway towards the mountains. The headlights pierced the dark and brooding sky. On either side of the road were banks of dirtied snow. Miss Davis was only half paying attention to the road as she listened to the news. On an impulse, she had done something, and now she was second guessing her instincts. She knew Kal had been reluctant to enrol in the distance education program, but he was so bright that … well, she'd filled out the forms for him and had sent them in. It had not been easy either. She'd stumbled from the beginning. First name of student: Kal. Surname: She had left that space blank and moved to the next question. Address of student: She had written White Camp, Mount Disappointment. Date of birth: She remembered Trindal saying Kal was 13 years old so had picked a month at random and written 1 June 1985. The question asking if the student was Jhunti, Aboriginal or Torres Strait Islander had also made her ponder. She just hoped he was accepted.

'And now for the weather', the announcer said. She dragged her attention back and turned the volume up. 'The low-pressure system that has been bringing all the snow is still with us and more heavy falls are expected today. Here in the city we can expect around four centimetres and another thirty centimetres for the high country.'

As if on cue, the first fat flakes of snow began to hit the windshield.

'It's going to drop to a chilly minus seven in the city tonight, so put that electric blanket on high', the announcer said. 'A new cold front is approaching, and there's a blizzard warning for the high country tomorrow. Temperatures are expected to drop to minus fifteen with wind speeds of sixty kilometres an hour and a wind chill factor of minus twenty. Thursday in the city, we can expect snowfalls of about four centimetres and a temperature of minus two, but there'll be white-out conditions in the high country. Next weather update in one hour.'

Miss Davis put the wipers on and glanced at the clock. She shook her head. She was going to be late again. Today was the first week back after her longer-than-usual break, and she had Kal and Trindal's lesson plans all worked out.

She turned off the highway and followed a single set of tyre tracks towards the mountains. The tracks were brown against the coating of white snow. As she drove around a sweeping bend, her car slid into the opposite lane. She frantically turned the wheel but did not jam on the breaks, knowing that would send her into a spin. Once back on the correct side of the road, she decreased her speed. Her heart was pounding, and her skin began to prickle with fear. Would she be able to make it up the mountain today? When she got to the group of shops at the base of Mount Disappointment, she pulled in, deciding she needed a strong coffee to steady her nerves before crawling up that terrifying mountain track. She'd just gotten out of her car when another car came to a slithering stop next to her and several members of Dog clan got out.

'Hello, Miz Daviz', Aunt Talks Too Much said with a grin. 'What a lucky chance that we found you.'

Miss Davis turned towards them, pulling her coat across her chest to keep the cold wind out. She had the distinct impression that they hadn't 'found' her, but had been waiting for her to arrive.

'Hello', she said. 'What're you doing here?'

'The road to camp is closed.'

'No way to get up the mountain', Uncle Mends Things said.

'We've come to get our cheques', Remmy said.

So, Miss Davis thought, the moment of truth had arrived. When she had done some investigating of the enrolment records, she had found that some of her 'students' had been attending school for twenty years. It was obvious the Nahill were scamming the department, but that placed her in a dilemma. If she told her supervisor the truth about how many students she really had, she'd be in trouble. The department was sure to blame *her* for attendance going from thirty-five to a handful. Either way, they would close down the school, and she would be out of a job. If there was an investigation into how long it had been going on, her supervisor would be fired for incompetence, and that would be the end of her getting a reference. The other scenario was that both she and her supervisor would be charged with embezzling the department. Now she knew why the other teachers had left so quickly. It was a great choice, either play along, kiss her teaching career goodbye or go to jail.

Aunt Talks Too Much put on her most winning smile. 'We've mainly come to get the children's homework, so everyone can keep studying even if the schoolroom itself is closed today.' She flashed her gold tooth. 'The rules are that as long as the children are doing their work, they get a cheque. You have prepared all their assignments, haven't you?'

Miss Davis swallowed heavily. She only had homework for a few of the children as most didn't stay. If she refused to hand over the cheques, she knew they'd complain about her not having prepared enough lessons, and she'd be in big trouble.

Maybe she should do what every other teacher had done – turn a blind eye to this scam and put in for a transfer. One of the men stepped forward.

'Do you have work for my daughter, Dopsil?' he said, holding out his hand.

Miss Davis gave him an appraising look. She had never seen him before and doubted his daughter even existed. She returned her attention to Aunt Talks Too Much.

'If the road's closed', she said, 'how did you get here?'

'We walked.'

Miss Davis shot a dubious glance towards their cars.

'We leave the cars down here for the winter', Aunt Talks Too Much said.

'We walk there and back', another said.

'No way anyone can take a car up there now', Aunt Talks Too Much said firmly. 'We are trying to help. Do you have the lessons for Laughs a Lot and the others?'

Miss Davis hesitated for only a moment before she reluctantly opened the back door and took out her briefcase. She pulled out some pages with names on the top and handed them over.

'I also have these for Trindal', she said, handing over two books, 'and these for Kal', she gave them a box of cassettes and some fresh batteries. 'This is for Lal.' She took out a picture book.

'And the cheques?' Uncle Mends Things said, peering inside the case.

Miss Davis stood undecidedly until Aunt Talks Too Much waved Kal's cassettes at her.

'You expect them to do their school work, don't you?' she said.

'So that means they get cheques', Uncle Mends Things said, holding out his hand.

Miss Davis changed feet, her boots squeaking in the snow as she contemplated the envelopes. It was one thing to hand over homework, but she should keep the cheques shouldn't she? Uncle Mends Things nudged his wife and gave her a 'do something!' look. The big, fat flakes came more thickly and obscured the surrounding bushland. Aunt Talks Too Much took a step back.

'We do not want to cause trouble', she said. 'I will tell Kal, Trindal and Nemid there is no school and no cheques until the road is open. Here', she made to hand back the homework.

Miss Davis didn't take it. She knew Kal and his family depended on this money but… did she trust that Kal would do his homework, she asked herself? Yes. Well, she reasoned, that was almost the equivalent of being at school for the day, wasn't it? Yes. So technically, was this exchange any different to a normal school day? With a sigh, she gave the wad of cheques to Uncle Mends Things.

'Thank you', he said.

'See you next week', Aunt Talks Too Much said.

She and the others all raced into Mrs Li's shop. Miss Davis stood for a moment longer feeling the snowflakes falling onto her hair and lashes. Numbly, she got back into her car and returned to her office in the city. By the time she got back, she was feeling guilty that she hadn't at least attempted the mountain. She made a vow that next week she'd definitely walk or drive up then made a cup of tea and settled down to begin work on next week's lesson plans for *everyone*.

Up the mountain in White Camp, the three remaining residents sat before a feeble fire. Icicles hung from the ceiling beams. The walls were coated in a white frosting of ice. When they had run out of food and wood, Nemid and the boys began ransacking the other cabins. They had started with Laughs a Lot's where they'd found small caches of both food and dry wood. Once these were exhausted, they broke into one Dog clan cabin after another. Most held only a few days' supply of wood and food but, as Nemid said, every day they stayed alive was another day they were closer to the thaw and salvation.

Tonight they were in Aunt Talks Too Much's cabin. After dining on baked beans and dry breakfast cereal, they were relaxing in front of a fire fuelled by pieces of her wooden furniture. Outside, the clear skies were littered with stars. Nemid knew it was going to be a very cold night. He glanced up and noticed new ice crystals forming on the ceiling. He tossed another chair leg into the fire.

'Time for bed', he yawned.

They pulled their thick blankets about themselves and settled down for the night as the temperature outside plummeted. Suddenly, a crack like a gunshot echoed through the still night air.

'What was that?' Kal cried as he sat bolt upright.

'Shhh', Nemid soothed, stroking the boy's hair, 'it's nothing to worry about. It's just a tree bough cracking. Snapping tree boughs are common on very cold nights.'

His reassurance seemed to make Kal even more wary.

'Over time', Nemid explained, 'the cracks and imperfections in wood fill with moisture. On nights like this the water freezes, expanding and shattering the wood of any trunks or branches that are diseased or weak. This is the time when nature does its big clean up. The cold gets rid of old boughs, and the melting snow and rain wash the debris away making the earth clean and ready for new things to grow.'

Reassured by this explanation, Kal lay down and went back to sleep. Nemid lay down and pulled his blanket closer, wishing they'd brought their woven plastic mat with them as the floor boards were freezing beneath them. He made a mental note to fetch it tomorrow. He resumed his silent deliberations. He was already recognising the warning signs of exposure in all of them, the sallow skin, the dark circles under the eyes and a deep weariness that made even the simplest of tasks feel like a major effort. He wondered what his chances were of going down the mountain and into the white world to seek help. A slight smile crossed his lips at this folly. Even if they had the strength for such a journey, the whites would like nothing better than to watch them all freeze to death.

He glanced at the dying fire and wondered if he should throw more wood on it to see them through the night. It seemed such a waste when they were in their blankets. He sighed and did nothing. Even with their strict rationing, he was unsure if they would freeze to death or starve to death first. Nemid again debated returning to Red Camp, but in good weather, the journey took a few days. Who knew how long it would take now. There was a reason people didn't travel during the snow season. If you were caught outside in these conditions, you would die. Breathing in the very air itself could permanently damage your throat and lungs. Besides, he mused, they'd all lost so much weight, they had no fat supplies to call on. All of them were desperate for the fatty salmon steaks and fish relish that was a Nahill staple in the snow seasons. Again, he cursed himself for not bringing more supplies.

He closed his eyes and tried to sleep, but his thoughts refused to stop battering his mind. He had to think. There must be an option he was overlooking. They had tried burning the boards from the houses around them, but the smoke had been so acrid and foul smelling, it had made them cough and become sick. It was the same for the wood from the food storage barrels. They'd burnt everything they could find in the school room, including the books, posters and furniture. Beside him, Trindal coughed. Nemid put his arms around the boy and hugged him close.

Feeling the first tendrils of panic weaving their way through him, Nemid tried to calm his mind by thinking of other things such as why Water clan had forsaken this place? What had happened here? The previous few nights his dreams had been haunted by images of that last Healer sitting alone in her cabin. He wondered how long ago she'd died. What was her name? Would anyone know? Had all her companions died first? Had she elected to stay behind or been deliberately left here to die? Had she meant to leave but then been snowed in unexpectedly? He wondered what her last days were like. Had they been like this? Had she lain here waiting for death? Had she starved or frozen to death? Had she beseeched the Great Spirits in vain for someone to come and save her like he was doing now to save his own family? They had all become so weak, he thought wearily, perhaps there was nothing for it but to endure. It was the Nahill way.

Every week, there was a new excuse as to why Aunt Talks Too Much had not brought the children's completed homework. Eventually Miss Davis realised she was never going to get any of the homework back, so they struck a new bargain. Miss Davis would only come every second week. With time on her hands, she continued her investigation into Kal. She went to the local library and went through the newspaper archives looking for any stories about lost or missing children. Over coffee one morning, she showed what she'd found to her friend, Tricia, a fellow teacher.

'There you are', Karen said, 'that's how many boys have gone missing in Australia in the last thirteen years.'

Tricia ran her eyes down the list.

'Well' Karen qualified, 'boys with green eyes.'

She took the list from Tricia and pointed to the top name.

'This boy', she said, 'Caleb Willard looks a lot like my Kal. He disappeared from a caravan park in Brisbane in January. Even though Kal's smart, I can't see him getting all the way down here *and* learning fluent Nahill in just a few months.'

Tricia studied the other names and descriptions. She tapped another boy's name.

'This one, Christopher Daniels, was reported missing three years ago.'

Karen nodded.

'Yes, I thought he was a possibility.' She stared down at the news story photo of the distraught grandparents and the flushed face of the boy's father, Barry Daniels. 'I'd love to tell them he's here safe and sound, but look where Christopher's from – Chador's Crossing. That's on the other side of the country in the wheat belt. I looked it up', she smirked at her friend. 'If Kal is Christopher Daniels, he's travelled over eight hundred kilometres. What eleven-year-old does that?'

'Good point.'

As Karen and Tricia continued down the list, they discussed each boy and Karen explained to her friend why she had discounted each one. Tricia sat back in her chair, a thoughtful frown on her face.

'Maybe he's not missing', Tricia said.

Karen's mind ran over possibilities. Was Kal Nemid's biological child? Had Kal's parents died hiking or skiing in the adjacent national park or been killed in a car crash? Had they been so poor, they abandoned him, or were they drug addicts who'd traded him for money? Maybe they had just given him to the Jhunti? Maybe they were gamblers, and Kal had been left as payment for their debt?

'Maybe', Tricia said, dragging Karen's mind back from her reveries, 'his family were victims of that murderer Ivan Milat and Kal escaped?'

'Maybe', she said thoughtfully.

'Do you think the Jhunti bought him to work as child slave labour?'

Karen sipped her coffee.

'I wonder', she said slowly, 'if the Jhunti allow children to be traded, adopted or fostered from one family to another?'

'In some cultures, that's common practice', Tricia said. 'Is it possible that Kal has been living with them his whole life?'

Perhaps, Karen thought, this's all a mare's nest. Perhaps there was no mystery here, just a boy being raised by his grandfather.

'What do your instincts say?' Tricia said.

Karen was silent as she remembered the time Trindal had scolded Kal for speaking of a dead person. In her gut, she just knew he'd been to a white school up to at least year six. She put her cup down.

'No, I don't think so. There have been too many instances where he seems new to Jhunti life.'

She stared out the window. It was almost dark outside even though it was only 3:30 pm. Thick snow was being thrown against the panes by the latest storm.

'I have a feeling he's afraid of something', she said and brought her gaze back to Tricia.

A look of understanding ran between them.

'You know what?' Tricia said. 'I think we need help. Do you remember Joyce? Her mother is a whiz at family history and knows all these people in the historical society. If anyone knows how to track down a missing person, it is them.'

'I'll take all the help I can get.'

'Let's start with another coffee', Tricia said, signalling to the waitress.

Karen's eyes returned to the snowstorm raging outside. She wondered how Kal and Trindal were getting on. She'd included a few fiction books in the last pack she'd given to Aunt Talks Too Much and imagined them sitting in front of a warm fire, Kal reading to everyone. She wished she were with them, spending all winter snug and warm in front of a roaring fire looking out at that beautiful vista.

Over at Red Camp, Ashekii's guilt had been at him night and day. Nemid had not taken enough food to last the whole snow season as all had assumed there would be ample supplies at the camp. When they'd discovered the truth, Ashekii had promised to make one last trip before the snows set in with a car full of food. He'd meant to do it right away but had been waylaid, and then that first savage blizzard had come followed by days of heavy snow, which made it impossible to go anywhere by car. One part of Ashekii's brain told him it was too late and that Nemid was sensible and resourceful and would be fine. Still his conscience nagged at him. Even though he knew it was hopeless, every morning and night, he searched the skies, wishing for a break in the weather.

One night sitting with the others in the meeting hall as the snow came down, he listened to a story handed down from the ancient ones about monsters who lived in the deep waters. The original story was a cautionary tale not to annoy the whales, orcas and sharks and to show respect to the other large creatures of the ocean. But the true meaning had been lost in time, and the Nahill version interpreted the 'deep water' as referring to the lake, so the story was now a reminder to stay away from the lake so as not to be eaten by the monsters that lived there. The only ones who were immune from the monsters were Fish clan because of their alliance with all things that swam. As Ashekii listened, an idea suddenly struck him. Perhaps he could convince someone from Fish clan to take him over to White Camp in a boat. Yes, he thought, that was the perfect solution.

One sunny but freezing afternoon at White Camp, Nemid and the boys managed to find a clump of tubers and were digging away feverishly, their mouths watering at the thought of the succulent treat. In the last two days, they'd eaten only a handful of frozen grubs they'd managed to scrape out of a decaying log. So intent were the three of them on digging, they did not hear Ashekii approach until he was almost upon them.

'Surprise!' he beamed.

They all turned and their eyes widened in delight. Ashekii grinned at them, his eyes bright and his nose red from the cold. He wore a large pack on his back and was dragging a small sled with two sacks on it. Nemid dropped his scraping tool and strode over to his cousin with his arms out wide.

'It's so good to see this face.'

They hugged, and Ashekii felt how thin the older man was through his bulky clothes. The boys crowded around him.

'Where'd you come from? How did you get here?'

Ashekii hugged them all to him. The boys were nothing but skin and bone. When he pulled back, he noticed Nemid hastily wiping the tears from his eyes.

'Where is your car?' Nemid said eagerly.

He was going to admit Ashekii had been right and beg him to take them back to Red Camp. He couldn't wait to leave this accursed place. Dog clan could have it and it could rot for all he cared. Ashekii shook his head, looking very pleased with himself.

'No car would make it in this weather. After a bit of barter, I persuaded Fish clan to bring me here in a boat.'

Nemid's face paled.

'You went on the lake?'

'Yes. I couldn't believe how quickly we got here!'

Nemid's heart sank as his grand plan for escape disappeared. He would never risk taking his precious boys out onto that lake. It would kill them all. As if reading his mind, Ashekii put a hand onto Nemid's shoulder and gave it a reassuring squeeze.

'On days like this with no wind, the waters are flat. The crossing is easy and perfectly safe.'

What a wonderful choice, Nemid mused. We can die from starvation, freeze to death or drown. He shook his head.

'As Pac I must welcome and thank Fish clan', he glanced in the direction Ashekii had come with dread. They had visitors, and there was no food or warming fire to be had. This was going to be a very humiliating day for the Pac of White Camp.

'They've gone', Ashekii said. 'There is only so much room in the boat', he indicated his pack and the bags and the sled. 'Provided the weather holds, they will be back tomorrow with the rest of the supplies and to take me back. I hope you don't mind such a fleeting visit.'

Nemid brightened at both these pieces of news.

'Not at all, not at all', he said.

Trindal pulled at Ashekii's pack.

'What've you got in there?' he said, his eyes shining in anticipation.

'Is it food?' Kal said eagerly. 'Our last meal was frozen bugs!'

Ashekii shot them a sceptical look then cocked his head towards the camp.

'How about we go to your cabin so I can unload?' Ashekii said.

With that, he turned and walked up the hill towards the camp. He handed the boys the rope so they could pull the sled along. Nemid watched them, torn between staying and going. The tubers were almost out. A little bit longer and he'd have them. But if he left, they would be dug up and eaten by animals just as hungry as he and the boys. His glance went to Ashekii's retreating form. His stomach gurgled hungrily. Licking his lips, Nemid reluctantly gathered up their digging tools and followed the others.

When they entered the cabin, Ashekii was immediately struck by the heavy white frost glistening on the walls and the icicles hanging from the ceiling. His breath came out in white clouds. He wondered how the cabin had become so cold so quickly, but then decided they must have allowed the fire to go out last night and left early this morning. Trindal went to the fireplace and began to gather some of their precious tinder to start a fire. Ashekii unslung the pack from his shoulders and glanced around. Everywhere he looked were piles of dogfood sacks, glass and plastic bottles, and rising above it all were towering stacks of flattened beer cans. Nemid came in and shut the door.

'Please, sit.'

He indicated an old tyre, which he'd made into a seat by filling the middle with a dry dog food sack stuffed with shredded plastic. Ashekii sat down, pulling his pack towards him.

'I have brought the Pac of White Camp a gift', he said and pulled a large earthenware jar of salmon paste from his pack.

'Yayyy', both boys cheered.

Kal reached for the delicacy eagerly. Ashekii handed the jar and a small bag of fresh meat rolls to Kal. Kal took them with a little bow. Knowing this was the only food in the house, Kal surreptitiously took out a meat roll and offered it to Ashekii.

'Please accept this as a token of our gratitude for your visit', he said and bowed again.

Ashekii took the roll.

'The honour is mine', he said, pleased that the boy was learning some manners at last. 'How have you been cousin?' he said to Nemid.

Nemid gave him a slight smile. 'Until we are self-sufficient, we make do. What do you think of my roofing tiles?'

Ashekii studied the stacks of flattened tin cans.

'You've been busy', he said.

'Yes. Boys, show him your new clothes.'

Trindal went to one corner of the room and held up a new coat made from woven plastic strips and goat hair. Ashekii raised an eyebrow.

'Is that comfortable?'

Trindal shrugged, not wanting to admit that it was the most uncomfortable, noisiest, scratchiest thing he'd ever worn. It had no give whatsoever and made him sweat. When Nemid wasn't looking, he and Kal used their new coats as toboggans. Nemid took up a strand of shredded plastic and began weaving. 'I'm making them pants', Nemid said, indicating his work.

Ashekii noticed the look of dread on the boy's faces.

'What news from Red Camp?' Nemid said, his fingers deftly moving back and forth.

For a short time, Ashekii talked of the births at the camp. Neither

Kal nor Trindal recognised the families that he spoke of. Then he talked of the deaths. One man had died because he'd been caught out in a blizzard, another had fallen down a hill and several old timers had also passed. A number of newborns had not survived the freezing temperatures, two women had died in childbirth and several children had been taken by the river.

Ashekii fell silent as his throat was dry from his journey. He had been waiting for them to offer tea, but the blackened kettle remained sitting coldly to one side. He rubbed his cold fingers against his legs and glanced at the feeble fire.

'Shall I throw on a few logs?' he offered.

'We don't have any', Trindal said.

Nemid was embarrassed that he appeared so impoverished before his cousin. Buoyed by the promise of food arriving tomorrow, he determined to put on a good face. He moved his weaving aside.

'Please excuse me for a moment', he said.

With an effort, he heaved himself up and hobbled out the door. Ashekii frowned after him. Once the door was shut, he looked back at the boys.

'Why does he limp?'

'He spends a lot of time weaving', Kal said.

All eyes went to the mess of shredded plastic.

'He certainly seems fond of that stuff', Ashekii said.

'Before that it was cans', Trindal said, indicating the stacks.

'And before that it was tins', Kal said, pointing at the myriad of items made from tins.

'We think…', Trindal began then stopped.

He glanced fleetingly at Kal.

'We think Nedda's gone crazy', Kal finished for him.

'Why d'you say that?' Ashekii said.

Kal opened his mouth just as the door opened.

'Here we are', Nemid said hobbling over to the fire with an armload of sticks.

Kal and Trindal's eyes widened. That was all the kindling they had. He dropped them to one side and casually tossed a few of the bigger pieces on before slowly settling and resuming his weaving.

'Nedda?' Kal said. 'Tell Ashe about your plans for white garbage.'

Nemid smiled, and a fanaticism came into his expression.

'As you can see', he said to Ashekii, 'we have done very well from the bounty that the whites discard. I think we should ask the whites to give us all their garbage, and we shall use it to make many useful things. With what they throw out, we will all have everything we need, and at the same time, save this from being buried inside the body of our mother.'

'I see.'

Ashekii gave his cousin a measured look, and it suddenly dawned on him what was wrong. Nemid and the two boys had been left on their own in this cabin during the time when Nahill were at their most social. Snow season was when, as a community, they helped each other to get through the brutally cold long nights, the frightening blizzards and the interminable boredom of forced inactivity. He'd once heard of a man caught up in the mountains through the snows who'd become convinced he could make a pair of shoes for himself out of a kangaroo bone.

'Here', he said, going to the fire, 'let me make some bread to go with this fish paste.' He opened one of his sacks and took out several handfuls of corn, then began to grind it. At the same time, his mind whirred as he tried to work out a way to persuade Nemid to come with him back to Red Camp. He tipped the flour into a bowl and added some water. 'What about a story while I'm doing this, Trin?'

'Which one?'

'How about … where children come from. The tale of Archia and Ves?'

'Yes, that's a good one.' Trindal's voice changed slightly to the sing song voice of the storyteller. 'A long time ago', he said, 'Archia and Ves, two of the Great Spirits, were engaged in an argument. Ves thought once a being had led a good life, they would be ready to die while Archia thought that given the choice, everyone would want to live forever. The argument lasted for several eons until the other Great Spirits could stand it no longer. They said they had to find out once and for all, so Ves and Archia gathered up dust and created people to settle their argument, intending to return them to dust when they had their answer. All the Great Spirits then created the Earth and put people upon it. The people learned to speak and walk and explored their world. The Great Spirits were enchanted with the little creatures and watched them avidly as one might a fish in a pond. Meanwhile, Archia and Ves began a new argument over which of them was to present their case first. Deciding this took a long time. Eventually Archia and Ves agreed and called all the People of the Earth to them. Once they were sitting before them, Archia presented his argument as to why he thought, given the choice, they would choose to be immortal.

'You would be able to solve all the mysteries you encounter', he said, 'you could love forever. Just think of how well you could hone your skills. You would never get old, and your bodies would never wear out. There would be only beauty and no suffering or hunger, pain or sickness.'

Trindal continued. 'The People of the Earth turned their eyes towards Ves.

'However', Ves said, 'being immortal would mean that there would only ever be a set number of you created, otherwise the world would be overrun.'

'But this means', Archia said, 'that everyone would know each other and never feel alone', he finished with a smile.

'However…', Ves said.

She presented her argument as to why she thought, given the choice, they would choose to be mortal. She said that mortals would be able to experience the wonder of birth, the delight of eating sweet berries, the bliss of falling asleep and the joy of dreaming.

'You would also feel pain and suffer illness', Archia said.

'And the relief of getting better.'

'But', Archia said, 'a mortal life would be filled with uncertainty.'

'And variety gives everyday events meaning', Ves said.

She continued to explain that, if mortal, people would understand the need to get things done in a timely fashion as there wouldn't always be a tomorrow. They'd experience the different stages of life from birth to wisdom then the surety of dying after a life well spent. She said that when they died, their bodies would return to the earth to nourish her, and their souls would be called home to the garden of the Great Spirits. With new people being born all the time, there would always be new and interesting people to meet during their lives.

The Great Spirits looked at each other to make sure the arguments were finished. Then they turned towards the people.

'Now tell us', Archia said eagerly, 'which would you prefer? To be mortal or to live forever?'

The People of the Earth went away to discuss it, and after a long, long time, they came back and said they wanted to be allowed to die. Ves could hardly keep the smugness from her smile, but Archia was flabbergasted.

'But why?' Archia said.

The People of the Earth told him that they loved the world that the Great Spirits had created for them and wanted to give back to her. They also said that they wanted to have children as they believed that to live wisely they would need the perspective of children.

Archia would have sent them back for another think, but the other Great Spirits intervened. They said Archia had the answer to his question, and it was time for the People of the Earth to be returned to the dust from which they were made. However, Ves was so taken with these children she and Archia had created, she persuaded the others to let her keep them. And so the People of the Earth were given the Earth and charged with caring for it and all the other creatures that now inhabited it to live happily together.'

Trindal shifted in his seat.

'The lesson of this story', he said, 'is that creation does not occur from nothingness; it necessitates the destruction of that which came before. Just like in the forest, new life feeds on death. It is the cycle that we agree to every time we eat something. We are the People of the Earth. We chose to be mortal.'

Ashekii finished making the bread and handed servings around to everyone with lashings of fish paste and pumpkin relish. They ate it greedily. Ashekii glanced at the feeble fire then at the frost on the walls of the cabin and suddenly realised they needed his help. He understood his cousin was afraid of the lake, but he would not take no for an answer, even if he had to physically drag the old coot into the boat.

'I don't suppose', Ashekii said, 'that I could persuade you to come back with me?'

To the children's surprise, Nemid shook his head.

'We have too much to do here, but thank you for asking.'

Kal and Trindal bit back their disappointment. They would never contradict their grandfather. Ashekii seemed to take this refusal well, and they talked of small things. As the night progressed, he mentioned that resentment towards Dog clan was at an all-time high once Gleris had told everyone the Pac's cabin had been used for goats.

'When they heard of the disarray in which you found the place', Ashekii said, shaking his head.

'It is nothing that cannot be repaired', Nemid said.

'Expect an influx after the thaw', Ashekii said.

We may be dead by then, Nemid mused morbidly. At least with these fresh supplies we will no longer starve, but there is a good chance we may freeze with the worst blizzards still to come. But he'd take his chances of freezing against the very real probability of drowning. The lake was to claim no more of his children. An ache went through his heart, and he lowered his gaze. Ashekii could see exactly what was going through Nemid's mind and searched desperately for something that would make him change his mind.

'Others will accompany Gleris', he said casually. 'It's just a shame she is the one who is making the decisions on who can come.'

Suddenly he had Nemid's attention, and he looked up from his reveries.

'She's doing what?' Nemid said indignantly.

'She's choosing who comes', Ashekii said with an air of nonchalance that Nemid found irritating. 'I mean, it makes sense. She's the only one who has seen this place first hand, apart from the three of you that is. What a shame you will not be there.'

'You have seen it. Why can't you be the one to choose?' Nemid said.

Ashekii held up both hands in surrender.

'I'm not dragging the Drekesh into this.'

Ashekii left that to sink in as he gave the boys another helping of bread and toppings. Nemid's jaw tightened. He snatched up his weaving again, muttering softly to himself.

Ashekii kept his expression impassive as he continued. 'You have no idea how popular she has become. Everyone wanting a fresh start is courting her favour.'

He sat back onto his tyre and wiped his hands on his pants. He yawned and leant against the wall. A biting cold shot through his shoulder from the frost. He leant forward again and picked the grit from between his teeth.

'I suppose as Pac you will be able to refuse any unsuitable transplants when they arrive. Still, after a trek like that...' he didn't finish the sentence.

Both knew Nemid would be extremely unpopular if, after traveling all that way, he told people to go home. Nemid knew just who she'd pick first, those worthless cousins of hers. They were selfish and lazy to the bone and didn't get on with anyone. While Red Camp would be overjoyed to see the back of them, Nemid didn't want them here either.

'She has no right to choose', Nemid said firmly.

Seeing that the spark had hit home, Ashekii silently congratulated himself. He stretched and yawned.

'Time for bed, I think', he said.

Nemid shook his head, suddenly dreading the thaw and the influx of new people.

'Can someone point me towards my mattress?' Ashekii said.

'We burnt them all', Kal said, 'but we have these.'

Kal guided him over to the pile of shredded plastic that served as their mattress.

'We pull this over us', he said, lifting the large thick plastic blanket. 'Trin usually takes the middle as he feels the cold worst.'

'I do not!' Trindal protested.

'You do too!' Kal shot back then returned his attention to Ashekii. 'Just ignore him. Ever since the goats left, he's been a total baby.'

'Goats?'

Kal nodded and explained where the goats used to sleep and how they'd been warm as anything snuggled up next to them.

'And where are the goats now?' Ashekii said.

'Dog clan took them', Trindal said. 'They took everything.'

He and Kal then explained how they'd moved from cabin to cabin, burning everything and eating all the reserve supplies.

'We even went to the cabin of the last Healer', Trindal said.

Ashekii turned towards Nemid.

'The last Healer?'

Nemid explained about the scattered bones and the tribal sticks being burnt by Laughs a Lot. Ashekii crossed his arms over his chest as he shook his head.

'Is there no end to Dog clan's pettiness? Feelings will run high when Council hears of this', and he gave Nemid a pointed look.

'The boy is simple', Nemid said, 'he did not know what he was doing.'

'Sadly, that is not how others will see it.'

'Then do not tell them.'

'I don't plan to, but when the others get here, I'm sure the story will come out.' Ashekii paused to let that sink in then, as if speaking to himself, he continued. 'Of course, with insults like that needing to be addressed, it would be very easy to interest some of our best Drekesh to relocate.' Ashekii made sure to keep his expression neutral as he continued. 'You know there isn't a lot for most of us to do at Red Camp. To come here and put things right would be the opportunity of a lifetime.' He nodded to himself. 'I had better mention this to Gleris.'

Nemid was ripping plastic into shreds with fervour. That Gleris was a fool, and he knew full well that she was not up to this job, but Ashekii was right, it was not Ashekii's place to choose who was to come. That job belonged to the Council or, better still, the Pac of

White Camp. Nemid thought of the lake and felt a chill of fear run through him but … it was his duty.

Leaving his words to do their work, Ashekii shoved the bedding around before lying down. He was struck by the smell of goat manure, mould and mildew that permeated everything and was glad he was only staying one night. The boys curled up beside him and, as they pulled the blanket over, Ashekii raised his head to look at his cousin.

'Coming to bed?'

'No. I want to finish this.'

Nemid made a show of adjusting his weaving. With a smug smile, Ashekii resettled himself and was soon asleep. They all awoke in the morning to find Nemid bustling about the cabin, packing their few possessions and making everything secure.

'We shall leave when Fish clan comes', he said.

And just like that, Ashekii had three house guests for the rest of the snow season.

The only sound was the squeaking of feet trudging through the fresh snow. Chani tried to place her feet into the same footprints of the Healer in front of her. Her breath came out in white clouds, and the chill wind made her pull her heavy cloak more tightly about her.

They were on their way back to camp after attending a birth at one of the outlying villages. The baby had been stillborn, and it had left many questions in Chani's mind, questions put there by her conversation long ago with Nemid, questions that she'd completely forgotten about until now. She found herself thinking of her father and the boys. She hadn't realised how much she would miss them. Nemid had always just been there and now that he wasn't, there was an ache inside her that nothing seemed to fill. She didn't dare tell anyone else as the other Healers had such a low opinion of males. They would not be able to fathom how she could not only miss them but find that she was unable to replace their company with that of women and her young Healer friends.

The line reached a small copse of trees that provided some shelter from the wind. 'Let's rest here', said Healer Mirash.

They brushed the snow from a gnarly tree and sat down, lowering their packs to the ground. A crow cried out in the distance. Healer Mirash waved. 'We are well and need nothing', she called out to it.

The crow took off. Both it and the Healers knew it was going to tell the Great Spirits of their progress. Healer Mirash glanced at the girl and noticed the concentration in her expression. Healer Mirash had heard stories about Chani, that she asked a lot of odd questions, questions that sometimes made people uncomfortable. She didn't understand how that could be as all apprentices asked questions; it was part of learning. She'd also noticed that Chani didn't mix well with the other young ones. It was nothing anyone could put their finger on, and when she'd asked why, the other girls admitted that Chani was 'a bit weird' but had not been able to explain why. It was why Healer Mirash had asked for Chani to accompany her on this visit. She wanted to observe the girl more closely and get to know her better.

'Questions?' she said.

Chani looked at her mentor.

'Will that baby go to the garden?'

'Of course. Everyone does.'

'But it doesn't have a name, and it wasn't alive. Will it be just a body up there like it was down here?'

Healer Mirash thought for a moment before replying.

'We are not just bodies. We are also spirits. What happened to that baby was that something caused its spirit to leave. It is something we must be mindful of. It could have been that the baby spirit changed its mind or that the Great Spirits called it back. It could have been frightened away, for instance, if there were too many men around as birthing is women's business. It might be that the baby spirit didn't like the family or that someone put a curse on the family that stopped the baby spirit from bonding with the body the mother had prepared. That is why we placed the amulets around the house, but really, it was too late to call us in. They should have asked us to come much earlier. If they had, perhaps things would have turned out differently. You know everyone goes to the garden.'

'But how can everyone fit in there?' Chani said. 'How will we all know each other? If we die with an injury or like that baby, are we trapped inside a broken body forever? And what about white people? Do they go there too?' Chani stared at Healer Mirash and saw that the older Healer was taken aback.

'Why do you ask such questions?'

'Doesn't everyone wonder about these things?'

Healer Mirash was about to say no then thought better of it.

'What's really on your mind?' she said.

'I have a friend', Chani continued. 'Have you heard of Kal?'

Healer Mirash nodded, turning so Chani didn't see her grimace of distaste.

'I was wondering', Chani continued, 'what would happen if he died? Would we meet in the garden? And if so, how would we recognise each other with so many people up there? And if he doesn't go to the garden, where would he go? Will I be able to visit him? I'd be really sad if I couldn't.'

Healer Mirash had heard enough. Everyone was right about this girl. Her thinking was completely wrong about everything! This was what happened when you let men have access to a Healer child. She'd have a lot to say to Healer Deikter when they returned to Healer Camp. Perhaps the best solution for all of them was to grant the request for Chani and Deikter to go to White Camp. At least that way, Chani and her questions would be away from the rest of the impressionable Healer girls. Healer Mirash stood up and shouldered her pack.

'Time to go', she said. 'If we hurry, we can be home before nightfall.' With that, she walked off and set such a cracking pace that Chani had no breath to ask more questions.

17

Every day during their stay at Red Camp, Ashekii found a way to spend time alone with Kal. In the morning, they would practice combat lessons, and in the afternoon, Kal would do his exercises. One day, as Ashekii showed Kal a new throw, he looked up to find Trindal watching them.

'What are you doing here?' Ashekii said.

'I want to learn too', he said. 'Kal isn't the only one Mash picks on.'

From that moment on, they practiced together.

Meantime, Pac Nemid was in great demand. He was dragged from cabin to cabin where people asked him about his time away, whetting many appetites with stories of reclaiming White Camp.

A few mornings later Kal and Trindal were told that Chani was back, and both raced over to see her, keen to tell her of their adventures. Trindal wanted to tell her about driving in a car and seeing picture books and learning to read and going to school and talking with a white lady and eating white people's food. Kal wanted to tell her about the goats and Laughs a Lot and about Dog clan and that it was true that they were thieves and liars just like everyone said. They stomped up the stairs to her cabin then knocked.

'Yes?' she called.

'Guess who', Kal teased.

With a little scream, Chani ran toward the door and threw it open.

'You're back!' she cried.

Chani gave Kal a huge bear hug. He laughed and hugged her back. Her arm snaked out and encircled Trindal too, and the three of them laughed and jumped up and down as they held each other.

'What're you doing here?' she cried. 'How long are you here for? Would you like something to eat? You're not sick, are you?'

Kal laughed. 'One question at a time Cha', he said. 'How about letting go of Bean Pole, so he lets go of me?'

Chani's cheeks coloured, and she gave Trindal a final squeeze and let them both go. They sat on the floor in front of the fire.

'Would you like a drink of something?' she said, and without waiting for an answer, fussed about them and made them herbal tea, handing each a cup and taking one for herself. The three stared at each other in silence then laughed again. Chani went into the other room and returned with a half-made rug and a bag filled with balls of plaited yarn.

'Here', she said, 'you can help me with this. I'm making it for you anyway. Ash told me you needed one.'

She dropped the rug onto the floor and handed them both fat needles made from Echidna spines.

'It's easy', she said. 'All you do is shove some yarn through the end of the needle like this', she demonstrated, 'then just sew along the edge like this', she poked her needle through one of the edges then pulled the yarn through, knotting it at the end.

The boys both threaded their needles, and each took a corner and began to sew. She watched them as they did their first row.

'That's great. Now go back the way you came', she said.

Satisfied, she returned to her own row.

'Tell me all about White Camp', she said, her eyes shining.

'It's really pretty there', Kal said. 'There's a huge orchard and a really big field.'

He then went on to describe how he'd helped prune the apple trees with a knife made from bottle caps and about the goats and meeting Laughs a Lot.

'Who's Laughs a Lot?'

'Dog clan.'

Chani made a face.

'Lal's OK', Kal said.

'And guess what?' Trindal said excitedly. 'We came back in a boat!'

Her eyes widened, suddenly afraid that they'd taken such a chance.

'We were respectful', Trindal reassured her. 'We hid our eyes and didn't look into the water.'

'The lake's real close, so when it's hot, we can go swimming', Kal said, 'only I can't swim. Can you?'

'What's swimming?' Trindal said.

Kal opened his mouth to try to describe it. Instead, he laughed and shook his head.

'It doesn't matter. It's a white thing.'

'I've been going to school', Trindal said proudly.

He went on to describe stickers and books and maps and lollies and sausages and all the other wonders from the white world that he'd encountered since leaving Red Camp. Chani listened with rapt attention, her eyes shining.

'I can't wait to go to school and to read and write.'

Trindal held up his needle.

'I'm out of yarn. Now what?'

Chani went over to his side, tied that piece off then gave him a new ball. He rethreaded his needle and continued.

'So where did you go?' Kal said.

Chani explained about being called out for the stillbirth. She frowned then decided to unburden herself. She told them about her questions to the older Healer about why people died and where they went afterwards.

'What did Healer Mirash say?' Trindal said.

Chani let out a frustrated breath. 'That's just it, she didn't.'

'Grandfather always says', Kal said, 'that there is a difference between beliefs and facts. He says we might not know all the facts and that's OK.'

Trindal nodded.

'Yeah, he's big on that. He says it's always good to question beliefs, even if it is just in our own heads.'

Chani was thoughtful for a short time then looked at Kal.

'According to white legends, what happens to people when they die?'

Kal shrugged.

'I don't know. I mean, most of the time we're trying to work out how they died. Like they'll say this guy died of a heart attack or that person died from falling down and breaking his neck. I guess you'd need to speak with a priest or something about the why part. Got anything to eat?'

Chani bit back her annoyance. She'd been all ready to have a long discussion about this, but neither Kal nor Trindal seemed in the least bit interested.

'Boys are always hungry', Chani muttered, tossing a ball of yarn at Kal before standing up and going to make them some food.

One day the icicles dripped and slid from the roof and trees into the snow drifts. The snow itself softened, and patches of brown dirt appeared. Green grass peeked out. Slowly, the forest came alive. Birds chittered morning and night, and everywhere new growth poked through the thinning snow drifts. Footsteps squished in moist earth. Outside, the smell of new life was everywhere. It felt good to be able to walk around without having to wear thick layers of clothing.

Down at the salmon stream, Kal laughed and couldn't believe how much he was enjoying himself. Ashekii examined Kal's fishing spear. It was about six feet long and had multiple prongs made from sharpened kangaroo bones. Ashekii showed him how to hold it before they both walked out into the stream. The water only came up to Kal's shins, but it was very cold. Ashekii positioned Kal so the fish would approach them with the sun in their eyes. He corrected Kal's posture and grip several times, making sure Kal held the spear at a 45-degree angle to reduce glare. He demonstrated how, if Kal stabbed at the apparent location of the fish, he would miss. He indicated that Kal must aim just ahead of the fish to adjust for water refraction. Both stood still, their eyes darting over the sun-glittered water as they watched for the tell-tale dark shadow of an approaching fish. Kal drew his spear back and threw. The men cheered as he held up his first salmon, his grin so wide, his cheeks hurt.

All the snow had melted, and the early morning light sparkled off a trail of blood. Kal watched as Ashekii ran his sharp knife back and forth separating the flesh from the hide of the dead wallaby.

'You try', Ashekii said.

Kal squatted and took out his hunting knife, which he handled with more dexterity now that he'd grown a bit and was much stronger. Grabbing the skin with one hand, he was about to slice when Ashekii stopped him.

'Not like that. This way.'

His blood-stained fingers went over Kal's as he gently angled Kal's hand so that he was holding the blade parallel to the flesh instead of at a right angle to it.

'Go gently at first', he instructed.

He ran the knife blade along the flesh, and Kal could feel it give way beneath the blade.

'Good', Ashekii said. 'Proceed.'

The boy continued to slice along the skin line. Ashekii smiled in approval, and Kal glowed under his gaze. Once Kal had cut the various pieces of meat from the animal and placed them onto a separate nest of branches, Ashekii showed him how to clean his blade and how to sharpen the knife.

'Always remember', Ashekii said as he watched Kal draw the blade carefully along the sharpening stone. 'Long, straight strokes. Better. Test your blade now.'

Kal sliced a blade of grass as he'd seen Ashekii do.

'Very good', Ashekii smiled and gave Kal an approving pat on the shoulder.

Kal's cheeks flushed at the praise.

'Can I ask something?' Kal said.

'A question from you?'

'Sorry.'

Kal ducked his head self-consciously. Ashekii raised his foot to give Kal a playful nudge. The boy instantly skittered away, his knife falling to the ground as his hands went up to protect his head. Ashekii stood and put his hands on his hips. He let out a frustrated breath.

'You think I'm going to kick you for asking questions?' he said heatedly.

'I shouldn't have said anything. I'm sorry.' Kal's heart was racing. He'd made Ashekii angry with his ridiculous questions. This was just like with his father. 'I'm sorry.'

Ashekii let out an infuriated cry, and Kal steeled himself, waiting for the beating he was sure was coming.

'No!' Ashekii said. 'I will not have this!'

He grabbed Kal by the arm and dragged him to his feet.

'Stand up', Ashekii said and shook him. 'Stand up like a man. No more whimpering like a dog! Head up, shoulders back.'

He made Kal stand straight, his corrections leaving bloody hand prints on the boy's sweating skin and clothes.

'Now look me in the eyes', Ashekii said. 'Look at me!'

Kal summoned every ounce of his courage and looked up to meet the warrior's fierce gaze.

'Better', Ashekii said. 'Now listen to me. Asking questions is how we learn. You will become an adult no matter what you do, but if you don't ask questions, you will be a foolish, ignorant man. You don't want to be a foolish, ignorant man, do you?'

Kal slowly shook his head.

'Good. Then from now on, remember that each question is a step on your journey to becoming a wise man. Understand?'

Kal nodded.

'Speak!' Ashekii snapped.

'Yes, honoured Drekesh.'

'Ask smart questions, and people will think you are smart.

Understand?' Ashekii paced as he warmed to his topic. 'You should be proud. Not many in the camp have the privilege of having a Drekesh take an interest in them.' He stopped pacing and turned to study the boy for a short time. 'From now on when we are together, you will speak to me like a young warrior. No more cringing and no more tears like a child. It is an insult to me that you think anyone would touch you while I am here. I will not punish you unless you break our laws. Understand?' He gave Kal a steady gaze.

'Yes, Ashe', Kal said loudly.

'Very good. Now we need to get back to our work.'

18

The more Nemid told his story, the more resentment swelled that Dog clan had the gall to lay claim to a Nahill camp. The story of Dog clan's outrageous behaviour grew with each retelling: Water clan cabins being used for goats; the drinking, smoking and general neglect; the offer of 'selling' wood to a family in need; the disrespect towards the sacred objects; and, most outrageous, leaving the last Healer's bones to rot. The Nahill were scandalised and fuming. The Red Camp storytellers were scrambling to come up with a story about who this Healer had been and what fate might have befallen her for her to die alone at White Camp.

The result of all this was that when Nemid asked for Water clan volunteers to accompany him to resettle White Camp, old and young answered the call. However, planting season was upon them, and everyone was needed in the fields. On the way back from planting one day, Nemid, Ashekii and Ashekii's wife Hahina were speaking quietly to each other as they walked.

'There is talk of other clans wishing to relocate to White Camp', Ashekii said to Nemid, 'and it would not do for one of them to get there first and lay claim to the camp and Pacship in your absence. It would be best if we went soon.'

Nemid was all too aware of this distinct possibility.

'We will need Drekesh who will be loyal to us', he said.

From the way Hahina and Ashekii glanced at each other, Nemid could tell this had been something they'd already discussed long and hard.

'Oh, very well then', Hahina said exasperated. 'I suppose someone has to keep you out of trouble.'

'That would be a great honour', Nemid said, laying a hand on his chest. 'Thank you.'

Ashekii shot him a wry grin. 'I will bring a few of my most trusted Drekesh to help', he said.

'If we take a large party to White Camp', Hahina said, 'Dog clan may be so overwhelmed and disgusted, they will leave.'

As soon as the corn was planted, Nemid and his party of six Drekesh and ten families set off for White Camp. Head high, Nemid took the lead, elated that he was bringing Water clan back to White Camp.

Trindal hummed to himself as he walked and thought this was just like old times when he moved every few weeks going from camp to camp. He liked traveling and meeting new people. His easy-going nature made him easy to get along with, and he quickly made new friends. In fact, he'd found that routine bored him and he liked variety. He was excited and ready for whatever lay ahead.

Kal had a sinking feeling that they had to leave Red Camp because of him again. By now, he'd realised that his presence in the camp was a bone of contention. Every day, he expected Nemid to march him to the edge of the reservation and tell him that he was too much trouble. Kal had tried his hardest to learn the ways and language of the Nahill, but it never seemed enough. He was fearful of what was to come.

Their path led them always uphill. The animal tracks they followed snaked back and forth. Every now and again, Kal caught the sound of Nemid singing from his position in the lead. When he asked Nemid about this later, he was told it was a travel song. These songs contained key information about landmarks and topography to help people remember how to get from one place to another without maps.

The first night, they made camp in a clearing on the top of a hill with boulders on three sides. Kal stared off into the distance as the horizon turned golden in the setting sun. As the birds began their evening chorus, all bidding each other goodnight, the Nahill spoke in hushed voices as they prepared their evening meal and made ready their beds for the night.

'How about a story?' someone said.

Trindal settled himself, trying to think which would be the most appropriate story for this situation.

'We owe our lives to the good will of the traditional owners of this land', he said as he'd been taught by Aloth. 'We pay homage to their elders past and present. Without their generosity, guidance and wisdom, we the Jhunti, would have perished a few seasons after our arrival.'

He bowed his head as he sent his thanks then began.

'Long ago we did not have fire. The Great Spirits did not feel the cold. They made things hot just by placing their hands on them. One day, the first Jhunti told the Great Spirits they were cold. Now, before this time, there had been so few Jhunti that the Great Spirits could warm them all by taking them in their arms and hugging them. But now there were lots of Jhunti, too many for the Great Spirits to hug, so they wondered what to do. After a while, they looked to the Sun.

'Sun', they called, 'can you send one of your daughters or sons down here to keep the Jhunti warm?'

The Sun shook her head. 'No. If I do that, it will be too hot for everyone.'

So the Great Sprits thought some more.

'How about', they called to the Sun again, 'you send a mouse down here to keep them warm?'

'Still too much', said the Sun.

Again, the Great Sprits thought.

'Maybe just a few strands of your hair?' the Great Spirits said.

The Sun pulled out several strands of her burning hair and tossed them to earth. The hairs were so long they went from one horizon to the other setting everything ablaze. Before the whole world was reduced to ashes, the Great Spirits called on the Rain Spirit, Thondara, who quickly sent a thunder storm to put the flames out. After this, the Jhunti were not just cold, but they were wet and miserable.

After more talking, the Great Sprits hit on a new plan. They ground up some pepper bush and convinced the Wind to blow it right into the nose of the Sun. After a moment, the Sun sneezed, and the small piece of fire that came from her mouth hit the earth. The Great Spirits showed the Jhunti how to keep it from going out. From this time on, when someone sneezes, others say it is the Great Spirits reminding us of where fire comes from.'

The next morning, the camp roused as the first grey light showed on the horizon. They had a hasty meal as children were readied, packs refilled and the fire stamped out. Kal yawned and stretched as he glanced around for Nemid. He saw him to one side of the campground speaking with a young woman dressed in green and brown with short black hair. He had been told this was a Trill. Ashekii joined Nemid and the Trill, and the three of them walked a little way up the trail. The young woman pointed to the right, and again they talked before the Trill gave a parting gesture and melted silently into the bush. Nemid and Ashekii returned to the group.

'The Great Spirits have sent us a treat', Nemid beamed. 'Two valleys away, a whole grove of Beha bushes are groaning with ripe, early-season fruit!'

A cheer went up, and the stragglers quickly finished packing. As they set off, someone sang the Beha bush song. They spent a whole day gorging on the tangy fruit. The next day, the group recommenced their journey but made camp early when they discovered a large clump of tubers. Having lain undisturbed for a long while, the tubers were of enormous size. That night, Trindal told the story of the first tuber.

And so, they continued their journey, singing songs by day, and by night, Trindal told stories. The whole trip had a festive atmosphere and felt like one big adventure. Just as they had made camp one night, Kal again saw a Trill speaking with Nemid and Ashekii. This time it was worrying news. The Trill reported that a large group of white people and Dog clan were at White Camp playing a game. Nemid realised it was probably Two Up night. He glanced at his small band of Drekesh. What might happen if they were overpowered by the sheer numbers of Dog clan? Nemid was keen to send Dog clan, and everyone else, a message that White Camp again belonged to Water clan. He also wanted to teach Dog clan a lesson so they wouldn't come back. But if his takeover failed, not only would the Nahill lose face, but Nemid would lose his Pacship, and Kal would be forced to leave. Nemid reminded himself that the Great Spirits were the ones in control of everything and left their fate in the Great Spirit's hands. As Ashekii gathered his Drekesh, Nemid thanked the Trill for her news. She vanished back into the forest. For the next while, Nemid and the Drekesh discussed battle strategies and tactics. When they were satisfied, they called everyone together.

'White Camp is a short way ahead', Nemid said. 'Trill report a large contingent of Dog clan and white people present.' He then outlined their plans. 'Although our numbers are small, it is important that when we arrive, we show Dog clan that we are in charge now. They must understand that things will be different and that their old ways are over. Are there any questions?' He waited for a moment, but the only sound was the caw of a crow. The Great Spirits were listening, just as he knew they would. 'Very well', he said, 'we shall attack at first light, so ready yourselves for war.'

'A real battle at last', one of the Drekesh crowed with relish.

As the others sharpened spears and knives, the Drekesh painted their faces and bodies with white ochre and covered all around their eyes with black charcoal. If they were injured, this would trick Great Spirit Deema, the one who collected the newly dead, into thinking they had died some time ago and pass them by. They sent prayers to Great Spirit Steppa, the spirit of war to steel their hearts and guide their actions, and to Great Spirit Yosh who cared for the brave. After bidding goodbye to their loved ones, they were ready.

The Drekesh approached the camp at first light. All were disgusted with the state of the once magnificent White Camp. The rubbish, bottles and stench made even the most hardened warriors want to weep. They channelled their feelings into a steely determination to rid the camp of the scourge that was Dog clan. Taking their knives from their sheaths, they slowly made their way up the hill.

All the warriors peered alertly around them as they went, checking for enemies. Their muscles were taut, a sheen of sweat glistened on their painted skins, their fists were clenched around their weapons and they were ready for battle. The very air of the camp throbbed with tension, and it seemed like even the birds held their breath. Soon they found a small group of white men sitting on the logs next to what was left of a bonfire. They were drinking beer from cans and talking in soft voices as they watched the embers and wisps of smoke from the dying fire. Squaring his shoulders, Nemid went to stand before them.

'It is time for you to go now', he said in firm tones.

The men eyed him with blurred vision before standing, gathering their remaining cans and staggering up the hill towards the car park, which was littered with dozens of cars, some with people sleeping in them. Startled cries could be heard as the Drekesh tapped on car windows, opened doors and roused the occupants by yelling at them in Nahill. Nemid and Ashekii were the only ones who spoke English, so it was they who directed the whites to leave. The bleary-eyed drivers took one look at the grotesquely painted faces and hastily drove away.

Reassured that the enemy were now contained within the cabins, the Drekesh made a signal towards the forest. The rest of the Nahill emerged and joined the Drekesh. Together they went from cabin to cabin rousing Dog clan from their beds. Suddenly the air was filled with indignant shouts. In no time items of clothing, furniture and anything else from the white world flew through the open doors and out onto the ground. Soon, people in various stages of undress, clutching shoes and clothes under their arms, ran from the cabins and towards the car park.

The Drekesh shouted Pac Nemid's new rules at the remaining members of Dog clan. Rule one was that no items from the white world were permitted in White Camp. Rule two was that Dog clan was only permitted four cabins. The rest of the White Camp cabins were for Water clan. Those who balked at the rules were swiftly escorted to the car park.

Aunt Talks Too Much and Uncle Mends Things came out of their cabin to face a pack of indignant Dog clan members. Both wore brightly coloured floral pyjamas and fluffy white dressing gowns. Their hair stuck out in all directions, and Aunt Talks Too Much's face was smeared with old make up. She scrubbed her sleep-flushed face and dragged her fingers through her hair, pulling it out of her bleary eyes. As soon as she saw Nemid, her lips formed into a firm line. She should have known that old troublemaker was behind this. A wave of nausea hit her as her hangover kicked in. She swallowed heavily and glanced at the crowd hanging along the edge of her balcony. If she was going to throw-up, she thought, she best make sure it landed on as many Nahill as possible.

'This is Water clan land', Nemid said. 'I have decided that Dog clan is to be tolerated, but only if you live the Nahill way of life.'

The Drekesh fanned out behind Nemid. He squared his shoulders.

'Those that live on this reservation must dress as our ancestors did using only the materials we produce ourselves.'

Uncle Mends Things lit a cigarette, avoiding his wife's eyes as he waited for her to explode.

'Next', Nemid said, 'there is to be no more drinking alcohol or smoking. In fact, there are to be no white goods consumed here at all. We Nahill can look after ourselves and do not need the intervention of white society.'

Aunt Talks Too Much took Uncle Mends Things' cigarette. She put it to her lips, drew in a long drag, held it for a moment, then blew the smoke right at Nemid.

'Thief!' she yelled, pointing at Nemid. 'You stole from us! We expect recompense in full!'

The colour rose to Nemid's face as he felt the others looking at him.

'There will be no more eating white food', Nemid said. 'We have brought enough to keep everyone fed until the first harvest, which you will help with if you wish to eat.'

Lemon came to stand beside her mother, pulling a denim jacket over her peasant style shirt. 'He can't make us do any of this, can he?' she said.

'No way', Wisha said, coming to stand on the other side. 'We'll just go into town.'

She pulled out a pack of cigarettes and lit two, handing one to her father.

'The cars', Nemid said, 'are only for emergencies. Nahill walk, they do not drive.'

'WE ARE NOT NAHILL!' most of Dog clan yelled.

Unperturbed, Nemid continued.

'We are fortunate to have Healers arriving soon', he said. 'You are to rid yourself of any white medicine, and in the event of sickness, you can ask if one of our Healers will do you the honour of attending you.'

'You can't stop us doing what we want', one of the Dog clan cousins said, crossing her arms over her chest.

With a flick of Nemid's finger, Drekesh escorted the woman to the car park and stuffed her into the nearest vehicle. They released the handbrake and gave it a shove down the hill.

'From now on', Nemid said, 'you are to contain yourselves to these four cabins. Your livestock and possessions are not to stray or they will be forfeited. If any of you do not like these new arrangements, leave this camp now.'

The members of Dog clan all looked at Aunt Talks Too Much, waiting to see what she would do. Aunt Talks Too Much glanced in the direction where her cousin had been marched away by the Drekesh. She was so angry, she couldn't speak. Taking another drag on her cigarette, she tried to think about what to do, but her brain was still foggy with drink. Her eyes went to the row of Drekesh, all with weapons drawn, and she knew that even though there were many more Dog clan than Nahill, they were no match for the highly-trained Drekesh. She flicked her cigarette butt at Nemid. It bounced off his chest and fell onto the ground. He crushed it with his boot heel then picked it up. One of the Drekesh took it from him and handed it to a child who threw it into the fire pit. Aunt Talks Too Much watched her butt smoulder, burst into flames then disappear, consumed by the fire. Deciding that adequately expressed her feelings, she turned and stalked back into her cabin, slamming the door behind her.

The following week, a dozen Dog clan cars were parked in the dirt driveway of a large weatherboard house on the outskirts of a town called Clarkesville. The house was on a two-acre block dotted with fruit trees. Laughs a Lot's herd of goats strolled about grazing, their tails flicking back and forth as they ate. A Billy goat followed them, occasionally nudging one of them hopefully, but his advances had so far been rejected by all. Flocks of chickens were supervised by strutting roosters. Several of the caravans were parked near the trees, most facing a large blackened fire pit. Smoke rose from the small fire burning underneath a huge metal cooking pot. A dozen old people were sitting in a circle around the pot of stew. Occasionally one of them would heave themselves out of their chair and stir the pot with a long, wooden paddle before resuming their seat.

At the front of the house, three men in their twenties were digging a large hole. Two more were hooking up the hoses that would feed water into the new duck pond come swimming pool. Out the front of the property, an old bus was parked on the grass verge. It had two flat tyres and grass grew up through the axels. To Dog clan this property was known as 'the Dog house', and they were all very proud of it. It served as a halfway place for those not willing to live a totally white life but unable to settle into the reservation lifestyle. Every adult had fond memories of staying at the Dog house as a child.

The two most important parts of the Dog house were 'the cupboard' where people left things for each other, like a kind of Dog clan post office, and the fire pit. Dog clan still thought of the Jhunti reservation as their home, but unlike the Nahill, most of Dog clan led what they referred to as a *blended life*. Unlike the puritanical Nahill, practical Dog clan did not see any nobility in shunning western culture just for the sake of clinging to a way of life that was obsolete. In fact they prided themselves on being the only clan that seemed able to adapt and embrace the most beneficial parts of this new life. They took what they found useful from white and Jhunti culture alike. It was like browsing in the forest, they reasoned. Surely it was sensible to pluck ripe berries from this bush and fruit from that tree, and when the pickings get scarce, to move on. It didn't make sense to them to try and make one bush grow fruit all year round. So they migrated between the different camps at the Jhunti reservation and the Dog house.

In the bedroom at the back, Sindri, zipped up her white vinyl knee-high boots before she straightened to survey herself in the mirror. She smoothed down her khaki shorts and white baby-doll camisole from which erupted her ample brown bosoms. A white man was lying in the bed behind her.

'Coffee?' he croaked.

She glanced back at his bare torso which was covered with hair and tattoos.

'No time', she said in English, donning a pair of round, pink, framed sunglasses. 'It's payday, and we gotta get goin'. You stayin' for the party tonight?'

The man groaned and sat up. 'I thought we were goin' fishin' today', he said and lit a cigarette.

'I told ya, it's payday', she took his cigarette. 'We'll go tomorrow.' She took a drag then blew the smoke out. He scratched the side of his head and reluctantly made to get up.

'Need a lift?' he said.

'Nah, but thanks for askin'.'

At that moment, a child's scream came from another part of the house, and she heard a door slam.

'I better go', she said.

She blew him a kiss for the cigarette and strode out the door. From every direction came music. One person played country and western, another listened to NSync and a third sang along to a rap song. The rest of the sounds came from one TV playing cartoons and another blaring an advertisement for fishing lures. She heard explosions from a PlayStation battle game that all the kids were addicted to, and mixed in with this was the babble of voices, laughter, arguments and conversation from old and young. The cacophony of sounds was a morning chorus that, to her, meant all was right with her world.

'Dinosaur droppings!' a young male voice yelled as a sneaker came flying along the hallway.

'Hey!' she snapped in the direction the shoe came from. 'That bloody near hit me!'

'Sorry, Aunty', teenaged Gilmore called, sticking his head out from around a doorway.

'I thought', Mash said, 'you were a circus midget!'

Both boys cracked up laughing, and Sindri shook her head knowing this was a quote from that stupid cartoon the boys watched obsessively. Mash threw Gilmore's shoe back and hit his shoulder.

'Ow!'

'Boys!' yelled an annoyed female voice from the other end of the house, 'I've had it with you two!'

'Mash started it.'

'Did not!'

'Did too!'

'Did not!'

Sindri took a drag of her cigarette as she kicked another sneaker aside.

'Can someone tell me what time it is?' she yelled up the hallway.

'Going for eight thirty', someone yelled back.

'Shit, we better get a wriggle on. Come on you two.'

Both boys materialized into the corridor. Each wore baggy low-rider jeans and basketball sneakers. Howls of laughter from other children came from the room Mash was in. Sindri held up her hands to stop Gilmore throwing yet another sneaker.

'No more, we're late. Out to the car, both of you.'

'Do we have to?' Mash grizzled, pulling on his sneaker.

'Yes, it's payday. Now, hop to it.' She shooed them ahead of her up the hallway in a fresh cloud of smoke, frowning at how low they wore those stupid jeans.

'And pull your pants up' she said, 'I can see things I don't wanna see.'

The boys made a token effort to hitch up their pants as they ran on ahead of her. She stopped at another room. Half a dozen boys of various ages were glued to the morning cartoons on the TV.

'All of you, to the car!'

Without waiting, she walked down the hallway until she heard young female voices coming from another room. She pushed open the door as the crooning of NSync's latest album got louder, a line of dancing red lights displayed the rising and falling beat from a cassette player in the corner. Four girls, aged ten to fourteen, sat in a floral pyjama cluster on one of the beds. They were watching two other girls standing at the full-length mirror. The other girls were older and dressed in denim overalls with only one strap fastened. Under these were pastel shirts with floral patterns on them. Every girl had long black hair braided in thin plaits that had taken the girls days to put into each other's hair. The tallest one was Wisha, Sindri's oldest daughter. The other was Aunt Talks Too Much's daughter Remmy, who had rings on every finger, including her thumbs. Seeing her mother, Wisha smiled.

'Morning mum. Rem 'n me were talking about what you said last night, and we were wondering, how about if...'

'No', Sindri said firmly.

'But, mum...'

'You're not getting tattoos.'

'How about a navel ring then? Everyone has them. Please? They don't cost much.'

Suddenly all the eyes were upon Sindri. Although she wasn't sure what a navel ring was, she shook her head.

'No.'

'But, mum', Wisha pouted, 'if it's the cost you're worried about, we could probably do it ourselves. My friend Jane did it with just some ice cubes and a needle. You leave the needle in boiling water for a few minutes to sterilise it, and it's perfectly safe. She could do it for me. Pleeeeeeese?'

Again, their hopeful gazes were upon her. Sindri rubbed sleep from her eyes. It was too early for a battle of wills, which was probably why they had picked now to bring this up.

'No', she said. 'I do not want to see any rings hanging off you. You're not a bloody cow.'

Wisha turned to face her mother, a pleading expression on her face.

'Can I get my tongue pierced then? I promise you'll never even see it.'

'No.'

Wisha's features hardened and she put her hands on her hips. 'You never let me do anything!'

As Sindri ground out her cigarette, she noticed Remmy and Wisha's white sneakers.

'You're not wearing them home are you? Think of the mud.'

The girls looked down. 'But if we change into boots', Remmy said, 'we'll need new outfits.'

'You got two minutes', Sindri said gruffly. 'It's payday, and we're running late.'

The girls began pulling out clothes to go with their Doc Martins. Sindri shut the door and continued down the hallway making a mental note to pay more attention to who those teenagers were socialising with.

She walked past the lounge room where two kids sat on the couch, game controllers in their hands as they blasted the enemy. One was her younger daughter Lemon, a stout girl with chubby cheeks and a take-no-prisoners attitude. The other was Lemon's ten-year-old cousin Hasty, named after his speedy birth. Both were dressed in camouflage cargo pants, Lemon in a black t-shirt and Hasty a khaki one. Both wore laced up, black combat boots.

'Eat this', Lemon chortled and another soldier exploded. Her barking laugh sounded just like the rat-a-tat-tat of her blazing AK47 machine gun.

'Two minutes', Sindri said and continued her way to the kitchen.

The volume of the TV in the boy's room went up another notch, and the sound of gunfire and tyre screeches of a cartoon battle echoed up the hallway.

'Turn that down!' Sindri yelled without looking back.

The volume remained at the same level. She got to the kitchen to find her Uncle Mends Things finishing off a piece of toast. He wore a tweed jacket, brown Velour pants and dessert boots.

'Good morning', he said indicating the loaf of bread. 'Ready for breakfast?'

Grabbing the pack of cigarettes from the table, Sindri lit another and shook her head.

'Just coffee', she said, pouring herself a cup. 'Where is she?'

'Fixing the fuel pump on the car', he said.

Sindri leant forward to look out the kitchen window. A small crowd stood in a semi-circle around Aunt Talks Too Much, who was doing something under the bonnet of one of their dilapidated cars. Sindri glanced at the kitchen clock. It was 9.00 am. It would take them a good ninety minutes to get out to the reservation, longer if the roads were bad. They better hurry. She took another sip of coffee and smoked her cigarette as she watched her Aunt fixing the car.

A collective cheer from outside interrupted her musings. The car engine coughed, and suddenly a blue cloud of exhaust smoke billowed out as the engine revved. Uncle Mends Things jumped to his feet.

'Time to go!' he called up the corridor. 'Everyone into the car!'

Sindri downed the last of her coffee and finished her cigarette. The TVs and stereos went silent, and a gaggle of children erupted from the different doorways. Everyone pushed and shoved through the back door to get to the cars.

The third term school holidays had gone far too quickly for Karen Davis. It seemed as if no sooner had school finished than it was time to revise her lesson plans and get her preparations finalised for the last school term for the year. It was with a feeling of renewed vigour and anticipation that she turned the big Education Department four-wheel drive towards Mount Disappointment and drove out to the Nahill camp.

The sound of the teacher's car slowly climbing the side of the mountain made Laughs a Lot smile. He dropped his spade and ran out of the field and up the hill to the car park. He was so happy to be back at White Camp. He found the Dog house too noisy and the other kids teased him. Besides, apart from tending to the animals, there was nothing to do and he'd soon gotten bored. After a lot of complaining and begging, his mother agreed to let him come back. Two Dog clan families from Blue Camp had accompanied him. Best of all, he'd been allowed to bring back his favourite goats and chickens with him and so Dopsil and her aged band of girls were safe for now.

When Miss Davis arrived she was met by Laughs a Lot. He was dressed in the same plain but serviceable tunic and leggings that Kal and Trindal wore. He was grinning even wider than usual and bursting with excitement.

'Good morning, Lal', she said as he swung open her car door.

'They're back!' he cried with delight.

'Who's back?'

'Everyone!'

Not quite understanding, Miss Davis climbed out of her car and followed Laughs a Lot across the car park. As soon as she reached the path down into the camp, she stopped. There were Jhunti everywhere. Some were in chatting groups, some were repairing cabin rooves, some were lugging bags of food down to the storage shed, others were leading reluctant goats towards the paddock and, as she followed Laughs a Lot down the path, she could see a large group of them in the field wielding hoes and tilling the soil. The groups of Jhunti stopped speaking as she passed, their eyes drilling into her. For the first time, she felt intimidated by these wild people and was very aware that she was the only white person here. If anything happened to her, no one would know. Her heart raced and sweat prickled her back as she strode onwards. She kept her expression as one of friendly interest, keeping a pleasant smile on her face even though her fingernails were digging into her palms.

With unwavering steps, she followed the young caretaker, who now also felt like her protector. People silently parted to let them through, and she was relieved when they reached the school.

'Lal?' she said as she unlocked the door. 'Who are all these people?'

Laughs a Lot scratched his head then pointed to the closest family.

'That is Rainez from Big Camp. The boy with her is Phelas. He's the step son of Mena. His mother died several snows ago when a sack of corn fell on her. He says he was very sad for a while, but he likes Mena and her family. His sister Rema stayed at Big Camp with their aunt Tresh who is the daughter of Lalsa. Tresh has three girls named…'

'Enough', Miss Davis said holding up a hand.

So, she thought, there *were* other camps. She'd suspected as much, but Kal and the others were always so reluctant to speak of them. Her curiosity piqued, she considered how to pose her questions as she opened the doors. They went inside and Laughs a Lot made straight for the school bell.

'When did they arrive?' she tried again.

'You mean Phelas and his family?'

'Yes, and the others, all of them.'

Laughs a Lot dragged the bell down from the shelf and headed towards the door, unsure how to answer her question. He didn't remember the exact order in which people had arrived. It had started with a few then there had been lots then more and more. Every day there were new faces, and his relatives were not happy about it. They had been furious to find their cabins ransacked. He was glad it hadn't been his fault. Laughs a Lot was at the door now and began to ring the bell. This took his full attention and he forgot all about Mizz Daviz's question.

Miss Davis stared after him for a moment then gave a mental shrug and walked to the front of the room. It took her a moment to work out what was different. All the wooden furniture and old books were gone. Even the posters had been taken. She looked back towards the door.

'Where is everything?' she called out.

At that moment, Kal and Trindal entered wrestling a new table through the door. Nemid followed them with two new chairs.

'Put it there', she indicated where her old one had been.

They positioned the furniture then the boys leant against the table, regaining their breath. Both had changed from boys to young men, she noticed. Their shoulders had filled out, and in the six months since she'd last seen them, both had grown at least three inches.

'What happened to my furniture?' she said, eyeing the new table.

'We burnt it', Kal said.

'We were freezing', Trindal said.

'I have made these as replacements', Nemid said.

'But we couldn't replace the books or posters', Trindal said.

'We're real sorry about that', Kal finished.

The only sound was the bell as it echoed around the camp. Miss Davis had so many questions she didn't know where to start. She placed her bag on the new table. It was bigger than the old one and the chair was much sturdier than the dainty one she used to have. She looked at Nemid.

'Lal was telling me there are other Nahill camps', she said casually. 'Where are they?'

'Lal is Dog clan', Nemid said dismissively. 'I will get the others.'

As if that explained it, Nemid gave her a curt nod and left. Miss Davis stared after him for a moment then turned her attention to the boys.

'Where did all these people come from?'

'The forest', Trindal said, 'like we did. Do you want us to try to find more books?'

'I could ask Mrs Li if she could get some posters', Kal said.

Both boys gazed at her earnestly. Miss Davis opened her mouth then closed it again.

'Forget the books and posters', she said. 'How did you go with all that homework I sent you?'

'What homework?' Kal said.

Miss Davis explained how she and Aunt Talks Too Much met

regularly at Mrs Li's shop. How she had given her everyone's cheques and homework. While she'd gotten a few drawings back from Laughs a Lot, whenever she'd asked for Trindal or Kal's work, there'd been excuses. Trindal and Kal exchanged glances, their jaw muscles tensing as they realised that Dog clan had been stealing their cheques. Kal wanted to tell Nemid right away, but at that moment, a pretty young Jhunti girl walked in the door.

Chani tried to bite back on her excitement. At last she was going to school. She had dreamed of this day for a long time and was beyond excited. Today she was going to have all her questions about white people answered. She was going to learn their secrets and to read and write.

'This's Healer Chani', Kal said.

'Nice to meet you', Miss Davis said and was given a flash of white teeth in a beautiful smile.

'Hello', Chani said in the brisk, no nonsense tone of a Healer. 'You are to teach me to read and write. Shall we begin?'

Suddenly, a noisy explosion of children erupted through the door. The laughter and voices quickly hushed when they saw there was a Healer in the room. Instead, they all stood still, dutifully giving the Healer priority. Miss Davis glanced at them and was pleased that at least these children had been taught to respect her authority.

'Good morning children', she said.

The children did not look at her. Their eyes darted this way and that, their expressions a mixture of apprehension, curiosity and amazement. Laughs a Lot ambled back in and replaced the bell then went to the teacher's bag, removed a picture book and sat down. Chani tapped her fingers against her leg, unused to waiting for an answer. Miss Davis went to the front of the room.

'Welcome, everyone', she said in her outside voice. 'Please sit in rows starting here.' She pointed to the floor in front of her desk. When the children remained standing in their tight group, she turned her head towards Chani, silently appealing for help. Chani realised the woman needed someone in authority to take charge of the situation.

'Sit', she said briskly in Nahill.

All the children instantly obeyed. Miss Davis surveyed her new class. She counted sixteen children whose ages varied from six to fourteen. Flustered, having come prepared for her usual contingent of three students, Miss Davis adjusted her thinking.

'Well', she said, twisting her fingers together, 'Let's start with introductions.' She placed a hand on her chest and spoke slowly and clearly. 'My name is Miss Davis.' She pointed to the first child. 'What is your name?'

The boy stared up at her blankly. A sudden flash of realisation hit Miss Davis.

'Do you speak English?' she said hopefully.

He remained silent. She cast a hopeful glance at the others.

'Hands up if you speak English.'

The only hands to go up belonged to Chani, Trindal, Kal and Laughs a Lot. She felt a pang of embarrassment that, after all this time, she'd not learnt even one word of Nahill, not even hello.

'Then why are you here?' she said, more to herself than the children.

She glanced towards Chani, hoping she'd translate again. Chani's cheeks coloured as she realised that this white woman must think Chani had snuck in here on her own. As if she would do such a thing. Maybe she didn't believe a Healer would be allowed to mix with the general population. It had taken much negotiation but Chani had been granted permission to be here by the Feren herself, and the Feren was the highest-ranking Healer there was. Chani's back stiffened.

'I have permission from the Feren', she said defensively. 'You are to teach me to read and write.'

Miss Davis stared at Chani for a moment, a hint of annoyance on her brow.

'All in good time', she said. 'Right now I want you to help me find out every one's name. Could you translate for me?'

Chani's eyes widened at being spoken to like that. The children's attention went from the rude white woman to the indignant Healer, spellbound. Kal and Trindal exchanged looks. Kal made to go forward but Trindal stopped him.

'No', he whispered then hurried to Miss Davis's side. 'Please allow me to do the introductions', he said jovially.

Chani stalked towards the door.

'This was a big mistake', she hissed in Nahill as she passed Kal. 'I don't know why any of you bother.'

Kal pushed himself away from the wall and followed after her as Trindal began to introduce Miss Davis to the children.

'Cha, wait up', he called after her rigid back.

She slowed so he could catch up to her. Together they strode through the camp, chickens and dogs scurrying out of their way.

'I had no idea', she said indignantly, 'how badly behaved white people were. I was willing to forgive you as … well, you were just a child, but she is a grown a woman! I expected more.'

Nemid was walking down the hill, dragging two long timber poles. He didn't see them as he was bitterly wishing he had some better tools. Could they borrow some from Red Camp, he wondered, or trade for them?

'Honourable Pac!' Chani called. 'A moment of your time.'

One look at her irate stance and Nemid knew the first day of school had not gone well.

'It is good to see these faces', Pac Nemid said.

'That teacher has no manners!' Chani said.

He put his poles down. It didn't take long for Nemid to get the picture.

'Honoured Healer', he said, 'I know white people are strange. That is why you need to go to school, to learn about their odd ways and find a way to accept them. It is for the good of your tribe that you are doing this, remember?'

They stared at each other for a long moment before she gave one curt nod and walked back towards school. Nemid turned his attention to Kal and indicated for him to speak.

'Wait till you hear what Dog clan did', Kal said heatedly.

Hardly pausing for breath, Kal told him how Dog clan had been stealing their cheques for the whole of the snow season and lying to Miss Davis. When he'd finished, his face was flushed, his eyes blazing with outrage. Nemid stood in silence for a short time, his arms crossed over his chest in thoughtful silence. It irked Kal that Nemid wasn't upset, but he knew better than to question him. Nemid glanced down towards the school room, then towards the Dog clan houses, then to the car park and suddenly the way forward was clear. He thanked the Great Spirits for their guidance then looked back at Kal. He wanted it clear the boy had nothing to do with what was about to take place.

'Please take these poles to our cabin', Nemid said in an authoritative voice. 'Then, I want you to fetch the rest of the poles I have cut.'

'Yes Pac', Kal said, knowing better than to argue when Nemid used that tone.

He begrudgingly lifted the ends of the poles and dragged them down the hill, wishing they had tractors. He dropped his first load in front of their cabin then went back into the forest to collect more. He was still hauling poles when Trindal ran up to him.

'Where've you been?' Trindal panted. 'You missed all the excitement!'

'What excitement?'

'Dog clan! Nemid cut off their education cheques. You should have seen them. I dead set thought Aunt Talks Too Much was going to explode!'

Kal dropped the poles.

'What? I don't understand. Start from the beginning.'

Trindal told Kal how Nemid had come to the school and added the names of all the Water clan kids that had turned up so Miz Daviz was really happy. Then Dog clan arrived. When they'd demanded their education cheques, Nemid made them form an orderly line as Miz Daviz called the roll. When they were unable to produce the child the cheque was for, that name was struck off the list and the cheque returned to her bag. Kal chuckled and shook his head.

'And then', Trindal continued with glee, 'grandfather informed Miz Daviz that the camp had no electricity. I was about to call in the

Drekesh because I thought Uncle Mends Things would hit him!'

Kal's eyes widened.

'What?'

'Ah huh. They left with only one cheque, for Lal.'

'Oh boy', Kal said, 'I wish I'd been there!'

Both laughed.

'Help me get these back', Kal said. The boys picked up the last poles and began dragging them towards Nemid's cabin.

'You should have heard them', Trindal continued as they trudged along. 'They vowed to bring damnation down on Water clan, and all of them vowed payback.'

'Hah', Kal scoffed, 'fingernail pickings to them.'

'There's more. After they'd gone, grandfather went through the roll with Miz Daviz and told her which of the other 'children' would no longer be attending. She said she'd known about the scam for a while but knew that if she told anyone they'd shut down the school entirely. Now the camp is full again, she doesn't have to worry about that.'

Trindal then went on to say that Miz Daviz had agreed to organise a trust fund for the camp into which all the education cheques would be paid. They could use this to buy hammers and nails and all the things that are needed to fix the cabins and help them through next snow season.

'Hey', Kal said, 'what happened to his no white stuff rule?'

'I guess he changed his mind', Trindal said and shrugged. 'Grandfather also said that reliance on government handouts had made Dog clan lazy. He said that soon the camp would be self-sufficient and then no one would care about the education cheques.'

They reached Nemid's cabin and threw their poles onto the rest of the pile. Both wiped the bark and dirt from their hands onto their tunics.

'I wish I'd been there', Kal said again. 'Show me how the Dogs looked when they realised they weren't getting any more money.'

Trindal's eyes widened and his mouth dropped open into an incredulous expression; his eyes narrowed as his expression turned to one of rage. Kal laughed. Trindal looked past Kal and spotted some of his new friends emerging from the forest.

'I'm going to tell the others', he said.

'I'm going to tell Ashe', Kal said.

Each boy turned in a different direction and ran off.

At the car park, Aunt Talks Too Much and her fellow members of Dog clan were milling about muttering curses at the Nahill. All said they should leave the stinking Nahill and the equally stinking White Camp for good. Aunt Talks Too Much's attention was caught by a flash of blonde hair. Kal was outside her old cabin speaking to his water-eyed scum brother Trindal before dragging their poles down to Nemid's cabin. Everything people said about those with water-eyes being unlucky was true, she mused. She watched the boys break apart and run in different directions. They reminded her of scurrying rats ... white rats, she mused. Everything was Kal's fault, she seethed. If Kal had not upset everyone at Red Camp, Nemid would have stayed there and left Dog clan and White Camp alone. Hatred ran through her as she watched Kal. She wished a pox on him and the Nahill. Uncle Mends Things ambled over to her.

'Come on love', he said.

She roused herself and followed him to the car, bidding White Camp, and the Nahill, good bye and good riddance forever.

19

All through the season of the Butterflies, White Camp was a mass of activity. Everywhere, the camp was alive as more people arrived, some to help for a few seasons and some to stay. Everywhere one went, people fixed, cleared or cleaned. The sound of hammers and saws became as common as the chirping of birds.

The field of the three sisters also underwent a transformation. Teams of Nahill toiled from first light till dark until all three of the sisters were planted, a marathon effort after so many snows of neglect. There was a cheer when the first trickle of water ran through the newly dug channels, making its life-giving way to the fields. After this, the Nahill performed the ceremonies of thanks with especial fervour. Day by day, life was being breathed back into this, the most beautiful of the Drekesh camps.

At the far end of the field one day, Kal heard the school bell but was too busy. He ignored the bell the following week as well. The third week, a small child arrived with a note asking Kal to come and see Miss Davis. He shoved it into his pocket and continued weeding. Late in the afternoon, he heard the sound of her car start and remembered the note. Wearing only his labourer's loin cloth, he ran full tilt from the field up to the car park. When Miss Davis saw the mud splattered, blonde boy running towards her, she didn't recognise him. He stopped abruptly before her, his chest heaving as he tried to catch his breath, his long blonde hair stuck to his face and… Her eyes widened as she realised it was Kal. She turned off the engine and got out of the car, a thrill of excitement running through her at being correct.

'So you *are* white', she said. 'I thought so.'

He stood stock still, his eyes wide like he'd seen a ghost. She shook her head.

'No', she said. 'I haven't told anyone.' He let out a relieved breath. 'I have some wonderful news', she continued. 'You've been accepted into the education program.'

He frowned and wondered what she was talking about. She smiled.

'I applied on your behalf, and they said yes!'

'You…', he swallowed to wet his parched throat, 'you told them about me?'

'I know, it's a little unorthodox', she said, 'but it's done now, and all you have to do is go to one orientation day and then you can study for all your certificates… *here*!'

A gust of wind blew a piece of paper from her car. He bent down to pick it up. His scars stood out clearly against the tan of his skin. She gasped. He knew that sound and quickly straightened up.

'They beat you?' she said in a horror-struck tone. 'Why didn't you tell someone?'

Her face hardened.

'This is outrageous', she glanced around. 'I knew you were afraid of something, and now I know what! There's no need to be afraid Kal', she reached for him. 'They can't force you to stay here.' She grabbed his elbow and tried to push him into her car. 'Come on. Someone like you shouldn't be forced to work in fields all day anyway.'

He pulled his arm from her grasp and began shaking his head as he backed away. Suddenly all the things he'd wanted to tell her, the vague plans of going to the lake together and asking for her address evaporated. All he wanted was to go back to the fields.

'I can't leave here', he said.

She lowered her voice, her eyes scanning the empty car park.

'They haven't threatened you, have they? They can't do that.

Slavery is against the law, and where I come from, no one beats a child and gets away with it.'

Unable to explain further without telling her about Barry and his old life, Kal turned and headed back towards the trees. The scars from the lash were clear on his skin and the sight of them made Karen Davis's blood boil. How dare they do that to a child!

'I'm going to have them charged', she called after him. 'You tell Nemid that the cops are on their way!'

When he didn't stop, she tried one last thing.

'Trevor?' she called. 'Are you Trevor Moore? Or James Sanders?'

He was almost to the trees.

'Christopher Daniels?'

Hearing his old name sent a jolt of terror through him. He started to run, his heart hammering in his chest. She'd found out who he was. She'd said his name. Did that mean Barry would find him now? He ran blindly, shoving foliage aside in a panic, putting as much distance as he could between himself and the person he had thought he could trust. What had he learnt about adults? Never trust them. Never. Never.

He'd been meticulously silent about his past. No one knew his real name or where he came from or how he had got here. He'd never told Nemid or Chani or Trindal or Ashekii. No one was supposed to know this, no one. His life depended on it!

Eventually he stopped running and tried to get his breath as feelings of panic raced through him and blood pounded in his veins. He leant down, his hands resting on his knees as he gulped down air. The memories of his old life flooded back. He'd last seen his father on a Tuesday night. Chris was in the shower. It was near the end of term and he was pondering how to convince Barry to let him stay with his friend Stewie for the holidays. Chris didn't hear the gate or the front door. He towelled off, brushed his teeth and dried the basin then hung his towel, making sure the folds were perfect. After collecting his dirty clothes he headed to his bedroom. He had just pulled on clean underpants when the hairs on the back of his neck began to prickle as he heard footsteps. He listened, trying to gauge his fathers' mood. It took only a few steps for his throat to go dry and the terror to set in. Acting on instinct, he quickly pulled on his jeans instead of his pyjamas bottoms. His hands were trembling as he stuffed a pair of socks into his pocket and shoved his bare feet into his sneakers. He was just reaching for a t-shirt when he smelt alcohol. He didn't have to turn around to know Barry was standing at the doorway. The first blow from the riding crop bit into flesh which had been softened by the hot shower. Chris cried out in pain and dropped to his knees.

'Please dad', he begged.

'You're no son of mine!' Barry yelled and laid into him.

Chris tried to make himself as small as possible but with no shirt to protect his back, the effects of the leather crop were brutal. A few strokes broke the skin, and he could feel warm blood trickling down his ribs. That was when Chris became convinced that his father meant to kill him this time. He had no idea how he did it, but suddenly he was on his feet and running for his life. Out of the house he sped, snatching up the emergency pack he kept hidden outside. He continued on till he reached the truck stop just out of town. His emergency pack was a small canvas bag that contained a t-shirt, a lightweight woollen jumper, a packet of dry biscuits, a tetra pack of fruit juice and his hunting knife.

He had climbed into the back of the first semi-trailer he'd found and cried himself to sleep, his whole body radiating pain as the towns sped by. When that truck stopped, he'd jumped into another one, and another.

With a sniff, Kal wiped the sweat and tears away. His breathing slowed and his senses returned. Kal had no idea how far the trucks had taken him or where this reservation was. He didn't know what state he was in or where the nearest town was, and he didn't care. What he did know was that he felt safe here, at last, and he was never going to leave. Right then he vowed that never again would he go to school or speak to Karen Davis; it was just too dangerous.

That night Kal groaned in his sleep as his head thrashed back and forth. In his dream, harsh voices came from the kitchen, and his mother was crying in the hallway. A door closed and she was gone. A deep sense of loneliness settled over his heart as a tear ran down his cheek. His eyes opened and he sat up, sniffing as he wiped his cheeks with the back of his arm.

'Mmm?' Trindal murmured sleepily from his mattress.

'Dream', Kal whispered.

'Mmm mmm?'

'Yeah. Go back to sleep.'

'Mmm hmm.'

Trindal rolled over and lay still. Kal sniffed again and lay down. It was just another stupid dream, he reassured himself, just another dream. He yawned and closed his eyes, determined to think of something else. He thought of what he would do tomorrow. There was that fence post that needed to be replaced, and he'd have combat training with Ashekii. He wasn't sure what he thought about combat training. None of it came easily to him no matter how hard he tried. Ashekii said he had to tap into his inner warrior, but Kal wasn't sure he had one. He wondered if he'd ever have one. A picture came into his mind of himself dressed as a Drekesh with a spear in his hand. He was tall and broad shouldered like Ashekii. His hair was long and black as he readied himself for battle. Nemid was staring at him with pride, and Trindal watched him with envy as he bested one opponent after another. He felt strong and powerful when suddenly his school books flew and hit him, the hard corners bighting painfully into his skin.

'You're nothing!' his father barked at him. 'You're useless. You're stupid. I wish you'd never been born!'

Barry's face was red with anger. He grabbed Kal's arm and dragged him out to the shed. The shed where no one could hear his screams.

Kal gasped and sat up. His heart was pounding. The scars on his back were throbbing. Damn his father. Damn these nightmares; would they never stop? All he wanted to do was run, run away as fast as he could. Deep breaths, he told himself. Deep breaths. He pulled on his tunic and leggings as his heart rate began to settle. It always felt better, safer with his clothes on, less vulnerable. Did he still want to bolt or stay? He decided what he needed was to go and stand outside for a little while.

He quietly let himself out of the cabin and looked out at the horizon. It was already streaked with the pinks and purples of sunrise. Great Spirit Larath had exceeded herself today, he thought. She had chosen colours to warn them that Great Spirit Thondara would be sending rain soon. He sent them both a silent prayer of thanks. The first whiff of smoke drifted to his nostrils as a morning fire was lit. Off in the distance a baby cried. To the right a rooster crowed, and chickens began to cackle as they flapped their way out of their pens. A door slammed, and someone laughed as the camp awoke around him. He sniffed and wiped his nose on his arm feeling better and his mind calming. With one final deep breath, he went inside to begin his day.

When Kal got back from the fields that night, there were fresh strings of bad dream amulets draped across every window and doorway.

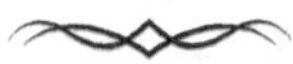

A tinge of grey blended into the horizon, and the morning air was crisp. In the fields, the three sisters were almost ready to harvest. In Pac Nemid's cabin, Trindal opened his eyes and looked around, wondering what had roused him from his sleep. He could just make out a figure pulling on a tunic.

'Kal?'

'Ah huh.'

Trindal raised his head and blinked a few times.

'Bad dream?'

Kal pulled on his pants.

'No. I'm going to meet Ashe', he glanced at his brother. 'It's been a while since you did any combat training. Wanna come?'

Trindal rolled onto his side, pulling the blankets up over his shoulders.

'Combat training's boring', he yawned. 'We keep doing the same stuff over and over.'

'At least', Kal said, 'you don't freeze up every time someone throws a punch at you.'

'You still do that?'

'Yep. Ashe deserves a medal for sticking with it.'

'What's a medal?'

Kal pulled on his boots and shook his head, cross with himself for using a white word.

'It's a kind of prize given to people who do brave things. I would have given up on me a long time ago if I were him.'

And, Kal thought, that was exactly what he was terrified would happen if he showed even the slightest hint of being sick of the unrelenting hours of combat training.

'After practice', he said, 'we're going to check the nearby salmon streams. I haven't seen them yet. Have you?'

'No. Isn't it a bit early for the salmon run? They don't start till after the snow melts'

'Ashe wants to see what kind of shape the streams are in. It's Water clan's duty after all, and he doesn't think anyone has checked them for a long time. Want to come?'

'Nah.'

Trindal resettled his head.

'Did you notice', Trindal said, 'there's a new family moved into that end cabin?'

'Next to Freth?'

'Ah huh. I met them yesterday. There's one boy and two girls about the same age as us. I said I'd show them around today.'

'Who are their people?'

Trindal sniffed.

'They're Water clan, cousins from Black Camp. Renah's cute and very nice, and I think you two would get on well, if you get my meaning.'

Trindal waited, hoping Kal would take the hint. Kal flexed his feet and made a slight adjustment to the tightness of his boot straps.

'They'll probably invite me to dinner', Trindal said. 'Want me to get an invite for you as well?'

'No, but thanks.'

Trindal rolled his eyes.

'You have to get out there, Kal, or no one's ever gonna claim you!'

Kal stood up and reached for his thick coat.

'Nemid has told me he'll have my hide if I start messing around with clan girls', Kal said. 'I'm to leave everything to the matchmaker.' He shoved his arms through the sleeves. 'And', he said staring at Trindal, 'he's told you to stop kissing everything in sight, as I recall. Before there's trouble. Understand?'

'I didn't do anything!'

'You didn't get *caught* doing anything', Kal corrected him. 'You've been lucky. Don't push it. I'll see you tonight.'

He opened the bedroom door, and for a moment his figure was silhouetted against the pale light that was now coming through the front window. The door closed. Trindal was heartily bored of working all the time. From sun up to sun down, it never stopped. There were times he wished he were back roaming with his various family members. At least then he'd been able to sneak off to explore places on his own and had managed to shirk most of the heavy work. Here there was no hope of that. He had already decided he wasn't like Kal, who seemed to thrive on hard work, routines and discipline. Trindal rolled over to face the wall, yawned and closed his eyes. He was asleep again in a handful of breaths.

When he woke about mid-day, he strolled out and found cold pancakes. He munched on one as he walked out onto the veranda and surveyed the camp, which was alive with activity. People walked past with baskets, and over at the fire pits they were refilling the log pile. Dogs barked and chickens pecked at the ground, some followed by a string of little chicks. The cabin straight ahead of them had someone on the roof fixing the tin. Trindal saw some of his friends sneaking off into the forest. He glanced around then hurriedly ran out to join them.

A few nights later, Trindal, Nemid and Kal were eating their evening meal. Kal glanced at Trindal who was shovelling his food down like there was no tomorrow. Every few mouthfuls, he would glance furtively out the window until something caught his attention. He stared at it for a moment then scraped up the last of his food and shoved it in.

'I'm finished', he said through his mouthful. 'I might go to bed. Night.' He went into the bedroom and closed the door after him.

Kal took another spoonful of soup when he heard a familiar sound. 'Back in a moment', he said getting up. He went into the bedroom and shut the door just as Trindal put one foot out the open window. Kal went to him and grabbed his arm.

'Where're you going?' he whispered.

'Out.'

'Out where?'

Trindal tried to push his hand off.

'What's it to you? You never wanna come anyway.'

'You sneaking out all the time is not right.'

Trindal let out a frustrated breath.

'You wanna know what's not right? Someone who spends all his time with old farts like Nemid and Ashe.'

Trindal managed to get free of Kal's grip and, with unexpected nimbleness, jumped lightly out the window and soundlessly dropped to the ground.

Kal leant out the window. 'Come back here', he hissed. 'What'll people think?'

'I don't care.'

'Well, you should.'

Trindal waved a dismissive hand. 'You're just jealous 'cause some of us like this thing called fun! See ya, Capitan Boring', and with that, he ran down the hill.

Kal stared after him. For a moment, he debated forcing him to come back but knew Trindal would just take off again. The reality was that Trindal was right. In this complex, highly political, easily-offended foreign culture that hated white people, Kal did prefer the company of Nemid and Ashekii. In fact, the only time he felt safe was when he was in their company. Kal closed the window and returned to his meal.

'Gone again?' Nemid said.

'Yeah.'

Nemid glanced at the closed bedroom door.

'It is not right to let a boy run off so much', Nemid said sadly. 'This one fears he is not being a good parent. Perhaps I am too old.'

'Don't say that', Kal said heatedly. 'You're just fine. It's 'cause of those new kids. He was OK before they came.'

Nemid took a gulp of his soup and mentally berated himself. Between sorting out squabbles, helping new arrivals settle and preparing the three sisters, whole seasons had disappeared. Nemid kept promising himself that he would make it up to Trindal, but the time just slipped away. Every time the Drekesh brought Trindal back with another admonishment, Nemid felt guilty and that it highlighted what a very bad parent he was. Leath was the one who had been so good with children, not him. Oh, how he missed her.

'Time, Eyas', he said sadly, 'we never seem to have enough time. What does Trin do when he goes out?'

'Gets up to mischief', Kal said. 'I heard it ranges from trying to catch night hawks to throwing stones onto the roof of Dog clan cabins. They're trying to convince Dog clan their cabins are haunted so they'll leave.'

Nemid smiled.

'Let us hope they succeed', he said.

Kal looked at him in mock horror.

'That is beneath you, Pac Nemid!'

They both shared a conspiratorial grin.

2 0

A thick fog glittered with dew as the first light of dawn showed on the horizon. The three sisters had been harvested, and two lights were on in Nemid's cabin: one in the main room and one in the room shared by Trindal and Kal. Trindal squatted beside his mattress, going through the contents of a small leather pack as he hummed a happy tune to himself. He was wearing the traditional Nahill tunic and leggings, and his hair was pulled back into a neat ponytail. He and Nemid were going to Big Camp for the snow season, and Trindal couldn't wait. He would get to visit more of his relatives, and the nights would be filled with games and fun and stories. His friends said Big Camp had lots of pretty girls and lots of storytellers unlike here where everything was mind-numbingly dull. Speaking of dull, he glanced at Kal. Kal's eyes were bloodshot from lack of sleep. The door opened, and Pac Nemid looked in.

'Ready, Trin?'

'Yep!'

Trindal jumped up, a huge smile on his face. Taking his pack, he strode out into the main room where two light meals of meat rolls and a special blend of herbal tea sat on the table for the journey. Trindal and Pac Nemid ate their rolls and drank their tea. Nemid's gaze went from one boy to the other. He knew Kal would miss him, but it was time Kal grew up and became more independent. No girl would want him if he was constantly clinging to Nemid's tunic. He had decided Kal should spend some time with other men, so Ashekii had reluctantly volunteered to mind him while Nemid dealt with his other problem.

Trindal was being so free with his affections that it was beginning to affect the morale of White Camp. Being the grandson of a Pac gave Trindal certain privileges, and the boy – young man – Nemid corrected himself, had been using these to full advantage. The Drekesh had asked Nemid to curtail Trindal's activities before parents demanded retribution.

Kal looked at Trindal. 'Are you sure you've got everything?'

'Yes', Trindal said with a hint of annoyance.

'What about your hunting knife?'

'I've got it.'

'But did you check that it was sharp? Have you remembered to take a sharpening stone?'

Kal went to the hearth.

'Here', he said fetching a stone from beside the fire, 'take this one, just in case.'

Trindal made a face. 'Are you nuts? I'm not carrying rocks in my pack. Sharpening stones are everywhere!'

Kal tossed the stone back. 'Good point. Did you take the good sleeping blanket? The old one has holes in it from when the goats had a tug of war with it.'

'Yes', Trindal said patiently, 'I took the good one, and I've got my steel and flint and food and everything.'

He shoved the last of his roll into his mouth and stood up. Nemid stood too, and both put on their packs. Kal tapped his fingers nervously against his thighs as he followed them to the door.

'Are you sure you don't want me to come with you?' he said. 'It'll take me five finger-snaps to pack.'

Nemid put a hand on Kal's shoulder. 'You know whites are not allowed at Big Camp', he said. 'We'll be back when the snow melts.'

Kal tried to bite back the feelings of betrayal and abandonment that he'd been fighting ever since Nemid told him they were leaving.

'How about if I came part of the way?'

Nemid could see the panic on the boy's face. He gave Kal's shoulder a squeeze.

'That's a fine offer', he said, 'but your place is here.'

Kal could not bring himself to look at Nemid. He was being abandoned again, just like with his mother, and there was nothing he could do about it. He never got any say in anything!

Trindal pulled open the door. 'See you after the snows', he said and strode out.

Pac Nemid gave Kal a little shake until the boy looked at him.

'This is Trin's time', he said quietly. 'Ashe will take good care of you. Try to keep out of trouble.'

With one last squeeze of Kal's shoulder, he strode off down the path. Kal stood in the open doorway watching them walk towards the lightening horizon until their shapes were swallowed up by the trees. He shut the door, blew out the lamps then went into a corner and sat against the wall. Hugging his legs to his chest, he put his forehead against his knees. Nemid was gone. Trindal was gone. Kal felt like he was falling from a great height, and he rocked back and forth to soothe the panic. He hadn't felt this alone in a long, long time.

A few weeks later, Kal and Ashekii were walking through the forest when Ashekii stopped and pointed to a trail of ants as they toiled their way along the ground. He and Kal bent over and followed them along the forest floor.

'See?' Ashekii said. 'These ones are going out from the nest in search of food.' They came to a tree at the base of which the line of ants magically disappeared. 'Here', he said. 'If we dig down, we will find their nest.'

They straightened up.

'We will not disturb them today. Ants are our friends. When they work fast, it means rain is coming. When they disappear, it means it is about to snow. Come, let us keep going.'

Ashekii resettled his knife at his waist as they began to jog.

'I have to go and see Mitrah today', he said more to himself than to Kal. 'She still owes us for that meat, and Hahina has been on at me to make her pay up.'

'Why don't you ask Whenro?' Kal said.

'Whenro? What's he got to do with it?'

'Because he is the cousin of Mitrah's father, but she calls him Uncle. As her Uncle from her father's side, he is liable for her debts. He has extra leather at the moment and could pay us. You wouldn't have to bother Mitrah again.'

'We need more leather?'

Kal nodded. 'Inah has chewed through her toys.'

Ashekii shook his head. That baby was unnatural the way she chewed up everything – and she only had a few teeth!

'Your solution to Mitrah's debt is sound', he said. 'I wish I'd thought of it myself. It is tactful and allows both Mitrah and I to save face and not go through the farce of her promising to pay me and both of us knowing she will not. A neat solution. I will ask Whenro.'

Ashekii felt a wave of relief that he would not have to face Mitrah again, and his step now had a jaunt to it. Suddenly he stopped. Kal took another step then glanced back.

'What?' said Kal uncertainly.

'How do you know that?' Ashekii said.

'Know what?'

'Tribal law? Who taught you about kin debt?'

Kal opened his mouth then closed it again, angry with himself for upsetting Ashekii.

'Answer me', Ashekii said.

Kal hung his head and began to tap the fingers of one hand nervously against his leg.

'Well?' Ashekii said. 'Who's been teaching you Nahill law?'

The answer suddenly came to Ashekii.

'It was Nemid, wasn't it?'

Kal's hair fell across his face, and his cheeks went a deep red.

'What else did he teach you?' Ashekii said.

Kal's silence made Ashekii want to shake him. He let out a

frustrated breath and moved forwards. Kal's arms went up to protect his head. Now Ashekii was genuinely angry.

'Seasons of combat training, and this is the best you can do?' he yelled. 'It is an insult to my teaching!'

He strode towards the boy, and there was no mistaking his intent this time. Kal was petrified, but something in Ashekii's barb hit home. Instead of cringing, Kal assumed a defensive stance just in time to deflect the first of Ashekii's blows. Ashekii struck again, and Kal jumped to one side. Letting out a cry of frustration, Ashekii tried a side swipe, but Kal grabbed his arm and dragged him forward off his feet and shoved him into the dirt. Ashekii tried to roll over, but Kal had him in an arm lock.

'Better', Ashekii muttered.

'What?' Kal panted from behind him.

'Better', Ashekii whispered.

Kal leant forward to hear, and in one movement, Ashekii flipped his feet backwards and kicked Kal in the back, pitching him over Ashekii's head. Ashekii sprang up and grabbed, but the boy was lighter and faster and Ashekii missed him. Ashekii ended up sprawled on the ground. Kal stood back, shocked at what he'd done. Ashekii started to laugh. Kal stood uncertainly for a moment. Ashekii sat up and brushed the dirt from himself.

'Much better', he said.

He held out a hand to Kal, but before Kal could pull Ashekii to his feet, Ashekii jerked Kal to the ground and had him covered, holding Kal's arm at a painful angle.

'Never', Ashekii hissed into his ear, 'trust your opponent until both have agreed the battle is over. And once you have bested someone, the battle is never over. Understand?'

Kal nodded, his face pressed into the dirt. Ashekii let him go and stood up. Kal remained where he was as he tried to ascertain Ashekii's mood. It wasn't until Ashekii started walking again that Kal stood up and brushed himself off. He followed Ashekii, staying a few paces behind just to be safe.

'I swear', Ashekii muttered to himself, 'I am going to have a few words with Nemid next time I see him. Of all the stupid things to do.' He shook his head. 'That old fool has dropped me in a right mess, leaving me with a kid who knows tribal laws better than most Drekesh and...', he stopped short and turned on Kal. This time Kal automatically went into a fighting stance. Ashekii's face paled as something horrible suddenly dawned on him. Just how much did this boy know?

Kal had been following him everywhere as he'd gone about his business: family business, tribal business, *Drekesh* business. A chill went down Ashekii's back as a terrifying thought struck him.

A Drekesh had to master eight disciplines; laws, customs, history, etiquette, diplomacy, knife skills, spear throwing and hand to hand combat. The boy's knowledge of tribal law was impressive, and Nemid had been instructing Kal on etiquette and diplomacy. Trindal had been telling Kal history stories, and Ashekii himself had been training Kal in combat skills. A wave of panic ran through him. Was Askekii looking at the very first White Drekesh? He tried to swallow but his throat was dry. No, no, NO! Not wanting to believe his own eyes, he turned on his heel and began to run along the path, Kal following. Soon they were back at White Camp, but they didn't stop. Ashekii lead them on up to the Drekesh training grounds. The masters and trainees were all busy practicing.

'Wait here', Ashekii told Kal.

The boy stayed to one side as Ashekii went to speak with the masters. Several of them glanced at Kal, who nervously switched feet wondering how much trouble he was in. The trainees stopped their exercises and went to stand around the masters, listening to what, at times, appeared to be a heated discussion. It seemed like an eternity before Ashekii beckoned to Kal, who obediently came to his side.

'You're not in trouble', Ashekii said. 'Please answer our questions honestly and attempt our tests as best you can.'

Kal put his mouth to Ashekii's ear and whispered.

'Will Nemid get into trouble if I do this?'

'No.'

Kal gave him a piercing look that Ashekii had never seen him use before. It was as if the boy – young man – he corrected himself, was staring straight into him, assessing if he was telling the truth. There was only one other person Ashekii knew that was able to inflict this kind of intense analysis on someone; Nemid.

'Alright', Kal said.

And so it began. His first test, a gruelling session where the masters questioned him on laws and customs, went well. Kal answered every question correctly. Next was a test of his knife throwing skills. At first it seemed that he'd pass this one with ease, however, when the second wood round was rolled down the hill, Kal's knives seemed to bounce off it. It wasn't until later that they discovered an illegal wood round, with a surface so hardened that nothing would pierce it, had been substituted for the proper one. Next they questioned the boy about etiquette and diplomacy. Then they handed him a spear and placed targets at regular intervals. They asked him to put the spear into each of them. He managed the first three without any trouble. For the fourth, he steadied his hand and took three strong strides before throwing his spear. It only just made it to the fourth target. He picked up the last spear and weighed it in his hand. It didn't feel right. Without thinking, he examined it.

'Proceed', one of the masters said irritably.

Kal shook his head.

'It's not right.'

'Does he think we try to cheat him?' the master said.

Ashekii strode over and took the spear from the boy. He weighted it in his hand then shook his head.

'It is not right for this test', he said.

He went to the remaining spears and checked them all. It seemed someone had substituted lightweight practice spears for the real ones. He said that Kal could not be properly tested with them as it was not fair. Begrudgingly, the masters agreed and indicated for Kal to go to the combat area.

It did not take the other Drekesh long to realise where Kal's weakness lay. Even though Kal was used to being physically assaulted, his natural reaction to aggression was to run or cower and throw his hands up to protect his head. It went against every survival instinct he had to stand up to aggression and defend, fight back or attack. In the best of ten rounds, he only managed to defeat his opponent four times.

The masters wanted to reject him, but Ashekii pointed out something no one else had considered. Kal had been at the Drekesh training ground going from one exercise to the next all day. It was now late afternoon, and he'd not had a rest or anything to eat or drink. It was not fair that this was when they'd chosen to test his combat skills. He doubted that any other Drekesh trainee would have the stamina to perform under these conditions.

There were some who wanted to dismiss Ashekii's claims because he was related to Pac Nemid. However, none could deny their truth. Kal was trembling with exhaustion. He stood his ground and said he would undertake any further testing they required of him. The masters had a quiet discussion with each other. In the end, Kal was excused. He trudged back to Pac Nemid's cabin, collapsed onto his bed and slept till Hahina came to fetch him for dinner. The next morning, Ashekii said that the masters had agreed that he could train with them.

'They have decided that you know too much to not train properly', Ashekii explained. 'We do not want you to be only half a Drekesh. It would not be right.'

Kal's face lit up.

'You're going to train me to be a Drekesh?' he said.

'Yes, not that it will take much longer. You're most of the way there already.'

Kal was bursting with pride, and he wished Nemid was here to share this wonderful news. He was going to be Drekesh!

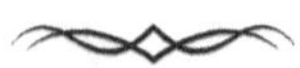

One night, half a dozen Dog clan cars coughed and spluttered their way up the mountain and stopped in the White Camp car park. Drekesh were sent to see what they wanted. With no income, Dog clan had lost the Dog house and, for the first time in living memory, they had to choose between living on the reservation full time or staying in the white world. The Drekesh indicated the suitcases in their cars.

'Not allowed', they said.

'But…', Aunt Talks Too Much protested, 'we've only brought our clothes. What are we supposed to wear?'

A short time later, a bonfire was going in the car park and Aunt Talks Too Much and the others were silently getting dressed into the Nahill fashion of tunic and leggings. The suitcases were thrown onto the bonfire. A semi-circle of Water clan Drekesh watched as Lemon and Hasty tossed their camouflage pants onto the pyre with a stoic set to their young jaws. They already knew they were going to hate it here with no PlayStations, no video player and no TV. What was a person supposed to do to amuse themselves, for crying out aloud?

Mash glanced at his mother, who nodded her head. Reluctantly he retrieved his beloved 'Rem and Stimpy' comic books from the car and tossed them into the fire. No more cartoons, he thought, life totally sucked. It was bad enough that he'd had to sell his Nike shoes, but he'd refused to sell his comic collection. He watched the flames consume everything that had any meaning to him. It was devastating. What were they supposed to eat now there was no home delivery pizza?

Next to him, Remmy had tears running down her cheeks as she stared at her NSync poster. So many nights she'd fantasied that she would meet the band and sparks would fly and she would join them. It was all so unfair. The girls had all been forced to unbraid their hair and remove their makeup. How would she cope with no nail polish or music? Her life was black. She knew she would just die if she didn't have Justin Timberlake and Brittany Spears in her life. As to not being able to have a hot shower, that was just disgusting and gross, and she had a good mind to follow Ravrah. Ravrah had just flat out refused to live at the camp and had moved in with her boyfriend. Ravrah hadn't been the only one.

Faced with the prohibition on cigarettes, alcohol or any other drug, a number of Dog clan members had chosen not to return. They'd all hugged each other and then waved goodbye to those leaving forever. It had been so sad. A tragedy. Not that the Nahill cared what anyone from Dog clan thought. Remmy had even had to remove her earrings and every other piece of jewellery. She may as well put on eyeliner, dress in black and become a Goth. She began to warm to that idea and wondered how charcoal would go as eyeshadow.

'Rem', Sindri snapped, 'get on with it!'

Instead of throwing her poster into the fire, Remmy began tearing it into little pieces to represent how her heart had been shattered. Sindri scratched her arm. Her skin was crawling from nicotine withdrawals. She wasn't the only one who was tense and snappy. She shot a glance into the forest knowing their every move was also being watched by Trill, although they had the good grace to keep out of sight.

Sindri wondered what was to become of the old people. They'd all gone to Blue Camp but how many of them would freeze this winter without the creature comforts of the Dog house? Everyone's lives had been turned upside down. No money from the Education Department meant no money for rent, food or petrol or all the other things they'd become used to. They had given their best cars to those who were staying in the white world. No cars meant the end of dropping in to visit the relatives who lived in Blue Camp on the other side of the lake. A tear ran down her cheeks. Bastards, she thought. Ignorant puritans. It wasn't fair. None of it was fair.

Aunt Talks Too Much was also going through nicotine withdrawals but refused to take her bad mood out on her relations. She was saving that for payback. It had been humiliating coming back to White Camp, especially seeing those Water clan usurpers living in cabins that up until recently had belonged to Dog clan. What did any of them know of real hardship? Just the sight of them made her sick.

Uncle Mends Things stepped forward and held out a branch that he had taken from one of the Dog house fruit trees. It had a single golden peach on it. Everyone could remember the taste of those delicious peaches. The juice would run down their chins as they'd feasted on them. In silence he tossed the branch onto the fire. As they all watched, the ripe, plump peach sizzled for a moment then burst into flames. Tears flowed down their cheeks like the juice from the forbidden fruit they'd never be permitted to taste again.

Big Camp stretched out through the trees with the Shashbai River running through the middle to Lake Meri Yallock. In the distance was the sacred island of the Great Spirits. On either side, as far as the eye could see, were clusters of mud-brick cabins. Almost all had a thin trail of smoke rising from their chimneys. Dirt paths wove between the dwellings, and fields filled with the three sisters dotted the landscape.

Nemid and Trindal walked along one of the paths accompanied by three of Nemid's Water clan cousins, who were helping him to find a Matchmaker. The Matchmaker had the delicate task of finding a suitable woman to claim Trindal. Nemid had changed his clothes to reflect the fashion of Big Camp. He wore a long tunic and a clutch of sashes – a blue sash to indicate he was from Water clan, a black sash to indicate he was a Drekesh and a red sash to indicate he was a camp Pac. Trindal also wore a long tunic and had the blue sash of Water clan and a white sash to indicate he was on a claiming tour. As they walked, the people they passed would bow as soon as they saw Nemid's sashes.

'Drekesh', some whispered reverently.

'Guide and protect', some would say, touching their chests before they bowed low.

When the two got to a set of cabins that, to Trindal, looked the same as every other group of cabins, they were met by a woman with frizzy black hair and the proud bearing of one from Tree clan. Her figure was solid and attested to the many dinners and feasts she had attended. As she spoke, she had a habit of clasping both hands in front of her, and when she was thinking, she would slide her thumbs back and forth. She had only agreed to take Trindal on as a favour and had been dreading it. Nemid's cousin bowed to her then indicated Nemid.

'Esteemed Amrix', the cousin said, 'allow me to present Nemid, Me pect Drekesh of Water clan, current Pac of White Camp. His mother was Neskatpi of Water clan, White Camp, his Grandmother was Chalish of Water clan, White Camp and his Great Grandmother was Serrashno of Water clan, Red Camp', she turned towards Nemid and indicated Amrix.

'Esteemed cousin, allow me to present Amrix from Tree clan. She is the best Matchmaker in Big Camp.'

Nemid and Amrix sized each other up with a look then inclined their heads towards each other. Her critical eye went to Trindal.

'Is this your grandson?' she said.

'It is', Nemid said, pulling Trindal forward.

Trindal bowed to Amrix, just as Nemid had taught him.

'This is an honour', he said.

He straightened and smiled at her. His manner had a kind of endearing impishness to it that one would remember, Amrix thought, so perhaps Trindal would not be so hard to place after all. As she studied him more carefully, her thumbs slid back and forth. He was pleasing to look at, and those blue eyes were certainly a beguiling feature. Many families would dismiss the boy because of his water-eyes and how unlucky some thought they were, but some believed just the opposite. Perhaps, she mused, some might even find such a feature intriguing. If he were well-mannered, they might be a conversation point.

Trindal remained formally erect, allowing Amrix to take stock of him. He hated having people assess his worth as potential husband material but was getting used to it. Nemid had told Trindal to always be on his best behaviour if he wanted to attract a good claiming offer, which meant that far from being fun, this trip was rapidly becoming boring with a capital B.

'Let us walk', Amrix said to Nemid.

The small group strolled along the street, and Nemid answered all Amrix's questions about Trindal's achievements. Could he find water, make a dwelling, make a fire and all the rest of the things a husband was expected to be able to do. Trindal walked beside them feeling superfluous and peeved that Amrix didn't just ask him directly.

'When did he make his first kill?' Amrix said.

'A short time ago, and Drekesh will attest to it.'

Trindal opened his mouth to say that he'd killed several times now, but Nemid's cousin silenced him with a sharp poke in the back. Amrix nodded, her thumbs rubbing back and forth.

'There are several families that are currently looking for a suitable match. I think he is too young for Bretel's Hoetath, but perhaps for Leniex's youngest, Usti?'

A shrewd expression crossed her face.

'He's storyteller-trained, isn't he?'

'Yes.'

'Dowry?'

'He has none now, but there are two who are available for claiming.'

She cocked her head to one side, puzzled. Suddenly a knowing smile crossed her face.

'You're going to remarry?' Amrix said. 'Oh, I am so glad. Now let me see, who can I think of that might be suitable for a camp Pac?'

'No, no', Nemid said quickly, 'not me. I do not intend to marry again. I meant my other grandson Kal.'

Trindal's jaw muscles tensed. He knew from experience that the moment Kal was brought into a conversation, no one even noticed him. A flash of anger ran through him. This was supposed to be *his* time.

'You have another son?'

'Yes. He's my foundling. He's older than Trindal. A very hard worker.'

Trindal moved forward.

'Kal's white', he put in.

Amrix was about to laugh at this joke then saw the set to Nemid's face.

'You're serious?' she said. 'But what kind of mother is going to allow her daughter to claim a white boy?'

Trindal allowed himself a smug smile and looked away. Nemid raised his head proudly.

'By the time of the claiming, he will be my adopted son.'

She frowned thoughtfully, her thumbs tapping against each other.

'Hmm', she said, 'the adopted son of a camp Pac? That's sounding more desirable. What was his first kill?'

'As yet, he hasn't…'

'And his profession?'

'Does that matter?'

She gave a derisive laugh.

'Of course it does', she dropped her voice conspiratorially. 'I've heard of families who lie about their boy's profession to get a desirable claiming offer. One even claimed her son was a Drekesh. Outrageous!'

'Drekesh is still popular then?' Pac Nemid said.

'Of course. It is surpassed only by a Councillor or Pac', and she gave him a pointed look. She placed a hand on his arm and lowered her voice. 'I will give you some advice. If you wish to secure a desirable claiming offer for Trindal, then I would not mention Kal to anyone. It is not just because he is white. You have to think about this from a mother's perspective looking to do the right thing by her daughter. Kal is too old to have no training, and he has not even made his first kill yet. I assume his dowry is as pitiful as Trindal's, and on top of that, he is white. To be honest, to find Kal a suitable claiming offer, you are going to need more than a good Matchmaker, you are going to need a miracle.'

Trindal let out a sigh of relief that the subject of Kal had been dealt with once and for all, and his good humour was restored. This was the first time in Trindal's short life that he'd had any kind of parental figure all to himself. He silently vowed to do whatever it took to attract a good match and to make Nemid proud. Once he was claimed, perhaps he and Nemid together could find someone who'd condescend to take poor Kal. Meantime, Nemid's focus was on Trindal and Trindal alone. There was a new spring in Trindal's step as they continued on their way.

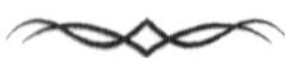

Sweat ran down Kal's face. He let out a cry and changed his stance with the other Drekesh practicing their combat skills. The Drekesh master paced back and forth in front of them, his hands clasped behind his back as he assessed them. Suddenly a stick was flying towards the head of one of the boys. The boy ducked, grabbing the stick and, dropping down, pulled the stick from the master's hand. With a savage kick, the master sent the boy sprawling.

'Never give your opponent an advantage like that', he said to the others.

Taking up his stick, he walked back along the line.

'Proceed!'

Kal's partner grabbed him and threw him to the ground. Kal rolled and finished in a crouching stance, ready to punch out. A swift kick was delivered to his ribs, and Kal went flying. A heavy weight fell onto his back, two hands went about his head, one on his forehead and the other on his neck. With just one twist Kal would be dead.

'Die white scum', Kal's opponent hissed into his ear.

The master indicated that the boy had won the round and that Kal was now 'dead.' The boy got off Kal and moved on to the next partner. Kal got up slowly, his ribs and back smarting from the blows. He wiped the sweat from his forehead and walked over to his next opponent.

Once this exercise was finished, the trainees relaxed and moved out to form a circle. The combat master pointed to two different trainees.

'Begin', he yelled.

The two boys assumed fighting stances and began to circle each other warily. The master pointed to another pair and made them lie on their stomachs before commencing their battle. The next pair was to fight on their knees, the one after had to use knives, the next sticks, and so on he went until all the young men were fighting in pairs. The Drekesh master went from pair to pair getting them to change their combat situations and use different weapons until all had fought in every position.

'Finished!' he cried. 'Up!'

They stood.

'Eyes closed', the master called.

Everyone closed their eyes, each hoping they weren't going to be his next victim.

'Open!' the master called.

They opened their eyes, and one found the stick coming right at him. Instead of ducking, he thrust himself forward, tackling the master to the ground. After a brief wrestle, he had the master pinned to the ground with the stick.

'Very good', the master said. 'An excellent manoeuvre. Up!'

The apprentice was on his feet, and the master stood adjusting his clothes. Suddenly he wheeled the stick straight at Kal. Kal dropped into a crouch, grabbed the stick with both hands and pulled it towards him, unbalancing the master who fell on top of him. They wrestled with the stick for a moment before the master made a jab at Kal's throat with his elbow. Kal only just moved out of his way. It was all the master needed, and he released the stick, his hands going about Kal's throat. Kal froze.

'No!' the master yelled into his face. 'Never freeze. Move! Fight or you will be dead! Again!'

He released Kal, and they resumed their tussle over the stick.

'Use your body', the master rasped between breaths.

Kal got the master in a strong hold but, knowing Kal's weak points, the master moved to one side then yelled at Kal and feigned a punch to his face. Kal released him, and his hands flew up to his head.

'No!' the master screamed. 'No, no, no! How many times must I tell you, do not listen to the opponent's voice, listen to his body. You had me, and I fooled you into letting me go. You know this is your weak point. You must overcome it. Again.'

Once more they began their tussle. Kal extracted a leg and kneed the master in the side. He fell over, winded. Kal didn't need to be told again, he jumped onto the older man, positioning the stick across his neck.

'Yes', the master said, 'much better. Up!'

Kal stood, his chest heaving and sweat running down his face.

The master indicated for all the trainee Drekesh to resume their drill stance. Kal bowed to the combat master as protocol dictated then readied himself for his next sparring match.

When Kal wearily trudged into Nemid's cabin late in the afternoon, he found Chani waiting for him with a bowl of warmed healing mixture.

'They all hate me', he said.

She tried to hide her smile at his dejected look. He stripped off and stood still while she daubed his fresh cuts, grazes and scratches with the mixture.

'I saw you talking to that Red Camp Healer', he said through gritted teeth. 'Any news?'

'Two babies have arrived this moon.'

'Yeah? That's good, right?'

'Maybe. They were both boys.'

She made a face and Kal sighed.

'Just because everyone wants girls', he said, 'that doesn't mean boys aren't any good.'

'Girls are much more useful', she said.

He took in a quick breath as she scrubbed a cut.

'Do you reckon', he said, clenching his teeth again, 'that they would have adopted me by now if I'd been a girl?'

She shrugged, but he knew he was right.

'The fungi harvest promises to be very good this season', she said. He smiled.

'I'm looking forward to it', he said.

He held his leg up so she could scrub his grazed knee.

'Someone is getting better', she said with a smile, 'not nearly as many injuries this time.'

It was late in the afternoon. Amrix had set up yet another 'first look' meeting for Trindal with an eligible girl. Amrix stood to one side chatting with the parents as Nemid took a small package wrapped in cloth from his pocket and handed it to Trindal. A young woman came to stand under a nearby tree, a haughty expression to her stance. She was heavily pregnant. Her long hair was ornately braided around her head as was the fashion at Big Camp.

'Remember', Nemid whispered to Trindal, 'best behaviour, and if she chooses you to join her favourites, say yes immediately.'

Trindal glanced at the girl.

'What if I don't like her?' he whispered back.

Instead of answering, Nemid gave Trindal a little push towards the girl who was staring up at the sky. Nemid silently crossed his fingers that this match would work out. Never had Nemid realised how delicate and difficult the claiming rituals were these days. After several weeks, Amrix had only found a handful of parents willing to let their daughters meet a boy with water-eyes, and none had submitted a claiming offer. Nemid had gone from being discerning about families and clans to entertaining offers from anyone. Amrix had been right to advise him not to mention Kal as these Big Camp families were skittish enough about Trindal. He knew they would baulk at having a white man as a brother. Even entertaining the notion might damage a family's reputation and standing. So he had firmly put any thoughts of Kal aside and focused solely on Trindal.

Trindal walked quietly over to the girl. He bowed low then offered her the present. She looked at it undecidedly for a moment then opened it. Inside was a carved wooden animal for her unborn child. She smiled and then looked at Trindal. He was cute, she thought, but he was too young. The only reason she'd agreed to meet him was because her parents had pressured her into it as a favour to Amrix.

'Thank you', she said.

Trindal gave her his most winning smile and indicated her belly.

'What portents from the Oracle for this one?' he said.

They began walking slowly as they chatted, and Nemid sent a silent prayer to the Great Spirits that this girl would make an offer for Trindal. The couple parted, and Nemid raised his eyebrows hopefully at Amrix. She made the sign she always did, which was that it was too early to tell. After a while, Trindal came to stand beside him.

'Well?' Nemid whispered.

Trindal shrugged. 'She liked the carving.'

'Did she like *you*?'

Again, Trindal shrugged. 'I think so.'

Nemid gave him a pat on the shoulder, and the two of them walked towards Amrix, who was talking to the parents. After a moment, she bowed and bade them goodbye.

'Never mind', she said, 'we'll try again.'

Nemid groaned. He had originally hoped to only be at Big Camp for the snow season as he dared not be away from White Camp for too long. Nothing was going according to plan, however, and he wondered if he would have to abandon this and return to his Pac duties at White Camp regardless.

21

Snow season and the season of the Snow Thaw came and went. Trindal was now spending most days with the Big Camp storytellers while Amrix searched for more possible matches. There was little for Nemid to do, and time sat heavily on his hands. He'd had no idea at the outset that finding a suitable match for Trindal would take so long, his own claimings having been settled over a period of two seasons. Amrix constantly assured him things were moving very quickly, by Big Camp standards.

After breakfast one sunny morning in the season of the Butterflies, Nemid could stand the waiting no longer. He put water and food into a small pack and strolled out of the cabin they'd been staying in. He picked a direction at random and wandered along the dirt path, hands clasped behind his back. As he passed the mud brick dwellings, he could hear happy voices and laughter. Brightly coloured party clothes were hanging from poles, drying in the morning breeze. Occasionally he was passed by a slave carrying buckets of water. He frowned and mulled over how different Big Camp was compared to the Drekesh camps where daily life centred around survival.

He thought back to when he and Trindal had first arrived. They were settled by the beginning of the season of the First Snow, a time when most Nahill made new things and repaired the old, but at Big Camp people spent their time entertaining, listening to stories and socialising. Then there was the season of the Snow Thaw. This was when visitors returned to their homes and when claimings took place. Here at Big Camp, they certainly observed the claiming season, however, the streets and market areas were abuzz with an influx of people here to curry favour, seek advice or try to influence the decisions of the Women's Council. After this was the season of the Salmon, which was when everyone else caught salmon, but here in Big Camp, activities centred on the first sittings of the Women's Council. The season of the New Leaves was, for most Nahill, one of the busiest times with everyone in the fields. Planting and tending the food crops usually lasted through the season of the New Wings and into the season of the Butterflies, but here in Big Camp, it was one long party season. Every residence was festooned with colour, and everywhere was gaiety. The air was rich with delicious food aromas.

The reason they could be so idle was because their slaves did the hard work and the tithe system. No one knew how it had come about, but Big Camp exacted food and material tithes from all the other camps. Nemid had never agreed with this and, during his youth, he had actively campaigned against it. Now he was a Pac, he was adamant that White Camp would not send anything. But that was a battle yet to come.

While Trindal was enchanted with the Big Camp lifestyle, Nemid grew ever weary of it. He couldn't believe that at one time he'd enjoyed living like this. On a whim, he turned onto the path that would take him past the area where he and his first wife, Trinuxa, used to live. Little had changed, he mused, as he passed the adobe dwellings. Each was bedaubed with the colours and symbols of the families who lived in them. This part of Big Camp was heavily populated by Tree clan.

Nemid came to a shady tree and stopped, turning to the right. A large storage shed stood where Trinuxa's house had once been. Trinuxa had been a good deal older than him, but they had grown to love each other. Nemid examined the area, searching for any trace of his previous life. There was nothing. After all the struggles the two of them had endured, it had amounted to nothing.

He could remember her cries of pain over those last seasons. It had been unrelenting, and he'd never felt so powerless. It had crushed something deep inside him knowing there was nothing anyone could do to help the woman he loved more than life itself. And then there was what he considered his greatest shame and failure... He stopped that thought, closed his eyes and felt fresh waves of helplessness wash over him. For all his wealth and power, he had not been able to save either of them. He'd been reduced to nothing … nothing. When he left this place, it was no wonder he had been just a shell of a man.

Suddenly he felt the need to get away from all thoughts of his old life. He strode away until he came to a field filled with the familiar sight of the three sisters. His pace slowed as he turned towards the field. The corn stalks were about shoulder height, the beans winding around them and the pumpkin leaves growing thickly about their base.

He stopped to breathe in the rich smells of new growth, compost and damp soil. It reminded him of home and a good, honest day's work. His eyes ran from one side of the field to the other, finding it soothing to see the orderly mounds. Here and there a man or woman could be seen carrying sacks of compost. Others were bent down weeding, and some were cultivating the soil with hoes or spades. A man approached Nemid. His tattered clothes were smudged with dirt and damp from sweat. He wore a head cloth to keep his long black hair out of his face and had a Tree clan tattoo on his cheek, which designated him as a Tree clan slave. He bowed to Nemid.

'Can I be of assistance sir?' he said.

'I've come to help', Nemid heard himself say.

The man regarded him in surprise. Since when did a free man help with the crops, he thought? Nemid strode past him and into the field. The sweet smell of corn and the mud squelching up between his bare toes felt wonderful. In no time, he was hunkered down pulling weeds.

It was now late into the season of the Dried Grass. Big fat March flies were buzzing through the air, biting any bare skin they found.

People wore their lightest weight tunics and bare feet. Everywhere smelt of eucalyptus oil from the leaves that lay baking on the dry soil. The ground crackled when walked upon, and the leaves and grass turned crisp and brown from the heat.

Laughter flowed from a dirt path through the forest. Thirteen-snows-old Shashina from Bird clan walked with the young men that were her current claiming favourites. The two Tree clan boys were from Big Camp, the Stone clan boy was from Black Camp and then there was Trindal. Her inclination so far was leaning towards one of the Tree clan boys as he was from a very prestigious family, but he was rather obtuse. Trindal had surprised her with his wit and charm, even though she had only agreed to include him as a favour to Amrix. As they spilled out onto a sandy beach, Trindal let out a cry of delight when he saw the lake. He ran down to the edge, hoisted his tunic and wadded in the cool waters, jumping each small wave. Shashina studied him. He was a handsome boy, she mused, and his grandfather was a camp Pac. Perhaps Amrix had been right to insist she give him a chance.

'Race you to the end', Trindal cried out.

The boys took off along the white sandy cove, Shashina right on their heels. When they got to the point, she looked back and could only just make out the smudge on the horizon that she knew was Big Camp. Panting, she realised she had never ventured this far from home before.

'Look', said Trindal pointing towards the cliff above their heads, 'there's a path. I bet it takes us to the next cove. Wanna check it out?'

Without waiting for an answer, he hopped along the rocks and scrambled up. Shashina found that having a prospect with a bit of pluck was a novelty, and she and the others quickly followed him. She was surprised and pleased that Trindal was taking such an active part in their adventure. She was growing weary of the smarminess of the other claiming prospects. They all danced attendance on her and agreed with everything she said no matter how outlandish.

Seeing the bigger boys nearly upon him, Trindal increased his pace. When Shashina had invited him to join them, he had taken one look at his competition and assumed that he stood no chance. Sick of being on his best behaviour all the time, Trindal had decided that he might as well enjoy himself before he got sent home. When they got to the top of the promontory, he stood with his hands on his hips catching his breath and staring out over the coves ahead.

'Look at that', he said in awe.

Before them were more coves and in the distance was the sacred island of the Great Spirits, also known as Toe Island. Legend had it that when the Great Spirits first arrived on earth, this lake was formed by their right foot, and Toe Island was formed when the mud squished up between the big toe and next toe. It was a reminder to all that the Great Spirits were real and that the stories of them once inhabiting the earth were true. Shashina came to stand beside him, pulling her hair back from her sweating face.

'I've never been this close before', she said.

Trindal pointed.

'A few more coves and we'll be right in front of it. Come on.'

He jogged along the thin dirt track, the others following. They continued from cove to cove clambering around landslides and rocks until they came to a sandy cove that was adjacent to the island. They all stopped and stared at the breathtaking vista. The island rose from the sea like a finger of white, and atop it was an unruly tuft of green ferns, shrubs and several stubby trees.

'It's beautiful', Shashina whispered.

'Someone from Blue Camp once told me', Trindal said, 'that there's a little cove on the other side just big enough for a raft. There's a track that leads up the rock face that's only big enough for one foot at a time. He said that once you get up there, you can just feel that it is a special, magical, sacred place.'

They all stared out at the island wishing they had some kind of water craft to get to it. At that moment, an engine roared, and they looked on, horrified, as a speed boat emerged from the other side of the island. The white occupants sat, some with drinks in their hands, as the white skipper navigated away from the island. One of the passengers threw a silver can overboard. The engine revved, and they sped away from shore. They increased their speed further, their propeller sending plumes of white water over the still blueness of the lake as they headed towards the buoys that clearly marked the boundary of the Jhunti reservation and Jhunti waters.

Shashina swallowed back a lump in her throat and, unable to look at Toe Island anymore, turned and began walking back along the beach towards home. The boys fell silently in line behind her. Trindal was tempted to abandon this farce and return to Big Camp on his own, but knew this would bring shame to Nemid.

After scrambling back along the cliffs, they spotted an inlet fed by a creek. They made their way to it then walked up the stream until the water was fresh and sweet. Kneeling, they drank their fill then flopped down in a cool, mossy glade to rest. To take her mind off what they'd seen, Shashina picked up a stick and pointed it at the Tree clan boy she was most interested in.

'If the Great Spirits granted you one wish, what would it be?'

He thought for a moment then smiled.

'That you would claim me.'

She laughed and rolled her eyes before moving her stick to point at the boy from Black Camp.

'And your wish?'

The boy chewed his bottom lip for a moment. 'I've always wanted to be able to hear what animals think.'

She smiled then moved her stick to Trindal.

'If I could have anything', Trindal said, 'I'd wish that I could remember all the stories in the world. That way I would always have new ones to tell people as I travel.'

Her stick paused for a long moment on him before she moved on to the other Tree clan boy. He was miffed that someone with water-eyes had impressed her when everyone said Trindal's inclusion had only been as a favour and that he had no hope of attaining Shashina.

'If I had one wish', he said, 'it would be to eradicate every white man from this world, so it would be the way the Great Spirits meant it to be.'

Shashina felt torn between wishing for the same thing and being aware that Trindal had a white father and an adopted white brother. It would, therefore, be impolite to deliberately be rude to him.

'You have a brother, don't you?' the boy said to Trindal. 'The one they call the White Rat?'

'Don't call him that', Trindal said.

Shashina turned towards Trindal. 'I've always wanted to know', she said, 'why your brother doesn't tell his people to stop coming onto our land. Surely he knows how we feel about it? If his family won't listen, why doesn't he speak to their Women's Council and get them to issue a directive for it to stop? We have so little, surely they can see it isn't right?'

All eyes were upon Trindal, and he looked away. He couldn't answer because he himself had wondered this very thing. It was different for Trindal; he'd been raised with the Jhunti and had never known his parents, both having died when he was young. Even their names had been lost in time, but even so, he was embarrassed and ashamed every time the topic of his mixed heritage was raised. It occurred to him that the slight advantage he'd gained with Shashina was now lost. His anger rose. He was so sick of being judged by what he looked like and not for who he was. He was sick of this whole charade. He would just have to concede that no one would ever claim him.

'White scum', one of the boys mumbled.

Something in Trindal snapped and he launched himself at the boy. The two of them tussled, and everyone, including Trindal, was surprised when he quickly subdued the bigger boy. Trindal sat on the boy's back, pinning the boy's arms down and shoving his face into the ground.

'Say you're sorry', Trindal said.

The boy hesitated, and Trindal jammed his face further into the dirt.

'Alright, I'm sorry.'

'Sorry for what?'

'I'm sorry for calling your brother white scum. Now get off me.'

Trindal gave the boy one more shove then stood up, sending a silent thank you to Ashekii for all those seasons of combat training. Shashina stood up, sick of boys. None of them were thinking about her or trying to make her feel better. All they could think about was fighting. Typical men!

She stalked away wishing they were closer to home. Trindal knew enough about girls to realise she was upset but decided he didn't care. In fact, he realised that he was heartily sick of this whole claiming farce. As someone who'd taken his likeability for granted and never had trouble winning people over, the constant rejection by these girls and their families was changing him deep down, and he didn't like it. And so, as he watched Shashina's indignant retreat towards Big Camp, her three claiming prospects running after her, Trindal decided it was time for change. He was old enough to look after himself and he had no real desire to start a family or get married. He'd only gone along with the whole claiming thing to make Nemid happy. He decided that when he got back, he would tell Nemid to return to White Camp and he would head off to some of the more distant settlements. They were always desperate for storytellers, and it was time he got on with his life's mission of collecting as many Nahill stories as he could. Instantly he felt better and even whistled a tune as he started back towards Big Camp at a leisurely pace.

He was surprised when he found the others waiting for him the next cove along. Shashina seemed in a better frame of mind, and he'd just bet that it was because the three boys had been grovelling to her. With no pressure to be on his best behaviour to please everyone, Trindal relaxed and became his normal self. A gust of wind blew Shashina's hair across her face. She raked it back with her fingers and smiled. In that moment, she looked very pretty, Trindal mused.

'Come on, slow frog', she called.

He fell into step, and the five of them made their way along the beach. Shashina was feeling bad for the way they'd all attacked Trindal for something that was not his fault. Even though she didn't think he'd be suitable for her, she didn't want to offend a camp Pac by being rude to his grandson. Enjoying the walk now, Trindal began whistling.

Shashina glanced at him.

'What's that?'

'It's a song I'm working on', he said. 'It's to go with the story I've been creating about the reclaiming of White Camp. I think it will make a good epic for snow season.'

Sensing he had a captive audience and a long journey ahead, Trindal began his new story. He started at the beginning with how he'd come to be at Red Camp, then meeting Chani and Chet Chet. He made sure to put a quaver in his voice as he spoke of Chet Chet's untimely death and the funeral they held for her then how Nemid had taken him in. As he spoke of his first trip in a car, everyone was entranced. Trindal's tale continued as he described the early days at White Camp and the strange creatures he'd seen in picture books. Using every trick he'd learnt from Aloth at Red Camp, Trindal gave each character a different voice and injected his story with joy and humour, sadness and hardship. In no time, they had arrived at Shashina's house. Trindal had just finished telling them about the last Healer, only in Trindal's version it was he that had found her bones. He turned towards Shashina.

'Thank you for asking me out today', he said. 'I have had a really nice time with you and your prospects.' He gave her a little bow then turned to the boys. 'It was an honour to make your acquaintance. I wish you all good hunting and a healthy life.'

He made to leave but Shashina put a hand on his arm.

'Wait', she said, 'you can't go yet. What happened when you told Pac Nemid about the bones of the Last Healer?'

'And what happened to Dog clan?' one of the boys said. 'I hope someone gave them a good thumping.'

'I wish I had more time to tell you all those things', Trindal said in a regretful tone, 'but Amrix told me to find her the moment I got back. It's alright', he added, looking at Shashina, 'I can tell it's a no, but it was nice to meet you.'

Not only did Shashina want to hear the rest of the story, but on the way back, she'd envisaged inviting her friends over to hear this firsthand account of an event that had scandalised everyone at Big

Camp. Having a private first telling of a tale that was bound to become a classic would be an event that everyone would be talking about … and she would be at the centre. Trindal turned to leave again.

'Wait!' she said. 'Don't race off. I didn't say no.'

Trindal shot a pointed glance toward the other boys. Everyone knew she had already chosen her favourite and it wasn't Trindal.

'Tell Amrix', she said, 'that you *are* one of my prospects. Now let's get something to eat.'

She indicated for them all to go inside. The boys eagerly filed into the building, but Trindal stayed where he was, torn. Being a prospect was the best offer he'd had so far, but it still wasn't a claiming offer, and the open road beckoned. He waited till the others had gone inside then turned to face Shashina and lowered his voice.

'To be honest', he said, 'I'm not sure I'm right for you.'

Shashina's eyes widened. With her connections and prestigious family, she'd never had any boy reject *her* before.

'What?'

Sensing he'd offended her, Trindal quickly explained. 'It's not you. I want to travel and spend my life collecting stories and meeting new people. I think you'd be much better off with one of them', he cocked a head towards the prospects. 'They'll want to stay here and raise a family with you.'

She straightened, unused to a boy speaking to her so candidly about what he wanted.

'But I want to hear the rest of the story', she said. 'I was going to invite some friends over. We're all dying to know the truth about what happened.'

Trindal pondered her words. Even though his tale wasn't quite finished yet, ever the entertainer, he was reluctant to turn down a willing audience.

'Well that's completely different', he said. 'Let's go.'

Pleased, Shashina led Trindal inside. Once her friends and family were assembled, Trindal did a quick recap of the story so far then launched into the new part he'd been working on with Aloth, the story of the last Healer. From the first moment, people were captivated.

As Shashina glanced around and noticed Trindal had everyone's rapt attention, it dawned on her that life with Trindal would be filled with times like this. His ability to create and tell mesmerising stories would make Trindal a much sought after storyteller, and as his wife, she would share that status and popularity. She pictured herself receiving entreaties from all over the reservation, all begging for Trindal to make an appearance. Of course it would be she who decided where they would go.

She looked at Trindal with new eyes and tried to imagine him with a deeper voice and the figure of a man. She decided she could do a lot worse. So many had rejected him, and it appealed to her that only she, in her wisdom, had seen the gem beneath. How superior she would feel when others finally experienced Trindal's talent and knew they'd let him slip through their fingers.

As she glanced at her single girlfriends, she knew she wasn't the only one having these thoughts. She decided she would have to act quickly. Silently leaving the party, she sent a slave to summon Amrix.

The warmth of the season of the Dried Grass had given way to the crisp nights and cooler days of the season of the Apples. One day Amrix came to their cabin early and told Nemid, in a thrilled breath, that Shashina's clan had invited him and Trindal to a full moon feast. Amrix said this was a sure sign that the end was in sight. She reminded Nemid to be on his best behaviour, to be agreeable and to impress them so they were all convinced that Shashina was making a good match.

'And remember', she said, 'this is not the place to mention Kal.'

'But what if someone asks if I have other children? Do you want me to lie?'

'Do you want Trindal to be claimed?'

Nemid's jaw clenched.

'If these people will not claim Trin because he has a white brother then I am not sure I will agree to the match.'

Amrix rolled her eyes.

'That's not what I'm saying. It's a matter of timing. Most young people have grown up knowing each other, so this has been rather hastily put together. They are aware that Kal exists, but there is no need to remind them that perhaps they should investigate more thoroughly.'

'Investigate? He's not violent. He just happens to have a different coloured skin. They should learn to be more tolerant. There's too much prejudice around here. Maybe I should have a word to some of my contacts on the Women's Council.'

Amrix patted his arm.

'Not until after the ceremony', she said soothingly. 'Now remember what I said. If the subject arises, steer it in a different direction. I'm sure someone with your background in politics won't have a problem doing this one small thing.'

After Amrix had gone, Nemid went for a walk until he found raised ground. He sat down and closed his eyes waiting till he felt the cool, evening breeze touch his cheeks. He entreated both his wives to come to him and help him as he felt conflicted. On the one hand, he wanted to do everything possible so that Trindal could make a good match, and Shashina was definitely that. On the other, having to remain silent about the need for a more progressive attitude towards white culture grated on his nerves. It wasn't just Kal that would be affected. A part of Chani's mission was to bring more white medical knowledge to the Nahill. It was why she had been taught English, why she was currently attending school to learn to read and why she had been brought up to be tolerant and to question why things were the way they were.

Since he and Healer Deikter had first discussed it, he'd been elated. Never should anyone have to suffer like Trinuxa. Again, he thought of Trindal. Time was getting on, and he did not want to spend another snow season away from White Camp. Already he had been gone much longer than any of them had anticipated. If

Amrix was correct, Trindal would soon be claimed and Nemid could return home. Perhaps there was no harm in placing his mission in the background for now and focusing on what was best for Trindal and the current job at hand.

A weight seemed to lift from his shoulders, and he silently thanked his wives for their wise counsel. He walked back to his lodgings feeling better and looking forward to meeting more of Shashina's clan tomorrow.

The next day, Nemid arose early and went out into the forest looking for anything special he could contribute to the feast. He returned well-pleased with a fern basket filled with late season berries.

As Shashina was from Bird clan, he selected his most impressive wooden bird toys as presents and arrived at the feast in time to help wrestle a large branch onto the fire. His gifts were well received. In no time, he ascertained that Trindal had been his agreeable self and charmed all the elders. As the night progressed, Nemid's company was in high demand as Amrix escorted him from one clutch of Bird clan relatives to the next, doing the introductions and facilitating conversation towards what a good match Shashina was making and, in subtle ways, pressing for a speedy claiming so Nemid could return to his Pac duties at White Camp. Nemid found Shashina's people friendly and easy to converse with. It was late in the evening, and Nemid was chatting with elderly sisters Ishin and Ashan. Nemid was about to make his excuses and retire to bed when Ashan asked about Dog clan. The reed-thin Ishin moved closer and lowered her voice.

'We hear', she said, 'that you had a hand in bringing them to heel.'

'Yes', her equally thin sister Ashan said, 'it was you that stopped them getting the favours from the white school.'

Nemid pondered for a moment then realised that by favours they meant money.

'Such a shame', he said and took a sip of his drink.

'We are told', Ishin said, 'that some are at Blue Camp and some have gone back to White Camp.'

The smile disappeared from his face.

'They are back at White Camp?' Nemid said sharply, suddenly

incensed that no one had thought to tell him what was happening in his own camp.

'Yes.'

'We hear it's quite a mess.'

The two sisters glanced at each other, both delighted to have such juicy gossip.

'Cars everywhere…'

'And furniture…'

'And something called bicycles.'

Ishin looked at her sister, both hands pressed together then flapping them open.

'What are those thin things called, the ones with white pictures in them?'

'Books?' Nemid said.

'Yes', Ishin nodded, 'books. And lots of shiny little things. Figurines and such.'

'And bottles that they drink out of all day and night.'

'The Drekesh say it makes them sing loudly and cry.'

Nemid's lips set into a firm line. They'd brought alcohol and other items from the white world back to camp after he had expressly forbidden them? He was going to have a lot to say to the Drekesh when he got back.

'They say there's always smoke coming from their mouths', said Ishin, miming someone taking a drag on a cigarette. 'Like this.'

Cigarettes too, Nemid seethed?

'And they all look so peculiar', Ishin said.

'Yes, the clothes, clothes and more clothes, and all in such garish colours.' Ashan made a face and placed one hand on her chest.

'The Trill said she'd never seen anything like it', Ishan finished for her sister.

'Apparently', Ashan said, 'their cabins are overflowing, so they're now putting things into the storage sheds.'

Nemid's eyes widened.

'But … but it's harvest time. Every bit of space will be needed. Do they expect us to starve just so they can keep a few trinkets dry?'

The two sisters shrugged then waited, drinking in everything Nemid said and did, knowing that the retelling of this would enable them to dine out for many nights to come.

'We hear it is worst at Blue Camp', Ishin said. However, Nemid was no longer listening.

His fingers curled into fists at the thought of Dog clan's selfishness and impertinence at bringing drugs and alcohol to the reservation and taking over valuable space in storage sheds needed for *food*. Why had no one stood up to them? Why had on one told him? What on earth was going on, and where the hell were the Drekesh?

'Outrageous!' he muttered. Then, suddenly aware of the intense gazes upon him, he bowed to the two elderly sisters. 'Thank you for bringing me this news. If you will excuse me?' Without waiting for an answer, he strode away from the celebration and to the home of an old friend who was also a Drekesh elder.

Nemid was again sitting on the outskirts of Big Camp, eyes closed, the breeze on his cheeks, as he sought the gentle company of his dead wives. Deep down he felt like a hypocrite. On the one hand, he had been the one asking for tolerance and openness toward the white culture, but on the other, he had just ensured the most Draconian of stipulations be placed on *everyone*.

In the heat of the moment, he had insisted that all living on the reservation must adhere to traditional Nahill culture. He inwardly cringed as he remembered ranting at the Drekesh elders about how allowing white culture onto the reservation was a slippery slope, that being too permissive was the fast path to destroying the Jhunti way of life, that the only reason the Nahill lifestyle had been persevered was because all Nahill chose to live this way, *all* Nahill not just *most* Nahill.

When it had been suggested that some members of Dog clan may not be able to fully reintegrate back into the traditional ways, Nemid had been insistent.

'Dog clan have brought this on themselves' he'd fumed. 'If they have allowed themselves to become soft, then it is on their own heads. They have pushed us too far. You only have to look at what they did to White Camp, the disgusting mess they made of it', his cheeks burned with indignation at the state in which he'd found his Water clan home. 'We cannot allow this to happen again. We have been caught napping once, and we shall not let our guard down again!'

Nemid's stomach clenched. How could he have said all those things to the collective of Drekesh elders? He had pulled them from their beds and insisted the tribe was in danger, insisted they act swiftly and with no mercy. It was as if all his seasons of inactivity and frustration exploded inside him. He'd felt he had no choice but to do something.

No, he told himself, this was not his fault, it was Dog clans' fault. How dare they make him become a conservative! It was not what he wanted at all. He'd spent the greater part of his life preaching tolerance, and now he'd become the harshest critic of white culture on the reservation. He'd been so angry, he'd shouted that the traditionalist views were the only ones that would ensure the future security of the Nahill way of life. *Shouted* ... at Drekesh *elders*! When word of this got around... Worse, he had not checked his facts with the Trill, just taken the word of those two old busybodies.

'What have I done?' he whispered. 'What have I done?' He covered his face with both hands and silently prayed for his dead wives to comfort him and help give him the strength to face Healer Deikter and their daughter Chani.

22

Chani strode up the path to White Camp with a cloth bag of freshly picked herbs over her shoulder. She was humming to herself when she heard muttering coming from inside the storage shed. As she neared the open door, she could see row after row of wooden barrels, most with lids tightly closed. She knew these contained the camp's newly harvested food supply of apples and the three sisters. She walked in, and her eyes swept the barrels.

'Who's here?' she called.

'That you Cha?'

She walked further in and saw a barrel lying on its side with a pair of feet sticking out.

'Kal?' she said.

'Yeah. What're you doing here?'

She came to crouch at the end of the barrel and peered inside. Kal was on all fours, his hands wrapped in linen, busily scrubbing the sides of the barrel with a rolled-up handful of thorn bush.

'I'm cleaning out storage barrels', he said. Before she could ask, he added, 'because I destroyed a red berry bush.'

Her eyebrows went up.

'How'd you do that?'

'It was an accident!' he fumed. 'There was a smoke bush in front of it, and that's what I was aiming at. As punishment, I have to clean out these putrid storage barrels ready for salmon season. When I opened the first one, I thought I was gonna barf!'

He gave the barrel one last scrub then backed out. He was covered from head to toe with the grime and goo.

'Stand back', he said.

Picking up a bucket of water, he tossed it inside the barrel, dropped to his knees and again began to scrub, this time slowly rolling the barrel along to rinse it as he went. Chani studied him and felt bad. A new edict had come from the Drekesh elders that all Nahill regulations must be adhered to with no exceptions. Throughout the camp, people were being punished for even minor transgressions, just like Kal. No one knew why, and it didn't matter. The Drekesh were law, and if they said this was how it was, then this was how it was. Everyone was on edge, and there had been renewed interest in learning all the rules and respecting all the ceremonies and customs. Even the Healers had been more cautious.

'So what's new with you?' he said.

She held up her bag.

'Collecting late season herbs.'

Kal climbed out of the barrel and tossed his thorny scrubbing brush to one side. Walking to the back of the barrel, he took a deep breath then heaved it up. The filthy water poured out, ran along the concrete and out of the shed door. Kal put the barrel down and tossed one final bucket of water inside, again rolling it back and forth before he rolled it to the far end of the shed, tipped it upside down and placed a rock under one end so it would drain. Wiping the sweat from his forehead with the back of his arm, he tipped over the next dirty barrel and rolled it to his work station. Chani studied the rows of barrels.

'You have to do all of these?' she said.

'Yep.'

She stared at them for a moment longer then headed for the door.

'Bye', he said but she'd already gone.

He rewound the linen around his hands, wishing for the millionth time the Nahill had gloves, then gathered up his thorn scrubbing brush and crawled into the next barrel. He was rolling that barrel over to dry with the others when Chani walked back in wearing an old pair of leggings and a well-worn tunic. Her long hair was in one long plait to keep it away from her face, and she was busily winding linen around her hand. Kal frowned.

'Need something?' he said.

'I've come to help.'

Kal leant against the freshly scrubbed barrel and gave her an appraising look. 'Not wanting to sound ungrateful', he said, 'but why? This's my punishment.'

'Last week', she said, rolling up her sleeves, 'Denet and her friend were given this punishment. She scrubbed one hand of barrels', and Chani held up five fingers.

'Maybe', Kal said, 'that was 'cause she's a girl. This's pretty hard work.'

'And maybe', Chani said indicating the dozens of dirty barrels, 'this is because you are white.'

Kal gave her an appreciative smile.

'OK', he said, 'I'm not going to argue with you about it. If you want to help, could you fill those buckets with water?'

As Chani took the four buckets out to the nearby stream, Kal moved the next barrel into position then climbed inside. He was scrubbing hard when Chani returned and placed the buckets on the floor.

'What next?' she said.

A hand emerged from inside the barrel.

'Lids', he said, pointing to a stack of dirty barrel lids resting against the wall.

She went to the first one, bundled up her thorny scrubbing pad and began to scour the built-up fish scales from the wood.

'These stink', she said, wrinkling her nose.

'Not as much as being inside them', he said.

They scrubbed in silence for a while.

'I'm still enjoying school', she said grinning. 'I'm the first and only Healer to go to school.'

'Why's that?'

'Because I'm special.'

He laughed and a spurt of water shot out of the barrel towards her. She grinned and continued her cleaning.

'Did you know that there are different lands?' she said.

'Ah huh.'

'Have you ever been to any of them?'

'No.'

'Have you ever seen the ocean?'

'No.'

'Have you ever been in an aeroplane?'

'No, but I've seen plenty of them. They use them for crop dusting out on the wheat belt.'

She wondered if she should ask what crop dusting was. Instead she rinsed off the lid she'd been working on, put it to one side and started on the next. Kal climbed out of his barrel and tossed in some water. Getting on all fours, he crawled back inside. They worked in silence completing another four barrels with lids before stopping and sitting on the floor to rest. Chani pulled out a plastic flask of water.

'Tell no one', she whispered, indicating the forbidden container.

He sniffed and wiped his nose on the back of his hand.

'Do you know what's going on with all these new rules?' he said.

She took several long gulps then handed the bottle to Kal. He drank greedily then handed it back.

'No', she said, carefully hiding the bottle in her pack. 'I did hear talk that it's coming from Big Camp. Have the Drekesh said anything?'

Kal shook his head.

'All I know is suddenly we have to obey and enforce all these regulations that never mattered before.'

She lowered her voice and leant towards him. 'There's talk of pulling out every piece of glass in the camp.'

He barked out a laugh.

'I can't see that happening, can you?'

She shook her head. He sniffed and gave his nose another swipe. Chani frowned thoughtfully for a moment then seemed to decide something.

'Do you still have bad dreams?' she said.

'Ah huh.'

'Do they make sense?' she said. 'I mean, do you understand them?'

'Sometimes. Why?'

She sighed.

'I've been having dreams lately that don't seem to make any sense. The dream begins with two eagles. One is me. We sit together on our cliff nest with two eggs content beneath this one. The sky is blue. All is well. The eggs both hatch but then come thunderclouds and a storm. The winds are so strong they blow us against the cliff face. The babies are left unprotected. The wind snatches them up and carries them away. We are powerless to stop it. My mate tries so hard to go after them, but is thrown repeatedly against the rocks of the cliff face and is killed. When the storm goes, this one is left alone, crying on her empty nest.'

She shook her head. 'It's so strange', she said. 'I've never had dreams like this before. I asked the Oracle, but she was no help. What do you think they mean?'

Kal began to pick the mud from his toenails.

'I dunno', he said. 'Maybe it's telling you not to nest on the side of a cliff?'

She gave him a playful punch.

'I'm serious', she said.

'I dunno. I sometimes dream I'm flying. I like those dreams. I feel so free.'

'This one makes me feel sad.'

'Well maybe you have two babies and then…'

'But Healers never have two babies. Never. Healers always have one baby, and it is always a girl. We make sure of that.'

'How?'

She put a grubby finger to her lips. They were both silent until he stood up with a groan. He held out a hand to her and helped her up.

'Break time's over', he said. 'I want to get these finished before the light goes.'

He rolled the next barrel over as Chani wrapped her hands in the linen cloth.

'Cha?' he said. 'I really appreciate you helping me with this.'

She gave him a reassuring smile and wondered why he was the only one she had wanted to tell about her dream.

'Has Nemid sent any word back from Big Camp?' she said.

'No. Bean Pole must be uglier than we thought.'

'Don't be mean', she scolded him.

They both scrubbed in silence. Chani rinsed off her lid and put it with the others. Kal rinsed his barrel, rolled it over to the other clean ones and brought the next one back. He clambered inside, scrubbed for a moment and then stopped. Almost afraid to hear the answer, he cleared his throat.

'Cha?' he said quietly.

'Mmm?'

'You don't think he'll stay down there, do you?'

She looked at his feet, taken aback.

'Why would you even think that?'

'I don't know, it's just … I know he used to live down there. I was wondering if maybe he might decide to stay.'

'He can't. He's Pac of White Camp. Besides, it is for his sake that I have moved here from Red Camp.'

Her indignant tone made Kal laugh.

'What's so funny?' she said.

'Nothing.'

She could imagine him making a face and shaking his head. If he hadn't been inside a smelly barrel, she'd have thrown something at him.

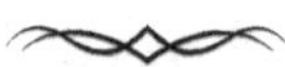

From the porch of her cabin, Aunt Talks Too Much watched as Kal and Chani left the storage shed and made their way up the path. Look at them, she seethed, their lives continuing as before while ours is in ruins. With no furniture, they were forced to sit on the floor like animals. The Drekesh had been very clear that if Dog clan wanted to share in the harvest, they were required to work in the fields like Nahill. It had been humiliating, particularly when the Nahill children had the audacity to give them basic instructions. It was all the fault of the White Rat. How she despised him and that Healer child of Nemid's. She wished a pox on all of them. As Kal and Chani went towards the stream to bathe, Aunt Talks Too Much glanced back at the storage shed.

'How would you like it if you suddenly had no food?' she muttered to herself. Her heart began to beat faster as an idea came to her. Maybe the time for payback had arrived!

As the sun began to set, the whole of Dog clan left their cabins and silently melted into the forest. Aunt Talks Too Much and her family walked along the path that led to the fields where the Dog clan goats were permitted to graze. Laughs a Lot strolled towards them and smiled.

'Hello, Aunt Talks Too Much', he called.

'Damn', Aunt Talks Too Much hissed at the sight of the simpleton.

She put on a smile. 'Hello Lal', she said, 'we're coming to bring the goats in as a surprise for you.'

He gave her a suspicious look. Despite spending a season with the Billy goat, none of the six Dog clan goats had become pregnant. The verdict was that they were all too old. Laughs a Lot knew what that meant. It was now just a matter of time before the whole herd was slaughtered. As a result, he made sure every day was happy for them and gave them extra pats and even snuck them apples when no one was looking.

'I don't mind doing it', he said.

'Don't be silly', Remmy said. 'You've been working all day.'

'Your mother says you are to go home', Aunt Talks Too Much said firmly, 'and we are to get them in for you.'

He stopped and stared straight at her.

'Are you going to eat them?'

The others shook their heads.

'No', his aunt said gently. 'We're going to put them to bed and give them an extra nice meal.'

He stood undecidedly for a moment then nodded.

'Alright. Just remember that Dopsil is the boss, but she's a bit grumpy at the moment. You have to give her a pat first and say nice things and then she'll follow you. Oh, and Nod had a sore foot this morning and her sister Katil is also sick. Just have a look at them both as you bring them back to make sure they're OK.'

'We'll be extra careful.'

He gave them an appreciative wave and jogged up the hill. Aunt Talks Too Much and her family continued towards the goat field. Before they got there, however, they all crouched down and stole through the orchard to the storage shed. It took all their might, but they managed to open the seldom-used door on the downhill side of the shed. Going inside, they inspected the bins. Row after row was filled with the new harvest.

'Get to work everyone', Aunt Talks Too Much hissed, 'and for the Spirits sake, do it quietly!'

A few moments later, the rest of Dog clan arrived and silently helped themselves to barrels of beans, corn, pumpkins and apples. Loaded up with as much as they could carry, they silently went into the forest. Each person made several trips until they were sure they had enough for the winter. Satisfied, several returned to the shed and tipped some barrels over so the contents spilt onto the floor.

In the meantime, Aunt Talks Too Much and her family moved toward the goats. The small herd was not in the mood to be moved by strangers, and instead of following docilely in a long train like they did for Laughs a Lot, they ran this way and that, refusing to be caught, cajoled or corralled. All the better, thought Aunt Talks Too Much.

'Here Remmy', she called.

The girl came to her. Aunt Talks Too Much lowered her voice.

'Go back to the shed and make sure to use the downhill door', she said. 'Collect as many apples as you can carry and bring them back. Hurry now, it's almost dark.'

Remmy took off at a run, and Aunt Talks Too Much re-joined the others trying to collect the goats. When Remmy returned, they had managed to get the goats crowded into a corner of the fenced-off pasture. Aunt Talks Too Much took one of the apples and sliced it into quarters. She threw them to the goats, who quickly gobbled them up. Taking another apple, she cut that into pieces and walked towards the path. At every step, she dropped another piece. The goats followed, each trying to be first in line to get the apple. And so they went, with Aunt Talks Too Much quickly chopping apple and dropping pieces behind her. Uncle Mends Things, Remmy, Lemon and Mash brought up the rear. The sun had set by now, and all around them were the songs of the birds settling in for the night. There were lights in cabin windows and smoke was coming from every chimney.

They progressed in a slow but steady procession, appearing to any casual observer as if they were leading the goats to their night time housing just as Laughs a Lot did every night. However, once the storage shed was between them and the rest of the camp, Aunt Talks Too Much turned to the right and started up the hill again.

'Remmy', hissed Aunt Talks Too Much.

The girl ran to her mother.

'Here', Aunt Talks Too Much whispered shoving some apple pieces into Remmy's hand. 'You go up there first.'

Remmy did as she was told, dropping apples as she went, the side door already wide open. Slowly but surely, the goats followed the apple trail. They got to within a few paces of the door and stopped, all staring balefully at the open door and the darkness within. Their ears flicked back and forth, and their noses twitched as they caught the scent of the feast that awaited them. They stood uncertainly for what seemed like an age. Aunts Talks Too Much was about to drag a few in forcibly when Dopsil took another few steps forward and gobbled up more apple pieces. Remmy tossed more apple into the doorway, and again Dopsil moved forward. She was almost to the door. The watching family held their breath, waiting and willing them to go inside before one of the Nahill saw them. It was agonising, but all knew better than to try to rush them or spook them. Remmy tossed a few more pieces of apple deeper inside the shed. Again, Dopsil assessed the situation, her ears flicking back and forth and her nose twitching. At last, she made her way forward, and it was as if someone had undammed a stream. Smelling food, all the goats pushed and shoved each other to get inside to the feast.

'Quick', Aunt Talks Too Much hissed.

The family hurriedly shut the door and bolted it behind them. From inside they heard barrels falling and the hiss of grain and beans spilling onto the concrete floor. All shared the same smug expression. Let's see how Water clan likes it when someone takes their food away.

'Off you go', Aunt Talks Too Much hissed.

They all ran towards the goat pen. Meanwhile, Aunt Talks Too Much scouted around the back of the shed. Making her way as quietly and inconspicuously as possible towards the door, she unbolted it as she walked past and left it slightly ajar. Meanwhile, Uncle Mends Things was at the goat pen. He carefully shut the gate while the others broke off one of the posts so the fence drooped just low enough for a goat to climb over it. By this time, Aunt Talks Too Much had joined them and, in the growing evening darkness, they ran back into the forest to claim their share of the stolen cache of food.

Yelling made Ashekii and Kal get to their feet. Going outside, they saw light down at the storage shed. There was the sound of goats bleating and the pounding of hooves as they scattered in every direction. Ashekii and Kal joined others running to the storage shed. Silence filled the air as they all gaped at the heart-wrenching sight of overturned barrels and most of the camps' winter food on the floor soiled by goats.

'How did they get in?' someone said into the silence.

As if a flood gate had opened, everyone talked at once.

'The door must have been open.'

'Who left it open?'

'Who was the last in the shed?'

'Not me, I've not been there in days.'

'Nor I.'

'Well someone must have.'

As the talk continued, Kal stared at the door. He was sure he'd locked it, hadn't he? A chill of fear ran down his spine. Had he? He'd been cold and pissed off and anxious to get clean. Maybe in his rush, he had not bolted it properly? He replayed the sequence of events in his mind. Yes, he was sure he'd bolted it. Well, ninety percent sure.

'Kal was cleaning barrels this afternoon as punishment', Aunt Talks Too Much said. 'Maybe he…'

'I fastened the door.'

'Are you sure?'

'Chani was there', he said. 'She can attest to me shutting it.'

'Why was a Healer helping you?' someone said.

'The goats didn't open it themselves', someone else said.

'I bolted it', Kal said, 'I'm sure I did.'

'Really? Then how did they get in?'

And on and on it went. The camp Council was called on to adjudicate.

Things worsened the next day when all of Dog clan's goats had to be slaughtered.

'It was because of what they had eaten', Aunt Talks Too Much told anyone who would listen. 'Those poor creatures were in so much pain, blown up till we thought their stomachs would burst. It was pitiful to see. We had no other choice. It was the only thing we could do.'

Even Uncle Mends Things had to admit, with her wringing of hands and sorrow-filled eyes, she almost had him convinced that her distress was genuine. That night all of Dog clan feasted on goat meat stew, all except Laughs a Lot who stayed in bed crying.

23

The procession of travellers leaving White Camp wound their way slowly down the valley. The party consisted of six men carrying heavy packs of goods to trade. There were a dozen women also with loads, and straggling behind were a line of children, all with packs of varying sizes. They toiled their way along the track, which switched back and forth as they descended the hill. When they got to a well-used campsite, they stopped to eat and rest. All were on their way to Big Camp for the snow season. After a short time, they were joined by three more travellers. One was a tall, thin woman, a senior Healer known for being very strict. The other two were Healer Deikter and her daughter Healer Chani. The travellers took one look at the women and bowed.

'Esteemed Healers', they murmured.

'We will be joining your party', the old Healer said. 'We have business in Big Camp.'

Healer Chani glanced back for one last look at White Camp. She would not be seeing it again for two snow seasons, possibly more. While a part of her was sad to be leaving, the other part of her was excited. Word had come that she had been selected to become a special apprentice to Healer Uxue at Big Camp. Healer Uxue was a legend in Healing circles. It was said she could perform miracles and had the ear of the Great Spirits. Chani was not sure why, but for some reason, the healer had agreed to mentor her. A shiver of excitement ran through her at the thought of all the things she was going to learn. As they resumed walking, she smiled and hummed, only just stopping herself from doing a little happy dance. She was indeed a very fortunate girl, doubly fortunate because her mother had agreed to accompany her.

Healer Deikter glanced at her daughter, relieved that she'd been able to remove Chani in time. It was a shame about Kal, but she'd done what she could. That boy had a talent for making trouble. The current climate of intolerance towards all things non-traditional was not helping. Who'd known that Chani had inadvertently broken an ancient law by helping Kal with his punishment? A season ago no one would have cared, but now… She had decided it prudent to spirit her daughter away until people came to their senses.

Of course, all this was that fool Nemid's fault, she mused. She'd told him to keep a close eye on the boy, but no, Nemid always knew best. He'd gone off on some stupid claiming quest to Big Camp and left the boy with that hot-headed cousin. What did he expect would happen? Drekesh weren't trained to sit calmly and think things through.

Well, now all their plans were in ruins, and she'd have to come up with a new strategy. *Men*, she fumed. The world would all be so much simpler if they didn't exist.

Ashekii studied the people in the meeting hall. Everywhere, there were loud, animated voices. Some people shook their heads, and others had their hands clenched into fists. The assembled camp council consisted of clan heads and respected elders. As they settled themselves, they looked justifiably disgruntled. With the need for everyone to adhere to all these rules and regulations, they were being dragged in to adjudicate something every day, and they were heartily sick of it.

Ashekii glanced at Kal, who stood silently before the council. His fingers were lightly tapping against his leg, this old habit being the only sign of his nerves. Ashekii had told Kal that no matter what happened, he must not speak or try to argue his own case, and so the boy was standing with his head up and shoulders back. When Ashekii studied the boy's stoic, impassive expression, he felt a wave of pride despite himself.

A stick banged on the floor. People quieted, and stragglers hurriedly sat down. A Councillor pointed to Ashekii and indicated for him to speak. Ashekii got to his feet and cleared his throat. He briefly outlined what had happened, that Kal had inadvertently destroyed a sacred bush and, in line with any other person who'd transgressed, he'd been given a punishment.

'Now tell us about the Healer helping him.'

Ashekii explained that during Kal's punishment, his *sister*, and he stressed that relationship, who just happened to be a Healer, had assisted him, inadvertently breaking another rule of which none, himself included, had been aware.

'He had a Healer helping with his punishment?' a woman said indignantly. 'Since when do Healers do that?'

Ashekii recognised the woman as being one of the Big Camp Healers and inwardly cringed at the bad luck of having her here.

'What's Healer clan got to do with this?' said someone else.

'He never should have been taken in!' someone yelled out.

'All whites are scum!' yelled another.

Several people jeered. Ashekii glared at the speaker.

'If you want to kill him over a few berries then just say so.'

Aunt Talks Too Much stood up, her face red with anger.

'He's not here because of berries', she said. 'He's here because he was disrespectful towards our most powerful and wisest of clans.'

'And because he killed our goats', added Uncle Mends Things.

'What goats?' the Big Camp Healer said, looking at Ashekii.

Ashekii described the matter of the goats, which he stressed he'd thought they were going to resolve between the clan leaders. He voiced his dismay that such a small transgression had been escalated to a point that warranted this special gathering and hinted that he believed it to be a waste of everyone's time. A number of the council women nodded as he spoke, and he was aware of their annoyance at having been summoned.

'What has happened with the goats is a sad thing', he said, 'but perhaps not as terrible as the Dogs have suggested', he shot a hostile glance at them.

'Whose job is it', Remmy said loudly, 'to check that the door is closed each night?'

There were red faces from the Drekesh who had long ago stopped checking even though, by law, it was their duty to ensure the food supplies were safe. Ashekii crossed his arms.

'It was the broken goat fence that was to blame, so the fault lies with Dog clan', he said.

'The Drekesh should have checked the door was shut', yelled Remmy.

Half a dozen young Drekesh warriors jumped to their feet and began shouting. An Elder banged her stick on the ground and called for order again.

'How long were the goats in there?' she said.

'Long enough to destroy most of the harvest.'

She shook her head at such a catastrophe; many would go hungry until next season's harvest.

'And what about us?' Aunt Talks Too Much said heatedly. 'All of our goats have died because of their incompetence. Are we to starve through no fault of our own?'

'And all because of the White Rat', someone snarled.

There were fresh mutterings of anger, and Kal felt more furious eyes upon him.

'Who didn't put their goats away securely?' Ashekii demanded.

'That is irrelevant!' Uncle Mends Things said. 'Kal must not have closed the door properly.'

Ashekii turned on Uncle Mends Things and pointed a finger at him.

'Your fence was broken, Dog clan; they are your responsibility, and it's your fault they got out!'

'If the door had been properly fastened, it would not have mattered, Drekesh.'

'Why didn't the Drekesh check the door? That is their job!'

Ashekii glanced at the faces of the councillors. He could see they were getting sick of this farce and had hopes for them throwing the whole lot back to the clans for them to sort out, as was correct, he thought. His heart sank as a procession of Healers walked in.

'Apologies for our tardiness', said the senior Healer, 'but we were attending to sickness.'

There was silence in the hall as all waited till the six Healers took their seats. The tension in the hall increased noticeably, and suddenly everyone was aware things had just become very serious. Ashekii's eyes went to Dog clan and saw their delight as all knew that now the Council would be forced to deal with the matter. Ashekii again lamented how Kal had become synonymous for all the transgressions of all white people.

'Now see what's happened', Aunt Talks Too Much said heatedly, 'his foolishness has resulted in Healers being dragged away from our tribe's sick. How many more Jhunti lives must be lost because of the whites? Banish him and be done with it!'

'Over a bush that will grow back next season?' Ashekii cried in dismay.

'He did more than that.'

And so the accusations raged back and forth until the stick was again banged on the floor. The Council studied those gathered before them then glanced at each other. The senior Councillor gave a slight nod.

'It is our decision', she said, 'that the true fault lies with the Drekesh!'

There was a collective gasp from those gathered.

'The Drekesh', she continued, 'are to blame because as far as the law is concerned, it was their responsibility to ensure the safety of the camp's food supplies.'

'And what about us?' Aunt Talks Too Much said.

The Councillor nodded.

'Yes', she said, 'as to the matter of Dog clan compensation, it is for the White Camp Drekesh to replace the Dog clan goats that were lost.'

There was a lot of muttering, but most agreed, begrudgingly, that the decision was correct. It seemed like the proceedings were at an end when one of the Healers went to the council and had a quick, whispered conversation with the senior Councillor then returned to her seat. As people stood to leave, the Councillor again banged her stick on the floor. She agreed with Healer clan, this boy was nothing but trouble and they'd all be well off if he left.

'And for the insult to Healer clan', she said, 'Kal is hereby made Brehole and banished from Jhunti land forever.'

Kal felt the bottom drop out of his world. Ashekii was shaking his head.

'That is too extreme', he said and approached the councillors. 'Please reconsider. He needs to stay here to learn our ways, so he will fit in. If he is no longer welcome here, we will send him to Black Camp. We have cousins there who would take him.'

'That is our decision', the Councillor said and stood up.

Ashekii glanced at Healer clan and saw the smugness on several faces. He wondered just what Kal had done to piss them off. He looked back at the councillors who were all standing up, preparing to leave.

'Then Nemid and I will go with him', Ashekii said.

The councillors turned towards him, even the Healers were staring at him with scepticism. Sensing there was something new afoot, everyone quietened.

'Are you saying', the Councillor said, 'that Pac Nemid would give up his Pacship and leave *us* for *him*?'

'Yes', Ashekii said, praying to every one of the Great Spirits that his gamble worked. 'We would do it to make a point. We are both me pect Drekesh. The Drekesh protect. Drekesh guide through example. Drekesh encourage through actions. Drekesh remind others of what's important. This is what the Drekesh are trained to do. With all due respect, this ruling is not fair, and more than that, it sets a precedent. It is so harsh that it will mean that our numbers will soon dwindle as people are banished into the white world for minor transgressions. Kal, Nemid and I must go into the white world and establish a new settlement for Nahill who have been banished for misdemeanours. Come Kal, let us gather our things and send word to your grandfather.'

The councillors glanced at each other, each thinking the same thing. White Camp's rejuvenation was very recent, and no one had considered a successor for Nemid's Pacship. With no shortlist of contenders, this Pacship would be hotly contested and take a lot of work. The whole tribe was getting ready for the first snow. Time was short, and yet the camp would need a new Pac as quickly as possible to stop petty squabbles exacerbating over the long and tedious snow seasons. Each of the councillors groaned at the thought of all that extra work.

'Wait!' another Councillor said. 'Perhaps we should reconsider?'

The first Councillor turned on her, fury in her eyes.

'You are saying we were wrong to punish him?'

'No, but Ashekii is correct that if this, one of our harshest punishments, has been meted out for...', she sighed and shook her head. 'We always punish in order to teach. If Kal is banished, what does that teach him? It is as Ashekii says, what does it teach everyone about our system of rules and punishment?' She glanced at Healer clan then back at her sister councillors. The councillors huddled together for a few moments, having a whispered discussion. When they parted, the second Councillor looked at Kal.

'We have reconsidered', she said. 'For the crime of making a Healer abandon her work to help with your punishment, you are banished until the harvest after next. The matter of the totem food has already been dealt with by Water clan. And', she pointed a finger at Ashekii, 'he better not cause any more trouble... *Ever!*'

Ashekii bowed. 'Thank you, Excellency', he said.

Everyone bowed as the councillors left followed by Healer clan. As soon as they were gone, everyone began talking at once. Ashekii came up to Kal.

'Can she do that?' Kal said in a whisper.

'Make us replace the goats? Yeah, and it's going to cost us a pretty sum too. A curse on Dog clan's eyes!'

He let out an exasperated breath.

'No', Kal said, 'I mean banish me into the white world.'

Ashekii wasn't listening. His mind was whirring through what he was going to have left to trade for replacement goats when the camp was already going to have to trade for food supplies.

'Their word is law. Besides, it's only till next harvest.'

Ashekii turned, and Kal followed him back to his cabin. When they reached it, they found Laughs a Lot loitering to one side. As they approached, Laughs a Lot beckoned to Kal. Ashekii gave Kal a push towards him then went inside. As Ashekii explained what had happened, Hahina's lips set into a firm line.

'You endanger your own position by showing too much favouritism towards him', she said.

'He's just a boy.'

'A boy who does not learn', Hahina snapped.

'They were too hard on him.'

'Now you're sounding like Nemid', she said. 'Tell me the last time you heard of a Healer helping someone with their punishment?'

Ashekii shook his head.

'Then Chani should have been punished too.'

'Shhh', Hahina hissed and glanced around. 'Saying such things is most unwise, husband. Even though she is your blood, we must never forget that she is Healer born.'

Kal came in, sat down and stared morosely at the floor.

'What did Lal want?' Ashekii said.

'He asked if Aunt Talks Too Much had mentioned that all the goats who died had been sickly, injured or too old for milk.'

Ashekii and Hahina stared at Kal for a long moment then Hahina crossed her arms over her chest.

'I see', she said in a tight voice. 'Well, perhaps we will remember to take that into consideration when negotiating for their replacements. I need a walk', she stormed out.

After she was gone, Kal tilted his head to one side, studying Ashekii.

'Did you mean what you said? About coming with me into the white world if I'd been banished?'

'Yes. If we're going to banish people for minor crimes, very soon there will be no Jhunti left on this reservation.'

They sat in silence, mulling over their thoughts.

'When shall I have to go?' Kal said.

'Tomorrow. I'll see you to the border myself.'

He gave Kal what he hoped was a reassuring smile. Kal sighed then stood up.

'I'm going to bed.'

'Goodnight, Eyas.'

Nemid had spent the night worrying that something would go wrong at the last moment. However, in the morning they were summoned by Drekesh and escorted to the claiming mound. The ceremony went off without a hitch, and once the public declarations of the union had been made, it was over at last. At the feast that followed, two old women with dyed red hair came over to Nemid and hugged him.

'It's so good to see you again', said one.

'It's been too long', said the other.

Nemid returned their embraces. He'd been expecting some of his first wife's family and fellow council members to drop by to pay their respects.

'Esteemed councillors', Nemid said then bowed. 'I had hoped you would be able to attend.'

The two women inclined their heads and Nemid straightened.

'We were sorry', said one, 'to hear about the loss of your family.'

'Yes', said the other, 'devastating to have it happen again.'

They both gave Nemid pitying looks that he was used to but heartily sick of.

'Without death', Nemid said with practiced ease, 'we would not have children.'

'And speaking of children', one of the women said, leaning toward Nemid, 'what's this we hear about that white boy of yours being trained as a Drekesh?'

A chill ran down Nemid's spine. How had they found out about his secret training of the boy?

'I'm afraid I am unaware of that which you speak', Nemid said.

'Where's that Healer?' one of the women said, beckoning to someone.

As a woman dressed in Healer robes approached, Nemid's eyes widened as he recognised Chani. She had changed from a child to a young woman since he'd last seen her. He bowed to his daughter. The two councillors inclined their heads towards her, and Chani gracefully acknowledged their salutations.

'Now what were you telling me', the first Councillor said, 'about that white boy being trained as a Drekesh?'

Chani smiled at her father.

'It's true. Kal is under the tutelage of the White Camp Drekesh masters.'

Nemid had no idea how Kal had managed to persuade the Drekesh to take him on, but now was not the time to ask Chani about it. He was overjoyed to see her today of all days, and he could barely maintain his composure. He refrained from hugging her, which would be most unseemly for a Healer, but hoped she'd been told of what a good match he had arranged for Trindal.

'There', the councillor said, looking at Nemid. 'I told you so. What's going on at your camp that you permit such a thing?'

Nemid gave her a tight smile.

'It is not for us to question the wisdom of the Drekesh masters', he said.

The two women exchanged glances, disappointed that there was not going to be a scene over such sensational news. Nemid excused himself from them and took Chani by the elbow.

'This is indeed a delightful surprise', he said.

'I cannot stay long', she said, 'but when I heard about Trin's claiming, I wanted to see you both.'

Trindal made his way over to them. He bowed to Chani then stood back. She brushed Trindal's hair from his face.

'Well, well', she said, 'don't you look all grown up?'

'You too', he said. 'Does Kal know I got claimed?'

Chani shook her head.

'Not yet, but I'm sure word will get back to him soon enough. Introduce me to your lovely wife.'

All too soon Chani had to leave. Trindal was then requested to accompany his wife as she mingled with dignitaries, relatives and other guests. A hand was placed on Nemid's arm. It was Amrix who was chatting to Shashina's aunt, a drink in her hand.

'Congratulations', she said, beaming. 'Oh, I love it when everything works out … and a fine match I secured for him too.'

'Yes', said Nemid happily. 'You have been as brilliant and astute as everyone said. I am deeply grateful to you.'

She placed a hand on her chest, flattered. 'It was my pleasure', she said. 'I must confess I was a little worried for a while there. However, it has all worked out in the end and that's what matters.'

Nemid smiled.

'Yes', he said, 'provided it all works out in the end.'

He was about to tell her of Kal's Drekesh apprenticeship when she leant towards him.

'Now before you run off, there's someone I'd like you to meet.'

Nemid was not at all surprised when Amrix introduced him to a particularly vibrant older woman who just happened to be a widow.

Ashekii helped Kal to pack his few possessions and get ready for his 'trip home to visit his people', as Hahina put it.

'Ready?' Ashekii said.

Kal shouldered his pack and nodded. With one last hug for Hahina and her children, Kal followed Ashekii outside. Standing waiting for them was Ashekii's band of Water clan Drekesh to see Kal safely to the edge of the reservation. Silently, they jogged into the forest. The air was moist and cold, and the ground was damp under foot. After a short time, the vegetation grew thicker and the sounds of the waking forest filled their ears. Everywhere, the birds sang their morning chorus.

Kal soaked it all in, knowing it would have to last him for many seasons. He reminded himself not to cry. He was a trainee Drekesh, the grandson of a camp Pac and he was lucky that the banishment was only temporary. After what seemed like no time at all, they came to the edge of the forest. Before them were the paddocks that belonged to white people. The road to the camp was to the right. The Drekesh all stood, hands on hips, none wanting to tell the boy to leave. Ashekii busied himself filling Kal's pockets with meat rolls.

'Thank you' Kal said.

Ashekii put his hands on Kal's shoulders, and they stared into each other's eyes.

'Remember all you have learnt', he said. 'Be a good trainee Drekesh out in the white world. Be strong and brave and bring honour to our family and clan. See you in a few snows.'

They embraced. Kal sternly told himself not to cry. Tears were for babies, and he was a man now. He wanted to make Ashekii proud of him. With a final squeeze, they parted, and Kal started walking towards the road. The Drekesh headed back into the forest. Kal turned, hand raised in salute just as rays of sunlight peeped through the thick trees. The band of Drekesh dressed in their dark brown tunics with linen leggings, their long black hair shining in the light looked very small beside the huge forest trees. Kal stared at them, willing himself to commit this scene to memory. There was a flash of movement in a tree top, but by the time he'd located it, the Trill was gone. He waved to the Drekesh, they waved back and then disappeared into the forest. It felt like he was waking from a beautiful dream.

Kal frowned as Ashekii's words came back to him. See you in a few snows. Was that *Two snows?* He'd thought his banishment was till the harvest after next which was only one year, but two snows meant two years, didn't it? His eyes went to where the Drekesh had been, but they were gone.

'Two years', he muttered then let out a resigned sigh. Ashekii was always right.

Shoving his hands into the pockets of his new jacket, he started walking along the road. The crunching of the gravel under his feet reminded him of when he'd first arrived. How many years ago was that? He counted the snows. Had he been living with Jhunti for only four snows? It had seemed like a lifetime. That meant he would turn fifteen this November. He felt way older than fourteen. Maybe, he mused, Nahill time was different to white people's time. He marched on, humming the courage song.

EPILOGUE

As daybreak neared, the forest stilled. One by one the birds began their morning chorus. There was a crisp chill to the air that spoke of the season of the First Snow being not far away now. Nemid's breath was coming out in white clouds as he climbed the steep path to his favourite look out over White Camp.

He'd been back in camp only a few days and was adjusting to life on his own again. At first he'd focused on the benefits of not having Trindal or Kal around. There was less mess, and when he made food, it was still there later on. There was also much less noise with no running feet thundering along the veranda, no doors slamming open or shut, no fighting or bickering and no raucous laughter waking him up. But it felt too quiet. For a short time Nemid had considered moving into the single men's quarters but decided it would be impractical. As camp Pac, there were times when people needed to have a quiet word with him, *without* other ears overhearing. Besides, this cabin had been the residence of the Pac for as long as anyone could remember. He would get used to his new life, he decided, and reminded himself that it was only for a few seasons. Kal would be back in no time.

He climbed up the last few rocks onto a small outcrop. Suddenly a vista of the whole of the forest reservation opened out to him. From this height, he could clearly see the sun on the horizon. Its morning tendrils bathed everything with orange and gold. To his right was White Camp perched on the side of the mountain. To his left and on forever was what was left of the Jhunti domain. This was his favourite vantage point, and being up here always helped him get his thoughts into perspective.

He stared down at the camp before him. His heart pounded with pride as he marvelled at all the changes to the camp since he'd become Pac. With the money from the education cheques, they'd been able to buy all the things they needed to fix everything. Now it resembled the camp of his youth. All the cabins had roofs and were water and wind tight, all the broken windows had been replaced or repaired, the animals had secure waterproof housing to protect them from foxes and all the animal fields had strong fences. The apple trees had been fertilised, were weed-free and pruned, ready for their hibernation. The fields were ready for planting in the season of the Snow Thaw, and great stacks of green waste sat composting in piles to one side. The smoke houses had been repaired, ready for the season of the Salmon.

He drank in the breathtaking view and in the far distance, he could just make out the white mist created by smoke coming from hundreds of cooking fires in Big Camp. He pictured Trindal wrapped safely in the arms of his new bride. Nemid knew Trindal would be happy and well cared for by her family. He frowned as he thought of Kal and hoped his family welcomed him back. Nemid wasn't sure how long it had taken Kal to walk to the reservation but knew it wouldn't take as long for him to walk home as he was bigger and stronger now. He hoped things went well for him this time.

Nemid returned his attention to White Camp. As the sun rose higher, smoke rose from the many chimneys, some in thin trails as fires were started and others in a steady stream as people readied their morning meal. There were a few people walking through the camp, hands shoved deeply into the pockets of their warm jackets. Chickens were loosed from their pens and moved between cabins, pecking and ruffling their feathers. The pack of camp dogs emerged from under their cabins, shaking themselves and stretching before seeking each other out and running in an excited pack up the hill, yapping and wagging their tails.

Nemid wondered if Chani would try another dog. Last heard, Trill had said she was working in a village not far from Big Camp and that she seemed well and happy. A pang of loss went through him. While they'd always lived in different cabins, Nemid had never been separated from Chani before. From Chani, Nemid's thoughts went to Kal and the events that had lead up to his expulsion.

Nemid was convinced that Healer clan was behind both Kal's banishment and Chani's hasty removal from school and his influence.

But why? This was the reason he'd been unable to sleep last night. Had they deduced Deikter's plan? That would certainly explain it. Deikter's plan was simple. She wanted Healers to use white medicine to help their people. To do this, Chani needed to speak, read and write English. She would then learn how to set broken bones, cure infection, fevers, tooth pain and many other things. Most of Healer clan would be against such a detour from tradition. It would undermine their authority and shake Nahill belief in fate and wellness, but it had to be done.

The more Nemid and Deikter had talked about it, the more they'd realised how crucial Kal's role was. Was this what Healer clan suspected? Was this why they'd insisted Kal be banished instead of punished? Or, had Healer clan done it to punish Nemid, to send him a warning and remind him of what could happen?

He crossed his arms over his chest, hugging himself in a way that was reminiscent of Kal. He reminded himself that Kal and Chani would be back in two snows, just a few seasons away, and there was much work to do before then. He had so many plans for White Camp and was determined that it would be the better for his Pacship. He wouldn't admit it out aloud, but now that he'd tasted leadership in his own right, he would not willingly give it up.

Fortunately, the puritanical measures his late-night rant had stirred up had mostly subsided as people refused to give up their glass windows and metal cooking pots. He was pleased and had learnt a valuable lesson. Nemid planned to transform White Camp into a place of peace and tolerance so that Chani's life's work would go smoothly. When Kal returned, Nemid planned to have at least one member of Women's Council ready to push through his adoption. Once this was final, he would make sure Kal became Drekesh. Not just any Drekesh, but the best Drekesh a man could be. He would be the Nahill's first White Drekesh. Then Kal would be claimed by a powerful and influential family. Nemid had enlisted Amrix's help and had been very specific about his requirements. He expected to hear back from her next claiming season.

Nemid scrutinised the winding mountain road that lead to the camp, and it occurred to him that perhaps change was a two-way thing. It wasn't just the Jhunti that should be more tolerant. Perhaps if white people knew a little more about Jhunti culture, they too would be more respectful. Perhaps if he worded things correctly, they may even gain a deeper appreciation for this beautiful land and the wondrous creatures and plants that inhabited it. He was reminded of a story his father told him about a dragonfly. When it was a pupa in the water, it thought that was all there was to life. When it was a flightless insect on the river banks, it thought that was all there was to life and when it grew wings and took on its full magnificence, only then did it realise it had at last become all it was supposed to be. He nodded to himself as everything suddenly fell into place in his mind. Everything made sense. The Great Spirits had done all this to give Nemid the motivation to do what needed to be done.

He sent his thanks to the Great Spirits for helping him to understand. He stood up and picked his way down the mountain, shoulders back and head high.

ACKNOWLEDGEMENTS

I would like to acknowledge the enthusiasm and wisdom of my husband Miles, who has been with me through every step of the writing process. Without his input, I would not have gotten this far.

I would also like to voice my gratitude to all my test readers for their feedback and interest in this project, in particular: Erica Stecker, Carolyn Worth, Mary Jadresko, Mary Lancaster, Jane Eddy and Mary Rahilly.

Many thanks to Catherine Deveny for her 'Gunnas' workshops, which is where I met the firecracker Julie Postance, without whom I would not have had the confidence or knowledge to take my work to the next level.

My gratitude also goes out to my family and friends for putting up with the constant hours of me typing on the computer or asking them questions like 'does anyone know how much corn you need to plant to sustain one person for one year?' A special thanks to Bronwyn Kolotelo for coming up with the answers to some of these questions.

Lastly, I'd like to thank my editor, Maria Williams, for her guidance and expertise in helping me to raise my words to such an eloquent standard and teaching me about how to write more effectively.

ABOUT THE AUTHOR

JULIET SUMMERS lives on twenty acres of bush adjoining a forest two hours from Melbourne, Australia, in a mudbrick house that her husband designed and that they built together. She is surrounded by nosy wombats, clowning rosellas, bossy kangaroos, curious wallabies and busy echidnas.

Every day in the forest brings new wonder. A few weeks ago they had snow, but today the Spring orchids are flowering. The skies are full of bird song, and everywhere are babies. The air is crisp and clean, and at night, the stars pepper the sky and everything is still.

www.ingramcontent.com/pod-product-compliance
Lightning Source LLC
Chambersburg PA
CBHW031931110726
47902CB00001B/133